DATE DUE

EMPRESS OF THE NIGHT

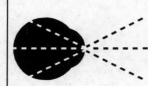

This Large Print Book carries the
Seal of Approval of N.A.V.H.

EMPRESS OF THE NIGHT

A NOVEL OF CATHERINE THE GREAT

EVA STACHNIAK

THORNDIKE PRESS

A part of Gale, Cengage Learning

GALE
CENGAGE Learning

Farmington Hills, Mich • San Francisco • New York • Waterville, Maine
Meriden, Conn • Mason, Ohio • Chicago

GALE
CENGAGE Learning·

LIBRARY OF CONGRESS CATALOGING-IN-PUBLICATION DATA

Stachniak, Eva, 1952–
    Empress of the night : a novel of Catherine the Great / by Eva Stachniak.
— Large print edition.
        pages ; cm. — (Thorndike Press large print historical fiction)
    ISBN 978-1-4104-7105-5 (hardcover) — ISBN 1-4104-7105-5 (hardcover)
    1. Catherine II, Empress of Russia, 1729–1796—Fiction. 2. Large type books. I. Title.
PR9199.4.S728E47 2014
813'.6—dc23   2014013988

Published in 2014 by arrangement with Bantam Books, a division of Random House LLC, a Penguin Random House company

Printed in Mexico
1 2 3 4 5 6 7 18 17 16 15 14

To the memory of my mother

She exercised a constant self-control over herself, and herein 'appeared the greatness of her character, for nothing is more difficult.

JACQUES CASANOVA DE SEINGALT ON
CATHERINE THE GREAT

And you shall fall, in no way different,
As withered leaves shall fall from trees;
And you shall die, in no way different,
As your most humble slave shall die.

GAVRILA DERZHAVIN,
QUOTED IN *THE ROMANOVS*

CAST OF MOST IMPORTANT CHARACTERS

Empress Catherine II, previously Grand Duchess Catherine Alekseyevna, born Sophie Friederike Auguste of Anhalt-Zerbst

Father: Christian August of Anhalt-Zerbst
Mother: Johanna of Holstein-Gottorp

HER FAMILY

Emperor Peter III, Catherine's husband, previously Grand Duke Peter Fyodorovich, born Karl Peter Ulrich, Duke of Holstein-Gottorp

Empress Elizabeth, aunt of Peter III and daughter of Peter the Great

Her Children

Grand Duke Paul Petrovich (married to Grand Duchess Maria Fyodorovna)

Grand Duchess Anna Petrovna (fathered by Stanislav Poniatowski)

Count Alexei Bobrinsky (a love child with Grigory Orlov)

9

Her Grandchildren

Grand Duke Alexander Pavlovich (married to Grand Duchess Elizabeth Alexeyevna)

Grand Duke Constantine Pavlovich (married to Grand Duchess Anna Fyodorovna)

Grand Duchess Alexandrine Pavlovna (to be betrothed to Gustav Adolf of Sweden)

Grand Duchess Yelena Pavlovna

Grand Duchess Maria Pavlovna

Grand Duchess Olga Pavlovna

Grand Duke Nicholas Pavlovich

HER LOVERS/FAVORITES

Serge Saltykov

Stanislav Poniatowski, later the King of Poland

Grigory Orlov

Alexander Vasilchikov

Grigory Potemkin (Grisha, Grishenka)

Alexander Lanskoy (Sashenka)

Alexander Matveyevich Mamonov (Mister Redcoat)

Platon Alexandrovich Zubov (Le Noiraud)

HER ATTENDANTS

Varvara Nikolayevna Malikina, a servant and confidante; Darya (also Darenka), her daughter

Vishka (Maria Savishna Perekusikhina), Catherine's confidante

Queenie (Anna Stepanovna Protasova), Catherine's confidante

Zakhar Ivanovich Zotov, Catherine's valet
Doctor Rogerson, court physician

COURTIERS

Count Alexei Orlov
Count Nikita Ivanovich Panin
Prince Lev Naryshkin
Count Alexander Andreyevich Bezborodko, first her secretary, then minister
Adrian Moseyevich Gribovsky, Catherine's last secretary
Count Morkov
Prince Adam Czartoryski, a Polish noble, Alexander Pavlovich's best friend
Valerian Zubov, a soldier/courtier, brother of the last Favorite
Count Cobenzl, Austrian Ambassador
Prince Repnin, former Russian Ambassador in Poland, governor-general of the newly acquired Eastern Provinces after the last Partition of Poland, Adam Czartoryski's natural father
Alexandra Branicka (Sashenka), Potemkin's niece
Princess Catherine (Katya) Dashkova, Catherine's friend

POLITICAL OPPONENTS

Emelyan Pugachev, the leader of the serf/ Cossack uprising of 1773–75
Tadeusz Kościuszko, the leader of the Polish uprising of 1794

She is dressed in a robe of silver brocade. A golden mantle trimmed with ermine and silver tassels covers her feet. Her eyes are closed, cheeks rouged, lips slightly parted.

In the Grand Gallery of the Winter Palace, illuminated by rows of thick wax candles, the imperial coffin rests on a raised platform beneath a canopy draped in black velvet. Imperial courtiers stifle their sobs. Grief-stricken subjects line up to kiss their late sovereign's hand. Imperial Guards stand at attention. The choir intones *Memory Eternal.* The priests in their black vestments embroidered with silver chant the prayers for the dead. The air is choked with clouds of sweet incense.

Crowds have gathered in front of the Winter Palace, along the Embankment, on the streets and bridges. This is the time of lamentation, when the soul of the newly departed still lingers, awaiting forgiveness for sins, gathering strength for the passage to the next world. Ancient Russian customs call for special foods and the

13

street vendors oblige with pancakes, fish pies, and *kissiel* made of oatmeal. To fortify the spirit, shots of vodka are sold by the glass.

But something rings louder than sobs and requiem chants. Russia's beloved Tsarina, Catherine, Empress of all the Russias, is lying in state and yet no courtiers, ministers, or high priests make laudatory speeches, praise the long prosperous years and glorious conquests of her extraordinary reign. The poets, too, are silent. No odes, no ballads, no dirges sing the despair of Catherine's orphaned subjects.

At the Nevsky monastery, with the whole Imperial Family gathered around him, His Imperial Majesty Tsar Paul I, the rightful heir to the Romanov blood, orders the monks to fetch his father's coffin from its anonymous grave. Two Russian sovereigns will make their last earthly journey together.

Old debts must be paid, old sins punished.

Thirty-four glorious years of Catherine's reign have been erased with a wave of her son's hand. How can the mind grasp that such a time has come?

■ ■ ■ ■

PART I
NOVEMBER 5, 1796

■ ■ ■ ■

9:00 A.M.

The pain is sharp, piercing, a burning dagger's thrust inside her skull, somewhere behind the right eye. It hits just as she lifts her quill out of an inkwell. Her hand freezes. The quill, dropped, stains the letter she was just about to sign.

The mantel clock begins to chime. She recalls being frightened as a child to see the hands of a clock turned back, believing time itself might go back and she would be forced to live again through everything she had already lived through, depriving her of the adventure of the future.

The pain doesn't stop or diminish. It is already nine o'clock and she is still behind with the reading she must finish before her secretary arrives. She considers calling Zotov, her valet, but dismisses the thought quickly. The headache will go away by itself, but once her old servant begins to fuss, she won't be able to send him away.

17

Pani, her Italian greyhound, sniffs her mistress's hand with fierce concentration, licking the skin of her palm. The dog is slender and fine-boned, a direct descendant of beloved Zemira, who lies buried in the Tsarskoye Selo gardens.

"I've nothing for you there," she mutters. She tries to pat Pani's head, but her right hand is strangely wooden, stiff and unwieldy, so she settles for an awkward caress, noting thick drops of pus in the corners of her dog's eyes. Just like Zemira, Pani is prone to lingering infections.

Outside her study, pattering feet and muted voices dissolve into furtive silence: The Empress is working. The Empress must not be disturbed.

She stands. With her left hand she grips the edge of her desk, clumsily, sending the papers flying. *How intriguing,* she thinks, watching the vellum pages glide on invisible currents, hover in the air, silent like birds of prey. Pani, too, watches, head cocked to the side. A wagging tail thumps at the floor.

The cup of coffee on the desk must be cold by now, but a drink will do her good. Her right hand is still heavy and stiff, so she picks up the cup with her left. The first bitter sip is refreshing, but the second one makes her choke.

She spits the coffee out. On the encrusted wood, on her papers. Brown, watery splashes she should wipe right away, but instead she lets her tongue probe the inside of her mouth, the soft, ribbed folds of her palate. *Like calf's brain,* she thinks, her mother's favorite dish.

She tries to put the cup back on the desk, but her hand refuses to obey, and it shatters on the floor.

If she walks a bit, will the headache dissolve?

Her first step is wobbly, unsure, making her clutch whatever is within her reach. The corner of her desk, the chair.

Behind her something falls down. Something big and heavy.

Her right knee is still sore. It's been like this ever since that dreadful fall three years ago, when she toppled down the stairs on her way to the *banya.* Zotov had heard the noise and rushed after her. Made her sit on the marble step for a while. Only when she assured him the dizzy spell had passed did he help her stand up, slowly. She didn't think she had been truly hurt, bruised and frightened as she was, but the knee is not letting her forget the fall.

9:01 A.M.

Each step, unsteady as it is, is a marvel. The muscles contracting and releasing. The feet shuffling forward, one after another. Like the mechanical doll her granddaughters loved to play with, before Constantine, her grandson,

19

cut it open to see what was hidden inside.

The steps take her out of her study, past the small alcove where her pelisses hang beside the silver-framed mirror, toward the door that leads to her privy.

In the alcove mirror, her body is reflected as if in quivering water, broken into uneven, ill-fitting parts, each wrinkled and malformed. Her face fares no better, the sagging flesh, the neck that resembles a turkey's throat. Her eyes are bloodshot, watery, blinking. *I've never been beautiful,* she thinks. *But what did Helen of Troy have to show for her looks? The ravages of war and the pursuit of men she had not chosen?*

The privy smells, faintly, of wet animal fur and rotting roots. The door closes behind her with a thump. The squeak of the hinges is oddly sharp, circling around her like the sound of a tuning fork. As if time looped, refusing to unravel.

Her fingers gripping the edge of the water closet resemble claws of some ancient bird, not quite accustomed to such feats of agility. And yet they hold on, help her balance. *How magnificent,* she thinks, *this effort of muscles and bones, sinew and blood.*

Slowly she lifts the fingertips to her nostrils and sniffs at the sweet, sharp smell of ink. Something from the past floats by — images of a race, frothy waves crashing against the shore, stretching over tawny sand. Seagulls shriek out of jealousy or greed. In the shallow water a horse's head lies entangled in a tattered fishnet and tufts of seaweed, baring its teeth. A swarm of eels wiggles out of its eye sockets, slithers through its open jaws.

A memory, she thinks, *not a dream.*

9:04 A.M.

With the headache pounding in her temples, voices bubble inside her. Phrases echo in her mind: *I am Minerva. I am armed.*

Something odd is happening.

A thought is not just a thought. A word is not a mere word.

She thinks of an apple and an apple appears. It is slightly greasy to the touch. It has plump, sunburnt sides and a splash of green around the stem bowl. Its skin is freckled with darker spots.

She stares at it for a while before setting her teeth on the skin and pressing hard. The apple snaps off with a cracking sound, then shatters, filling her mouth with juice.

The joy she feels is ancient, the joy of crushing through living tissue, life nourishing life.

Why am I thinking about an apple?

There is no apple. Her hand is empty. The word *apple* that rattles in her mind means temptation.

Is this what she should be thinking of?

21

The question intrigues her for a while, until another agonizing throb shoots up the right side of her skull and a flash of light stings her eyes.

9:05 A.M.
In the vestibule, servants talk.

"Are you sure Her Majesty hasn't called for me yet?" Gribovsky asks. Her secretary's voice is anxious, thin with unease.

"Quite sure, Adrian Moseyevich."

"But it's past the usual time."

"Her Majesty has her reasons."

Something is happening to her, but she has little time to think what it might be. Each movement demands her utmost attention, angles to calculate and adjust, muscles to flex and to steady. She listens to each breath that enters or leaves her nostrils.

Her heart, a traitor drummer, pounds its own rhythm. Or is it like a frantic courtier sent to warn her of some approaching calamity? Fire? Flood? The mob armed with scythes, marching on the palace doors?

Her lips are parched. The blue porcelain jug in the privy is too heavy to lift, so she dips her fingers inside and sucks on the drops that cling to them. The water is stale. She should ring for Queenie, who must be outside, with the others.

Why is there no bell in the privy?

The headache has diminished, but the inside of her skull feels fragile and exposed, as if an ax has split her open. Is this how Jupiter felt giving birth to Minerva?

"What time is it?"

"Still early, Adrian Moseyevich," someone answers curtly. A woman laughs. A door opens and closes. Footsteps grow fainter. A dog barks. Something rattles against the windowpane; there is a loud bang followed by a thump.

"You know who he is. His father ran a bookstore off the Great Perspective Road. By the Fontanka. Then it got flooded."

"What are you scribbling there, Adrian Moseyevich? Have some hot tea. It's a chilly morning."

"The dog is still missing. Do you think someone stole it?"

"A thief would've brought it back, already, for the reward."

"The poor beastie must be dead by now."

The voices outside the privy door float back and forth; whispers fade away. Rumbles quicken like wooden carts on the ice mountain, right before they pick up real speed and become unstoppable.

9:09 A.M.
In the privy, she manages to hike up her pet-

23

ticoats and lower herself on the commode seat. Like a big hen settling onto a nest. The seat is cold and sticky, giving way under her weight with a squeak.

The voices in the vestibule swirl, punctuated by moments of soothing silence. The world around her slows. The pain is still there, but it, too, feels distant, easier to bear. Time is sluggish. There is no need to rush.

Inside her belly, muscles let go, release the hot stream of urine. For a while, all she wants to do is sit and absorb the profound pleasure of relief. Sink into silence. Just be.

Out of this silence comes another memory. A monkey, Plaisir, was the French Ambassador's gift. A mere baby when he came, dressed in a velvet jacket, breeches, and a feathered hat. His tiny paws clutched at her finger when she held him, and he buried his pink face in the folds of her dress. His eyes were big, beseeching.

Cebus capucinus. White-headed capuchin.

The two keepers ordered to mind Plaisir at all times had scars on their hands and arms from bites and scratches, all the way up to their elbows. No chain was enough to restrain the little rascal. Once free, the monkey always found a way to her study. He opened every drawer in her desk, tore papers, spilled ink, chewed at her quills, peed on her chair. He put his finger up his anus and then smeared excrement on the walls. When she screamed at him, he covered his ears and made a grimace of such relentless misery that she laughed.

On one of his mischievous sprees, Plaisir smashed a jar of her face cream and ate its contents. A few hours later, he crept under a chair in her bedroom and wouldn't come out. No treats, none of his favorite toys would tempt him. "Leave him," she ordered the servants. "He'll come out when he gets hungry." Only he didn't. He just shrank and died.

9:10 A.M.

To stand up, many muscles have to be kept taut, many bones lifted. In the meantime, every heartbeat calls for her attention.

The memory of Platon's hoarse voice interrupts her concentration. "Why are you hurting me, Katinka? You are all I've got. Without you, I'm dust."

The voice of her lover is insistent, pleading. She pictures Platon standing next to her, so crushingly beautiful in his charcoal-colored ensemble, his features pure. Nose, jawline, lips. If she could draw, she would sketch him in black ink. Then smudge the edges to soften him.

Have I hurt you, Platon? How? And when?

This is a problem she could solve. Unravel the puzzling configuration of cause and effect, if only she thought about it long enough.

She has always been good with ciphers. Numbers that turn into letters. Words that stand for other words. To solve a puzzle one needs to look for patterns, the rhythm of repetitions.

But why does Platon begin to whistle, and then sing?

Russia reaches farther-higher
Over mountain peaks and seas.

How can she solve a puzzle that shifts its shape, flickers like a firefly, and then disappears into the dark? How can she solve a puzzle when all she can be certain of is the searing pain in his voice?

9:11 A.M.
"Crying all night . . . again . . . poor child . . . this is not the end of the world, Her Majesty told her so many times . . . but the young never listen . . ."

The voices in the antechamber veer off, like nervous horses bent on flight. Sometimes whole phrases come through the walls, sometimes only words.

"It hurts more when you are young."

"Such a shame."

"How could he . . ."

She should try to hear more, learn what the servants are talking about. It's useful to know what is not meant for your ears.

But the headache is not going away. Each pang is a blow, enclosing her in a roaring fog. Voices, groans, a loud drumming sound. Her palms moisten with sweat.

Such headaches have plagued her before. The bursts of blinding light are not new, either. It's not surprising. She has been working too much, too hard. But what looks done one day disintegrates on the next. No wonder that the weight in her chest gets heavier.

The Polish campaign is over, but the Polish partition treaty is still not finished. The Prussians want to keep Warsaw, but won't yield anything of value in return. As always, they want Russia to get their chestnuts out of the fire for them!

Nations are like merchants. They form and break alliances according to the rules of costs and profits. A country that wishes no expansion will wither. Stillness is an illusion. Empires need to grow or face defeat. This is why she has taxed her body beyond its strength. In the service of her empire. Are other monarchs working as hard as she is? Without stopping?

She needs a good long rest.

The Earth hides many secrets.
This is a good thought. Useful and pleasant.

In Siberia, serfs dig out giant bones buried several fathoms underground. "Fossilized ivory, Your Majesty," scholars tell her. "Brought here by the current of an ancient river." But ivory does not grow in the shape of bones. Elephants must have once lived where now there is nothing but snow. If one is patient, the strangest transformations are possible.

Remember these words, she orders herself. *Write them down as soon as you are back at your desk. Use them when you talk to Alexandrine.*

Outside her privy, noises grow and diminish. Feet clatter. Something metallic bangs, then rolls away. The dog's nails are scratching the wooden floor. Voices she hears are too loud, or sound hollow, as if coming from inside a deep well.

Her servants are jostling among themselves. Queenie is asserting her position. Vishka opposes her, slowly, with measured, relentless cadences. It matters little what they are talking about. Prices of silk, salt, Crimean wines. The likelihood of the Neva freezing soon. Predictions — even those professed by experts — are hardly ever accurate. Conviction is merely a sign of the speaker's self-assurance.

A telltale sign of arrogance.

9:13 A.M.
The commode has a soft leather seat. When

28

she moves, the leather creaks. Back and forth. Slowly, gently. The swaying of the body soothes. This is how being in a cradle must feel to an infant.

Inside her belly a throb, a mounting pressure of blood. As if her menses have returned. Which cannot be.

The flashes of light are gone now, replaced by elongated floating shapes that drift through her field of vision. Glowing against the ray of pale morning sun that comes through the small window up high. Sometimes blurry, sometimes transparent. Sinking to the bottom when she tries to look at them closer.

Within her very body there are layers of inscrutable marvels.

Everything moves, united in a common goal. The heart pumping blood. The saliva gathering in her throat, silky and smooth. Her mouth is full of something soft. Like silk or gauze. Or a ball of wool that cats like to play with. She can hear her own breath. Her body is a universe in itself, a cluster of patterns that are still stunningly mysterious.

Remember only what matters.
This memory is all I have, *she decides.* Since I was a child, I have always known how to use what I have.

"You are ugly, Sophie," a voice says. The

29

brother who has stolen her place in their mother's heart is lying in bed, his weak body a thin bump under a satin-covered eiderdown.

She is no older than seven, her hands and scalp are covered by scabs, her bones threaten to bend out of shape. "A hunchback," she sometimes hears the grown-ups whisper. Their voices are poisoned with pity.

The summer has ended and the red spots are coming back, ripening slowly into silvery scabs. Even when the scabs peel off, her cheeks, her scalp, and her arms are scaly and rough. No amount of rubbing can help. She has to wait for another summer when, hidden from prying eyes behind a silk screen, her chemise removed to expose the skin, she will lie on a sun-soaked towel. After a few weeks, pink spots will retreat and her skin will become smooth again.

"You are ugly, Sophie."

Her brother's eyes flicker with glee. William thinks he has defeated her. This sickly, crippled brother of hers, the cause of Mother's panicky whispers, her soothing caresses. Her insistence that nothing should ever be denied to this cherished boy.

"And you are going to die," Sophie tells her brother. There is no hesitation in her voice, no doubt. "Just like Augusta did," she adds before he covers his ears. Their sister lived for ten days, and the earth on her tiny grave is still soft.

"Mother!" William screams. "Sophie is scaring me again!"

Her silly brother won't fight with her. William trusts weakness and pity, oblivious of the price they will exert in the end.

He is a fool. A tittle-tattle. A weakling.

Down the stairs comes the hurried tapping of her mother's heels.

She, Sophie, can brave Mother's anger. She can withstand any punishment. She doesn't care. "You'll die, William" — her lips mouth the words until Mother's hand slaps her hard, until blood seeps from a broken lip. Salty and sweet.

I've come to Russia from Zerbst, with Mother.

I was called Sophie.

From that journey she remembers vast expanses of snow-covered fields, which — the Russian Guards tell her — will be lush with wheat and oats and barley in a few months. Stretches of thick, dark forests where foxes and mink grow the softest of pelts. Towns and roadside villages where onion-domed churches entice the eyes with bright colors and the peal of bells. Carved frames and shutters of peasant huts. Night that comes early, swiftly swallowing what in Zerbst would still be the light of day.

31

Her feet swell from the long hours of sitting in the carriage and hurt when she steps out of the carriage and tries to walk. Not that much, but enough for Mother to order one of the Russian attendants to carry her daughter to the inn when they stop for the night. They are illustrious visitors, Mother announces to yet another bowing postmaster who may not fully appreciate the honor bestowed on his smoky tavern. The Princess of Zerbst is traveling on a personal invitation from Her Majesty Empress Elizabeth Petrovna. Who — if sudden death didn't intervene — would now be her sister-in-law.

Mother's much-repeated statement elicits vigorous nods from their German maid and polite ones from the Russian servants. It's hard to fathom what the subsequent tavern-keepers make of it. Russian words flow fast. Even the few she has already learned elude her.

It's best to start from the beginning.
Da means *yes.*
Nyet means *no.*
Mozhet byt means *maybe.*

"Isn't Sophie charming, Peter?" Empress Elizabeth asks when they arrive. Excitement tints her cheeks the color of ripe apricots. Or is it a new shade of rouge?

Peter, Sophie's second cousin, now Russia's Crown Prince in need of a wife, lifts his head. His eyes — slightly bulging — dart from her to his aunt and back to her.

Here in Moscow, Peter looks thinner than he was in his home in Eutin, where Sophie first saw him. Like a starving man, if an heir to the throne could lack nourishment.

The cold of the long winter journey still lingers in her bones. Ice gardens blooming on the carriage windows. The chill of moldy roadside inns, numbing toes and fingers. The foggy cloud of her own breath. The endless expanses of frozen fields, thick forests blanketed with powdery snow. The fear, persistent and unyielding, that if — by whatever mishap — the carriage that was speeding toward Russia stopped, the frost would creep up inside and kill her.

And what does Peter see when he looks at her? Her clear white complexion? Her strong teeth? The budding breasts, held up by tight stays? Her hazel eyes, flecked with blue? Where do his thoughts race? To Eutin, where she assured him he was so very smart? Where he whispered in her ear: "If they make me the King of Sweden, I'll run away with the Gypsies and they'll never find me."

"Do you like Princess Sophie, Peter?"

Around them — in this sprawling Moscow palace with creaking floors and empty anterooms — everyone catches their breath. She, a mere princess of Anhalt-Zerbst, notes the curve of her cousin's thin throat and a frown of his eyebrows.

A long moment of waiting, and then Peter nods.

It is a slight nod and it doesn't seem like much, but there is a whole world behind it. A world of what is now possible. Of not being sent back to Zerbst, not having to hide her thoughts behind pliant smiles. A world of bold strides. Of sweeping vistas. Of spring that will melt the snow.

A world she craves so much that her hand clenches on the folds of her skirt. A world that makes her think of a stallion dancing around before a race, tail raised, taut muscles quivering under the skin. Just awaiting the sign to sprint forward, knock everyone out of its way.

The courtiers crane their necks. Behind her, Mother fails to stifle a gasp.

Keep your eyes down, Sophie!
    Don't spoil it! Not now, not when you are so close!

The Empress of Russia rises from her throne. Elizabeth's glittering gown must be heavy and stiff, but she moves like a dancer, head high, spine straight, steps light and graceful. Scarlet silk embroidered with gold thread displays intricate flowers in bloom. Her mantle is lined with ermine. On her neck rests a triple string of black pearls. "Garish . . . ostentatious . . . so very Russian" have become Mother's favorite words.

Imperial arms, soft but strong, encircle "the beloved moon children," press them to a heaving chest. The silken embrace is tight. "My Sophie. You'll never disappoint me."

Her forehead is pressed against something pointed and hard, which will leave an imprint on her skin. Sophie breathes in the scents: attar of roses, bitter almond, and the sharp foxy smell of sweat.

"Wipe that stupid smile off your face, Sophie. You are not his wife yet."

Mother's lips curve in a forced grin as she licks her finger and smooths her daughter's brows. Or tucks a strand of her hair under the new velvet hood.

"Listen to me, girl!"

Sophie is still. She does listen. She doesn't stare, especially not at the Empress of Russia, who has just announced to the whole court that this snippet of a princess from Prussia will soon turn Peter into a proper man.

She, Sophie, makes sure she walks one step behind her mother, and never speaks first. Mostly she listens. When a question is asked, her reply is always brief. "I love what I've seen of Russia . . . no, I haven't seen this much snow ever . . . yes, the Empress is most kind and generous . . . the Crown Prince is very handsome."

Her voice is velvety soft. Her eyes stay lowered, taking in the frayed hems of dresses and scuffed shoes. But an imperial promise, however fleeting, however vague, cannot be erased. It's an ancient wisdom. One cannot step twice into the same river.

Here in Moscow, houses are mostly wooden. Streets meander, dissolve into impossibly narrow lanes. Sleighs must make long detours to reach their destinations. Outside the butcher shops, the snow is stained red, spattered with fresh blood. By a tannery, the air is so acrid it makes her gag.

In St. Petersburg, which she saw only briefly on her way to Moscow, palace façades were made of stone. Streets were wide and straight. A giant ice mountain stood on the frozen river. Painted carts sped down its steep slope, faster than a galloping horse, faster than the gust of northern wind. "Too dangerous, Sophie. I won't let you do it," Mother had said.

But Mother couldn't stop her from seeing the elephants. Their folds of gray skin, curled trunks, the yellow sabers of their tusks. Ears like giant sails folded against their domed heads.

On that dark afternoon lit by flaming torches and barrels of burning tar, these gray, swaying giants balanced on hind legs and waved their feet in the air. They played ball, threw rings into the air and caught them in

36

mid-flight.

She had laughed and clapped her hands so hard that they hurt. Beside her, Prince Naryshkin, her host for the evening, whispered his warnings: *An elephant can crush a raging bear, bend the bars of an iron cage.*

Beware the wild beast, Sophie.

But don't stop looking!

The trumpet had sounded, the elephants lined up, fell on their front knees, and lowered their giant heads. In front of *her,* a princess of Zerbst.

This is the memory she clings to at the end of each Moscow day, curled up in bed, burying her face in the soft fur blanket. It makes her forget that there is humiliation in wanting. That gifts from Zerbst are too meager to impress even the palace servants. That smiles and kind words don't go far.

"We must hold our heads high, Sophie," Mother scolds her. "Our line is far more ancient." Mother does what she has always done, consults a tree of descent, which she has committed to memory. Family connections are sturdy ropes along a shaky footbridge of prestige. Aunts, cousins, brothers, wives, husbands. Prince of Brunswick. Prince-Bishop of Lübeck. Good blood has many tributaries.

Zerbst, Mother brags, bustles with magnificent balls and military parades. A rickety drawbridge takes on the luster of a thoroughfare. A statue of a butter maiden becomes a landmark talked about in Berlin itself.

Mother doesn't hear the snickers at her boasting. Whispers that die as soon as she comes near. The looks that remind Sophie how uncertain their future is.

And Peter?

Every morning, Peter comes to their rooms to announce his plans for the day. Plans that make no mention of the world outside the palace doors.

"Look at my drawings, Sophie," he says. "These are the uniforms I want my soldiers to wear."

Or: "Have you really spoken to King Frederick, Sophie? What does he look like? What did he say to you?"

There is brightness in Peter's blue eyes when he talks of Berlin or Holstein, brightness that dies out when she asks him anything about Russia. If she persists, he snaps at her with impatience, or anger. Why would Sophie of Anhalt-Zerbst want to know what a Russian chancellor does? Or which of the maids sleep in the Empress's inner rooms?

"But you'll be a Tsar one day, Peter. Don't you want to know?"

"I won't be a Tsar for a long time," he replies, which could've been a wise answer, but it isn't. For Sophie knows it is not a prince's wish for his Empress aunt to rule as long as she can, but a desire to escape his destiny.

The past, which cannot be changed, is far away. The future, which can be altered, is uncertain. For now, both need to be pushed into some far-flung crevice of her heart.

The present is the puzzle she needs to crack.

S volkami zhit', po-volch'i vyt'. If you want to live with wolves, howl like them.

Russian doesn't easily yield to fourteen-year-old lips, already set in their ways. "Once again, Your Highness. Only softer. Russians do not like foreigners!"

Monsieur Abadurov is her tutor, and he teaches her that Russian nouns acquire new endings depending on their position in a sentence: *"Bolshoy chleb,"* he says, "but *chleba net."*

In Russian, names turn into other names. Alexander becomes Sasha. But Alexandrine can also become Sasha, so there is no way of telling from the name alone if Sasha is a girl or a boy. Sasha can also turn into Sashenka. Just like Grigory turns into Grisha or Grishenka or Grishenok.

Puzzling? Yes, but easy enough to learn by heart. It's harder to understand the meaning of Russian tales. In a German story, a man is a fool when he screams in fear at the sight of

39

a hammer hanging on the wall because, one day, it might fall down and kill a child standing underneath. In Russian *skazkas,* a fool understands the language of birds and beasts. He may be slow and covered in grime, but the fool is the one who marries a Tsar's daughter and becomes the wisest of rulers.

S kem povedyoshsya, ot togo i naberyoshsya. You become like those you spend time with.

Up close, Empress Elizabeth's skin resembles a fresh painting. Caked powder masks the redness of her nose, the scratches on her neck, the livid patches of bruises. Dark, moist circles gather under her arms, but perfume is stronger than sweat. Beauty is made of layers, each protecting some secret of the night. In the palace corridors, handsome young men eat the Empress with hungry eyes when she passes by. If she drops a fan, a feather, a ribbon from her hair, they squabble for it like wild dogs.

"Don't displease me, Sophie, and Our Lady of Kazan will protect you."

For Elizabeth, the murky, incense-infused silence of the chapel is the only place where thoughts of death and eternity trump earthly pleasures. There, under the soulful eyes of icon saints, the Empress speaks of mercy and settles her accounts with God.

This, too, is Russia. Wrapped in the sweet scent of frankincense. Lit by the votive lamps that illuminate the long, gaunt faces of the saints. Lost in the contemplation of that other, true world. Russia doubts knowledge. Mistrusts reason, for all evil comes from opinions. Embraces suffering and acceptance of God's will. Russia is like a cipher, forever changing. When you crack one pattern, another takes its place.

Peter's hounds lie by the fireplace, panting. One is sniffing at its balls. The other emits a low growl as she enters, but its tail is wagging, so the growl is not a threat. "Why are you crossing yourself like *them*, Sophie?" Peter asks when she bows in front of the icons in his room and crosses herself in the Orthodox way, right shoulder first, three fingers bunched. "No one can see you now!"

She has come to his room to play chess, a game fraught with dangers. Her silk shoes pinch her toes, so she has kicked them off.

"Why can't you be more like your mother, Sophie?" Peter asks, as he advances his pawn three squares, hoping she won't notice. His fingers are long and slightly crooked. His eyelashes are almost white. "Your mother is not stubborn like you are!"

Peter's uniform, the Preobrazhensky greens the Empress orders him to wear, is unbuttoned and stained at the cuffs. "Speak to him

41

about Holstein, Sophie, if that's what he wishes," Mother urges. "You don't want to be sent back to Zerbst!"

A game of chess is a game of choices. Sacrifice a pawn to capture a knight. Assess each position, predict the next few moves, watch out for incongruities. Or let your opponent cheat and think himself invincible.

If I please Peter, I'll displease the Empress.
If I please the Empress, I'll displease Peter.

Peter soon tires of playing. "Look, Sophie," he says. "Look what I've got."

A black silk kerchief is covering something on the table. No other woman has seen what he is about to reveal to her. It is a hundred-year secret. It has been sent to him from Eutin.

Peter mumbles something, but what she hears makes little sense. "Kaspar — the executioner . . . with his own hands . . . at midnight . . . no moon . . ." Then, pompously, he asks himself if he should even consider showing his secret to a mere woman.

Sophie waits patiently. Peter is a chatterbox. He doesn't know how to keep a secret.

Peter lifts the black silk, revealing strips of paper covered with German script. *"Passauer kunst,"* he says in German, beaming with pride. The Art of Passau.

She extends her hand to touch the nearest slip.

"No!" he screams and smacks her fingers.

She hides her irritation, turns it into a question: "What are they, Peter?"

"There is magic in them," he says, his long fingers hovering over the paper strips. "The one who carries them will become invincible."

She doesn't laugh. She doesn't mock the exultation in his voice.

"Were they made for you?" she asks.

Instead of answering, he points at a piece of paper. "This one has been waiting for me for over a hundred years."

"How do you know?"

"I know."

He doesn't have an answer, so he evades her question. If she persists, he will only grow angry, claim some divine revelation, known only to the initiated. This shouldn't surprise her. People do the oddest things to assure power. Maids spit over their shoulders when they see a black cat. She has heard of a woman at the Tartar market who ate a candle with a holy image melted into it. One of the Empress's own maids hid a package with bones and hair under her mistress's bed.

"What will you do with them, Peter?" she asks instead.

Surprisingly, this time he does answer. Some, he tells her, he will chew and swallow. Others he will carry on his body. Tied by a thin linen strip. Close to the skin.

"Will you tell me what's written on them?"

"No!" There is a sudden burst of terror in his voice, and he covers the curls of paper with the handkerchief again. As if she could destroy his magic just by looking at it.

Boltun — nakhodka dlya shpiona. A chatterbox is a spy's treasure.

Russia is not only ruled by a different calendar, but it also follows her own holy days and sacred obligations. "Lutheran guests do not have to observe our customs," her tutor announces.

"But they can be told their meaning," Sophie says.

"Each pilgrimage is a different journey, Your Highness."

Empress Elizabeth has left for Troitse-Sergieva Lavra, the monastery where St. Sergius had many visions. In one vision, a multitude of birds flocked to him. It was a sign that the saint's followers would be plentiful.

"How did he know it was a sign?"

"He heard God's voice and then he became a great teacher."

"What did St. Sergius teach?"

"That even the Son of Man did not come to earth to be served, but to serve."

She considers the story of a wise monk who

44

insisted on the importance of simplicity and service. A life spent in labor and prayer, sustained by plain food and clothes. Far away from the lures of court.

This, too, is Russia.

"The most pious land in the world," her tutor assures her. Orthodox Christianity is truer to the teaching of Christ than the Catholicism of Rome or the Lutheran Creed. Because it is not contaminated by worldly pride. Because it is not guilty of the sin of presumption. Even the Tsars have learned that tampering with the Church's practices will bring the wrath of heaven.

She doesn't tell her tutor that her father would have disagreed. "Why is the Empress walking to the monastery?" she asks instead. "Why can't she ride in her carriage?"

"Because deprivation of the body is part of repentance."

"Repentance for what?"

"That, Your Highness, I cannot tell you. We each sin in our own way."

Mother is not that reticent. Away from the Empress, she bristles with confidence. Her voice carries through the thin walls of their rooms. ". . . on her fat knees . . . begging the Virgin to forgive her for every time she takes a guard to her bed!"

Deprivations? Fasts? Ha!

The Empress of Russia is insatiable. Elizabeth craves rich food, strong drink, and the caresses of men. Caresses a girl like Sophie should know nothing about.

Now, with the Empress gone on her pilgrimage, Mother lies with Chevalier Betskoy.

They laugh. They whisper. They laugh again.

Her father is not here to stop them.

The Russian maids make signs with their hands, imitating a pair of horns on a man's head. They wink at one another when they carry out basins of sop water from Mother's rooms.

Like mother, like daughter, Sophie hears. The apple doesn't fall far from the tree.

Under a tapestry showing a stag pierced by an arrow, there is a hidden door. It is locked, and nothing but dense, murky darkness is visible through the keyhole. On her dressing table, jars of cream change places. In her drawers, even the locked ones, papers have been moved around. Someone must have opened the box with her beauty spots, for one of them has fallen on the carpet. Someone has gone through her linens, leafed through her books.

The spies are watching her. What are they looking for? A mistake? Or merely proof of her willingness to be worthy?

Bez kota mysham razdol'ye, her Russian

tutor writes in big even letters for her to copy. Without a cat, mice feel free.

With the Empress gone, the palace corridors have emptied. The servants whisper and laugh among themselves. Guards yawn. Pages fidget when summoned, forget what they have been asked to fetch.

Peter has stopped speaking Russian. "Send your tutor to hell, Sophie," he tells her. His writing table is still covered with papers, but it is no longer Passauer art. Peter has a new project. He wants to gather the maxims from all the letters he has ever received from King Frederick of Prussia: *A general should never engage in battle unless he has an advantage over his enemy. A retreat is sometimes necessary.*

"Copy them for me, Sophie," Peter orders. "Your mother says you have a very good hand."

Gde tonko — tam i rvyotsya. It'll snap where it's the thinnest.

"Please, Mother," she pleads.

But Mother looks at her with the calculating eyes of a rival. "What do you want from me now, Sophie?" she snaps.

"Send Chevalier Betskoy away. People are talking."

47

"People are always talking, Sophie."

Mother's eyes say more. That her daughter knows nothing of her disappointments. That a woman's happiness has to be snatched when it's still possible. That even a good and honest man can leave a woman empty and wanting.

"What if they tell the Empress?"

Mother's hand raises too fast for Sophie to duck. The slap across her cheek turns her head sideways. "I'm here because of *you,* Sophie! I've dragged myself away from my home for your sake! Is this how you repay me?"

The cheek smarts and swells, pulsates with blood.

"We are in Russia now, Mother."

"And what is this supposed to mean, Sophie? That we should forget who we are? Let these barbarians turn us into puppets dancing on *their* strings?"

Mother's hand raises again, but this time Sophie is faster and steps back. The hand hesitates in the air and falls limp to her side.

During the day, when Mother leaves on her errands, elderly court women come and sit in her room. They are supposed to keep Princess Sophie company or watch over her when she rests.

Anyone who matters a smidgen at court has gone with the Empress on the pilgrimage.

The women who come to sit with the Princess of Anhalt-Zerbst know that. They have become invisible, they joke. Too old for men, too insignificant for other women to bother with.

They speak of the Moscow chill, hard on the bones. Of the servants, lazy at all times, who skimp on the logs to sell them on the side. Of the lackey who sold a canary at the market and replaced it with a dead bird, thinking his mistress wouldn't tell the difference. Then they sigh and grow silent, racking their brains for topics that might amuse the young Princess of Zerbst.

When she relieves them from their duty by pretending to fall asleep, they talk about her.

"Poor Sophie. Weak, isn't she? A child, really. At fourteen, they tell you how you are a woman, but you are not."

"Imperial marriages are bargains, and this one looks like a bad one . . ."

With her eyes closed, her breath even and deep, Sophie listens.

"Grave mistakes are easy to make, and even easier to notice and report. Servants have big eyes and keen ears. No one is ever alone here."

"The Empress wants her? But the Empress is fickle. It's not hard to change the imperial mind."

The mere mention of Mother makes their voices break into merry laughter. They imitate

Mother's gasps and haughty declarations of superior German ways.

They shake their heads with amusement at Mother's wanton foolishness. Mockery of one's betters? Hints of imperial shortcomings? Pray, how does it differ from slashing your wrists with a knife and letting yourself bleed to death?

Only a deluded fool entrusts gossip to paper and ink. Hides it in her own bedroom. For any spy to find.

Poor Sophie. So eager to please, that child.

It's not the first time and not the last that a child will have to pay for her mother's sins.

"No more rubbing my daughter's cheeks with ice!" Mother, tense and stony-eyed, screams at the maids in the morning. Everything irks her. The soft Russian wraps, the velvety coverlets, the pelisses of silver fox fur. The gilded doorframes. The gold-plated basin. "No more Russian dishes, either!" From now on, her child will eat simple plain food. Boiled beef. Bread soaked in broth and red wine. Half a glass of weak ale to quench her thirst, sweetened with a spoonful of honey.

The maids scurry like frightened rabbits in front of a galloping horse. "Your services are no longer required," the court doctor has been told. Princess Johanna of Anhalt-Zerbst is no fool.

"You are not really sick, Sophie," Mother

seethes. "You just want me to fuss over you. I know you!"

"My daughter is perfectly well," her mother declares when the doctor arrives. "She is just tired. Aren't you, Sophie?"

The court doctor wears a pair of tight silk gloves, which he peels off with ceremonial slowness. He has quickly glanced at the contents of her chamber pot and smelled her vomit. Now his fingers probe her tongue, the inside of her lips.

"Please, madame. Let me examine the patient."

The doctor scrutinizes the skin on her neck and arms, feels the glands on her neck. "No traces of smallpox," he announces cheerfully. A young woman, he explains to Mother, possesses a delicate and fluid constitution. The balance of humors is easily upset. An emetic will purge the digestive tracts of poison. A concoction he calls the vinegar of seven thieves for rubbing onto the skin to quicken the flow of blood. Venetian tonic for building up strength.

The doctor trusts the Princess of Anhalt-Zerbst would find nothing amiss in these remedies. He is delighted to see that he is right.

The light is miserly, filtering through curtains drawn to keep the drafts away. Wrapped in a thick dressing gown, Sophie sits on a daybed, her feet buried in furs.

Peter hasn't come by, but he has sent his servant girl with an inquiry.

The servant girl is tall and bone thin. Her hair is tied back, hidden under a lace bonnet, but in her eyes there is energy and brightness. And a warm flicker of curiosity as she casts a quick glance toward the bed.

"Who are you?" Mother asks sharply.

The servant girl does not lower her eyes. "The Grand Duke has sent me to say that the Princess of Anhalt-Zerbst has promised to copy Frederick the Great's maxims for the Grand Duke," she recites in a measured voice. "The Grand Duke wishes to know if the Princess intends to be indisposed for much longer."

Mother scowls. Even in Russia, a servant girl should know her place. "I asked you who you were!"

The girl hesitates, not too long but long enough to earn Mother's huff of annoyance. "A reader to His Highness, the Grand Duke. Her Majesty wants to make sure the Grand Duke doesn't tire his eyes."

"What do they call you?"

"Varvara Nikolayevna, Your Highness."

A reader, to Peter? For how long? What does she read to him? What does she see that I don't?

52

■ ■ ■ ■

But Mother no longer pays the servant girl any heed. "We have to keep Peter happy, Sophie," she says as if they were completely alone. "We cannot be thought of as uncaring."

"No, Mother," she replies, but unlike her mother, she cannot ignore Varvara Nikolayevna's presence. It's not just that she would've liked to ask her about Peter. There is something about this girl that reminds her of Father, of his encouraging nod when her eyes filled with frustration over some childish task. Of his hand on her shoulder, preventing his daughter from trampling onto a bird's nest.

"Write what I tell you, Sophie! In your best hand," Mother orders.

Dear Peter, I'm very sorry to have upset your important and admirable endeavor. I promise to get well very soon, and in the meantime, I'd like to resume our work while I'm still resting.

When she is finished, Mother snatches the note from her hand and examines it, scowling. "Your letters, Sophie," she says, "are too small and too uneven. And there is a smudge of ink in the corner. Do you want Peter to think you are a slob?"

"No, Mother."

"Write it again, then!"

Mother's skirts twirl as she paces the room, impatient, lost in her own calculations, her own schemes. Outside the door, a heel stomps the floorboard. A man clears his throat.

"Hurry up, Sophie!"

She copies the note again. Mother, satisfied this time or simply impatient, folds the paper and flattens it at the edges. The servant girl is standing motionless, head high, lips tight, her eyes shining with thoughts known only to herself.

"There, take it to your master, and be gone," Mother orders.

Varvara Nikolayevna, her head tilted slightly, takes a stiff step forward, and for a moment it looks like Mother might slap her. But then outside the room a man's spirited voice breaks into careless laughter, and Mother's whole body softens. As soon as Peter's reader extends her hand for the folded note, Mother hurries out of the room.

The note disappears in the folds of Varvara's dress.

Paintings hang in the corridors. On one, a bearded man is bound to a plank, a blade glitters, a crowd awaits the spectacle of execution. On another, armored men ride sturdy Tartar ponies, bred and raised on the steppes. These horses may look small, but they can cover miles without tiring. The saddles have short stirrups. Why? To let a mounted archer stand when riding. Why? To shoot with more accuracy, for when you sit in the saddle, you are jostled about and lose your aim.

Sophie is fourteen. Not a stranger to saying one thing and meaning another. But she is a foreigner here. Her eye must be trained to see what is of the essence. Her ear must hear what is hidden.

"Talking to servants again? Where is your dignity, Sophie? Your pride?"

Her mother is wrong.

Friendships are forged in chance encounters, in the faint light of the unshuttered windows, on frosty Moscow days. In the palace corridor, on the way to the imperial chambers, in the antechamber of Peter's rooms, where the Princess of Anhalt-Zerbst is kept waiting like a merchant or a debtor.

Questions are a good beginning. Questions followed by a beseeching smile, a playful shake of the head. The initial ones are innocuous, easy to answer: "What is kvass made of, Varvara Nikolayevna? What is the Russian word for a bee? Have you ever seen an elephant? Aren't they marvelous creatures? So graceful and yet so strong! Is *Varvara* Russian for Barbara?"

Only later, when murmurs give way to easy laughter, other questions are possible:

"Have you been at court long?

"You are a bookbinder's daughter? A ward

of the Empress? A foreigner, too?

"An orphan?

"Alone?"

In the end, it is not only what one asks about but how. Every answer, however brief, however flippant, is a clue. Words hide inside other words, hint at the gravity of what is unfolding outside these drafty rooms. So do the hesitations, the sideways glances. Are they distractions to lead the newcomer astray? Or warnings to be treasured and pondered? Like that page she has copied from a book and then found burnt on a silver tray?

Nobody survives alone.

Not here. Not at this court.

She puts out her hand to grip the arm of her chair, to steady herself. "Will you help me with my Russian, Varvara Nikolayevna? Sometimes?"

"Yes, Your Highness."

"Will you read to me, too? Happy stories. With good endings. There is enough sadness in the world."

"If the Empress permits."

"Then I'll ask her as soon as she returns. And I shall praise you to her. Tell her how kind and helpful you've been. How I wish she were here already!"

"Too many requests are waiting for her, Your Highness. It's better to wait for the right moment."

"How will I know when the right moment

arrives? Will you tell me?"

But Varvara Nikolayevna does not answer. "Praises are not always good, Your Highness," she says instead. "It's best you don't mention me to the Empress at all."

"Why not?"

"It's best not to reveal what we truly want. It's best to hide our impatience and our fears."

Like mother, like daughter.
An apple may fall close to the apple tree, but it doesn't have to stay there.

Noises wake her at night. The wooden walls are thin. In Mother's room, the floor squeaks. A wardrobe door creaks. A stumble, a giggle, clicking of glasses. The wine is pronounced inferior, but it will do. Must do. It's a cold Russian night, after all.

"Wait until we move back to St. Petersburg," Chevalier Betskoy warns. "There, it's even colder."

"How much colder?"

"Think birds freezing in mid-flight and falling out of the sky. By three o'clock, it's already pitch dark."

"I don't believe you!"

"You should."

Soon, so soon, Mother's voice thickens and breaks. "Not here . . . wait . . . let me . . ."

A bedframe rattles against the wall. Breathing gets raspy, greedy. A giggle snaps, turns into a deep moan of pleasure.

Mother is gasping for air. Calling the man who is with her *beloved . . . my treasure . . . my only, true happiness.* "You don't know what hunger is," Sophie hears her whisper. "How much he has suffocated me. For how long."

Her bedroom is shrouded in darkness. In the small alcove, the sleeping maid gnashes her teeth and moans something in Russian that sounds like a plea for mercy or a favor. The girl is a sound sleeper and won't wake up unless yanked out of her dreams by force.

But Sophie is wide awake. Mother destroys everything she touches. The present and the future. Stains it all with gossip and greed, with lust that serves nothing but her own pleasure.

If Sophie doesn't stop her now, they will both be packed off back to Zerbst in disgrace.

She gets out of bed and walks toward the window. Outside, on the moonlit street, the snow has banked into tall drifts. A horse-drawn sleigh is making its way past them, the peal of harness bells teasing her ears. Empress Elizabeth won't be back for another three long weeks. The Empress who once placed a *kokoshnik* on her head and called her "my beloved moon girl, my hope."

Her mind moves over the possibilities, feels

them for ripeness. Rivalry? Possession? Pride?
Would the Empress come back to save a dying girl?

Za chem poydyosh, to i naydyosh. If you go looking for it, you will find it.

Lips become parched if you keep them parted long enough, without licking them. Cheeks can be made to redden with a vigorous rubbing. But will looking sick be enough? An ordinary cold would help, a runny nose, bloodshot eyes, voice made raw by a sore throat.

She considers opening the window, but it has frozen into the frame and won't budge. Besides, the night watchman might hear her struggle with it. Then her eyes rest on a vase filled with cut orchids. The chambermaids are lazy, even with an imperial gift. The water, unchanged for days, already smells of rot.

She picks up the vase and lifts it to her lips, taking one bitter sip, then another. Slimy strands stick to her tongue and teeth, but she holds her breath and doesn't gag. Human will, Babette, her governess, has taught her, is more powerful than animal instincts. Human will is the iron gate to mankind's true salvation. Reason can overcome emotions that try to divert us away from our goal.

A stomach can hold the stinking water and the slimy remnants of the rotting stems.

Longer than she has thought. As long as it is necessary.

"No bleeding," Mother says sharply when the court doctor arrives this time.

The doctor raises his thick, graying eyebrows.

"But why?" he asks. His voice is reassuring. He explains the necessity of restoring the balance of humors. Surely the illustrious Princess of Anhalt-Zerbst will not object to medical wisdom?

"No bleeding," Mother insists. Her own brother came to Russia to marry. He fell ill, was bled, and died.

If it happened before, it can happen again.

The doctor rolls his eyes. "A woman's reasoning," he whispers, loud enough for those close by to hear. He has come prepared for such a contingency. His voice is stern: "If bleeding is not allowed, the Princess may die."

"No bleeding!" Mother shrieks. "I won't let you butcher my child!"

The silk pillows are soiled with vomit. The maids cannot empty the chamber pot fast enough. Their pale faces cringe. With revulsion? Or fear?

"Look at me, Sophie," Mother orders, unable to conceal her unease. It's a chink in her armor, which would've pleased her daughter at some other time.

The slimy taste of the flower water lingers on Sophie's lips. No amount of vomiting can erase it. When she tries to raise herself up, her head spins so much that she has to squeeze her eyes shut.

The court doctor rests his hand on her forehead and shakes his head, shooting Chevalier Betskoy a man-to-man look. How can Princess Johanna of Anhalt-Zerbst be so blind? So ignorant? Shouldn't a man interfere? Right now?

Mother has always been stubborn. Only Father knows how to distract her into compliance. Chevalier Betskoy makes one mistake after another. He returns the doctor's look. "Perhaps we should summon Her Imperial Majesty," he says. "Before it is too late."

"Sophie is *my* daughter," Mother seethes through clenched teeth. "What can a barren woman know that I don't?"

The imperial sleigh pulls into the palace yard in a whirlwind of snow. A barking dog is shooed away, the lash of a horsewhip brings forth a yelp of pain.

Doors open. Rosary beads click.

"My Sophie! Poor lamb! What have they done to you? A few days I'm away, and this is what happens?"

Servants are peeking from behind screens and half-closed doors, eager for the spectacle of the imperial rage directed at someone else.

61

What do they see? Whose side do they take?

"The moment I leave, common sense and decency go to the Devil!"

It is all directed at Mother.

Mother, a German bitch, ready to let her own child die because she is too busy fucking.

"*Durak,* and you listened to her!" the doctor hears when he mumbles his explanations for why the bleeding has been delayed for so long. "You, too, wished me to come home to a funeral?"

The Empress moves briskly about the sickroom. Skirts rustle, heels pound the floorboards. "Fetch Lestocq," Elizabeth bellows. "I trust no one else."

The maids scurry around. One is holding a wicker basket covered with a white lace kerchief. Another, a Holy Icon. A cat meows.

"Has anyone even had the presence of mind to call a pastor? Or have you all chosen a coffin for this child already?"

Mother is standing on the other side of the bed. Chevalier Betskoy is right behind her, inching his way backward, out of sight.

Where is Peter? Does he think she, his fiancée, might die? Is he sorry for her? Does he even care?

Sophie cannot see with her eyes closed, but the snorting noises must come from Peter. And the stifled grunts of disbelief.

They are all here.

They are all watching.

■ ■ ■ ■

The doors open. Count Lestocq is announced. "I came as soon as I heard, Majesty," he mutters as he rushes in, ordering his assistant to open his lancet case. "Without a moment's delay."

A draft floats inside, a frigid, slithering stream of winter air.

The Empress's onetime lover, the man who helped Elizabeth seize Russia's crown, the Count lifts the coverlet. Not too much, just enough to expose his patient's small, shapely foot.

The sharp lancet blade opens a vein right above Sophie's ankle. It hurts, but not much. A stream of blood flows down. A bandage tightens. She feels nothing at first, but then a lightness descends, dizzy, luminous. Her heart slows. Her breath deepens.

She lifts her eyelids a mere slit, enough to discern the Empress bending over the bed. The skin of imperial cheeks has not been touched by powder today. The front tooth is darkened and chipped. The pale lips are muttering a Russian blessing she, Sophie, doesn't quite understand.

Mother, oblivious to what has just happened, is doggedly protesting her innocence. "My daughter, Your Imperial Majesty, has merely suffered from indigestion. She has not been in any danger."

"Enough, you ingrate," the Empress hisses. "Look at this child. Look how pale she is."

The box with lancets closes with a snap. There will be no better moment to open her eyes wide. Unclasp her hands and raise herself on her elbows. No better moment to avoid her mother's frantic glances, the pearly drops of sweat on her high forehead. To ignore how she drops to her knees, shuddering. A lot can be said without words. What has been assumed can be denied. What has been defined can be refashioned, turned inside out.

Beside the rock that is the Empress of Russia, Mother is an empty seashell, enticing but hollow and so easy to crush.

"I have a request, Your Majesty."

The imperial ears do not miss the slightest alteration of her small but clear voice.

"I don't want a pastor. Please, could Father Theodorsky come pray with me instead?"

The Empress fixes her with her stare. Then she raises her eyebrows. *What is it that I have just heard, Sophie?* her eyes ask. *A sign of your cunning? Or a vow of compliance?*

Or both?

In the fireplace, birch logs crackle and hiss, sending a wave of warmth toward her.

It is time to fall back on the silk pillows. Let her thoughts dwell on the enticing vastness of this land, an immensity that defies the senses. Bring back the memory of the frozen fields, of dark, thick forests covered with snow, of rivers locked under ice. Time to envisage what she, Sophie of Anhalt-Zerbst, has heard about but not yet seen. Chains of mountains that fill the horizon, endless meadows of the steppes, where grasses are tall enough to hide a man on horseback.

Time to make her face say: *I'm not like my mother. I'll not disappoint. No matter what the price.* Time to blink, make tears well up and flow down her cheeks.

Beside her, seated on her bed, the Empress of Russia blinks and stirs. Her large, soft body has made the mattress sag. Her hand lifts, reaches forward. It is perfumed, its pink nails buffed and rubbed with rose oil.

Why this moment of hesitation? Has she, Sophie, been too crude? Too hasty? Has she betrayed her deepest wishes, the price she is willing to pay for them?

She has been warned. Told to wait for the right moment. *Watch and learn from those who have seen more,* her new friend has whispered.

But what has been done cannot be taken back. Sophie has placed her bet. Now all there is left is to wait.

The imperial head turns away from her.

"Listen, you ingrate," the Empress of All the Russias tells Mother. There is the unmistakable note of triumph in the imperial voice. "Listen to what this sweet child is asking me to do."

The thoughts that come are of a cat in wild catmint. Pawing it, chewing, leaping about with joy.

Sophie of Anhalt-Zerbst has a new Russian name: Catherine Alekseyevna, after Elizabeth's own mother. According to the Russian custom, she should be called Catherine Christyanevna, for her father's name is Christian, but the Empress decided that it would've sounded too foreign to a Russian ear. And a Russian Grand Duchess, a wife of the Crown Prince, should not sound foreign.

Varvara Nikolayevna, who knows the ways of the court, says that the Empress has declared Prince Christian of Anhalt-Zerbst a man of no substance. A parasite who feeds off his wife's connections. A man whose name would only have impeded his daughter's position. "Don't let anyone see your tears," her new friend whispers. "It's not that hard!"

In her notebook, Catherine Alekseyevna is carefully writing down the Russian proverbs her tutor is giving her to learn by heart:

Delit' shkuru neubitovo medvedya. It is foolish to divide the pelt of a bear that has not been killed yet.

Every night, the maids untie her stays, wipe her breasts with almond milk, rub her nipples until they harden, brush her hair. Slip thin cambric undershirts over her perfumed body. Her breasts are full, her womb is alive.

They lead her to the marital bed — the bed blessed with a Holy Icon and sprinkled with holy water — and leave hastily.

She waits. Sometimes she sits in bed holding her knees. Sometimes she runs her hand over her breasts and then her belly and her thighs. Sometimes she runs her fingers through the curls of her pubic hair, which is black and thick like a mink pelt.

She thinks of the day she arrived in Moscow, when she was stripped naked and her German clothes were taken away. How she was dressed in a silk chemise, light as gossamer, and a brocade dress. She thinks of the wedding in the Kazan cathedral — when she stood beside Peter and the Archbishop blessed them and anointed them with holy oil. Of the wedding feast, where whole landscapes were made of sugar: a sugar castle with a sugar garden, sugar trees laden with sugar fruit. She thinks of the Empress putting her ringed hand on her flat belly, ordering her to give Russia another heir to her throne. A healthy Romanov boy to succeed his father.

She thinks of Mother, who has left for Zerbst without a word of farewell and who hasn't written to her yet. Of Father, who wasn't invited to her wedding.

Sooner or later, Peter, her husband, the future Tsar, always comes into the bedroom. He, too, has no choice.

There are many faces Peter may put on. Of boredom. Of indifference. Of petulance. Or of rapt concentration, but this happens only when he manages to fool his minders and smuggle his toy soldiers into the bedroom. Then she, his bride, can watch him place them in formations, recreate battles long ago lost or won, battles over which he has total control.

She can ask him questions, then, and Peter will answer. Explain a tricky maneuver, a clever evasion that once assured a Prussian victory. Or she may make herself useful. Straighten the line of pikemen with spears held at an angle to keep the enemy horsemen at bay. Or pick up fallen heroes.

She reminds herself how a few months ago Peter almost died of smallpox. How she despaired when those who called themselves her friends withdrew from her, knowing that if Peter died, the Empress would send her back to Zerbst. She might be fending off Mother's scorn now, sifting through threadbare marriage offers. Hearing that she was always both too proud and unlucky. Always hungering after what was not meant for her.

"It'll happen, you'll see." Varvara Nikolayevna always knows what to say at the worst of moments when hope vanishes. "Some men get easily scared and grow soft."

The smallpox swelling is almost gone from her husband's face. The redness, too, has dissipated or has been hidden under a layer of concealing cream. Besides, she tells Peter, a man doesn't need to worry about a few pockmarks.

"I know that," he snaps.

He eyes her with suspicion. He hears her with impatience. He thinks her too clever for her own good. Madame Resourceful, he mocks her, who always has a solution to all problems — whether anyone wants it or not. In the palace corridors he hastens his steps to avoid her. In their marital bed he gives her a wide berth. When she tries to touch his hand, he recoils.

"Stand up, wife," he yells. *"Schnelle! Schnelle!"*

Sophie jumps out of bed and stands at attention. He tells her to bend and pick up his sword. He orders her to march across the room. Present the sword as if it were a musket. Lift her legs high, like a good Prussian soldier on parade.

He forbids her to speak. He watches her from the bed as she marches, his head resting on his hands.

"Why are you so silent, wife?" he asks.

"Because you told me not to speak, Peter," she answers, and for a moment her obedience pleases him and his face brightens.

"Enough!" he yells. "Come back!"

She puts the sword away and gets into bed beside him. The mattress is warm and smells sweetly. The maids have spread jasmine and rose petals under the sheets. Varvara has told her not to lose heart. To be patient. Men are like that sometimes. Shy. Afraid to show their weakness. It doesn't have to mean anything.

She is patient.

She is waiting, in silence, until Peter laughs, turns his back on her, and begins to snore.

In Russia, death is pictured as an old, bony woman with a scythe. Silent and relentless, impossible to outwit. A hag asking through her toothless mouth: "Who will govern when *I* come to the Empress's bed?"

In the inner chambers of the Imperial Palace there is no need for subtlety. A country needs an heir, a child patiently groomed for power, a Tsarevich of imperial blood.

A fruit of the imperial marriage. A Grand Duchess's sacred duty.

So why is her womb still empty?

Her ill wishers, her slanderers, hide in the back passageways, in the corridors, behind two-way mirrors. They call her a barren tree,

a withered blossom dropping without forming fruit. To the Empress, who has brought
her to Russia, they whisper: *Another year has
passed. What is the use of a tree that yields no
fruit? Hours flow faster than we think. What if
what we took for signs of divine approval were
the whispers of the Devil?*

A woman has to please her husband, not to
hide in books. Or ride a horse astride like a
man. Or ask too many questions.

If Catherine smiles, her slanderers call her
flippant; if she wipes the smile from her face,
they call her proud.

She has made a bargain and has not delivered. Her punishment has only just begun.

She has no more friends at court. Anyone
who has dared to show her any kindness has
been sent away. Prince Naryshkin has been
told the Grand Duchess has no time for idle
prattle. Maids have been dismissed for whispering a few words of comfort. Varvara Nikolayevna, too, is gone, married, already
awaiting a child. Varvara, who once warned:
"This court is a dangerous ground. Life here
is a game, and every player is cheating."

"I've chosen you over others," the Empress
seethes, poking at her belly. A punch, harsh
and insistent, is meant to hurt, and it does.
"Where is my heir now? How much longer
do I have to wait, Catherine?"

71

Six years she has been married, and her husband has not touched her. This is her shameful secret. For isn't it always a woman's fault?

She must have repulsed him somehow. With her looks? Her words? Her actions? Was she too haughty? Too quick to speak? Not obedient enough?

Sometimes when she is alone, she opens her shift and sniffs at her body. Is it her smell that stops Peter from desiring her? Or her bony hips that refuse to take on a layer of soft fat? Are her breasts too small, or too big? Her skin too rough? Her chin too pointed? Her teeth too rotten? Her lips too parched?

In the palace chapel, Russian saints look at her with empty eyes. *We have suffered in silence,* they say, *and so should you. Such is the Russian way.*

It is the month of May. The Imperial Court is visiting Gostilitsa, Count Razumovsky's country estate outside St. Petersburg. Their host, in embroidered yellow caftan, Empress Elizabeth's portrait pinned on his chest, welcomes them with bread and salt. At his home, his esteemed guests, the Count announces, have no duty but to amuse themselves.

On the way to her Favorite's house, Empress Elizabeth has complained about the foul smells, the horses, which were far too slow, and her new dress, which was too tight and made her skin itch. She has ordered three stops to relieve herself behind a screen the servants unfolded for her. At the last stop, she spotted crows circling the carcass of a mule and ordered a change of route, adding another hour to the four-hour journey.

But by the time the carriage rolls into the courtyard of the Gostilitsa mansion, Elizabeth's irritation has vanished. Everything now pleases the Empress. What a relief to leave the Winter Palace behind, she tells Count Razumovsky. To breathe the country air. To see the birch grove, the lush meadow, the lake where wild fowl is nestling among the reeds. She wants to row a boat herself, she wants to fish, for nothing tastes better than a fish caught with one's own hands.

Count Razumovsky is a considerate host. The handsome red boat with padded seats is ready for his beloved Empress to embark. The fishing rods are waiting, fresh worms wiggling on the hooks. Settled at her feet when Elizabeth deftly rows the boat to the middle of the lake, he holds the tin bucket at the ready.

For a whole hour, the courtiers await their return. No one else wishes to follow their mistress. No one wishes to catch a bigger fish.

When the boat finally bumps back to shore, everyone gathers to admire the catch. Elizabeth beams as, one by one, her ladies-in-waiting recoil at the mere thought of touching the wriggling flesh. "You would've made my father laugh," the Empress says, motioning to a bearded servant who stands by with a tray of knives.

"Are they sharp?" she asks.

When the servant nods, the Empress rolls up the sleeves of her blouse. She picks up the longest of the knives, with a stag-bone handle. She tests the sharpness of the blade with her index finger.

All small fish will be boiled whole, for *ucha,* the fish broth. Only the bigger ones will be filleted and fried.

The ladies-in-waiting flock around the Empress, clucking their tongues in awe as their mistress stuns the fish with a hammer, cuts off its head, makes a slit through its belly, and empties the bowels. "Follow the backbone to the tail," she says, as the knife cuts across the body. "This is what Papa always said."

She, Catherine Alekseyevna, Russia's Grand Duchess, adds her voice to the cries of astonishment and admiration. She is not fond of fish, preferring boiled beef and pickles, but no one needs to know that. When one of the stunned fishes suddenly begins to thrash about, Catherine gasps like everyone else.

For a moment, it looks like the Empress will not let her catch out of her hands, but the fish is slippery and fast. One splash and it is back in the lake.

Peter slaps his long arms along his body and makes a strangely apt imitation of a wiggling fish. No one laughs, but he doesn't seem to notice.

"What do you find so funny, Peter?" the Empress asks.

The question makes Peter giggle.

"Please, Peter." Catherine pulls at her husband's sleeve, but it is a mistake. Her plea — however gentle — makes Peter more reckless. Why? She has puzzled over such moments before, the way one puzzles over the insistence with which moths return to the flames.

"Nothing like country air in the spring, Catherine," Elizabeth says, ignoring her nephew. She wipes her bloodied hands on a towel a servant girl is holding for her. "Take a long breath. Fill your lungs."

Catherine obeys. The air is cool, scented with wood smoke, but the act of breathing does nothing to diminish her unease. Spring has made the Empress even more impatient. This is the season for procreation, for newly born colts, yellow chicks, ducklings waddling through mud behind their mother.

"Let the Grand Duchess hold it," Count Razumovsky says and places a duckling in

Catherine's hands. The duckling turns its little head and bites her thumb, but so lightly that she scarcely feels it. The duckling wiggles in her palms, soft, downy, warm. It is like holding the essence of life itself.

She bends, opens her hand, and lets the duckling slip out and follow the mother.

The house they are assigned for the visit is a three-story wooden one, newly built on a hill. Their bedroom is on the third floor. Nearby is the dressing room and a room where her chief maid sleeps. The second-floor rooms have been readied for the ladies-in-waiting and maids-of-honor.

The first day of the visit is one long feast. The serf men, in their long white tunics with embroidered collars and hems, direct the guests to refreshments, placed in the backyard, along the corridors of the grand house, and in the dining room. "Our simple Russian treats," their host says. Long tables have been covered with immaculate white cloths and garlanded with wreaths of spring flowers. Silver platters are covered by hillocks of rolled-up *bliny,* layers of smoked fish, roasted pheasants, glazed hams. Roasted piglets hold pinecones in their snouts, their charred skin precut like checkerboards. On dessert tables, beside enormous cakes, stand bowls of candied fruit dipped in chocolate. Fiddlers play lively folk tunes. Serf girls in embroidered shirts and skirts, wearing red, yellow, and blue beads, sing a melancholy song about *Snegurochka*, a Snow Maiden who is lonely and cold until she falls in love. But when her heart warms up, she melts.

Peter, forbidden to smoke in the Empress's presence, is sucking on an empty clay pipe. As always when they are in the company of others, he pays his wife little heed. His eyes trail after the peasant girls. Sometimes, like a truant schoolboy, he ventures to one of them and pulls on her beads or the folds of her bulky skirt.

When they are alone together — which is almost all the time, for such is the Empress's order — deprived of distractions, Peter can be drawn into a conversation. The best topics are always his memories of Holstein. Most of them are fanciful accounts of his Prussian childhood. By the time he turned seven, that imaginary Peter had valiantly conquered a band of brigands that had terrorized the countryside, chased the Gypsies who had kidnapped a little girl, rescued her, and handed her back to her weeping mother. Often in these stories it is Monsieur Brummer, his one-time tutor and now Marshal, who turns out to be his biggest adversary. "Brummer tried to stop me from charging," Peter would say, "but I ordered him to shut up."

Catherine still believes in patience. In chipping away at resentment.

Catherine is still young.

She listens to her husband's stories in admiring silence, offering her reassuring nods. When Peter stops, she asks questions. "What did Brummer say when he saw you aim your musket?" is the best one. It always evokes an elaborate picture of the former tutor crushed by awe, falling to his knees, professing his guilt for having doubted his charge. Caught up in these tales, Peter becomes restless. His boasting voice raises and thins, turning into a shrill wail. He waves his hands, or jumps up and down as if he needs to pee. The scenes his imagination evokes soothe him, but he is unable to keep track of what he has told her. So an attack on a Gypsy camp sometimes involves muskets and a regiment of Holsteiners, sometimes just a few servants with whips. The only constant is Brummer's humiliation and his admission of blindness for having failed to realize Peter's true merit.

The feast at Count Razumovsky's estate lasts all night. When dancing ends, sing-alongs by the bonfire begin. When voices become hoarse, there are games: blindman's buff, cat and mice, Cossacks and robbers. Or the tongue twisters Elizabeth favors. She, Catherine, causes general merriment when her tongue gets helplessly entangled in: *Stoit pop na kopne, kolpak na pope, kopna pod popom, pop pod kolpakom.*

A tongue twister Elizabeth excels in.

At dawn, when the Empress finally sends everyone away, Catherine and Peter return to their house. The servants draw the thick curtains of their bed tight, so that the light will not disturb them. They are both exhausted from the dancing and the games. Their eyes smart from bonfire smoke. They fall asleep at once.

Catherine wakes instantly when Choglokov, their chamberlain, minder, and one of the Empress's spies, tears the bed curtains aside. Choglokov is half dressed; tufts of curly gray hair peep through the opening of his nightshirt.

"Get out of here! *Fast!*" he shouts.

She has not time to ask why. An odd grating sound is coming from the fireplace. The walls creak. Heavy objects fall. Glass shatters. Outside, dogs bark in a frenzy. A piece of plaster spirals from the ceiling and crumbles on their heads. One of the ceiling beams begins to crack; chunks of dark wood rain to the floor.

Peter snorts and jumps out of bed.

He doesn't look at her.

The floorboards sway beneath her, as if she were on a barge in a storm. Her husband dashes out of the room. In his haste, he stumbles over the threshold and hurts his foot. The last she sees of him is his bent figure, limping away.

A window breaks, scattering glass shards. More layers of plaster are falling from the ceiling. Her hands are like two chunks of ice. Her heart pounds. *This is the end,* she thinks, even before she hears the guards outside, shouting, "Where is the Grand Duchess? Has anyone seen the Grand Duchess?"

The door bangs open. The guard who rushes inside her bedroom wears Preobrazhensky greens. He is tall and big-boned, with a mop of dark, thick hair. His arms are strong enough to lift her up as if she were a feather. She doesn't know his name. He is one of the many Palace Guards who stand at attention in the corridors. Who stare into the distance, oblivious — it has seemed to her — to all that was happening before them. If she has seen him before, her eyes have not rested on him long enough to etch his features into her memory. It is only now, when he holds her in his powerful arms, that she notes his swarthy, handsome face. The dark shadow on his jowl.

There is something else she sees.

On the face of a man who holds her and sweeps her out of the collapsing room there is no impatience, no petulance, no irritation. His eyes, locked on her, soften and sparkle. There is such delight in them, and such desire for her, that gooseflesh travels up her arms, a shiver through her loins. It softens the lump of fear in her throat. It melts what has been frozen.

It pleases her to see how hard he tries to be somber and dry, all business. Assuring her that she will be safe. That he won't let a hair drop from her head, for such is his duty to Russia's Grand Duchess. To die for her, if need be. To save her from all harm.

His name is Serge.

Later, there will be many stories of that day. How Russia's Grand Duchess had been rescued from a collapsing house by Serge Saltykov. How Peter, her husband, stretched on a crimson chintz-covered ottoman and wrapped in a sable blanket, kept asking what manner of vanity and silliness could make a woman take so long to get out of her bedroom. How Count Razumovsky threatened to blow his brains out when he heard that his own builders had removed the supporting beam. How the Empress — worried about her lover — refused to admit that the Grand Duchess had ever been in real danger at all.

But she, Russia's Grand Duchess, will remember the feel of a man's hand around her waist, the smell of snuff in her nostrils. Her own arms locked around his neck as he carried her to safety. His voice, as he raged against building a house in winter, over the frozen ground. "When the earth begins to thaw," he said, "the limestone boulders that held the foundations will no longer stay in place."

And then, with his eyes lingering over her, he added, "Only a fool wouldn't know this."

A game of chess is a game of choices. Sometimes you have to sacrifice a knight to checkmate the king. A game of chess is long. It's not wise to make your moves predictable. Not when change is still possible. When time is on your side.

Many traps have been laid. Many eyes and ears have been charged with following her every move. Many tongues repeat her every word.

But she is no longer alone. Now she, too, has her eyes and ears, tongues and gazettes, spies who steal their way into the inner rooms of the Winter Palace. The stories they bring back to Catherine come from dusty corridors and palace alcoves, from servant rooms and the Imperial Wardrobe. These stories are more precious than jewels. They tell her whom to stay away from and whom to bribe. Whose lies triumph in the gossip circles that gather nightly in the Imperial Bedroom. Who will be grateful for a kind word, a discreet loan, a whisper of warning.

Knowledge is power. That much she has always known.

Armed with her spies' stories, she can weave in and out of traps. Offer bribes that are neither too big nor too small. Rewards that please, not disappoint. Warnings that are heeded with gratitude she hoards against the future.

Power lies in hearing what is not meant to be heard. In understanding what motivates those who plot against you. In knowing what could make them turn about-face, come to your side.

A maid-of-honor who has reported your words to the Empress can be swayed with a ruby ring and promises of gratitude. A princess of the realm whose family hates you can be charmed with an unexpected visit and assurances of special friendship. Maids caught sifting through hidden drawers covet a trinket, or fear an exposure of some indiscretion. A stolen ribbon can condemn a seamstress; a broken china cup, a scullery maid.

The best of spies, Catherine has also learned, are not bought or tricked into compliance. The best of spies believe in her. See in her the answer to their dreams. Want her to save them from their own fears. To reach for the crown of Russia.

In the darkest hours before dawn, Varvara Nikolayevna, who is back at court, says, the Imperial Bedroom is lit by thick wax candles. Maids trim them constantly, for Elizabeth believes that flickering flames bring bad luck. The Empress is superstitious: If an owl hoots, servants with muskets are dispatched to scare the bird away. If a raven lands on the palace yard, it, too, is shooed away.

The Empress of Russia is terrified of the dark. Of an assassin's dagger. Of the Prince of Darkness, who can take many shapes. And of a twenty-three-year-old Grand Duchess who watches her from the wings, counting her gasping breaths.

"You know what she wants," Varvara Nikolayevna whispers to Catherine.

When Elizabeth's young lover leaves her bedroom, the Empress of Russia falls on her knees in front of the Holy Icon and begs Our Lady of Kazan to forgive her sins. It is then, her eyes softened by the sight of the divine baby nestled in the Virgin's arms, that Elizabeth, drunk on cherry vodka and lust, seethes. "Why can't that runt of a husband give her a child?"

Her slurred voice is steeped in derision. "And why doesn't that stupid *Hausfrau* know what to do?"

A drafty room in the Summer Palace is lit like a stage. Candles are placed on the windowsills, on tables, on a plank suspended from the ceiling. Thick wax candles that will last the whole night if need be. From the Holy Corner, Our Lady of Kazan gazes with her soulful eyes on the Grand Duchess Catherine, who, after nine barren years, will finally give Empress Elizabeth her precious heir.

Outside, in the garden, the sounds of pursuit. Meows followed by barks, growls, a quavering howl. The guard dogs are chasing stray cats down the gravel paths. "Throw a bucket of water on that damn dog!" someone shouts.

This is the month of September. The time when the Empress — who calls herself a simple peasant girl at heart — likes to hear of the year's abundant harvest. Haystacks fragrant with sweet meadow flowers. Cows fattened on summer grass, their udders swollen with warm milk. Birds flocking together, gathering on trees and fences, chattering away before they take off to warmer lands.

"Steady, Your Highness," the midwife mutters, leading Catherine firmly by the elbow. Her growing belly has altered her balance. More than once she has tripped on a perfectly even floor.

The midwife — Elizabeth's most vigilant spy — has guarded her from the time her menses stopped. Her shrill voice is spiked with constant warnings: "No necklaces, Your Highness, no beads, no raising your hands over your head . . . no sitting with your legs crossed . . ."

Month after month, Catherine obeyed, and the child grew and quickened and kicked inside her. Now, when her womb is about to release its prize, her hair has been combed and tucked inside a lace cap. The skin of her belly is sleek from goose fat, her bowels loose from rhubarb and prunes. It is only her trembling hands that betray her. Mother's whisper echoes in her head: *You nearly killed me when you were born, Sophie. You ripped me open like a sackcloth.*

"It'll be over soon enough!" The midwife is determined to soothe her, with lies if need be. The mother's fear is dangerous. It can scar the child in the womb. Turn it into a monster.

By now, the Grand Duchess, the wife of the Crown Prince, knows loss and fear, humiliation and loneliness, and the long, dragging hours of boredom. She knows how it feels to believe that nothing will ever change. That all exits have been blocked, that no light will ever penetrate the darkness of one's prison.

She also knows love. Love that makes her wake up at dawn with her lover's name on her lips, her arms seeking his presence. Love that makes her hungry, possessed. Love that prompts bold visions of imaginary escapes. In the one she evokes most often, Serge Saltykov climbs through the window and warns the midwife not to utter a word if she cares for her own life. "Come, Catherine, I'm taking you with me," he says, arms outstretched. His beauty takes her breath away, the swirl of his black hair, the sparkle in his hooded eyes. An unmarked carriage, Serge says, is waiting at the entrance to the Summer Garden. They must be quick. A swift dash out of the city, a safe house where faithful servants await.

"This love is not good for you," Varvara, who carries her own secrets, warns her. "Remember Serge Saltykov's wife?"

Why dwell on what no longer matters? Catherine closes her eyes, smarting from candle smoke. The man who thinks of her safety and her comfort encircles her with his arms, she imagines. Kisses her and their newborn baby, whose soft whimperings melt her heart.

"Steady, Your Highness. This way." The midwife's voice interrupts these thoughts.

A mattress is on the floor. "Horsehair." The midwife clucks her tongue approvingly. "The best. Won't ever get damp. Or infested with bugs."

Scents of rosemary and lavender waft by. Mixed with the heavy perfume of someone who has been in this room recently. The Empress herself? The Empress, who, having blessed her in front of the whole court, breathed a warning into her ear: "Hurry up, now, Catherine. Don't keep me waiting all night."

How does one hurry the time like this?

Her eyes slide over the table by the window,

fresh swaddling cloths rolled up in a wicker basket. Bleached white in the sun. Towels, sheets. Soft, too, Varvara has assured her, before vanishing into darkness. Well worn out, freshly laundered.

It is in Varvara's hands that she has placed a letter to her mother. *If you read these words, Mother, I'm no longer among the living.* A plea for forgiveness for any wrongs committed. A bequest of a few trinkets she can call her own.

From behind the thin walls voices seep, hushed, muted. Murmurs of prayers, of questions asked, answered, or ignored. Gasps of bewilderment at something said or implied. The Empress is there, with all her ladies-in-waiting. Elizabeth of All the Russias, who still cannot decide if, by fetching the Princess of Anhalt-Zerbst to marry her nephew, she has made a good bargain.

Her belly, big and bulging, is weighing her down. The child inside kicks. Sometimes a tiny foot or an elbow pushes against her skin.

"The blessed child is ready for this world, Your Highness," the midwife mutters, when another sharp pang makes her moan. She needs the midwife's hands to steady her as she lowers herself on to the horsehair mattress. They are the strong, capable hands of a woman who has eased many labors.

A deep breath. Then another, although she has heard that St. Petersburg air, thick with the vapors from the canals, is not healthy for the lungs.

A child, awaited for so long. Her payment to the Empress. Her ransom from the Empress. *A son,* Catherine prays. *Please, let it be a son.*

She hasn't seen her lover for four weeks now. There have been no letters, but she hadn't expected any. Serge Saltykov is not much of a writer. But still, she has been hoping for something. A flower, a book, a ribbon any serf girl might get from her beloved at a village fair. It's his child she is carrying, after all. It's his child that can kill her.

Her body longs for the caresses that would wash away the clammy touch of her husband's hands. Peter's heavings, his sweaty body reeking of nights spent in drink. It takes a moment, a mere flicker of time, to recall Serge's voice: "You are unlike anyone I've ever known, Catherine." To dismiss Varvara's warnings: "He's a philanderer. A seducer. Take your pleasure and the child Serge can give you. And then run."

Fear is poison. It can undo a man. Or a woman. It is best to trample fear like grass fire, before it spreads.

On that long night, pain measures out time. Pain the midwife assesses like a shrewd shopkeeper. Good enough. Better. Excellent. What does Catherine think of this child, which is still part of her? For nine months, she has tried to predict its nature. A strong kicker, a fighter. A child mindful of its mother's moods. If she is frightened, it freezes inside her. If she is happy, it melts and blends with her. If she forgets its presence, it moves to remind her that she is no longer alone.

If it's a boy she wants him to resemble Serge, with his sharp, dark eyes and lithe body, graceful, and so pleasing to a woman's eye. And her father, too. With his keen mind and the steady steps of an upright soldier prince.

If it's a girl . . .

No, it cannot be a girl. Her spies have already seen the imperial purchases. Not just sable and ermine for the cradle and silk coverlets, but a rattle with an ivory handle carved in the shape of a sword. And a tiny uniform of the Palace Guards. With red facings on the green cloth.

"Once this egg is hatched," the Empress says meaningfully, and grins. Varvara, who comes every day with news from the imperial inner rooms, describes how Elizabeth insists on choosing the wet nurses herself. Village girls who have just given birth expose their breasts so that their *matushka* can inspect them for blemishes, pinch the nipples to check the flow of milk. "I haven't seen the Empress that happy in months," Varvara tells Catherine.

The body will remember the pain of the child inching its way out, toward the light. The slow tearing of muscles and skin. The cheeks burning, the pearls of sweat gathering on the forehead. Hair wet and tangled, teeth chattering from strain and fear. Legs trembling as if she has just climbed a mountain and must still keep on climbing.

And all the time, pictures flutter in her head: Peter, the future Tsar of Russia, her husband, is grinning. He has just sentenced a rat to death by hanging. "Why, Catherine? Because the vermin has dared to chew at my soldiers' limbs." Serge's eyes slide off her unseeing. Why? Because he is chasing another woman, one who has not yet yielded to him.

From all these thoughts, the midwife's sharp cries pull her back. "Push, push . . . keep pushing. Harder." A slap on her face retrieves her from the soft, dark dream into which she's sinking. "*Now,* Your Highness! One more time!" Until something sleek and oily pops out between her legs. A bundle of flesh. Her child. Her baby. Choking, crying, for this must be a cry, this tiny jangled sound, a chime of such crystal clarity that her skin tingles. With longing. With love.

Catherine's eyes sting with joyful tears.

■ ■ ■ ■

"The egg has hatched!"

The Empress, wrapped in a blue satin cape, bends over the swaddled baby. Elizabeth is a big roosting hen, cackling, clucking her tongue. "My own blessed prince, my hawk, my treasure."

Priceless . . . God-given.

The courtiers crowd around on tiptoes, peering for a better view. Intent on milking this momentous time for all it's worth. They have dragged with them the whiff of the court, that unmistakable mélange of perfume, wood smoke, melted candle wax, and a discernible hint of excrement. It has been a long vigil.

For this moment they have abandoned slander. They gasp in admiration, shake their heads in awe. A prince is born. Russia's new heir. Russia's hope. The world has just become a better place.

Only the Grand Duchess of Russia lies forgotten.

It might be just as well, for Catherine detests pity. And false grins that try to pass for smiles. *Out,* she thinks. *All of you!*

The Grand Duchess lies on the mattress with sheets crumpled and drenched with her blood, her insides torn and empty. Left in this drafty room of the Summer Palace, where in a dreamlike trance she perceives her own brother, long dead, pointing his thin, crooked finger at her. Crying: "Mother, come here. Sophie is making faces at me!"

Sophie, the Stubborn Child who never listens to her mother, who shall be buried alive, her hand popping out of her fresh grave. Sophie, whose arms and scalp were covered with scabs, whose bones threatened to bend out of shape.

Outside, in the corridor, voices, thumps, scrapes. "Growling bear," someone says. "Sad destiny," another voice adds. Is it her baby they are talking about? Or her?

And then she hears: "You are alive, Your Highness. I am here. And you have a son."

It's Varvara, her spy in Elizabeth's bedroom. A crisp white bonnet covers her hair, making her look nun-like. Her chatter never stops, as if her words were a lifeline for a drowning woman. "When my Darya, my daughter, was born . . . when the midwife left . . . when I got over the fever . . . the first weeks are the hardest . . ."

Varvara's hands are soft, capable as she wipes away the sweat and blood. Folds the soiled sheets. Fetches a glass of cold raspberry kvass. If only Varvara's voice stopped wrapping itself around her, sneaking into the smallest of openings. Evoking images she doesn't need. Of a happy mother in a quilted dressing gown, in bearskin slippers. Her arms cradling her baby daughter. Her lips brushing her daughter's silky cheeks.

"Where has she taken my son, Varenka?"

"Into her own bedroom. He is safe there. She named him Paul. Paul Petrovich."

"How does he look?"

"He is beautiful."

What Varvara says is vague and trite and not very useful. Paul Petrovich is beautiful because he has beautiful fingers, tapered at the end, and a tiny tuft of hair. Paul is beautiful because he has a beautiful smile. "Please don't cry," Varvara pleads. "Please . . . It's all over now."

It's not all over. It's not right. It'll never be. Somewhere behind these walls a tiny child cries, his lips searching for her in vain. A baby born to a world in which his mother is forbidden to touch him, to rock him in her arms, to kiss his tears away.

Even a cow is allowed to lick her newborn calf. Smell its skin, its breath.

Is a Russian Grand Duchess a lesser being than a cow?

"Shh . . . you have to stop crying . . . someone might hear you. You don't want the Empress to think you don't trust her. That she cannot take care of your child."

A heart can take only so much hardening before it breaks.

■ ■ ■ ■

"Listen to me, Varenka! Stop talking and just listen.

"I want her dead! I want to see her fight for her last breath. I want to watch her die. Alone.

"I will say what I want. I don't care who is listening!"

There is fear on Varvara's face. Her eyes dart sideways. Her left cheek twitches. She shakes her head, claps her hand over her mouth. "Shh," she whispers. "It's just your pain speaking. It's not you. Shh."

Some lessons Catherine has failed to understand. Why? Because she was harboring illusions. She flattered herself. Refused to consider the evidence of her own eyes. Assumed that in the empire of love, some things are sacred.

Serge said, "There is no world without you," and she believed him.

Serge said, "I've given you a son. I've made you safe, but now I have to stay away. It hurts me more than it hurts you," and she believed him.

Serge said, "You have your fate in your own hands now, Catherine," but *this* she did not believe.

■ ■ ■ ■

It is winter already. She has ordered her bed to be moved into a small alcove, pushed against a blocked door. It is the drafts that she wants to escape, she tells her maids. Ever since she gave birth, her flesh cannot hold the warmth. She cannot stand upright for more than a few minutes before her feet begin to swell. In her tiny nook of a room, curled under a down coverlet and a fur blanket, she reads or — if words stop making sense — stares at the barricaded door. The ridges of the wood grain form an intricate pattern of horizontal lines; the holes show where an old lock has been carelessly replaced. Sometimes the wood creaks, especially at night, when all sounds are magnified by the cold and the silence.

Her belly still aches. The pain begins in one spot, where the baby's head ripped her open, and then travels upward. Catherine tries not to think of the son whom she is not allowed to see for longer than a tearstained blink. A swaddled baby with watery blue eyes and a tuft of blond hair.

Sometimes she succeeds.

Serge, her beloved, has raven-black tresses and black eyes. Could it be that Paul is Peter's child after all? The possibility fills her with revulsion. Not only because the very memory of Peter's clammy hands sickens her, but because there is nothing in him she wants her son to inherit.

Sometimes a well-meaning maid-of-honor comes with news of how little Paul cried all night. Or yawned with the most amusing grimace. Or sucked on his clenched fist. Or peed on the wet nurse when she removed the swaddlings.

After she was delivered of her son, a black stripe appeared on her belly. The skin has stretched and the old firm tightness of her muscles is gone. Would Serge like her the way she is now? She thinks of him in faraway Sweden, where the Empress has sent him so "the Grand Duchess will no longer debase herself."

He hasn't written to her. It's too dangerous. She doesn't even know when he will be allowed back. When this thought comes, she buries her hand between her thighs and presses hard, but such paltry measures always disappoint.

Now that Russia has a Tsarevich, the Grand Duchess cannot be that easily pushed aside. Court calculations have been adjusted. Is it better to back the Crown Prince or the mother of his heir and successor? Who will last longer, once the Empress closes her eyes? Who will withstand the palace intrigues? Please more hearts? The results of this hesitation are beginning to reveal themselves. Gifts arrive with assurances of devotion: swaths of fabric, cases of wine, rare books, invitations to name-day celebrations, requests to join her at cards. Peter's staunch supporters, Countess Shuvalova and her brothers-in-law, are still plotting against her, but Chancellor Bestuzhev — her onetime enemy — now pesters the Grand Duchess with promises of support.

In the Winter Palace it is either her or Peter.

The future Emperor comes to his wife's rooms every evening. Sucking on his clay pipe, sending clouds of suffocating smoke in her direction, Peter delivers his revelations. Russian ships are so rotten that a royal salute would sink them. Earthworms, boiled with oil and red wine, are the soldier's best remedy for bruises. Peter's eyes do not rest on her but seek her maids-of-honor, the true recipients of these daily visits. It is for them that Peter curls his wigs into fashionable pigeon wings and perfumes himself like a sultan. Or, rather, for one of them in particular. Elizabeth Vorontzova, whom everyone calls *Das Fräulein*. "Yes, Your Highness . . . No, Your Highness . . . How smart you are, Your Highness . . ." Vorontzova may be short, ugly, and coarse, but not to Peter.

She, his wife, tries to summon her rage, but fails. The truth is that nothing but her lover's presence can rouse Catherine out of despair.

She concocts Serge's lean face out of memory scraps, searches for his low, thick voice in the voices of other men, imagines his touch, his caresses, until the pain of his absence stabs too hard. It feels as if she were slowly being torn apart, piece by piece.

"Your Highness must hear me out," Chancellor Bestuzhev says. "There is no good way to say it. I won't even try."

In Sweden, Chancellor Bestuzhev informs her with a pleasure he doesn't even try to hide, Serge Saltykov strides like a peacock, clad in the glory of his imperial love affair. "Frivolous," the Chancellor says. "Indiscreet." Serge boasts of the Grand Duchess's passion for him, hints at what rewards it might yet bring.

"I don't believe it," Catherine screams. She has heard these words before. Rumors have always stuck to Serge. "Why does everyone wish me to stop loving him?"

The Chancellor of Russia nods gravely and changes the subject. *Das Fräulein*'s antics irk him more and more. Her preening. Her coarse jokes that make the Grand Duke laugh: A fly comes to the tavern and asks for a plate of shit with onions. "Only go easy on the onions," the fly tells the tavernkeeper. "I don't want to stink."

The Chancellor sighs and suggests that such jokes are easy to reproduce. He could supply Her Highness with a whole line of them, grand lords and ladies with urgent needs to relieve themselves in most unusual places, or the usual permutations of sexual couplings. "Your Highness could also make her husband laugh, occasionally . . . knowing how laughter provides release."

Catherine shakes her head.

Bestuzhev is not the only one who tries to poison her feelings for Serge. Everyone feels entitled to blacken her lover's reputation. Varvara ticks off her questions on her fingers, one by one: "Hasn't he sent his wife away just to be free of her tears? Hasn't he pawned his mother's jewels?"

Serge may be bad-mouthing her at the Swedish court, she concedes, but only because he believes that this is the only way to protect her. Put more distance between them. Stop the rumors that would hurt her and her son.

All she needs is to talk to him.

Hear him out.

Make him see that she has not changed.

And she will see him. As soon as he comes back to Russia for the New Year.

1755 will be the year of great changes.

She has begged Empress Elizabeth to excuse her from appearing at the New Year's ball. And now, her request granted, dressed in a white muslin gown, she ties her hair with a pink ribbon and perfumes her body. Before leaving, her maid has been ordered to put more logs into the fire. Soon the bedroom is warm enough to dispose of thick stockings and fur slippers.

She waits. Across the corridors of the Winter Palace that separate her rooms from the Grand Ballroom, the music resounds. There is laughter and screams of delight. Revelers wander the palace unhindered; lovers seek empty rooms where they can hide. Footsteps approach and then fade away.

Catherine opens a book, closes it again. The flames of the fireplace provide a temporary distraction. When the anxiety becomes impossible to withstand, she takes a sip of laudanum straight from the bottle, without even diluting it with water. The bitter taste spills over her tongue, but moments later, the warmth in her stomach calms her.

She bargains with fate. *If he comes right now, I will give alms to the poor.* When he doesn't come, she offers more. *I will sell my jewels and take five orphan girls. Ten, no, twenty orphan girls, and bring them up at my own expense. I will teach them to read, write, and count.*

Give them dowries.

Find husbands for them.

There is little she remembers from the rest of this night. A few of her friends come by — friends who've promised to keep an eye on

Serge. They try to be of help. Yes, they have seen her lover. Yes, they have passed on her assurances. Yes, he knows that she is waiting. That she is alone.

"So why is he not here yet?" she remembers asking.

The memory of their answers eludes her. The drowsy, foggy thickness has made her thoughts laborious. Her words slur.

Didn't Serge once say: *Aren't you my beloved? The queen of my thoughts?* What could have changed?

He does come to see her, a week later. After she lets her hair turn oily and rank, when no admonitions or her maid's coaxing could make her dress up and see anyone. When in the clouded palace mirrors her face looks frightened and starved. She looks, Catherine realizes, as if she has been quarantined during some plague to stop the disease from spreading.

Serge enters her room, unannounced, dragging in the smells of the road: bonfire smoke, wet leather, the sweat of horses. In his hand is a gift from Sweden, a bouquet made of pinecones and acorns, tied with a red ribbon.

"For Your Highness," he says, as if he were giving her something precious.

She waves her maids away. When they are gone, she throws her hands around his neck, rests her head on his chest. His heart beats fast, but his hands do not lift, his arms do not embrace her.

It takes her a moment to register that what she hears is Serge's tongue clucking with disapproval. "The Grand Duchess of Russia is making the court tongues wag. Haven't you heard the names the Shuvalovs are calling you?"

He takes her hands off his neck and makes her sit down. "I'm here," he says, "because you've forced me to come."

She hears him and yet she doesn't. She babbles of her pain, her fears, her terrible loneliness. She wants him to know how much she missed him.

When a tear rolls down her cheek, he wipes it with his finger. "I've never wished to hurt you," he says.

Serge's voice is soft. His words are ripe and fragrant, each bestowing pleasure. The court, he says, is a swamp of jealousy and intrigue. He has been warned that the Empress does not want him near her, and so he had to obey. He thought she would understand. Was he wrong? His lips glide down her bare shoulder.

"I understand," she mutters, through joy and relief. Serge is back. He loves her. She was right all along.

She opens his breeches and slides her hand inside.

This is where he stops her. His grip is painful. Harsh. His words strike like lashes of the knout. "Other women can afford to be blind, Catherine, but not you!"

"What do you mean?" she asks, still uncomprehending.

"You've just believed another lie."

"What lie?"

"Everything I've just told you is a lie. And you know it."

She covers her ears with her hands, but he pulls them away. He whispers, but his whisper is shrill, chilling the marrow of her bones.

"I'm a liar, Catherine. I don't care for any woman who has yielded to me. I wish it were not so, but this is how I am. I love only what I cannot have.

"No one has forced me to say it. I've given you many clues. But you've refused to see them. What other proofs do you want?"

She shakes her head to stop him, but he won't.

"You want me to flatter your feelings, Catherine, but I won't do it. Think of it this way: You spoil my game with your pain. You make me uneasy. I don't want to think of myself as cruel. Or ruthless. This is why I have to shatter this silly dream of yours.

"Listen to me. I'm not the only man like this. Some of us really only want the thrill of pursuit."

Later it will seem like one terrible nightmare, but at the time, each word is like a burning dagger thrust through her heart.

"I'll go away and not bother you again. I'm being sent to Hamburg anyway, so you won't have to see me. The Shuvalovs say —"

"Why should I care what the Shuvalovs say?" It takes all her will not to scream.

"Because every one of them is poisoning the Empress against you. Telling her that you are a meddler, just like your mother. That you want to steal her crown. That you will stop at nothing. And then, for good measure, they are telling your husband that you are unreasonable and arrogant. That you don't deserve him. That he should take a lover who wishes to please a man, not dominate him. Is that what you want? To be supplanted by *Das Fräulein* or some other scheming witch? To lose whatever influence you still have with your own husband?"

Her lips move, but no words come.

"I have a gift for you," Serge continues. "A better gift than some miserable pinecones I've just bought from a peddler in the street. A few words only: Your heart has room for far more than you think."

She cannot stop sobbing. She doesn't know how. Her shoulders heave; her throat threatens to choke her.

"Get yourself a new gown, Catherine. Do something with your hair. Put some rouge on your cheeks. Walk into the ballroom and show them who you really are.

"Not a duckling, Catherine. A hawk."

Three years, she thinks, when the door closes behind Serge. *I've given this scoundrel three years of my life.*

Fury racks her. Ancient, vast. Fury at Serge. At herself. Fury mixed with pity plunging into sorrow, to become fury again. She paces the room; her heels strike the floorboards like musket shots.

Her clenched fists beat her cheeks. She trips over something. It's a pinecone. A pinecone she flings into the fire, astonished at how swiftly it burns.

Her body slumps into a chair. An image appears — of Serge lying beside her, dangling a straw from his lips by a single thread of his spit.

She shudders.

But another voice is sounding already. Small but clear.

Betrayal is like poison. A dose too small to kill strengthens you instead.

For the February 10 ball, given to celebrate Peter's twenty-seventh birthday, she orders a blue velvet gown embroidered with gold oak leaves. Full lace ruffles for the inside of her sleeves. Velvet wrist covers trimmed with marten fur. She ties a scarlet sash around her waist. The months of pining in her room have

106

given her skin a translucent pallor. Giving birth has filled her breasts, added a soft layer of fat on her hips.

At the ball, she walks up to her husband without hesitation. Her birthday wishes for him flow with easy grace. When *Das Fräulein* winces, she, Catherine, Russia's Grand Duchess, turns to her. "Mademoiselle," she says, "your malice is taxing your features. If you do not check it, it might cause permanent damage."

There is silence after these words. Where is this new courage coming from? What has brought it on? Whose secret backing?

Catherine can see these suspicions as if they were squirming worms, wiggling on the moist, freshly dug soil.

Das Fräulein's elation disappears, pinched out like a candle flame. She gives her lover a quick, pleading look. But Peter is Peter, the same weak, vacillating man he has always been. He is also a coward, and cowards bow before force and hide behind anyone who offers protection. Nothing for you, from this quarter!

Das Fräulein is no match for Catherine.

The evening is long and the Grand Duchess of Russia has just begun.

V chuzhom glazu sorinku zametno, a v svoyom — brevna ne vidat'. In another person's eye you see the smallest of motes; in your own, not even a log.

Her words, Catherine can tell, are making rounds across the glittering ballroom. Fans flicker, courtiers hurry from one group to another, repeat what she has said.

"You've become intolerably proud," Peter informs her. "Everyone is complaining about you."

"Who is everyone, Peter?"

Her husband laughs, with dark glee. "I was told you would ask this. That this would be the first thing you would ask. But I know how to bring you to your senses."

"Let me ask another question, Peter," she says. "What exactly does my pride consist of?"

He wrinkles his pug nose as if to sniff the air for clues.

"You hold yourself too erect," he finally says. There is unease in his voice. Whatever words he imagined her to say, these were not it, or he has forgotten the answers the Shuvalovs must have drummed into him.

"Do you then wish me to stoop like a slave?" Her voice is stained with irritation.

"I know how to bring you to reason," he says. "You are arrogant. You need to be taught a lesson."

"And how do you intend to do it?" she retorts.

He is not prepared for her calm. She has cornered him; she should remember that even a coward is dangerous when cornered. But she is past such considerations.

Peter, his back leaning against the wall, draws his sword out from his scabbard.

"What do you intend to do with that?" Catherine asks in an icy voice. "Challenge me to a duel, Peter? Then I ought to get a sword, too, don't you think?"

He slides the blade back inside the scabbard.

"You are always so spiteful," he says, his face red.

"In what way?"

"You are putting down my friends. You humiliate them."

"Your friends, Peter?" she asks. "Who are they, these true friends of yours I'm so spiteful toward?"

"Countess Shuvalova says —" he mumbles.

"The Shuvalovs call themselves your friends," she interrupts him. "But do friends humiliate your wife in public? Do friends spread rumors behind her back? Do friends send a husband to chastise his wife without him really knowing why?"

Peter is staring at her, blinking, his once white skin reddened and pocked. The sour odor around him, vodka mixed with tobacco, makes her stomach churn.

"This is what happens if you don't trust me," Peter stammers. "If you had come to me and complained about the Shuvalovs, all would've been well."

This is a withdrawal, almost an apology, she knows. An offering of a truce she would have accepted only a few weeks before. Now she pushes it away.

"What could I complain about, Peter? Rumors? Innuendos? Wouldn't you wish proofs? Certainty?"

Peter is no longer capable of following her argument. Like a drowning man, he has latched on to the thought of defending her. A notion which is big, noble, and beautiful. "I would've warned them not to talk about you." His tobacco-stained fingers are still clenched on the sword's handle.

She frowns. "You shouldn't say anything else, Peter. You've had too much to drink."

The harshness in her voice surprises him.

"You . . . you . . ." he stutters. "Why have you . . ."

"Go to sleep," Catherine interrupts and walks away.

Later that evening, she is in a drawing room, playing cards with Lev Naryshkin and the British Ambassador. Lace ruffles enhance the shape of her hands. The wrist covers stop the cold from entering her bones.

The cards land on the table with a soft thud.

She has just let her companions win another round, three hundred rubles each, so they are both in an excellent mood when Alexander Shuvalov approaches them. An ugly man, with bulging eyes and a twitching cheek. Shuvalov is the head of the Secret Chancery; he's accustomed to seeing fear in those he merely glances at. Her spies tell Catherine that he can kill a man with one blow to his temple.

Before he speaks, she points at the tray on which bottles of champagne and Malaga wine have been placed side by side.

"I've heard that champagne spoils your blood," she announces. "Doctor Halliday advises me to drink Malaga, instead."

Alexander Shuvalov's twitching cheek makes him look like a maimed Cyclops.

"The Empress has asked me if I agree," Catherine continues. "I said I wasn't sure yet."

Lev Naryshkin chuckles. Her threats are plain: Everyone knows that champagne is the Shuvalovs' monopoly.

She picks up her cards, unfolds them slowly, one by one, and deals the queen of spades. "Can you beat this, Lev?" she asks, as Alexander Shuvalov bows stiffly and takes his leave.

Tsarevich, she thinks.

Paul is such a small child, lanky, with eyes that narrow and harden when anything new appears in front of them. His wet nurses never stop fussing. Never let him stand on his own feet without hovering over him like clucking hens. Clutching his elbows at the slightest sign that he might waver, let alone fall.

Is this why, after making a step or two on his own, he lifts his hands to be picked up and carried around? Whines and whimpers at the slightest delay?

Elizabeth is ruining him, Catherine decides. *Indulged at every step, how can he ever learn anything of use?*

The Grand Duchess is allowed to see her son only once a week. She steels herself for these visits, cordons off thoughts of regret, of what could have been but won't. The child is always dressed in too many layers, his face flushed and sweaty. He knows no solitude, no silence, no boredom that would force him to come up with his own amusements. Someone is always cooing to him, singing, filling his mind with peasant tales. The nursery is so crowded with toys that nothing holds his attention for long.

What can she bring him that he doesn't

have already? A bunch of wildflowers? A pinecone? A handful of shiny chestnuts?

"Look! Don't you want to touch it? Feel how smooth they are?"

Paul shakes his head or claps his hands over his eyes. Or buries his face in his nurse's apron, to titters of approval.

What have they been telling him? That his mama is a witch? A Baba Yaga of fairy tales who fattens children before she eats them up? Is this why he spits out the apricot confit she has brought?

"I don't know what the wet nurses tell him," Varvara says. Her eyes are sad, for she does know, but she has taken it into her heart to be a savior, a guardian angel who keeps bad news away.

"Can you not find out?"

Children outgrow their fears, Varvara assures her. Children forget what they have been told. Children change. A mother's love always wins.

There are so many questions the Grand Duchess shouldn't ask, her friends warn her. Does my son eat well? Does he wake up at night? Does he cry much? Why is he so timid? The Empress should have no reasons to think that the Grand Duchess doesn't trust her. "My son is in the best of hands," she should say. Or "No one on earth would care for Paul better than Her Imperial Majesty does."

She should smile, too, when she says it. A

broad smile of carefree confidence. Of trust. Of maternal gratitude.

She listens to these admonitions. She must. No one survives alone. Fortune needs to be nudged along. The Empress is ailing. The crucial moment is near. It won't be long now.

Day after day, her friends sneak into Catherine's inner rooms. They have learned to become invisible. A scratch at the door is a sign. A cat's meow. A red handkerchief under her pillow. A pat on her shoulder at the Russian Theater. A note pressed into her hand, with "*La Grande dame* is on her way" hastily scribbled across it. A warning delivered not a moment too early so Catherine would know the Empress has just set off for what she believes is a surprise visit. A visit that will find the Grand Duchess alone, not lost in some forbidden book but bowing to the Holy Icons, lost in fervent prayers.

Without her friends, Catherine would have perished long ago.

Lev Naryshkin whispers: "Not all men are like Serge, Catherine . . . One bad apple doesn't have to spoil the whole barrel," and he devises elaborate escapes from the palace for a few hours of freedom. Katya Dashkova knows what the Shuvalovs tell Peter. Varvara Nikolayevna hears the Palace Guards laughing behind Peter's back, mocking his tight Holsteiner uniform, which forces him to mince his steps like a child who needs to pee.

Saying that her husband resembles Frederick the Great as much as an orangutan resembles a man.

Not all men are like Serge, she repeats to herself.

Stanislav, loving and beloved, is — like her — a foreigner at this court, a traveler from Poland in search of knowledge. Lost, he confesses, in Russia's vastness. Bewildered by the sublime happiness he has not dared to expect.

In the winter dark, broken by flaring lampposts that fill the streets with rank hempseed scent, these words send gooseflesh up Catherine's arms.

On this sleigh ride, they cuddle under fox furs, submerged in their own heat, oblivious to the frost that pinches their cheeks. Their smells mingle, an intoxicating mixture of perfume and sweat. Their hands burrow inside the furs.

Outside the city gates, the sleigh picks up speed. Soon they fly through the frozen fields. The harness bells tinkle. The driver — bribed into secrecy — never once turns toward them.

Her hand is on Stanislav's thigh, fingers spread, bearing down. It is all there, the melting and the longing, the words of love whispered with burning intensity. At moments like these she almost believes that they will never part.

And then darkness strikes, thick and sticky and impenetrable. Catherine is lying flat on the snow, her body bruised, her head throbbing with pain. Above her, in the sky, the Big Dipper is speckled with silver leaf. Stanislav is kneeling over her, his hands clasped in a prayer, a supplication for her to live.

She has no memory of what has just happened, so she must piece it together from the broken whispers of her beloved. The horse stumbled and fell, the sleigh toppled; she slipped out of his arms, catapulted into darkness.

"My head," she whispers. Her eyes feel heavy; her thoughts thrum.

"You must've hit a boulder," Stanislav says. "I thought I'd lost you."

She lifts her head in spite of the wave of nausea that travels up to her throat. Her lips are parched; her tongue tastes blood. The driver, frantic with fear, is urging them to get back into the sleigh, which he has managed to set straight. The man is thick-skinned, with ruddy pockmarked cheeks. "Your Highnesses," he pleads, ready to fall on his knees, prostrate himself, "have pity on me."

The snow feels impossibly soft and soothing. Stanislav has placed some of it on her forehead, where it now melts and trickles down her neck. *What now?* his eyes ask.

"Help me up," she whispers.

He extends his hand, and she grips it. Carefully she lifts herself up, waving the terrified driver away. The first steps are painful. Her ribs hurt, and so does the small of her back. Her right knee is throbbing. She limps toward the sleigh, leaning on her lover's shoulder. Stanislav's chin trembles; his teeth chatter. He has prayed for her to live. He has offered his life and his happiness to God in exchange for hers. This is what he is telling her now, a list of his wishes for her, who is more precious to him than his own soul. "If you died," he promises, "I would've drowned myself in the Neva."

When she is back in the sleigh, seated, wrapped with furs, Catherine closes her eyes and tries to recover the moments erased from memory. But there is nothing there.

Her friends, her spies, her confidants report every shortness of the imperial breath, every fainting spell, every cough. "Elizabeth woke up screaming," they say. "Refused to say what she had dreamed about!"

"It won't be long now, Catherine. Your time is coming soon."

She listens and hoards these offerings, words overheard in the Empress's bedroom, the Chancellor's office, the servant hall, words gleaned from letters or documents not meant for the Grand Duchess's eyes. Secret, dangerous words she turns in her mind, commits to memory, which won't betray her as

117

paper might. They not only reveal what has been hidden. They also assure her that at this court, where some still call her "a *Hausfrau* with a pointed chin," others are risking their lives for her. Not because they like or pity her, but because she allows them to dream their own sweet dreams.

I won't disappoint you, she vows.

"What is *he* doing here?" Katya Dashkova asks in a stage whisper. Her nose wiggles, like a rabbit's. Her upper lip lifts in contempt.

He is Grigory Orlov, a Lieutenant of the Izmailovsky Regiment, a hero from the Battle of Zorndorf, but Katya doesn't care to remember his name, and even if she did she wouldn't deign to pronounce it. A Vorontzov by birth, she thinks any Orlov an upstart.

Sometimes it is better to be a foreigner. Forced to befriend no.t only the spoiled princesses of the realm but those who desire to raise themselves up, to make their own destiny. Who never forget that the guards, these "makers of the Tsars," once carried Elizabeth in their arms right to the Russian throne.

July days are hot, even in the morning, but a brisk walk through Tsarskoye Selo gardens is an irresistible temptation. Even if after a few rounds sweat soaks through Catherine's linen shift into the corset and her petticoats. The exertion of this hour is what will sustain her through the long court day. Make her less restless, less impatient.

Katya has slipped her thin arm through hers and is holding it tight. Too tight, but this has to be endured. Small payment for the pleasure of conversing on Voltaire's wit and *Das Fräulein*'s blunders at the Vorontzovs' dinner table. Or of Moscow's contempt for St. Petersburg, still a mere "garrison town" where greed runs unchecked and uppity "service nobles" dream of advance.

Mercifully, Katya never talks of her children.

Grigory Orlov happens to be in the palace gardens just as the Grand Duchess is taking her walk. Catherine suspects that someone, Varvara perhaps, has charted for him the route of her morning walks, for he appears before her with a predictable regularity. By the pond, at the end of the hedge-lined lane. By the oak tree. He is not shy: "You've been captured, madam," he said once. "I'm not that easy to catch," Catherine shot back.

In the flesh Grigory Orlov is always somehow bigger, more handsome than remembered. Massive, yes, but also agile and graceful. Taut and yet pliant. He holds his head high. His very presence makes her think of simple things. Bonfire flames lighting up the darkness. The sweet, thick treacle of honey. A feeling that no matter what the day has brought, nothing is going to touch her.

When she looks at him, he doesn't avert his

119

gaze. *Notice,* his eyes say. *Notice the cut of my steel-colored tunic, my shining high leather boots, the polished helmet I cradle in my hand. Give me the slightest sign, and I shall find my way to you.*

Why are you waiting?

She is waiting not because she doesn't like the thought of his hands touching her. Not because of the letters from her Polish lover who had to leave and who — she knows it — will never be allowed to come back, long letters from Warsaw filled with tender but impossible dreams.

She is waiting because she is Russia's Grand Duchess and she won't be had cheaply. What is hard to come by will always be more precious.

"Shall we turn back?" Katya asks, shooting Lieutenant Orlov a look of annoyance that he doesn't even notice.

"Yes," Catherine replies, and she does turn on her heel and walk away. She feels Orlov's gaze even with her back turned.

"If you don't take care of yourself, Catherine," Katya warns, "your friends will." *Das Fräulein* is already making sketches on how she will reset the imperial jewels.

In the imperial nursery, Paul is drawing scaly dragons that spit fire and eat up naughty children for supper. "Have you ever seen a dragon?" Catherine has asked her son, and

120

he said that he has. Many times. "In the corridor . . . under the bed . . . in the pantry."
Varvara tells her that at five, the heir to the
Russian throne still wets his bed and won't
fall asleep in the dark.

Grigory Orlov trusts the bulk of a man's
body, the power of taut muscles and sinews.
"Punch me in the stomach, Katinka," he
teases, laughing. When Catherine does, with
all her strength, her knuckles redden as if she
were striking a brick wall.

His skin has the glow acquired from riding
fast horses. His teeth are even and strong. He
doesn't display them merely out of vanity. A
soldier needs strong teeth to tear the musket
cartridge. Once she saw him bend horseshoes
with his bare hands.

Volkov boyat'sa — v les ne khodit'. If you're
afraid of wolves, don't go to the woods.

"Not all brothers are like yours, Katinka,"
Grigory tells Catherine when she recalls William's childhood taunts. Grigory is not a man
of many words. She has to coax stories out of
him, patiently, as one extracts the meat from
black walnut shells. Only when they lie
together, spent and sweaty, will he let her see
glimpses of his boyhood. Days spent climbing trees, catching fish in rushing streams,
falling asleep in a haystack and waking up at

121

night to the flaming torches of a searching party and their mother's tears. Never alone, always with his brothers, though it is Alexei whose name comes up most often. Alexei, who climbed the church roof at night and rang the bell at the belfry. Stole the keys to the pantry and got them all sick gorging on *bliny* and roasted pheasants.

There is a small house on the Vasilevsky Island, two lanes away from Peter the Great's museum, Kunstkamera. It has wooden stairs of polished pine, and banisters painted white. There are six rooms upstairs, a long parlor with a bearskin hanging over an ottoman, a dining room, a music room, and a kitchen on the ground floor. There are also servants' quarters, but Catherine hasn't seen them. The housekeeper and her husband, who live there, are Orlov serfs. So are all the gaily costumed servants: cooks, maids, footmen who peer at her from behind the doors, through the windows. Who whisper among themselves and laugh. The housekeeper, Annushka, remembers the young masters when they were boys. "All like whirling tops, always getting into mischief and bruises." She sighs, and her watery eyes light up. "Though Master Alexei was the worst of them all."

"Guest in the house, God in the house," the Orlov servants greet the Grand Duchess when she arrives. Not that it stops the knowing looks, the bemused admiration for their

122

dashing master, who, this time, has brought home the most precious trophy of them all.

In this house where she meets her soldier lover, Gypsy singers come to sing to them at supper time, or dance to the fiery rhythm of the fiddle. In this house she is spoken of as *nasha* — ours. "From here . . . one of us . . . bred in the bones . . ." With a family who will stand by her in the moment of need and the moment of triumph.

Katinka, he calls her. His Katinka. Grigory Orlov, a warrior who can slay an enemy with one blow, knows, with every fiber, every muscle of his body, that no one else, no other man, no other lover of hers, has ever been equal to him. He knows her hunger and her satiation. He knows that as soon as he touches her, the boundary between where she ends and he begins melts away.

The line between what is needed and what is loved can become thin.

Grigory Orlov calls Peter a pip-squeak and a monster. A German fiddler with a pocked face and a small, limp dick. No wonder, he says, that Peter couldn't father a child. "If he dares to lift a finger to you, Katinka, I'll slash his throat. I'll tear him to pieces and nail them to the first signpost."

Grigory Orlov will do what he says. Unless her fearless, reckless lover is killed first, leaving her to her husband's revenge. Born of resentment, even a weakling's rage can harm.

Peter can toss her out, like a rotting piece of flotsam thrown into the Neva River.

In public, she still calls Grigory Orlov "that oaf."

Dobroye bratstvo — luchsheye bogatstvo.
Good brotherhood is the best wealth.

"Men are like unbroken horses, Katinka," Grigory Orlov says. "Learn how to make them follow."

Catherine is an excellent horsewoman, but she has never broken a horse yet.

"Teach me," she says.

Horses are about flight and fear, he tells her. *A firm hand is needed to control them.*

All this and more she learns from Grigory Orlov's lips. And from the sight of him walking into the pen where a stallion stands tethered. He is a giant of a man whose every pore exudes courage. *You have to frighten the horse first. Show him who is the true master. Then he will follow you.*

The Orlov lessons are simple, and Catherine has always been a quick study. Taming of animals and taming of men are two sides of the same coin.

Grigory has no talent for a clever turn of phrase. His wisdom has to be gleaned from clipped phrases, extracted from grunts and

124

exaggerated sighs of impatience or derision. Like an alchemist, Catherine has to test and refine what she hears and sees, purify and transform what he tosses her way, until base metals turn into gold.

Don't seek approval outside yourself. Know that you are in charge, and a horse will sense it and accept your conviction. But if you don't have it in you, the horse will know it instantly and defy you.

Why?

Because your body betrays you far more than you think. Because you cannot hide your thoughts. Banish the ones you don't want.

Grigory throws her the line attached to the horse's halter. He stands back, watching her.

Nerves and muscles are taut, strung tight. Hoofs stomp the pen, ears twitch. Anything can alter the uneasy balance of this moment; anything could spark a blind panic that cannot be controlled. A passing shadow, a blinding glitter of a diamond pin, a screeching seagull on the lookout for spoils.

"Get him to retreat, Katinka. Keep going. Keep your eyes on his."

Power is about will and direction.

Power is about assuming your place with confidence.

Power is about rewards bestowed for what you desire, and punishment for what you reject.

125

Power is taken or lost with every step, every quiver of your voice. It's not just the words that matter, it is their tone, their pitch.

"Victory comes from confidence, Katinka. All soldiers know this."

When it is time to mount her ride, fear descends. In a flash, she sees herself, limp, on the ground, trampled, maimed, her face pummeled to a pulp. She doesn't have a man's body. She is not that strong. Her bones can be broken, her spine smashed. She has seen men crippled by falls. Pink foam on their lips as they mumble their pleas.

She lets the fear in, lets her heartbeat smash blindly against her rib cage. Plead for time, for more practice. Urge her to leave, invent some more important tasks. Admit her weaknesses, which — she knows — are many. *I'll count to five,* she decides. *This is how long I have to be afraid.* Courage is distilled from moments like this. By the time her hand reaches for the reins, by the time she is lifted into the saddle, there is no trembling, no hesitation. Her heart is forced into an even beat, her voice firm and steady.

A smile breaks on Grigory Orlov's lips. A smile of pride and praise.

It's her body that betrays her. At first she still hopes her menses are merely late. But that bright August morning she wakes up feeling sick and dizzy and chilled by fear.

Her spies in the Imperial Bedroom are whispering of Elizabeth's fainting spells and long processions of healers brought from the farthest reaches of the Empire. From her husband's chambers come snippets of joyful anticipation. *Das Fräulein,* who has always trusted the language of the gutter, proposes locking "that haughty German sow in the nearest pigsty."

This is not the time for a bastard birth.

"Mother of God, have mercy," Varvara Nikolayevna whispers when she hears the news. "How long without bleeding?"

"A month . . . no one knows yet . . . only you, Varenka."

Tears slip down Catherine's cheeks. Bitter tears of humiliation and defeat. Perhaps it's already too late. The Grand Duchess may hope she has avoided the watchful eyes, but her fall would make for such a tasty gossip. She who dares to think of the crown is defeated by her own belly.

For a woman, a bedroom can be a prison. And a tomb.

"Don't cry, please."

Varvara's voice penetrates the chaos of panic. Deception is hard work. It requires precise calculations. And the most trusted of servants. Varvara's fingers tick off the coming months. The renovations of the Winter Palace drag on. The courtiers are moving back and forth. The Grand Duchess can develop some plausible ailments that keep her away from official appearances. The swelling feet? Back pain? With winter furs and lined bulky dresses, an April child can be hidden until the very end.

The maids will be fooled with monthly blood. The bowl of sickness will disappear.

"If I die, Varenka —"

"You won't die. You are strong."

Only Grigory wears his joy like a mantle. Peacock proud that his child grows in her belly. Bigger with each day. Kicking her inside. An Orlov boy, strong and brave, like his father and uncles.

Not, he says, grinning, *like Saltykov's son. Paul is scared by his own shadow.*

"If you are born to hang, you won't drown." Empress Elizabeth is panting, her wrinkled cheeks flushed. Her feet are so swollen that bruised flesh spills out of silk slippers. Inside her, death crouches, patient. "Destiny will sniff after you like a bloodhound, Catherine," she says.

The dying Empress is mocking her. Elizabeth's lips curl into a sneer. "A petty princess of Anhalt-Zerbst still trying to outdo me? To prove me wrong?"

Time makes leaps and reversals once

thought inconceivable. In the new Imperial Bedroom, where even the stinging smell of fresh varnish cannot mask the stench of death, she, the Grand Duchess of Russia, is standing by a dying Empress's bed. Inside her a child kicks, a secret love child that might get her banished to some monastery cell where she will grow gaunt and shriveled, choking on forced prayers.

Or worse.

They are alone. The servants and the ladies-in-waiting have been sent away. They are now biding their time outside the bedroom doors, straining their ears, eyeing one another with suspicion. The palace spies — Catherine's among them — fight their own unending battles. Who is received in the inner bedroom and who has to wait in the antechambers. Whose warnings are heeded and whose ignored. And — most of all — who is entrusted with the most precious of imperial secrets. For a secret withheld from one but entrusted to another turns into a bond as powerful as love.

Elizabeth lies on her high bed, on her smooth silk quilts, in this room where darkness is banished, where thick candles are never snuffed. Thoughts of hell haunt her. The earthly sensations that determined her pleasures now define eternal pain. Flames will burn her skin, whips will lash it, boiling oil will scald it. Wiry devils will pour liquid gold on the most sinful parts of her body, tear it with red-hot pliers.

"I shouldn't have brought Peter here," Elizabeth seethes. "I should've let him rot in Holstein."

Her nephew is a fool. A runt. Peter is weak, wavering. He listens to anyone who flatters him. Peter will ruin Russia. Make it a Prussian footstool.

Elizabeth's eyelids droop; her chest is racked by labored gasps. The corners of her mouth crack open, oozing yellow pus.

How much longer will this drag on? A month? A fortnight? A week? Doctor Halliday, the chief imperial physician, accepts the gifts she, Catherine, sends him only to throw his hands up, professing his helplessness. Patients have defied his expectations before. It is all in God's hands.

The baby kicks right underneath her stomach, sending a wave of nausea up her throat. The Orlovs have planned it all. Grigory's brother, Alexei, will create a distraction. Varvara Nikolayevna will smuggle the newborn infant out of the palace.

If this baby doesn't kill her first.

The dying Empress stirs. "I shouldn't have brought you here, either," she mutters.

Bitter words. Gritty. Like ashes mixed with sand. "I know your secrets, Catherine. I know who spies for you and why. I know what you want."

A cold trickle of sweat rolls down the small of Catherine's back.

"Your Majesty is mistaken," she replies. "I have no secrets."

"They've been warning me." Elizabeth speaks with what looks like a smile but is probably just a grimace of pain. "A consummate liar, they've called you . . . with no thought for anyone but herself."

Catherine doesn't ask who has thus condemned her. Not that she doesn't want to know. But she won't give Elizabeth the satisfaction. She will not be forced to root through the rotten debris of her past in search of traitors. It's enough to suspect how much has already been betrayed. The belly tied with a girdle to make it look smaller? Grigory Orlov and Alexei, gathering support for her in the barracks? Enough to get them all arrested, executed for treason.

A ragged sigh escapes the Empress's parched lips. Her face says: *I could destroy you, Catherine, expose your despicable ambitions, drag you through the mud, but I don't want to.*

Before death takes her, Elizabeth wishes to drive a bargain. In exchange for the imperial silence, the Grand Duchess must swear to guard the throne for her son, Paul Petrovich. "Your last payment, Catherine, for bringing you here," Elizabeth gasps. "To Russia."

131

As if she, Catherine, hasn't paid enough already.

"Do whatever you need, Catherine. Push Peter aside. Send him back to Holstein . . . Be Regent until Paul is of age. Until my precious boy can be Tsar!"

What will she do now, this dying old woman? Make her swear obedience on Our Lady of Kazan? St. Nicholas the Miracle-Maker? Or will she threaten to haunt Russia's Grand Duchess in these rooms, a vengeful harpy of the underworld making sure she is obeyed even after death?

But the Empress of Russia knows that fear — however flimsy and desperate its source — is more reliable than trust. Or gratitude.

"There are those in the palace who know my will, Catherine." Elizabeth's feeble voice needles itself inside her. "They'll always remind Paul what I wish for him. And they'll watch you after I'm gone."

In the dark night of the Russian winter, the Empress, from whom power is chipped away with each tick of the clock, whispers: "Do you know of black nightshade, Catherine? The berries taste sweet, but a small handful of them will kill a man in seconds."

Perhaps.

Perhaps not.

"You are being watched, Catherine," Elizabeth mutters. "Even now."

■ ■ ■ ■

This baby follows its own cocky ways, wakes up when she settles to sleep, flips inside her or rolls about, oblivious of all the dangers it has brought with it. In the months past she was still hoping for a miscarriage, but an Orlov child has no intention of letting go of life. The thought is pleasing, like all reckless courage. And chilling, too, for by December Catherine is running out of excuses. Swollen legs, migraine headaches have elicited snide comments.

A secret of this magnitude is an obligation that grows. Varvara appears each morning, before dawn, an exacting ghost, her tasks all planned and mapped out. Every month, for five days, the Grand Duchess's sheets and undergarments are stained with blood. Every month, her belly is wrapped tighter, and the folds of her gowns are let out to accommodate it. Only on some evenings, with curtains drawn tight, with cotton swabs inside the keyhole, the swaddlings can be removed and the taut skin soothed with massage.

Even during the day Catherine fights sleepiness. Heavy deep sleep, dragging her into darkness. When she wakes she sometimes needs a moment to remember where she is, what danger she is in.

Five more months, four.

By the end of December, Varvara's news from the Imperial Bedroom is more and more alarming. It is no longer just the fainting spells or screams of raw terror. The doctors have taken to desperate measures. Tried to tap Elizabeth's swollen belly to relieve the pressure, let out the excess bile.

To no avail.

"This is the real end," Varvara whispers. "The long-awaited moment. And the Empress has asked me to bring the Grand Duchess to her."

By the time Catherine makes it into the Imperial Bedroom, tied up, swaddled in thick quilted petticoats, the room is swathed in darkness in spite of thick wax candles. Sobbing women surround the bed, refusing to budge, Countess Shuvalova among them, flashing the Grand Duchess a scowling look of raw hatred.

She is thankful for it, really, this gashing reminder of what is essential. When a tree falls in the forest, it lets in more light and frees space for new growth. This is the time for the battle of displays: *Your tears against my devotions. Your gossip against my prayers. Your scowls against my trembling hands.*

One step, then another. A bow to the Holy Icons, fingers touching the floor, the shoulders. Gestures that say *God Almighty is my witness. Eternity is my scene. Russia is my conscience. Look at me, you all,* Catherine's eyes say. *Look and compare.*

This is the battle she, the Grand Duchess, will not relinquish. Not when the Empress spurts blood from her mouth and her nose. When the old woman grips the sheets, thrashes about as if trying to keep afloat on a stormy sea. Not when the howling comes, harsh, high-pitched at first, then rolling, like that of a trapped fox. Not when her love child moves in Catherine, a twitch of pain and promise.

Not even when her husband comes and all fall on their knees before Emperor Peter III.

I refuse to believe the rumors, Stanislav, her Polish lover who still considers himself the master of her heart, writes from Warsaw. Once he had been her true comfort. Her thoughts of him are still spiced with memories of long conversations on fate and destiny and the power of human dreams. Love is no less real even if it retreats, melts into the shadows.

I'm making arrangements to come to your side.

Stanislav's letters are written in cipher. The awaited news — the death of the Empress — has come and gone. The courtiers have rallied around the new Emperor Peter III. Russia has her new Tsar, *batushka,* the father of the nation. The merciful grandson of Peter

135

the Great. Even in Warsaw, everyone knows that Peter has no wish to let his unloved wife near him. That he has humiliated her in public. That he appears everywhere with his mistress.

Deciphered, Stanislav's letters yield concessions, make room for necessary transformations. His beloved Sophie is a woman in need of protection. *That* Orlov he hears about so often is a soldier, ready to die for her. Besides, *that* Orlov has many friends among the Palace Guards who can protect her and thus be useful. Such are the exigencies of life. The price to be paid. Hard, but unavoidable. Once Sophie is out of danger, *that* Orlov will be amply rewarded and sent away.

Catherine throws these letters into the fire. When her silence does not stop Stanislav, she writes:

I forbid you to come. I'm watched day and night. Your presence will only add to my peril. Even your letters put me at risk . . . especially since they are in cipher. Refrain from writing to me so often, or — better — do not write at all.

Grigory Orlov doesn't know of this correspondence. "How could you've ever loved him, Katinka?" he has asked, laughing. Him, a delicate Polish count who believes that a turn of phrase is mightier than the thrust of the sword.

Secluded in her room, the Grand Duchess of Russia is like a queen bee, receiving reports from all quarters, each charting the expanding boundaries of her power.

Her friends, her supporters, her spies labor in the shadows, relentless, honey-lipped, armed with confidence and gold, fortified by threats and dire predictions about what must happen if things are allowed to go on as they are. The name of Peter III spells ruin for the Russian army and the Russian Church. Chaos and dissipation. Humiliation and defeat.

Power is built in increments, of bets of money and ambition, secrets entrusted and betrayed.

The Orlovs and their subalterns are whipping up the support of the Guards. Katya Dashkova carries imperial assurances and promises to St. Petersburg's finest salons, while Paul's governor, Nikita Ivanovich Panin, weaves his nets of courtly backing on the belief that Catherine II will reign as Paul's Regent.

Whispers travel fast. Gold changes hands, emboldens the hesitant or faint of heart. She, their future Empress, holds all the strings, knots them in ways only she knows how to unravel. Each knot is separate, connected by a stitch underneath the fabric. Together they

137

form a pattern that dazzles the eyes and lifts the heart.

Don't tell them too much, don't give them too much to think about, Catherine tells herself each dawn. *Keep your words simple. Straightforward. Easy to remember and repeat:*

Freedom from tyranny! Escape from this foreign madman who thinks of Russia as his punishment! Who wants to turn us all into Prussians. Unlike his long-suffering wife, Catherine Alekseyevna, who never fails to show her respect for what is most sacred to us all.

St. Petersburg's salons are tense with growing apprehension. In smoky back rooms, seasoned courtiers assess Catherine's strength and measure it against Peter's.

Her promises and pledges have already seeped all the way to the soldiers' barracks, where men know how to argue the merits of a woman's rule. The late mother of the nation served Russia well. Why not continue what has worked so well for so long?

Catherine's growing belly is well concealed. As long as she sits at her desk, her visitors leave none the wiser of what she is harboring inside. By now, this reluctant game of deceptions has become a source of pride. In the mornings, before she is dressed, she puts her hand on her belly to feel an invisible hand or foot slide up and down under her fingers. *Restless,* she thinks. *Like his father.*

Childbearing is the time of reckoning. She is thirty-three years old, carrying her third child. Paul, her firstborn, barely recognizes her; Anna — her second — was kept away from her so even her memory is a mere flicker. A small, cold hand that Catherine kissed just before the coffin closed.

The child has grown so large inside her that the disguises threaten to break. Repeated too often, her excuses come back mauled and menacing. "Madame Resourceful is haughty as she has always been," her husband declares. Katya Dashkova lets out a girlish cry and insists on fetching her own doctor to examine her swelling feet. "You still don't take care of yourself, Catherine," she scolds. "So we, your friends, must."

When the birthing pains come, when after a short stab the waters break and soak the bed, when the midwife arrives, whispering her prayers and admonitions, Catherine welcomes it all with relief. This birth will be a release. Necessary before she can take another step.

She is not alone. Grigory and his brothers have sworn to guard her with their lives. The Orlovs are brilliant tacticians. They know the power of diversions; they know how to deceive.

"A fire the likes of which St. Petersburg has

not yet seen," Grigory chuckles. A conflagration that will bring throngs of gawkers. "You'll see, Katinka." She won't, really, but Catherine doesn't interrupt her lover's ardor. The wooden building a few doors away has been emptied a few days before. "Volunteered by a faithful friend," Grigory says. One torch will be enough to set it ablaze. "Then you can scream all you want," he announces with such boyish pride that her heart tightens.

But by now Grigory has been shooed away. Giving birth is not done in men's presence.

Hours pass before the midwife tells her to push. Long hours soothed with Varvara's promises. The arrangements have been most careful. Varvara herself will smuggle the baby out of the palace. "I'll make sure it is well cared for . . . I'll visit . . . every day . . . myself."

It is tempting to think of another life. A well-lit parlor, Grigory at her side, around them children whose minds and hearts she can form and shape. For children need light and freedom. They need to ask questions that will be answered. Read stories that teach that nothing should be judged before it is tried first. To learn that when the light of reason shines on darkness, everything is possible.

But why dwell on what can never be? Why not think of what is possible instead?

By the time the child who could have been her death or her disgrace tears out of her and

140

is safe in the midwife's arms, a bundle of hungry cries, Catherine feels nothing but relief.

Nine months she has waited for this chance. To lock away what cannot be and open to what is possible.

It is April of 1762. The Emperor of Russia will never know that he has just lost his only chance to defeat her. Through the bedroom window come the wafts of smoke from the fire, animal squeals, and the excited screams of the mob.

Outside she can hear Grigory's steps, rushing through, impatient and bursting with energy. He is a father. He has a son.

Alexei Grigoryevich.

When evening comes, Grigory lifts her up and carries her to the open window. This is what she sees: a charred building from which flames still leap, a yard where half-crazed animals still run like demons, a figure carrying a bundle wrapped in a gray shawl, entering a carriage and speeding away.

After her love child is delivered and smuggled out of the palace, Catherine grows bolder. On Vasilevsky Island, buried in a printer's cellar, lie copies of her proclamation, which — as soon as she declares herself Empress — will be pasted on doors and pillars. These printed pages are her vow, her sacred promise. She will uphold the vision bestowed on Russia by Peter the Great, that giant among Tsars. Russians will again be proud of their Motherland; the old Europe will have no choice but to heed her sister nation, glowing with energy and strength.

When new doubts or warnings emerge, she pays them heed. *Are they true or false?* she asks herself. *Certain or merely possible?*

Has anything been neglected? Left to chance?

Can anything still be done?

Who should be ordered to do it?

She is not vain enough to believe herself omnipotent. Not all can be foreseen, or prevented. Not all kept secret. When the crucial moment arrives, she will still have to ask herself: *Shall I rule? Or will I perish?*

A white June night of 1762 is when all is decided. In a simple mourning dress of black silk, Alexei Orlov at her side, Catherine rides from Peterhof to St. Petersburg, along the dusty bumpy road to the army barracks. Soldiers of the Guard regiments are there to hear her plea: "Bereaved by the loss of our beloved Empress, I entrust myself and my son to you."

The Orlovs don't break their promises. Or throw their words into the wind.

In her hand a Holy Icon. On her forehead a greasy spot where the regimental priest has rubbed the drop of holy oil. The words Catherine has prepared and rehearsed are smooth and polished. *The glory of our beloved Motherland . . . the end of tyranny . . .*

The mourning dress cast aside, she puts on the Preobrazhensky greens. The uniform fits her like a glove. *I'm one of you,* it proclaims.

"We've done it, Katinka! Our gamble has paid off!"

Not a gamble, she thinks. Dark, patient hours of toil when alliances are stitched together. When what cannot be changed is undermined.

The men who throng to see and touch her are crazy with joy.

She has already chosen the words she will use to announce the new rule of reason and order.

It won't happen at once, she will warn. Russia is a vast country. Many diverse peoples will have to be united in one common goal. For where one twig snaps in no time, a tight bundle withstands a lot of pressure. But with hard work, prosperity will come. Soon the world will take note of the powerful Christian Empire of the East.

This will be her legacy.

Someone hands her a tumbler of water, tinted reddish with wine. She drinks in gulps, soothing her throat, raw from speaking in a loud voice.

"You've always been my Empress," Katya Dashkova gasps. "Always."

Paul, her firstborn son, is staring at her, blinking. When they brought him to her, he was murmuring something with great concentration, a poem, it turned out, for his papa's name-day feast. "I don't want to make a mistake," he insisted when Catherine told him he didn't have to practice anymore.

The child has been brought in haste. His wig has been powdered without mercy. His jacket has not been brushed. On his upturned nose, under a dab of concealing cream, a wart. Someone should be taking care of such matters. Someone more capable. Where has Varvara been when she could be of use?

Grigory and Alexei are everywhere. They storm through the Winter Palace, directing the human waves. Courtiers who want to be noted, who wish to assure the new Empress of their undying support. Petitioners waiting for a chance to thrust their harebrained schemes into her hand. Some weep. Some cluster together and whisper. A squealing voice in the back of the room proclaims the victory of justice.

Alexei Orlov has news of Peter. The deposed Emperor who fancies himself a great warrior sends messengers to St. Petersburg, one after another, surprised when they do not return. It is the messengers' stories that Alexei gleefully repeats. Peter, annoyed at his wife's absence, searching for her under the bed at Monplaisir Palace, as if she cared to play hide-and-seek. Peter flapping his frantic hands like a seal on an ice floe. *Das Fräulein* urging him to gather his Holsteiners and charge the capital. "Catherine is a usurper! You are the Tsar! You are a true Romanov! As soon as you show yourself to the people, they'll abandon her!" Peter stewed in cowardly sweat, stammering, "Y-y-y-y-yes!" Stumbling over his own tongue.

Usurper . . . a true Romanov. Alexei Orlov bares his upper lip as he spits these words. The white, jagged scar across his cheek is a reminder of an old fight he didn't back away from. There is no need to spell out the dangers any further. A coward can be used by others to instigate a revolt. The new Empress is not safe yet.

"Come, *matushka,* you have to show yourself," Alexei insists. "The people think this monster has kidnapped you! Sold you to the Prussians, in chains. Step onto the balcony. Calm the people's fears."

Everyone wants to touch her. Someone catches her hand and covers it with kisses. How many kisses should be allowed before she withdraws it? Two? Three? A hundred? Among unfamiliar faces that throng and melt around her, those of her friends and supporters stand out. They are here, dressed in their best, bursting with joy and expectations. They are all her creatures, but they are not one another's friends. Their eyes lock on hers, demanding proof of their own importance. Surely she cannot take Katya Dashkova's silly enthusiasm seriously? Or trust Varvara Nikolayevna, a bookbinder's daughter who pushes her nose into other people's business? Or even think for one moment that the Orlovs deserve more than they already have?

"Come, *matushka*! Show yourself to the people! They must know you and the Tsarevich are safe."

Alexei Orlov is beside her. Cursing under his breath that they should never have let all of these good-for-nothings inside the palace. "Now everyone is important," he seethes. "Where were they when we needed them?"

Paul is staring at the tips of his shoes. "Is it true that Lieutenant Orlov is not afraid of anything?" her son has asked Varvara. "Not even the Devil?"

"Take your son's hand, *matushka*," Alexei commands. "Follow me."

A small, slender hand stiffens in Catherine's. She can feel the narrow bones of the rigid fingers. Paul's steps are awkward, each movement punctuated by a waft of urine. Her son and heir has wet his pants.

Outside the palace windows, screams erupt again and again. The future is still in flux. In Oranienbaum, Peter has his Holsteiners at the ready. He has been Tsar for six months.

Outside St. Petersburg he is still *batushka,*
the Father of his people. Even if he is not
ready to fight for his throne, others will be.
The Shuvalovs are no quitters.

Catherine has no time to think it all
through. Not yet. Not now, not in these first
feverish hours, when everything is happening
at once.

She steps out to the balcony. Down below,
people are shoving forward for a better look,
stamping their feet, roaring their approval.
Soldiers, guards, priests, beggars. Joy mixes
with impatience and unease, a heady brew. A
young man has climbed a lamppost and is
waving his hat. Kerchiefed women are holding Holy Icons, bunches of field flowers.
Children crane their necks. An old man has
knelt in the road, making the Sign of the
Cross.

Catherine raises her hand.

They all stare at her, their new Empress,
still in the Preobrazhensky greens. Her very
presence on this balcony is a sign that all is
well. That her enemies have failed, that Russia is safe.

Do they believe in her?

Suddenly, all noises stop, and then she
hears someone shout, a cry that is picked up
and repeated until everyone is chanting: *Long
live Empress Catherine Alekseyevna! Long live
Tsarevich Paul Petrovich!*

She doesn't see her son's face, but she feels

Paul straighten. His left hand is still in hers, stiff and sweaty, and she lifts both up into the air, sparking another explosion of joy from the crowd.

This is what she remembers. The two of them standing together, mother and son holding hands, as the people of Russia rejoice below. And then she hears her son's wavering voice, asking: "Am I Emperor now?"

"There is no emperor," the guards announce. "We take our orders from Empress Catherine II."

Peter is my prisoner.
Peter has abdicated.
Peter has sworn allegiance to my rule.
All Peter wants is his flute, his mistress, and his Blackamoor.

Peter wants a quiet life, away from court. "Let me go back to Holstein," her husband asks. "This is all I've ever wanted."

Mercy can still take many shapes.

"He'll turn against you, Katinka," Grigory Orlov snarls. "A mad dog will bite the hand that feeds it."

Listen to those who have risked their lives for you!
The Holsteiners will stand by him. Prussia will use Peter against you.

There is already one mad Tsar in Schlüsselburg. You cannot afford another!

In the game of bloodlines there are those who have more rights to the Russian throne than a princess from Zerbst. Peter is a Romanov. Catherine is not. This is what they are saying in Moscow already. Why let another woman rule?

Peter is a man.

Peter, who stinks of tobacco and sour wine. Whose fingernails are black with dirt. Whose pockmarks flare red when he is excited or scared. Who for eighteen years has trailed her with the shifty looks of a coward.

"He called you a fool in front of the whole court, Katinka. He must be rendered harmless."

Catherine's head is swimming with all those voices, grunts, innuendos. Their urgent pushing, their dismay. A flash of light warns of an approaching headache.

"I have no time to think of him now," she says.

She has to think of Peter, though. Foreign dispatches arrive addressed to him. The orders he signed are still on her desk. Proposals he drafted. Letters he has left half written. Or letters he is still writing from Ropsha, where Alexei Orlov is guarding him. Letters he signs as her *very humble, devoted servant*. Peter wants to leave for Germany with *Das*

149

Fräulein. Her husband begs his wife and Empress not to treat him as a criminal, as he has never offended her. He appeals to her magnanimity.

> I beg Your Majesty to order that no officers should remain in the same room with me, since I must relieve myself and I cannot possibly do that in front of them . . .

Memory is a shape-shifter. A running nymph turns into a tree; a vain man becomes a flower. Memory sharpens its edges each time an image comes circling by.

Peter, his face pockmarked like a page splattered with ink, is screaming. *"Nein, nein! Dumme Schlampe!"* Stupid bitch.

In Ropsha there is a small lake. Empress Elizabeth liked to fish there. Peter is kept in one small room on the ground floor. A room with a bed, a desk. A window with thick blinds.

She is in the throne room, receiving well-wishers and petitioners, categories that defy separation. It is the eighth day after the coup, a Saturday. Catherine hasn't slept for more than a few hours. She wouldn't have eaten if her attendants didn't insist.

Her temples throb. Her hair has been hastily done, and she has a feeling that the string of pearls is slipping out from her tresses every time she shakes her head. After the easy comfort of the Preobrazhensky uniform, the court gown feels all wrong. The stomacher is too tight. The heavy folds of the skirt impede movement.

"Your Majesty needs to rest," Varvara fusses. "Just for an hour. Please. A bed is ready. I've darkened the room."

How tempting, to close her tired eyes, let thoughts settle, like dust on a summer road after a carriage has sped by.

To rest for a moment. In silence. In the dark. Alone.

The doors swing open. A messenger from Ropsha is spattered with mud. The rain has soaked his riding coat, filthy water is now dripping to the floor, staining the wood. "For the Empress's eyes only," the man insists, retrieving a folded letter from his chest pocket.

One stiff page, sealed with the Orlovs' ring. An eagle's beak that looks like a cat's paw.

Alexei Orlov's scribble, a truant schoolboy's hand. Catherine scans the page quickly, trying to make sense of it. Matushka . . . *most merciful . . . how can I explain . . . I am ready for death . . . it has happened.*

An accident? A quarrel that got out of hand? *. . . Peter is no more . . .*

Where does guilt lie? In the cadences of innermost thoughts? In orders not given? Or is wishing for something enough?

151

■ ■ ■ ■

A white night blends seamlessly with dawn. The air is singed with bonfires from the celebrations, scented with the roasted flesh of oxen and pigs. Clusters of revelers can be heard outside the palace gate, voices arguing over something, followed by loud belches or imitating the bleating of sheep. "There will be dozens of children born in March," Varvara has said, laughing.

The carriage that has brought Peter's corpse from Ropsha is standing in the palace courtyard. She, the new Empress, has covered her shoulders with a woolen shawl before sneaking here alone. The shawl is blood-red with botanical motifs: tulips with bulbs and petals, a few already wilted, revealing the shape of the stem.

Catherine studies her husband's dead face as if he could still trick her. A swollen throat makes Peter's neck look stubby. His lips are blackened.

Alexei Orlov, her husband's murderer, is standing beside the carriage. In the lilac dusk of northern night the scar across his face looks whiter and more jagged than she remembers it. His big hands hang loosely by his sides. "We had too much vodka . . . he called me an upstart . . . he called me a liar." Alexei's voice is brittle. *Forgive me or quickly make an end of me,* he has written.

There is no remorse in Alexei's eyes, only insistence. Empires cannot be ruled with hesitation. One bold strike will prevent others from rising. Foreseeing future troubles is not an idle game of predictions.

Blood has been spilled?

One cannot make an omelet without breaking eggs.

Mercy? Justice?

Mercy to whom and for what? Justice in what cases and for what price?

This is what Alexei's gray eyes tell her: *When you steal the throne from your husband, you better make sure he cannot take it back. If Peter lives, he will be an excuse for anyone wanting to overthrow you.*

If you don't strike first, you risk being killed.

If you leave enemies lurching in the dark, they will gather strength and attack you when you don't expect it.

If you want power, you must have the courage to use it.

She takes one last look at Peter. Dead, he looks smaller — childish, even. His shoulders are bony, quite narrow. There is a smell of *ladan* about him, the sweet Russian herbs of the underworld. The Orlovs have no quarrels with the dead.

She should do something. Touch Peter's cheek, perhaps, send him out of her life with some gesture of farewell. Adjust the scarf on his bruised neck.

She doesn't move.

There is no need to prolong what has already ended. The dead have no use for gestures. They do not feel the cold of the tomb.

"Take him to the Nevsky," she orders and walks away.

Fortune is not blind. Fortune is a series of well-chosen steps.

Every morning at six, Catherine sits at her desk, quill in hand, a steaming cup of black coffee beside her. To Frederick of Prussia she sends gifts of melons and dromedaries, followed by vague promises of possible treaties. To Maria Theresa of Austria she dispatches a rosary made of precious stones and assurances that Russia is a God-fearing Christian country. The balance of power requires shifting allegiances and constant vigilance. If Russia gets too big, she will be betrayed.

She has hung Peter the Great's portrait in her study. The giant Tsar, in his plain soldier's uniform, is making long strides over a verdant field, while dwarfish courtiers rush behind, struggling to keep up. Hand raised, the great Tsar is pointing west. It's a bit crude — with a serf painter's skewed sense of perspective — but she prefers it over the Tsar on his deathbed, with eyes closed, indifferent to the matters of this earth.

On her desk, maps lie. Old, new. Some still rolled up, some already unrolled, their edges held in place by whatever object happens to be around. An inkwell. A marble sculpture of Mercury. A volume of Montesquieu, pages she hasn't had time to cut.

Russia is her kingdom. To her south, the Ottoman Porte. To her west, Poland. Both drunk on chaos and constant flux, both weak, soft with indolence. The Porte is a vipers' nest gorging on illusions of past grandeur. Poland is a giant on clay feet; any grandee wields more power than a Polish king. Power demands such assessments. A keen eye for opportunities. Your weakness is my strength. Your fall is my gain.

The Empire needs to grow.

What do the weak trust? God? Fortune? Fate?

Poland is already Russia's vassal state, the boulevard for Russian troops, and it should stay that way. Since Poland elects her kings, Catherine wants Stanislav on the Polish throne. He can no longer be her lover, but she wishes him well. She has assured him of her goodwill, and she is eager to prove it. There are other considerations, too. Stanislav is not rich or too well connected. The Polish nobles know that. He'll have to bend every which way to stay alive. A crown will also put an end to his foolish plans of joining her.

155

There is pleasure in such thoughts. Pleasure of giving gifts that bind. *Do as I wish and you shall rise up in the world. Oppose me and you shall perish.*

Imperial thoughts.

Alexei Orlov takes her to the docks. The new ships in various stages of construction are like the skeletons of giant beasts. "Strong enough to defeat the Ottoman Turks," he declares, as she runs her hand over a freshly hewn mast.

Alexei's voice is brisk, businesslike. For a while after she absolved him of all guilt in Peter's death, he removed himself from St. Petersburg. Now he is back, filled with nervous energy, always pushing on. In her inner rooms where Grigory often brings him, Alexei makes sure he is always in her sightline. He doesn't avert his eyes when his brother, at some rare moment of leisure, tickles her feet with an ostrich feather.

Peter III, the imperial manifesto announced, died of natural causes. Of hemorrhoidal colic. In the Nevsky monastery where his body lay in state, her spies reported slow, orderly lines of subjects paying their respects. There have been a few hushed comments on the presence of the thick scarf around his throat. Some foreign diplomats made crude jokes on the dangers of Russian hemorrhoids. Worthy of noting, but nothing more.

Catherine doesn't think of Peter much. She

dreams of him sometimes, dreams that leave little behind them except a faint feeling of disgust. All his portraits have been removed from sight, his name erased from all official documents, his orders either rescinded or reissued as hers. Her Ambassadors still compile what is being said at foreign courts about her palace coup, but she doesn't lose sleep every time Maria Theresa calls her a Tsar-slayer or some Parisian hack writer compares her to Messalina or Anna Livia. One letter to Voltaire, filled with compliments and accompanied with an imperial gift, does more to improve her reputation abroad than her Ambassadors' protests.

They say it is women who like to be flattered, but men are no different. Come up with the right compliment, and hearts will melt. Marvel at a great man's genius. His erudition, polish, wit. Ah, your understanding of history! Your judgment of character! How astonishing to read works that do honor to the human race and then see them so little put to practice.

Grigory Orlov calls Maria Theresa an old crow. "Is it true, Katinka, that she is spinning wool for her own death shroud?"

"Now we can get married, Katinka."

She is sitting behind her desk, Grigory Orlov leaning over her shoulder. His fingers move down her neck. His hot tongue caresses

157

the lobe of her ear.

Their son, little Alexei Grigoryevich, is growing fast. A healthy boy — she reads in weekly reports — sturdy and strong. As soon as he is ready to start his studies, she will bring him to the palace, hire the best of tutors.

This is not the first time Grigory Orlov has come to her study unannounced. Or sat himself on the small ottoman, flipping through her papers, restlessly rolling and unrolling maps. Or reminded her that a pike plies the waters to keep the carp awake. On Grigory's lips the old saying means that soldiers need wars to keep them lean and focused. A war is a chance to advance, to change one's fortune. If men are left to idleness, they start plotting.

He is only saying this because his Katinka is a woman. A woman needs help. Needs advice.

The Orlovs have made her; the Orlovs can bring her down. Panin, who still believes Paul Petrovich should have been declared Emperor and she his Regent, has warned: "Madame Orlov will never rule Russia." Nikita Ivanovich Panin is Paul's tutor and the possessor of a mind Catherine plans to use in the service of the Empire. His warning, therefore, counts.

The Orlovs may stride the corridors of the Winter Palace with pride, but to the old

158

nobles they are upstarts who have rubbed shoulders with merchants and soldiers. And who need to be sent back where they belong.

She catches Grigory's fingers.

"Not now," she murmurs softly. "I need to be alone."

He gives her a puzzled look, as if she asked him to go to the moon. Or bring her a unicorn's horn.

"I still have papers to read," Catherine says, pointing to the wooden box on the side table. She needs one million one hundred thousand rubles for her court expenses each year. Nine hundred thousand for her own household. The stables by themselves cost her one hundred thousand.

"Don't you have accountants?" Grigory Orlov rolls his eyes. "Don't you trust anyone?"

From Warsaw, Stanislav writes: *Let me be with you in any capacity you wish, only do not make me a king . . . One doesn't love like I love you more than once . . . What is left for me? Life without you is nothing but an empty shell . . .* Frederick has received an offer from the British he finds more advantageous for Prussia than an alliance with Russia. He writes: *If you want my support against the Turks, give me something of real value in return.* Land, he means. Fields. Towns. Rivers.

"Let me finish one more letter."

"No," Grigory insists. "You've worked

enough."

This is a trivial disagreement, but not a trivial moment. Grigory's voice bristles with a new, harsh note. Is someone telling him to assert himself? Stamp all flames when they are still flickering?

"Let me judge when I've had enough," she replies. There is still a chink in her words through which laughter can sneak in. They can still turn this exchange into a lovers' spat, that familiar, playful tussle of duty and desire.

"No, Katinka. I know what you need."

His lips are more insistent. His teeth nibble her skin. His hand dives inside her dress, pinches the nipple of her breast.

"Stop it," she says.

He doesn't stop. His hand is diving deeper.

"No!"

Her voice is sharp, but she is not yet angry. Merely warning him to ease off, turn a caress into a soothing kiss of regret she could savor long after he is gone.

But he is Grigory Orlov. Reckless. Bold. *Yield,* his hands urge her. *You won't regret it. You never have.*

Why not? a voice inside her tempts. *Don't you deserve a moment of pleasure? Don't you work hard enough?*

"Not now!"

Grigory grabs her by the hair, pulls her head back. The side table crashes to the floor;

the box overturns. The papers scatter like dry leaves.

The fate of her papers doesn't concern him. Nor her broken side table. If she waits any longer his arms will pin her down. The taut, strong arms of a man who can stop a panicked horse in its tracks.

She softens like a kitten. She purrs. "You win," she whispers into his ear.

He freezes. For a moment, all is still.

He still hesitates, but then his lips come closer to hers. "My Katinka," he murmurs, with such utter relief that her heart sinks.

His arms soften. His grasp weakens.

She tears away from him so swiftly that he has no time to catch her. She rushes to the door and opens it, to the terrified look of a Palace Guard. Only then she realizes how she must look to him. Disheveled hair, torn dress, bloodstains on her lips. One of her shoes is gone, and she is limping. There might be a bruise on her cheek, too, for the skin smarts and feels hot.

"Pick up the papers," she orders.

The guard is young, smooth with easy grace. He lowers his eyes as he gathers the scattered sheets and hands them to her. She doesn't want to imagine where his thoughts go. She points at the box, and he picks that up, too.

"Take the table away."

The guard lifts the broken table, and she

161

rings for her maid. She will need ice for her cheek. A new dress. A new pair of shoes.

"Good night, Count Orlov," she says, turning to Grigory, who is standing like a pillar of salt, struggling to understand what has just happened. "I'll see you tomorrow."

Whatever he thinks matters little. Far more important is what she, the Empress, now sees for the first time in her lover's eyes.

Fear, not anger.

Supplication, not pride.

■ ■ ■ ■

PART II
NOVEMBER 5, 1796

■ ■ ■ ■

9:30 A.M.

Her right arm is dangling, limp, as if it belonged to someone else. Pain shoots up inside her skull. Something is wrong.

Bezborodko, the best of her ministers, has warned her against French assassins sent to kill her. "They crossed the eastern border, Your Majesty. Two young men, posing as exiles deprived of their fortunes by the Revolution. They will take any chance — a ball, a masquerade, an audience granted out of compassion. One will have a dagger hidden up his sleeve. Another intends to fire a flint pistol."

She has laughed it all off. "If they were truly on their way, would we know all that?" she has asked. "Should we fear an assassin who doesn't know how to keep a secret?"

Has she been wrong?

The French are liars. They speak of liberty and brotherhood and then let the mob loose in the streets. Drag their king and queen to

165

the gallows, in the name of justice. Like this charlatan Cagliostro, they claim to be able to create gold from urine. They forget that a barrier of fear, once broken, cannot be easily put back in place. That a man left to his animal instinct will not trade or build, but hoard and pillage.

Not much makes her sweat with horror. The thought of the mob does. Men who stick blades of scythes upright, who turn trees into gallows, ropes into nooses. And their women, who — like the French *poissards* told Marie Antoinette — wish to gather her entrails into their aprons and carry her head stuck on a pole.

Homo homini lupus. A man is a wolf to man.

9:32 A.M.
Heel taps in the antechamber are sharp, nervous. Someone is circling the room outside. Every third click of the heel is louder than the others.

"What are you doing here?" Queenie snaps at someone somewhere outside the privy door. "Go, go!"

Why is Queenie shouting?

A dog's paws scratch the floor. A nose sniffs at the crack underneath the door. Impatient, whimpering uneasily. Pani? Smelling what a human nose cannot discern?

Her right hand moves only when she wills it to move. The shooting pain in her head has changed frequency. The jabs no longer follow one another closely. Her head feels fragile, porous.

Her left hand clasps the door handle. One more jerky awkward pull and she will lift herself from the commode. *As soon as the pain begins to fade,* she promises herself.

Ballet dancers, she recalls, glide across the stage even if it hurts.

Now, she thinks.

Up.

But the muscles and bones betray her. She slides to the floor, a marionette with cut strings. Like the ones Peter tinkered with until they walked with exaggerated swaggers. Or twitched their noses like rabbits. Or collapsed into a helpless pile of wooden limbs.

9:34 A.M.

I'm not dead, she thinks. *I've merely fallen.*

She repeats these words a few times silently, for each takes a long time to register.

I? Have? Merely? Fallen?

Her field of vision has narrowed to those few inches in front of her eyes. She sees the wooden boards of the commode, their intricate, wavy lines, the circles with flecks of lighter wood inside.

Incomprehensible but beautiful.

The veins in the marble tiles beckon. White, brown, gray, red, colors that seep in and out of tiny cracks. Then there is the skin on her hand, freckled and full of furrows and bulging veins. And the hem of her cuffs, the stitching so intricate that she cannot trace a single silver thread, for it melts into the oak leaves and acorns. If she lifts her head just a tiny bit, she can see the stream of light coming from the window. Tiny particles of dust dance in it, the ballet of joyful pirouettes and mad chases.

Outside, behind the swinging door, a man's voice asks, "Have you seen Her Majesty this morning?"

Her servants are looking for her. Vishka, who always knows everything, swears she has not seen her mistress leave.

"Look," Vishka insists, "the pelisse is still here. Her Majesty would not have gone outside in this cold without her fur."

It's a game of hide-and-seek, Catherine decides.

Merriment bubbles inside her, drawing her into an old memory of childhood pleasure. She is under a bed, holding her nose to stop herself from sneezing, for the maids do not dust under beds if they can get away with it. Someone walks into the room and she is sure it must be Babette in search of her, but her governess does not wear satin. And there is someone else, for she sees a pair of men's shoes with silver clasps.

From under the bed, Sophie — for this is

her name then — can see the hem of the rustling dress lift. A frilly petticoat drops to the floor, revealing white stockings tied with scarlet garters, satin shoes on tapered heels.

A man's hand runs up the woman's leg. "I've been waiting for so long," a voice mutters.

The woman giggles, pushes the hand away.

"Now," he pleads. "While they all think you are in the garden."

"Is that what they think?" the woman's whisper teases. Carefree, and yet familiar.

Mother?

Can it be you?

Amid hushed peals of laughter, the bed above begins to sag and shake. A vest lands on the floor, followed by breeches and a white corset.

Murmurs flow. Promises of love. Of longing.

When the moans of pleasure reach her, Sophie slides her hand underneath her own petticoat, into the spot between her legs. She holds it there. Presses tight. Tighter. Until she feels a tiny tremor. Sweet and sticky like honey.

"Her Majesty has not left her suite," Vishka insists, and now her voice is husky with worry. "I was here all the time. Adrian Moseyevich is my witness.

"Knock at the door again, Zakhar Ivano-

169

vich," Vishka urges. "Her Majesty doesn't hear so well anymore."

Zakhar Ivanovich obeys, and Catherine hears a distant knock on the study door and then her valet's voice, loud and clear: "Madame, may we come in, please?"

9:35 A.M.

Outside the privy, the banging does not stop. "Your Majesty," Catherine hears. The man's voice is scared. "Is Your Majesty there? Can any of us come in? Anna Stepanovna, perhaps?"

Anna Stepanovna? Queenie!

A dog barks. The bark turns to a whimper, filled with longing. *There have been so many dogs,* Catherine thinks. Bouncy, wheezing, wily, full of pranks. *Which one is this?*

The pain inside her head has split into myriad small pains, some mere pinpricks, some searing blows.

Something has happened to me, she thinks.

She manages to turn her head sideways. She is lying on the floor. But why? Has she fallen? When? And why can't she get up? Or speak?

Something bad has happened to her. Something she has not anticipated. Something she has overlooked.

Am I sick? Poisoned?

Fear quickens her thoughts. Once fear is let into the heart, it will grow. There is a way to stop it, though. Think of faces with sneers stamped on them. Rejoicing at the thought of her misfortune. The faces of gossipmongers, spreading their lies. Old or new, but always spiteful. How upon seeing her son for the first time she called him "a Kalmyk monkey" and refused to see or care for him. How she intoxicates herself every morning with champagne and Hungarian wine. How she takes on lovers and kills them when they no longer please her loins.

It always helps to remember the malice, the sniggers. Nothing builds defiance more. Charts the course of action.

I need help. Now. Fast.

Mercifully, her servants have stopped asking their useless questions. Now they are trying to open the door. She can feel it push against her body. Hard. It hurts when they do that, for the sharp edge of the door is digging into the sore skin of her bad leg. Blood must be seeping into her petticoats, staining the fabric.

I need my blood to stay in me, she tries to say, but her lips do not move. Neither does her leg, when she wishes to shift it out of harm's way.

"Call Doctor Rogerson right away," a man screams.

Zotov, his name is Zotov.

He is her valet. She knows him well.

Zotov is bending over her now. There is a mole under his eye. A bushy wisp of black hairs sticks out of his nostril. Catherine smells garlic on his breath, and yesterday's dinner. Cabbage, sour cream, pickles.

A mole on a left cheek is a token of an unhappy life, Queenie has said. Or did she say the right?

Someone pulls her arm now; someone else lifts her legs. She hears grunts of effort. She is heavy, like earth itself.

The servants have put a mattress on the floor for her, as if she were to give birth again, but this is not possible, is it? She has already had her children. How many did she have? Three. What happened to them? One died. Another, Grigory's son, she sent away, for he angered her with his recklessness.

There are people in the room. Many people tiptoeing around her, unsure what to do. Some she knows; others are familiar but their names elude her. Her two most trusted maids, Queenie and Vishka, bend over her, their faces crumpled with fear. Their lips move, but words come much, much later, distorted, as if shouted into a barrel. "Is Your Majesty in pain? Doctor Rogerson is on his way."

Catherine listens and considers the words she hears. The inside of her skull is like a seaside rock on which waves crash. Some waves bring pain; others merely muddle her

172

thoughts.

Doctor Rogerson, her court physician, has come from Scotland. He is a gloomy gambler who likes to tell her that Scots do not like one another much. His hair is reddish and thick, like that of a shorn sheep. His cheeks are pockmarked, and there are livid bags under his eyes.

What will he say?

A bad migraine?

Poison? Aqua Tofana, perhaps?

Puzzling as they are, these questions are not particularly troubling. Or pressing. For the wave of pain subsides and now she feels calm. Her eyes close, and for a long while she floats above the marshy fields where green frogs croak among the reeds.

They are called *lagushki,* she remembers.

9:38 A.M.

"No, Adrian Moseyevich," Vishka screams. "You shall not leave this room. Not even for a moment."

Gribovsky is my secretary. He is good. He can be trusted. Grisha chose him.

What is Vishka so afraid of?

Vishka speaks too fast for her to catch all the words. "Anna Stepanovna, please, tell the doctor Her Majesty has fainted . . . but nothing more."

173

Feet patter. A door opens and closes. Outside a dog is howling, though the sound is muffled.

The fear in Vishka's voice is spreading like a fog over a field. It hangs heavy in the room, obstructs vision. This fear feeds on her limp body. On her failure to make her lips move.

A spring may seem to have dried out, but move a few rocks, wipe off the sand, and it comes back.

"Remember, Sophie?. Remember our dreams?"

This is her lover's voice. It has a tingling to it, evoking long evenings by the fire after a sleigh ride. Laughter and merry abandon. Long talks of taming the future. "Destiny, divine plan, cosmic forces," Stanislav said. "Your own free will," she replied.

Or this is how she wishes to remember it.

Monplaisir, on the gulf, with waves crashing on the rocks. A stone terrace. A long, wet, warm kiss. Sorrowful dog's eyes of a man who has to go away. Not wishes to, Stanislav tells her, is forced to. For a reason still hidden to him. For a lesson both of them will have to uncover.

Happiness is possible, Sophie.

I'm not Sophie.

We had a child. A daughter. Her name was Anna.

Anna died. Mother died, too. And Father. Father, who has not been invited to my wedding.

I would believe that any other woman could have changed, but you?

I shall either rule or perish. This is what I've learned.

There is a spatter of whispers, all tense, all marked with concern. Vishka is not whispering. *Stop fidgeting,* she barks. Bring a bucket. Mop up the mess in the privy. Don't just stand there gaping, staring like a magpie at a piece of bone. Move.

Her words produce grunts. Moans. A whiff of vinegar. "Don't spill the salt, you clumsy fool!" Vishka seethes.

Nothing is right. Nothing is as it should be.

She is Empress.

All she needs is to raise her hand. Speak and order shall be restored.

Her lips move.

There is no sound.

For now.

I've fallen. I'm hurt. I need time. I need to rest. I need to think.

Some memories are stashed away, safe from prying hands. Like a pearl necklace in dire need of restringing. The servants shouldn't

175

touch it, for any careless handling could bring a disastrous spill, the jewels rolling on the floor, disappearing in the crevices and nooks.

In one of these memories, she touches a mossy wall. Her fingers stumble upon an opening, a crack between the cold, wet stones. She peers through it. Beyond it is a miracle of flowering trees, shrubs, rosebushes, and vines. A tangle of greens, an orgy of colors and scents.

Under her fingers, she feels the iron prong of a small gate, which squeaks when she opens it. In the garden, a swing catches her eye. It is still moving, as if someone has just jumped off it, but there is no one near.

She is wearing a court gown of pink satin; her hat is adorned with long white plumes. Plump and rosy, she is a goddess of dawn. She sits on the swing and begins to rock back and forth, leaning as she wings back, bending forward as she rushes forth.

It takes a while before the swing reaches the highest point, but when it does, the sensation is exhilarating. The air rushes by, caressing her cheeks, billowing her skirts, threatening to dislodge the hat from her head.

That is when she sees him — a man in the shadows, watching her. Hidden among the greenery, pretending to be invisible. Something about him mesmerizes her. His air of absolute stillness? His teasing promise of mystery?

Whatever it is, for his eyes Catherine lets her shoe slip off and fall to the ground. Her foot is high-arched and gracefully slim. Her skin is alabaster white.

Look, she urges him, teases with a smile. *I may be capricious. What I want today I may disdain tomorrow. Catch this moment, if you can. It may not come again.*

She can almost feel how his body twitches and shifts. The brown, wiry body of a horseman who can tame the wildest mounts.

He mutters something. His voice is faint at first, but then she can hear him as if he were whispering into her ear: *I will make you weep for nothing, make you shudder at shadows no one else will see.*

She knows this voice. He is Grigory Potemkin. Grisha.

Without him, nothing will ever be good enough.

In the heady hours of the coup, it is the stranger's quick eagerness that strikes her. Thousands of adoring eyes, thousands of hands raised in a blessing or a vow of allegiance, but only one man has understood her predicament.

The borrowed Preobrazhensky uniform fits her like a glove; a naked saber gleams in her hand. Horses neigh; spurs clink. The multitudes that have awaited her for hours shout their joy. Drunk on the loot from the taverns, crazy with hopes and ambitions let loose by the unyielding brightness of a white June night. Catherine is just about to mount her horse when she realizes her *dragonne,* her sword knot, is missing.

A guardsman gallops toward her, tears the *dragonne* off his own sword, and hands it to her with a graceful bow. She catches a glimpse of a long, sensitive face, a cleft chin, a thick mop of auburn hair. Behind her, Katya Dashkova's frightened voice urges her to make haste. Peter is still Tsar, if in name only. This is no time for hesitation.

But the Horse Guard who has handed her the sword knot refuses to leave her side. His horse is flanking hers, knee to knee. "Your Majesty must forgive my boldness," he murmurs. "I cannot control it."

A horse I can control, but not the boldness of my heart, his twinkling eyes tell her.

Sergeant-Major Grigory Potemkin, Catherine soon learns, is a nobody. One of many who agreed to follow the Orlovs. He has been well rewarded for his service. Promoted to Second Lieutenant, offered a gift of six hundred souls or eighteen thousand rubles, whichever he chooses.

They call him Grisha.

How old is he? she asks.

Twenty-three.

Grisha Potemkin, a petty noble. A provincial boy from Chizhova. Delivered from his mother's womb in a village *banya* while his father was drinking his inheritance away in the company of his serfs. Grisha Potemkin ran barefoot through the meadows with peasant boys. Roasted beets in the bonfire ashes, chewed on raw turnips, hulled seeds from sunflower heads. An altar boy with grandiose claims of greatness that — this is what he believes — awaits him as surely as spring comes after winter. Bright, yes, but like his stout papa, ruled by sloth and arrogance. His teachers despaired, forgave, and despaired again. In the end, Grisha Potemkin was expelled from school for laziness and nonattendance.

Where is Chizhova?

Somewhere on the western borderlands. Far away from Moscow, even farther from St. Petersburg. A needle in the haystack of her empire. If you blink as you pass by it, you will miss it.

For Grigory Orlov, Grisha Potemkin is a diversion.

"What a clown! He can make anyone laugh."

"How?"

"Imitations. He can mimic Panin, Shuvalov, *Das Fräulein.*"

"I want to see him do it!"

179

Summoned to amuse his Empress, Grisha Potemkin strolls into an inner room of the Winter Palace with a tight, mysterious smile. His hair is silky, auburn-brown, as beautiful as she has remembered. Beside her, Grigory Orlov rubs his hands, as if this Lieutenant of Horse Guards was his own invention.

"I cannot do it, Your Majesty," Grisha Potemkin protests. "I'm not able to do any mimicry at all. Please excuse me, madame, and forgive me for disappointing you and your illustrious court."

His voice has an unmistakable German accent. He holds his head high, as if he were standing at the top of a flight of marble stairs, looking down on them all. His gestures are slightly feminine.

Catherine is aware of murmurs churning around her, of Grigory Orlov's rumble of mocking laughter. She knows what her Favorite, Orlov, is thinking. A new Empress is not predictable. Not fully sure in her own skin. What will a monarch of but a few hours do to a man who dares to imitate her?

She laughs.

Her life has just been transformed in ways she cannot quite fathom. What she has desired so long is hers, miraculously, a gift and a burden. Laughter breaks her open, releases what has been pulling tight at her insides. Holding fear, darkness, and the raucous exhilaration of victory.

And he, Grisha Potemkin?

He thinks he has won already. That he has conquered her with this laughter. Disarmed her defenses, drawn her to him. Impatient, young, Grisha Potemkin believes in transformations. In moments that herald a change of fortune. Moments he intends to grab and squeeze out like a lemon.

This is why he will follow her in the months to come. Throw himself at her feet, not once, not twice, but dozens of times. In the corridors of the Winter Palace. In the garden of Tsarskoye Selo. At the Peterhof courtyard, his knees wobbly on cobblestones, eyes shining with eagerness, the reddish tint of his hair catching the sun's rays. He will flatter her, compliment her lavishly. He will kiss her hand. Profess his love. Rebuked, he will still appear at her card table, lean over her shoulder to look at her cards, ignoring Grigory Orlov's mounting rage.

She will laugh or smile or shake her head in disbelief, and walk away. His attentions please her, but she doesn't want him to know that. Why spoil a child? Why soil such an innocent pleasure? It's best to watch over him from afar. Send small advancements his way. Gentleman of the Bedchamber. Assistant to the Procurator of the Holy Synod. Army paymaster. Guardian of Exotic Peoples.

Her *cavalier servente* is too young, too rash,

too eager. He needs her guidance, her warnings.

Warnings he won't heed.

Brilliant Empress, gaze at visions,
And behold, a woman great:
In your thoughts and your decisions
As one soul we all partake.

Time is not to be wasted on idle amusements. Time belongs not to Catherine, but to the Empire.

There is so much to do.

Russia is growing in spurts and starts. A decision to support one faction brings on the wrath of others. No move is innocuous. All power is challenged.

The old game of dare? The testing of one's mettle? Calculations made on paper fade when confronted with daily transactions of flesh and blood. The weak will challenge the strong, even against all odds. In matters of states, predictions breed like mice.

When she demands greater religious freedoms for the Orthodox faithful, the Poles cry that Russia is meddling with its most sacred laws. Stanislav, now King of Poland, pleads for time, for reforms that would strengthen his government and his monarchy. While his subjects denounce him as a Russian footstool and take to arms. While Ukrainian Cossacks join the melee, seething with rage against their Polish lords and Jewish overseers. With the Cossacks, when rage erupts, the earth burns.

In all her palaces, Catherine keeps copies of her most cherished books. Montesquieu. Locke. Beccaria. They are the essence of Europe, and Russia must be a European country, not an ignorant Asian backwater where all manner of cruelty is condoned.

Every day she is writing her *nakaz*. This will be her legacy for Russia, the precious jewel of justice and order. Not laws themselves — these she will leave for her creation, the Legislative Commission. She will merely draft the basic principles for the new laws that would bind all her subjects:

It is better to prevent crimes than to punish.

Laws and the legal system should aim at reforming the criminal.

Words cannot be called criminal unless accompanied by deeds.

Censorship can be productive of nothing but ignorance.

Torture is a crime.

Every citizen wishes his country to be happy, glorious, and safe.

Laws should protect but not oppress.

A ruler rules alone, but is subjected to certain fundamental laws, defined by tradition, habits, and custom.

"What are you always scribbling, Katinka?" Grigory Orlov demands. They have settled into a truce of sorts, but all is not well between them. Their son, Alexei Grigoryevich, brought to the palace and given the best of tutors, is one source of aggravation. Torn books, ink carelessly spilled on old volumes. "A soldier's son," Grigory gloats, "refuses to be chained to a desk."

"Monsieur Pompadour," Grigory Orlov calls himself. His favorite end to all their squabbles is to stalk away with his jaw clenched.

Irritation can be ignored. Or reports she finds among her papers in the mornings. A tavern bill for smashed furniture, including a cuckoo clock from which a wooden cuckoo has been shot with a flint pistol. Another drunken night at the palace *banya*, followed by a carriage ride through the city in the company of a naked whore. Another pregnant chambermaid dispatched to the Orlovs' estate. An order for a wallpaper decorated with libertine pictures of an amorous couple in which "the woman bears clear resemblance to Her Imperial Majesty."

A woman with small smooth breasts, rounded buttocks, and black, disheveled hair. Chased, pinned to the floor, mounted.

"Your Majesty should mind," Panin nags. "It's not good to be too forgiving."

At least he is not saying "foolish."

184

■ ■ ■ ■

Russia needs uniform new laws that would unite the country. She has sketched the general principles, given them to her advisers, adjusted them by cutting down those that were contentious, watering down others. Now, she said to her delegates, analyze my general principles, adjust them to what is possible. Draft the new laws.

To serve on the Legislative Commission is an honor. A historic moment for Russia. The beginning of her true Enlightenment.

People give many reasons why the words on paper do not apply to them. Russia lies in the North. Peasants can be made free in warm countries, but here, in the cold of the northern clime, they have to be forced to work. The state cannot do it. Russia is too large. Nobles have to possess the means to rule their serfs. The way they have always had.

Chattel. Slaves who do not own their souls. You rule them by the knout, Catherine thinks, angrily. *By the rack, and by the gallows.*

They talk of God-given powers. Of preserving what has always been. Sheremetevs. Rumantsevs. Dashkovs. They don't point out that Catherine is not of their blood, but they imply it. The Germanic need for order and clarity is commendable, but how do you make the same garment fit twenty different

185

peoples with different customs and religious beliefs?

Provinces want more power? Local governments want more autonomy?

Politics is many games. Watch and learn is one of them. Stir the brew and observe what comes floating out with the scum.

All citizens free under the law?

If this is so, then merchants want to own serfs, and landowners object. Or landowners want to trade or start a manufactory, and merchants object. Old nobles wish to be spared the need to rub shoulders with newly minted nobility. Allowed to register their complaints, state peasants get mired in stories of felled fences or a neighbor's cow eating their hay or some greedy official extending his hand for bigger and bigger bribes.

And on top, throw in a layer of sloth and greed.

Catherine gave every delegate a bound copy of her *nakaz.* By now, so many have lost their copies that half of her commissions do not gather at all, waiting for it to be reprinted. She gave them medals to commemorate their committee participation; they sold the medals and got drunk. As if she paid them to prove that every good thought and idea can be turned into mockery.

Rumors run wild. Why does the Empress want to free the serfs? To undo the canvas of the fabric that has served us well?

To undermine Russia?

Is it foolishness or hubris? Or merely a woman's reasoning?

Serfs harbor sloth and darkness in their souls. Give them an inch and they will take a whole *verst* and want more. Unchain them and they'll slash your throat. Or spill your guts and trample them with their dirty feet.

So far, the only thing the delegates agree on is to offer her the title of Catherine the Great or All Wise Mother of the Fatherland. She says she has been Empress for five years only and hasn't earned the privilege to be called the Great. The gesture pleases her, though, for one reason. There are no more suggestions that she should be Regent for her son or give up the throne when Paul reaches majority.

At her Moscow residence things go no better. St. Petersburg servants roll their eyes at the Moscow ways. The palace steward has been left too long without supervision. A simple dinner is a battle of wills, a parade of substitutes, flattened cakes, meats suspiciously freely treated with grated nutmeg. Obstacles range from serious — one of the cooks was stabbed by a thief caught pilfering sugar — to ludicrous — a hedgehog was fished out from a jar of cream.

Without vodka, one cannot understand, she hears.

She opens the door of her study — much

heavier than the Winter Palace one — and summons the serving boy, whose only job as far as she can tell is to sit cross-legged outside her door.

To hold it so that it would not slam?

The boy looks scared. He casts his eyes about. His ears twitch, like a horse's.

"No, you have not displeased or disturbed me," she calms him. "But I would like to learn something about you."

The boy's hands tremble.

"What's your name? Where are you from? Where are your parents?"

His name is Taras. His mama he remembers well. She looked so beautiful in her coffin. Dressed in her best clothes, which she had prepared herself long before she died. Embroidered and ironed. Killed by the evil eye, the boy explains timidly. A neighbor coveted their brown laying hen. His papa died when he was too little to remember.

A Cossack raid, fire, pillage? Was he a victim or perpetrator? Violence in its many forms doesn't surprise Catherine. The world is a hostile place. Being vast and flat is not an advantage. Russia still remembers the raids of the Tartar hordes. Every seven years, the saying still goes, calves become milk cows, girls grow into maidens. Ripe for Turkish slave bazaars.

"Your mama," she asks. "Did you help her? Carry water for her? Bring her kindling?" She doesn't quite know what children of the poor do. In Zerbst, they took care of fowl. Swept the yard with willow brooms. Ran errands, minded the younger ones.

"I helped her cry." Taras no longer stammers or hesitates in his account of his family's misfortunes.

"Do you know what freedom means, Taras?" the Empress asks, but this is too abstract a question, and all she gets is an uneasy blink. She has a better idea. "Repeat after me: *I am free to . . .*"

"I'm-free-to, Your Majesty," the boy hastily repeats. He is oblivious to the irony of the words he has just said.

"No, no. I want you to finish this sentence," she explains. "By yourself."

Taras fidgets. There is a tear at the side of his shoe, flashing a patch of dirty skin. Do Cossacks not wear socks?

Asking the child to finish a sentence like that is not the right way, either. Too much like a confession of sins.

"What are you forbidden to do, Taras?" she asks, instead. This is easier.

"Leave my post, Your Majesty. Let go of the door before a lord or lady passes through. Spit on the floor. Curse." Judging by the easy flow of the boy's voice, the list promises to be endless, so she cuts it short.

She inquires instead about the customs of Taras's village. Witches who poison the wells,

189

devils reincarnated as black cats, curdling the milk in cows' udders, creating monsters in the mothers' wombs. Has he ever seen a monster? No. But he has heard of many that were born. A goat with two heads. A child of whom it was said that it was neither a boy nor a girl. Tsar's men came to take them away. No one has ever seen them again.

Has he ever heard of Peter the Great?

Yes. *Batushka.* Good to his people. Not the Antichrist as some old men call him.

Taras is not quite at ease, but clearly elated. Will he remember this conversation with fondness? Tell his children about it, if he has any? He is bright, in spite of his fearful glances. About fourteen? A bit older than Paul? But Taras's sense of time is fluid. He does not know the year of his birth.

"Go now," she says, searching for a gift she could give him. A few coins? A ring? It would only be stolen or coaxed away. So she takes a clean page and makes a drawing. An Empress with a big crown, seated. In front of her stands a skinny boy, holding a door. *For Taras, in memory of our conversation,* she writes underneath, and signs it *Ekaterina Imperatritsa. Moscow, August 1767.*

Taras takes the paper from her with such joy on his face that her heart lifts. She watches as he folds it gingerly and slips it into his breast pocket. She shall leave instructions with the Moscow steward that this boy be taught something useful. Something that will let him earn his keep. Advance him, too. Read and write. Accounts. Calculations and measurements, if he has any aptitude for them. A growing empire will always need surveyors.

The world is filled with what is forbidden. By the mother, the priest, the master or mistress. Elders and betters. The dead and the living. Do not kill, steal, lie. Unless in battle. Unless in war. Unless God or your monarch orders you.

How do you herd cats? Sail in a sieve?

If you are Empress, you try.

It is his absence she registers. His exuberant laughter. His theatrical gestures. The witticisms only Grisha Potemkin would dare to lay at her feet. Like when she asked him a question in French, and he replied in Russian, for "a subject should answer in a language in which he can best express his thoughts, and I've been studying Russian for more than twenty years."

His palace quarters have been emptied in haste, leaving dust dancing in the sunlight. An iron bed stripped of linen. A washstand with a porcelain basin wiped dry. Nothing on the floor but crumpled pages of unfinished love poems, a whalebone button, a few broken quills. If she didn't know her *cava-*

liere valante better, she would order a recount of her silver. Only thieves leave like that.

Grigory Orlov shrugs. There is no figuring out Potemkin. Like cats, Potemkin has his own, mysterious ways. Here today, gone tomorrow. Chased, perhaps? "By a woman bent on marriage vows?" he offers. "A bad debt?"

Her spies are more forthcoming. Grisha Potemkin has withdrawn from all earthly pursuits. He lives alone, just outside St. Petersburg. He sees no one, studies religious books, prays for hours, meditates. He has grown a long beard.

Why?

There has been an accident. He has lost his left eye. Now he thinks himself odious.

Rumors have it that the Orlovs had had enough of Potemkin's impertinence. That they lured him into a tavern for a game of billiards, beat him senseless. Shaved his hair. Plucked his eye out. Told him to stay away from her.

"Nonsense, Katinka." Grigory Orlov's nose wrinkles as if he smelled something rotting. There is no darkness in her Favorite's eyes. No layer of ice in his voice. "Life has been good to me. Why would I wish revenge? Don't I have you? The Cyclops, Katinka, is not that important."

The Cyclops? A one-eyed giant? Strong, stubborn, and abrupt of emotion. Forging thunderbolts for Zeus, arrows of moonlight for Artemis?

Apt, Catherine thinks.

Soon other rumors come flying. A whack of a tennis ball started an infection. It turned bad. A peasant quack was allowed to treat Grisha with his remedies. The eye isn't lost, merely blinded. Hiding in the folds of flesh.

She sends a messenger friend to his house with a basket of presents and a note: *It's a great pity that a person of such rare merits is lost from society, the Motherland, and those who value him and are sincerely well disposed to him.*

She knows Grisha Potemkin won't resist a well-staged return, a black patch over his bad eye, a look of suffering on his long face. Slowly he will fill up the emptiness of his absence. Still reckless, still impatient, still dissatisfied with what she has offered him.

Waiting for the wheel of fortune to turn, make the impossible possible.

For some time now, the Ottoman Sultan has looked north with fear. He has sought allies in Paris, in Vienna, in Berlin, trading promises for support. In the secret backrooms of Europe, maps are redrawn almost daily, at Russia's cost. Does Maria Theresa of Austria deserve access to the Black Sea? What might Prussian Frederick consider a worthy compensation for his change of heart?

In 1768, when Russian troops are still fighting the Polish rebels, the Ottoman Porte declares war on Russia.

At the War Council, even the Empress is only a woman. To be advised, persuaded, cajoled. Urged to listen to those who know their trade. Catherine can negotiate with Prussia and Austria, buy their support with treaties or concessions. They, her Generals, Field Marshals, even her Lieutenants and Privates, will ride into battlefields, taste gunpowder when they tear musket cartridges with their teeth, dip their sabers in blood. Freeze in the winter trenches or bake in the summer heat. Turn the Turkish fleet into a ball of fire, storm fortresses, claim whole regions of fertile land.

They will come back heroes.

There is new sprightliness to Grigory Orlov's steps, a new assurance to his voice. He wakes at dawn and rushes to the stables. His horse is harnessed, ready for the morning ride. In the antechambers, a small army of petitioners wait for his return. Young, bold men with dreams of conquest. Eager to try their luck.

Monsieur Pompadour in pink slippers? A mighty eagle locked in a golden cage? How Orlov laughs when Catherine reminds him how he used to berate himself. It's all so simple, after all. A soldier is not a courtier. A soldier needs the thrill of battle, the challenge of a fight.

He will be gone, Catherine thinks, and wonders why there is so little sadness in this thought. *A separation will do us both good.*

Grisha Potemkin, she notes, has also requested to be sent to the Turkish front. *The only way I can express my gratitude to Your Majesty is to shed my blood for your glory . . . I cannot live in idleness.*

"What I desire more than life itself I cannot have," her spies report Potemkin saying. "Men court death for lesser reasons."

The long half-dark of dawn, the hours raked by anguish are the worst.

She is a creature of habit and loyalty. Dissolution of love is a loss, and Catherine doesn't like to lose. She makes herself recall Grigory Orlov's dispatches from plague-ravaged Moscow, where fear turned men into beasts. His strategy was simple, his orders straightforward. Burn whole sections of filthy, rotting shacks to the ground. Fumigate houses with vinegar. Quarantine anyone wishing to leave the city for any reason. Prevent even the smallest gathering. *The rule of law,* he wrote. *Absolute obedience. For their own good.*

Wasn't she proud of him then?

Isn't she proud of him now, when he is at

the Danube, negotiating peace with the vanquished Turks?

"Unfaithful, crass," Panin counts off on his white, pudgy fingers. Grigory Orlov's faults have been multiple and recurrent. With Orlov, it's feast or famine, she hears. High stakes, quick temper or easy tears. "Surely, Your Majesty, there are limits to womanly endurance. Or, for that matter, gratitude." At court, her body's cravings are open secrets. Harbingers of seismic shifts. Her minister and right hand wishes his Empress to imagine the possibilities.

Lieutenant Potemkin is *not* one of them.

"Your Majesty has many more suitable admirers," Panin says, with the indulgent smile of one receiving too many confessions. "Alexander Vasilchikov is modest, has impeccable manners," Panin tempts. A respite, a reward in her busy life. Doesn't she deserve that?

Catherine is not a mere woman. She is Russia's Empress.

Lieutenant Potemkin is such a show-off. He relishes drama and grand gestures. He is greedy, insatiable. Plagued by moods that swing from ecstasy to despair.

She is tired of drama. She has an empire to run.

"Your Majesty deserves comfort and peace," Panin cajoles. "The excellent young man I have in mind . . ."

The excellent young man Panin has in mind has beautiful black eyes. Alexander Vasilchikov tells amusing stories of a tamed squirrel that used to come to his boyhood room and beg for nuts. Or an orphan fox pup that grew up in his father's kennels and learned to bark like dogs. Vasilchikov never frowns; his voice hides no thunder. His hands are warm and dry; his lips soft like silk. He receives her many gifts with a sweet smile of gratitude.

Surely this is all she needs. A respite for the lover's hour, caresses that fade away, leave her free for what is of true essence.

From the Danube, dispatches arrive daily. Grigory Orlov grows impatient with the negotiations. The Turks are haughty. They refuse to admit defeat. In the next note, another tone slithers like a serpent across the grass. *Just don't forget, Katinka, that Panin has never liked us Orlovs. That he has always thought himself a cut above us all, you included . . .*

Catherine reads these words twice, trying to pin down what irks her so much in them. That Grigory is constantly teaching her? Telling her what to think? Or that he is equaling the Orlovs and the Anhalt-Zerbsts? "He dares to presume" — her mother's vigilant voice echoes in her thoughts.

Who is this Vasilchikov they tell me about?

197

Grigory Orlov writes in his dispatches. *What kind of folly is Panin feeding you now? Damn the blasted Turks. I'm on my way.*

She crumples his letters and tosses them into the fireplace.

You were the first to tire of me, she writes back. *I wanted us to grow old together. It is you who have betrayed me, but when I turn away, you want me back. Am I your chattel? Your possession?*

Panin has been right all along. She has been too patient. Too forgiving and for far too long. She is Empress. Busy with matters of state. Her time, her well-being, is vital. For her subjects. For Russia's future. She needs to be soothed, not taught lessons. Loved, not lectured.

Summoned, Panin saunters into the room, barely able to hide his glee. His wig is perfumed with bergamot. There is a glint of gold in his mouth where a tooth has been strengthened with gold leaf. He, too, should be taught his place. Once and for all.

But she needs him now.

Grigory is on his way, and she, the Empress of Russia, is not going to demean herself by trying to reason with a raging bull.

"Advise me," she orders Panin.

Panin obliges after a respectful bow. He has thought out the details already. Count Orlov, who has conquered the Moscow plague, cannot dispute the wisdom of quarantine. There have been reports of bubonic plague in the south. Not too many, but enough to stop anyone coming from there for forty days.

Gatchina would do. It is a comfortable estate, easy to guard.

She scans Panin's face for the slightest hint of irony. Eunuch-like, she thinks him, swollen with what she would like to believe is indifference but must be pride. Guard Grigory Orlov?

But Panin's gray eyes are serious, his plans rational and precise.

Twenty, forty men, if needed. Muskets at the ready. Ears deaf to threats and pleas. Pockets immune to bribes. Her order is all Panin requires.

Yes.

Time is on her side. Time will calm Grigory Orlov.

For now she must do whatever it takes to avoid words hurled in haste and pain. Words both of them will later regret.

"Is everything good?" Vasilchikov, her timid lover, asks. In his eyes there is unease. How do you tell a man that his caresses are too soft, his kisses too shallow?

In the shimmering glow of the Tsarskoye Selo afternoon, everything irks her. The *banya* is too hot. The rooms too cold, in spite of a blazing fire. Time stalls, drags, only to rush forward with frightening abandon. Images stick to her like tar. That moment almost twelve years ago, when, on the heady day of the coup, a young Horse Guard rushed to her side to give her his sword knot. Weren't they already riding together, side by side, then?

She remembers the silky sheen of Grisha Potemkin's hair, the flashes of sauciness in his eyes. Gestures, fast and bold. Thoughts that make her nipples grow tender against her stays. *He intrigues me, but I'm not besotted.* The unattainable tempts him. Potemkin wants to conquer, and what he conquers he will despise. She has known such a man already. She doesn't wish such a man again.

The listless man who for the last few months has been allowed to enter her bedroom, who trails after her like a stray dog, repeats his question: "Is everything good? Am I pleasing you?"

These are not wise questions. They invite nothing but lies. They warn of weeping fits, sulky displays of distress. She feels a tug of guilt.

The Empress turns an hourglass upside down, watches the sand slide through the narrowing tunnel.

"You must excuse me now," she mutters. "I'm tired. I wish to be alone."

She throws herself into work.

One can be too successful, too bright, too visionary. In European games, power is thrown on the apothecary's scales. If they do not balance, trouble ensues. Russian victories have made the Prussians uneasy and the Austrians frantic. The coded dispatches sent from court to court demand curtailing Russian gluttony.

How much would she give up for not fueling Turkish wrath?

She is tempted to give up nothing. For months, she pores over maps, adds and subtracts the numbers. How much does a war cost? How much does it bring in return? These are not crass calculations. Prussia and Austria want chunks of Poland. *The Empress of Russia can help herself to her share, too. A lion's share,* Frederick of Prussia tempts. *Far greater than what we get.*

It's a hard bargain. Isn't Poland hers already? Isn't Stanislav doing what she instructs him to?

How much shall she pay for peace? She cannot wage two wars, can she?

Giving up chunks of Poland? Is it worth it? What if she stalls? Refuses?

The Empire is like an old quilt in need of constant tending. As new patches are added, old ones thin and tear.

In the Urals, a Yaik Cossack is gathering disgruntled mine workers and runaway serfs.

They have just attacked yet another estate. Robbed the cellars, stole the gold and silver and ran away. At the foundling hospitals, the mortality rate is 99 percent. Doctors give her long lectures on the balance of humors and declare the medical art helpless against the immoral habits of the poor. Paul, her son, has reached the age of majority and hints that Maria Theresa is teaching *her* son and heir how to rule.

The throne is a lonely place.

From Gatchina, Grigory Orlov is sending emissaries. Brothers, cousins, even his old servants, whose toothless mouths blend pleas and spit. Grigory wants to see her, his beloved *matushka,* the only joy of his life, one last time. Only one. How can she deny it to him after all that has joined them? How can she be so cruel?

In her inner rooms, the timid lover's voice quivers. Vasilchikov's body gives off a whiff of stale cheese. He hasn't seen her for three full days. She has not replied to his latest question. She walked away while he was still speaking.

The memory of his touch grows faint and fleeting. The lover's hour is for caresses not accusations.

My mistake, my fault, she thinks of him. *Made of desperation.*

Should she not have listened to Panin? Should she have sent for *him,* instead?

He, Potemkin, is at the Turkish front. There is nothing they say about him that she doesn't know already. Nature has made Grisha a Russian peasant, and he won't ever change. He fears bad omens. Trails after charlatans and tricksters. Chews on raw turnips. He's moody. Indolent. Slovenly. Vain.

So why does he make friends faster than kvass breeds flies?

Her desk is piled high. Letters, proposals, petitions, drafts of treaties she needs to analyze and amend. Reports on the dyeing of silk, the feasibility of building a china manufactory, summaries of books she has no time to read. Five secretaries work around the clock and yet the tidal wave of papers does not diminish. "Still think you are better than me, Catherine?" the late Empress's voice mocks. "That you can do it all alone?"

Lieutenant Potemkin appears at court unannounced. He throws himself at her feet, like the thespian he has always been. Her ladies-in-waiting scamper away, lean against the walls, blend into tapestries on which nymphs escape their pursuers, hunters aim arrows at giant stags.

A lean, pale face. A black patch over his left eye. *A Cyclops,* she recalls Grigory Orlov's old taunt. Blacksmiths, she has since learned, cover one eye to minimize the power of flying sparks to blind them.

The same cleft chin, full lips. No longer a boy but a man toughened by hardships. *Attacked and outnumbered by the enemy, he was the hero of the victory.*

Still in love with her after twelve long years. *You can see my zeal. You will never regret your choice. I am Your Imperial Majesty's subject and slave.*

Let it be, she thinks. *I won't fight it anymore.* In her mind, for some time now, she has been making amends to the timid lover. An estate, a generous pension, a few trinkets from her latest Parisian shipment. How long will it take to move Vasilchikov's things out? A day? Then another day for Grisha to move in. She already has her first gift to him: a promotion.

The simplicity of these arrangements tickles like an ostrich feather.

"Stand up, Lieutenant-General Potemkin," she orders. "Your Empress is extremely grateful for all you have done for Russia. You are very, very dear to her heart."

He rises with awkwardness, which amuses her greatly, and gives her a pained look. "Why is my Sovereign dismissing me?" he asks.

"Dismissing you?" Has she not just given him a sign? Could it be that she has not been clear enough? But deep inside her, she knows that he has read her thoughts and found them wanting.

His good eye doesn't let go of her.

He shakes his auburn hair. He abhors coyness. He doesn't care about promotions, but now that his Empress has just given him one, he is going back to the south to earn the honor. He thanks God Almighty that the peace treaty with the Ottoman Porte has not yet been signed. That there are still skirmishes on the border.

Her shoe grinds against the carpet. There will be a hole there, afterward, matching the size of her heel.

Grisha Potemkin does not flinch against her anger. His last words to her before he leaves are: "Step on me, obliterate me, or take note of my love."

You won't think of him, Catherine orders herself. *It is that simple.*

Not easy, perhaps, but it can be done. There is her son's wedding to plan and arrange. Guests to receive. To dazzle with how much she has achieved already.

If this is not enough of a distraction, in the Urals, the Yaik Cossack declares himself Peter III. "With the help of a faithful servant I've escaped my wife's murderous hands," he announces, clearly with someone's expert help. "I've come back to free my people from this sinful German usurper. I've come to put my son on the throne that is rightfully his."

The Cossack's name is Emelyan Pugachev. Pugachev doesn't resemble Peter. He is short, fat, and illiterate. He speaks only Russian. But those who wish to believe can accept even wilder tales. The mob the traitor commands is no longer robbing wine cellars and stealing silverware. Pugachev's trail is that of slashed throats and spilled guts. It is moving east.

She knows them well. False Tsars. Usurpers commanding hordes of peasants. Filthy, bloodthirsty men who listen to their loins and their insatiable greed. Who want to bathe in blood and semen. Who sire nothing but terror and death.

How little it takes. Call yourself Peter. Or Elizabeth's daughter. Convince a few fools and a few cutthroats first. Promise them rewards beyond their earthly ambitions. Make them think all is possible. Boundaries will fall. Barriers will be dismantled. Justice will shine on the smallest of them all.

Command through hope and fear. Coax and threaten. Offer dreams that dazzle with easy possibilities. Watch the human wave gather more riffraff, feed on disappointments, thwarted ambitions.

Give what's not yours.

Grow deadlier with each promise.

Lieutenant-General Potemkin is back in St. Petersburg, but he doesn't appear at court.

Why?

If Her Imperial Highness wishes to know,

her faithful subject slave has to oblige. Potemkin has removed himself from court because he is in despair. The one he loves with all his soul doesn't return his passion. Only in a monk's cell, where he can contemplate eternity, can he find consolation. He will pray for his beloved every minute of his life.

He is back, she thinks.

He is back, she repeats to the mirrors that reflect her face, suddenly too round, too manly. The gold-framed mirrors nestled between giant windows or fluted columns. In front of which she stops to adjust pearls in her hair or the fichu around her neck.

On even the busiest of days, flashes of him take her by surprise. The muscular arm of an ancient hero might catch her eye on one of the new paintings that have arrived from Paris. Or someone might mention Lieutenant-General Potemkin's bravery at the front. The taking of Bucharest.

From the Nevsky monastery, messages come every day. His unfortunate and violent passion has reduced his soul to despair. This is why he had to flee the object of his torment. Even the most fleeting glimpse of his Empress aggravates his suffering, which is already intolerable. He has put all his feelings into a song:

207

As soon as I beheld thee, I thought of thee
    alone
But oh Heavens, what torment to love one
    to whom I dare not declare it!
One who can never be mine! Cruel gods!
Why have you given her such charms?
    And why did you exalt her so high?

Lieutenant-General Potemkin looks so gaunt, the messenger friend tells her, taller somehow, and yet diminished. He has grown a long beard, which he won't even trim. He lies prostrated in his cell for hours. Drinks nothing but well water. Eats nothing but coarse black bread and raw turnips.

Hasn't he done this once before?

"The man is declaring his love *and* telling me he doesn't dare to do it?" Catherine asks, laughing. "Both at the same time?"

"True love makes no sense, Your Majesty. True love is madness."

"Are these Lieutenant-General Potemkin's words?"

"Yes, but I'm not supposed to admit it."

"What are you supposed to say, then?" she teases.

Lieutenant-General Potemkin has visions. In one, he walks through the steppe and picks up words. The words are like dewdrops, clinging to the blades of tall grass. He shakes them into a golden chalice and then, when he is too tired to take another step, he drinks them.

"These are *her* words," he says.

"The words of my beloved.

"They restore my strength so that I can walk again."

Time can be portioned, cordoned off. That much for the affairs of state. That much for the affairs of the heart. The line can be drawn in between. If it is not enough, she will dig a trench. Flood it, if necessary.

My wasted years, Lieutenant-General Potemkin writes in the latest note the messenger friend delivers from the monastery. *Foolish with earthly hope, with dreams of impossible happiness clouding the visions of eternal love, the source of all feelings. Why would I wish to return to such anguish?*

She picks a new sheet of thick, ivory paper.

Because your Empress needs you, she writes. *Isn't that enough?*

The messenger friend comes back from the monastery and reports: "There is no reply, Your Majesty."

That night she walks, candle in hand. The corridors of the Winter Palace are wide and long. The floors are made of many kinds of wood arranged into squares. Sometimes the squares are adorned with petals or stars. Her heels make a staccato sound. She is wearing red stockings, embroidered with black tulips. She has let her hair loose.

New paintings have already been hung on the palace walls. Each a trophy. She stops by the *scènes galantes:* A stolen kiss. A capricious woman scorning her turbaned lover. The legacy of French or English generations now adorns the walls of a Russian palace.

I made you look east, she reminds those who call her insatiable. *Hungry Russia cannot be ignored. Russia must be fed.*

But there is a chink in these thoughts. Through it Catherine sees a dusty monastery cell with its hard, narrow bed and creaky floorboards, the flickering lamp under the Icon of Saint Grigory, who believed that a limited human mind cannot comprehend the unlimited God. *This is my whole life now,* one of Potemkin's notes ended. *The only happiness allowed to me, since what I desire can never be.*

From outside the palace windows come the steady steps of the night watchman, echoed by the warning barks of the dogs.

Grisha?

Her feet are sore from walking. One of the red stockings is torn at the toe. In the long corridors she discovers all manner of surprises. A servant snoring on a windowsill. Another one curled in a corner like a dog, mumbling. She leans over him, then hastily withdraws, for he reeks of vodka and vomit. On the ground floor, right beside the palace kitchen, an old toothless woman is looking for something. She bends and picks up an invisible speck, a piece of black thread, it turns out, for she is willing to show her treasures: a toothpick, a flake of sawdust, a broken ebony button. "Things disappear," she whispers in warning. "They are all thieves here."

Back in the Imperial Bedroom, Catherine tousles the bed to make it look like she has slept in it, although she knows that the maids will not be fooled.

Grisha, Grishenka, Grishenok. She catches herself mouthing his name, thankful that Russian allows for so many transformations: every one a sweet promise of tenderness.

A quill is in her hands; the amber lid of her crystal inkwell snaps open.

Come to me, she writes. *Please.*

"Place it in his own hands only," she orders the messenger friend, fighting an urge to kiss the seal, the wax still warm from candle flame. "Don't trust it to anyone else."

"Yes or no," they ask her.
  "About what?"
  "On the subject of love."
  "I can't lie."
  "Yes or no?"
  "Yes."

My darling soul. My heart. Batenka. Grisha. Gri-

211

shenka. Grishenok. Giaour. Moscovite. Golden pheasant. Tonton. Twin soul. Little parrot.

My beloved husband.

His bare feet step softly on the green carpet that covers the spiral staircase leading up to her bedroom. There is a pink bandanna 'round his head. He is chewing on a raw turnip and he is laughing. There is mischief and joy in Grisha's laughter. He tells her some delicious gossip, something funny and intriguing and utterly outrageous. At Prince Yusupov's party, naked serf girls stood on pedestals like statues, holding trays with grapes, while the guests walked by, tasting the sweet offerings.

"Imagine this, Katinka," Grisha says and laughs.

"You are such a Cossack at heart." She laughs back at him. "Look at your bare feet. A Prince with calluses."

"Am I?" he asks, and his good eye flashes her a sly glance. A Cyclops biting his nails to the quick. If there are no more nails left to bite, he will chew on a quill, a comb, her jewels. She has seen him crush a pearl in his mouth.

He cannot be tamed. She knew it even then, when he first lay with her in the palace *banya,* her eyes taking in the glitter of gold and silver, the sheen of precious stones.

There he was pouring wine into crystal goblets, peeling peaches, feeding her with his

212

fingers, sweet juice dripping down her chin. She was forty-five, ten years older than he. Her three children had stretched her skin and her insides. But when he pulled her toward him onto the leather bench, it felt wrong to have anything separate their bodies. Hooks, ruffles, buttons, cloth.

It's all here, with her, the memory of this evening. His face full of wonder, his belly trembling under her fingers. The soft velvet satin of his skin. His hand traveling down her naked back. His lips grazing her skin. A tangle of arms and legs. The thrumming of desire. The sensation of hearing him with her bones.

The sweet murmurings of love: *beloved, most desired, mine. For what I feel for you, no words have yet been found. The alphabet is short and the letters few. Could I love anyone after you?*

There was no timidity in him when he gave her pleasure. No shyness when he took pleasure for himself. And when she was still nestling in his arms, her lover, her Cossack, her wolf clapped his hands and a Gypsy band began playing right outside the *banya*'s door.

How bad it is to love so extraordinarily! It is an illness, you know.

Grisha has refused to take the rooms vacated

by the timid lover, so she has given him an apartment directly below hers, linked by a private staircase.

He comes up when it suits him. He may choose to be witty and ebullient, or silent and morose. He may lie at her feet and call her his goddess or walk into the room without even acknowledging her presence.

Or point at the map of divided Poland and ask: "Why did you agree to give up so much?"

"I had no choice."

"You don't know that."

"What would you've done?"

"Wait. Call Prussia's bluff. It would've worked."

"Perhaps."

"It would."

He doesn't mince words. Catherine has let herself be bullied. She gave up too much. A fox will come back to the chicken coop. Feathers will fly. "I'd have made a great King of Poland," Grisha says, and on his lips this is neither a boast nor a joke.

His mind is never still. The plans it churns glitter. He could rule Poland or take her army south and smash what's left of the Ottoman Empire. He draws new maps for her, each bolder than the last.

"I want you here, with me," she protests. "We've wasted enough time."

"Not because of me," he says. "Admit that, at least."

"Not because of you, Grishenka."

When he is not spinning his visions for Russia, he wants to know everything about her. Old lovers and dreams, abandoned plans and festering regrets.

He is jealous of every man she has ever let into her bed. He wants to eradicate their traces, erase their memory.

He wants to be her hero, her king, her admiral, her lover. He torments her with his questions until she finds herself writing sincere confessions:

Serge Saltykov: dire necessity
. . . the present Polish King . . . loving and loved . . . but a three-year absence . . .
Prince Grigory Grigoryevich Orlov . . . would have remained for life had he himself not grown bored . . .
. . . that, out of desperation, forced me to make some sort of choice, one which grieved me then and still does more than I can say . . .
. . . then came a certain knight . . .

His lovemaking is stormy, moody. He may devote himself solely to her pleasure. Play her like a harp, bring forth a cascade of shivers. Or he may push her head down, bury her face in his loins. Make her earn her turn.

When he draws away, she grips him and pulls him tighter. As if, without him, some calamity would surely strike.

Runaway serfs and other rabble who have gathered around Pugachev are drunk on victories. The ragtag army sweeps on, pillaging, raping, burning. They've seized scythes, sickles, hammers, pickaxes for weapons. Men, women, children have been skinned alive, hung upside down, their feet and heads cut off. Towns have fallen to peasant rage.

The messengers bob and cringe when they repeat Pugachev's drivel: Catherine stole the throne of Good Father Peter III because he wished to free the serfs and *she* didn't.

Pinpricks of ingratitude?

Stings! Lashes!

Pugachev is a shrewd foe. His promises — fattened on vodka and greed — are as vast as the Russian steppes: freedom from all masters, riches without end. What fodder for weak minds!

As long as she is fighting the Ottoman Porte she doesn't have enough troops to send against him. But once she signs a peace treaty with the Turks, vodka-crazed rebels are no match for the Imperial Army.

A few days later, Pugachev is on the run.

After Pugachev's final defeat, the Imperial Commission delivers elaborate reports. The Empress's questions have been straightforward. Was anyone behind the traitor? A foreign power? The Ottoman Porte? France? Poland?

The traitor falls on his knees, acknowledges he is an impostor, begs for mercy for his sins. No evidence points to foreign instigations. The rebellion is Russian, bred in the bones of disgruntled serfs. The nobles nod knowingly. Serfs obey nothing but the knout. We told Your Majesty so, didn't we?

Such are her thoughts when she reads the Commission's reports. Arranged in folders, the way she requested. Interrogation reports of the perpetrators, testimonials from victims, descriptions of damage to towns her troops have liberated from the rebels.

A folded piece of paper is attached to one of the reports. Catherine unfolds it to a flash of recognition. It is a drawing of an Empress talking to a boy-child. Signed with her own hand. *Ekaterina Imperatritsa.*

"How did this get there?" she demands, her mind scurrying back to the Moscow day when a Cossack boy told her of helping his mama cry.

The drawing was found hidden on the mutilated body of a young man. A promising Kazan clerk, particularly good at numbers. Betrothed to a local girl, a merchant's daughter. Before he was murdered, he was made to watch his fiancée being raped by Pugachev's henchmen. His tongue was cut off so that he could not curse them.

217

She tells it all to Grisha, sobbing in his arms. He rushed up from his rooms as soon as he heard her scream. He knows when she hurts beyond endurance.

She thrusts the drawing into his hand. The Empress seated on the throne extending her hand to touch a skinny boy with a serious face.

"It was hidden," she weeps, "in the lining of his clothes. His most cherished possession. That piece of paper killed him. It's so hard sometimes . . . to foresee . . . to know . . ."

Grisha's hand smooths her hair. He doesn't interrupt. When her voice falters, he bends his head closer.

This is what she tells him:

It hurts when an act of kindness kills the innocent. It is agony when the forces of darkness extinguish hope. When a mob brings out the worst in the human soul.

We are tiny boats of reason floating in the sea of ignorance.

Grishenka understands her with every fiber of his body. "I won't leave until you smile," he promises.

"When I grow up, Maman, I'll make Darya the Queen of Poland! Varvara Nikolayevna told me an emperor can do anything he wishes to."

Paul's voice. Paul, who clings to the memory of a servant long gone. Paul, whom she, his mother, still believes repairable. With a soft cushion of fat around his waist. With a face free from sullen indifference. His flesh seems to slide from his cheekbones, making his eyes bigger and more liquid. Paul, who applies himself so diligently to his swimming practice. Draws the plants he has gathered during the walks with his tutor. Writes compositions in short sentences, but not quite deprived of charm: *Russian court is magnificent and polite. The Empire is greater than all the balance of Europe. Peter the Great was tall and well made.*

But then, on another day, Paul is lying on the floor, his body thrashing. His two playmates are holding him down; one is straddling him, his hands extended, gripping her son's throat.

"What are you fools doing?" she screams, rushing toward them.

In an instant, the boy lets go of Paul's neck. Her son, freed, is coughing, gagging. Saliva is dripping down his chin. "We are acting, Maman," he mutters. There are bruises on his throat where the page's fingers have dug into it. "It's our play."

"What kind of vile play?"

Paul falls silent and lowers his eyes. "It is just a play."

"What about?"

"I don't know yet. We've been trying out a scene."

"Who were you?" she asks.

"A Tsar."

"What did he try to do?" She points at the boy crouching under the table. "Murder you?"

"Yes."

"Why?"

"To punish me."

"For what?"

In response, Paul mumbles something about assassins lurking everywhere. About sin that flows like the raised waters of the Neva.

"Paul, who is teaching you this nonsense?"

When he draws away from her, she sees the large dark spot on his breeches where he had soiled himself. She rings for the maids. "The Crown Prince is not well," she says. "Put him to bed at once."

Neither boy can explain anything. Their fathers will of course promise to get the truth out of them, but in the end will come up with little more than contrition and letters of apology.

The pages are more forthcoming. Threatened with instant dismissal, they confess that His Highness wished to be strangled. "Not to the end," they say. "Just a little bit." At first the Grand Duke wanted his friends to use a string he had cut off a curtain. But then he decided to be strangled with bare hands. The boys didn't want to do it, so he made them draw lots. Prince Kuriakin drew the strangler's lot and had to smear his hands with soot. So that the Grand Duke would see the imprint of his fingers on his throat.

Why?

The pages swear they do not know. Further interrogation produces a curious admission that, after the pretended strangulation, Paul was to lie motionless and his two friends were to cover his head with a large piece of parchment. He has prepared it himself. It is stored in the heavy oak coffer by the window. It has something written on it, but the pages have not been allowed to see it.

The coffer is locked. There is no key.

She considers sending a footman for a crowbar, but then she decides that her son is not that clever. He would hide the key in some obvious place. She scans the room quickly, dismissing places where the maids would have found it.

Her eyes fall on the giant Chinese vase that stands on a marble column.

She slides her hand inside. Rummages through some sawdust, and there it is, the key to her son's secret.

The coffer, opened, reveals a few surprises. A box with model soldiers. A curling iron. A polished musket bullet. A leather sash with brass buttons, all polished to a shine.

The parchment lies at the bottom of the coffer, wrapped in a layer of black silk cloth. It is barely large enough to cover Paul's face. The inscription on it is beautifully calligraphed.

It says: *Prince of light and reason.*

Court gossips recall the jesters of old. Anna Leopoldovna's saucy dwarf, who called her mistress vile names and clucked like a hen. Or rode into the dining room on the back of a squealing pig. Or sniffed the courtiers and cried out the names of their sins: sloth, vanity, greed.

Lust, bold like a court jester, winks at Catherine from among the papers. Makes her hurry through the sparkling palace corridors. Her servants look away. They know when not to see or hear when the Empress rushes down the green carpeted stairs. She is a woman who cannot wait for the night.

The gilded doors open with a tiny squeak, revealing the wide bed with silk sheets, strewn with cushions. Some of them she has embroidered herself. With rich, bold patterns. A dragonfly with transparent wings. A parrot with a long tail of red and yellow feathers. When hands are busy, the mind focuses best on what is most important: This is when petitions are assessed, ukases locked into words, ideas born and rehearsed, chosen or discarded.

Not a flicker of time wasted. Sweet or useful, each moment. Everything else has to go.

The sun may be up, but Grisha is still
asleep on the bed, dark shadow on his cheeks,
his hands sprawled, claiming space around
him. There is no stopping him, she hears. A
racehorse chafing at the bit. Cocky, proud.
As he should be. Even if he still needs to
learn the tricks of the court: Hide what you
really desire, calculate the odds, foresee your
opponent's moves well in advance.

Asleep, he grinds his teeth and turns on his
side. Outside, in the palace yard, servants are
sweeping the debris from this morning's
storm. Broken twigs, torn leaves, clumps of
straw.

She smiles as she warms her hands over the
fire. Loosens her skirt, petticoats; sheds her
court clothes like a snake sheds an old skin.

Grishenka mutters something in his sleep,
still unaware of her presence, her warm
fingers sliding down his belly, feeling him stir.

His good eye twitches, opens. His hands
grip hers.

"Who are you?" he murmurs. "What do you
want?"

She laughs in response, with pure joy.
Throws herself into his arms, slides her bare
legs down his body, feeling the shape of his
muscles, the sprinkling of coarse hair. Takes
him and is taken, melting with love.

223

Afterward, she doesn't leave his bed. Sometimes these quiet moments are even sweeter than lust. She rests her head on his chest, listens to the pounding of his heart. He is her comfort and her refuge. With him, she can forget the onerous business that awaits her the moment she steps out of his room padded with velvet and plush.

Wait. Squirrel the longing away. Hide your joy and your pain. Love, too, needs its secrets to survive.

One night she wakes up and finds his place beside her empty. The clock shudders and strikes two. In the garden, outside, an animal shrieks like a baby in fright. Groggy from sleep, still dizzy with memories of their lovemaking, she rises from her warm bed and goes in search of him. In her flimsy dressing gown, with bare legs.

"Master is not back yet, Your Majesty," his valet tells her, so Catherine sits in the library outside Potemkin's room, waiting. Shivering from cold. Three o'clock strikes, then four. The valet comes back, smiling in a silent apology for his master, yet unwilling to divulge another man's secret. She refuses an offer of hot coffee. Or his master's pelisse. Like a silly child, she wants to be sick, to pun-

224

ish Grishenka with worry.

Voices approach, laughter. The voices dissipate.

It is not him.

Is he hurt? Wounded in some brawl? Robbed in the back alley? Stabbed with a dagger, bleeding to death? Or has he found another, someone more pliant? Younger? Was his love an act?

Her thoughts are a river of absurdities. One more proof of his supreme power over her.

At half past four, stiff from sitting, aching from jealousy and longing, she rises and walks back to her empty bed. She cannot sleep. He might come by at any time. "I didn't know, Katinka, that you were up, worrying yourself into silliness," he will surely say. "If I had, I would've hurried back."

At six o'clock, the maid comes to help her dress. Told to be quiet, the girl strains her ears: "There is no one there, Your Majesty," she says.

It is past ten when Grisha lumbers in. His hair is a mass of tousled curls. The patch on his eye is smeared with something white. Chalk? Face powder?

"Have you slept well, Katinka?" he asks, as if they were in the midst of the most ordinary conversation.

She shakes her head. She is choking, on the edge of tears.

"Didn't sleep a wink, either," he says, as if there were no difference between their nights. On him, she can smell snuff, vodka, and the sweaty, musky scent of exertion.

"Where were you?" she manages to ask. Her voice sounds raw, erupting with jealousy she's furious to hear.

He frowns. "Just a night with my comrades," he says, yawning and stretching his arms, one by one. "Boring," he adds.

"I'm not interrogating you, Grishenka." Her voice is no longer able to hide the stain of tears. Somewhere behind them, doors sigh, feet patter. In the yard, a horse neighs with impatience.

He is watching her. Silent. How can anyone look at anyone's face so long, so intently?

"You are the Empress," he reminds her. "You can do what you want. Interrogate me. Torture me. Throw me into a dungeon."

This may be construed as surrender, only it isn't.

Quietly, on cat's paws, Potemkin walks toward the window, yanks the velvet curtains open. A clasp gives way, a fixture breaks from the wall. A fine shower of powdered plaster sprinkles his thick auburn hair. For a moment it looks like he might shake it off like a wet dog. But he merely licks his index finger, swipes it over the plaster dust, and puts it in his mouth.

She stares at him until he leaves, and then

she bursts into sobs.

I cannot live like this.

In the morning, Catherine locks the door to her study. The guard is ordered to admit no one.

At her desk, she arranges the papers according to importance, picks up the sharpened quill. Love can be locked away, compressed like powder in a barrel.

She can hear Potemkin's voice arguing with the guard. There is a thump, a clink of metal. The handle on her door rattles.

Flimsy, she thinks. *It'll break. Like a Turkish fortress.*

She braces herself for attack or surrender, accusations or confessions.

The door cracks open, but to her surprise he walks in slowly.

There is a droop to his bad eye; the eyelid never quite closes. She stifles the desire to lick the spot where the eyelashes sprout. A whack of a tennis ball, a poke of a billiard cue — she recalls the wild stories of his explanations for the injury. Like so many others, he doesn't like to confess the source of his wounds. "This?" Alexei Orlov had asked with mock exasperation, his fingers touching the scar across his cheek as if he has just discovered it. No one likes to be reminded of a fight lost.

"How can we stop hurting each other?"

227

Grisha asks her.

He repeats this question during the lover's hour, entangled in the sheets, his naked foot ripping the fabric. His nightshirt is pulled up, revealing the pelt of curly fleece.

Only this time, he has the answer. It is hidden in a drawing he has brought with him. "What have I done with it?" he asks, groping beside the bed, his hand fishing blindly, pushing her jeweled shoes aside. "I must've put it somewhere," he says, and leans out of the mattress, bending forward until his head is almost touching the floor. When he returns, there is a rolled parchment in his hands.

The drawing is beautiful. Leaves, roots, and a white cluster of flowers. "Did you make this?" she asks, but he shakes his head, pointing at the leaves crowned with spiked lobes. Some are opened like a flower with a red center. "Tempting if you are a fly," Grisha points out. Some are closed on an earwig, so only the insect's curled tail is visible. Others on a mosquito.

"An insect-eating plant," Grisha explains. The trapping mechanism does not shut when a dead leaf or a blade of grass falls into it. Only a living prey will trigger it. If an insect is small, it can escape through meshwork, for it would be too much effort to digest it. If the prey is big and strong and struggles, the trap will tighten faster.

She frowns.

Is this botany's answer? That she cannot free herself from his traps? That with each movement, she becomes more entangled?

Or has she trapped him? What will he accuse her of now? A look she gave or did not give? The days at court are filled with traps. She, whose gestures bestow power, cannot move without hurting someone's feelings.

She is aware of his head touching hers as they examine the drawing in silence, pretty enough to be framed and placed somewhere where she could see it. Not too often, but often enough to consider the matter of traps and empty threats.

"Don't think of traps, Katinka." Grishenka's voice breaks into her thoughts. It still astonishes her, how he answers the questions she hasn't yet asked.

The plant, he tells her, is interesting not because of its ingenuity but because it bespeaks profound transformation from one mode of existence to another. This plant is on the verge of breaking through to the animal level.

She, too, can read his thoughts. If a plant can become an animal, lovers can separate and yet stay closer together. United in ways others can never fathom.

"A hybrid on the verge of spiritual advance," Grishenka tells her. "Our teacher."

The vision that he spreads before her is of

two giants, walking hand in hand. Towering above the crowds. Free with their desires. Indulgent of their weaknesses. Proud of their strengths. The court will watch them with rapt attention, but they will be like two conspirators, laughing at the bewilderment they cause.

"Spoilt children of Providence, Katinka. We'll want something to happen? All we'll have to do is desire it."

His mind is busy, bubbling with plans. His good eye probes the defeated Ottoman Porte like a butcher taxes the flesh on a fat hog.

The Black Sea is never frozen; its ports need not shut down for the winter. The south is warm and fertile. Where wild hordes of horses and Tartar brigands roam, he sees future towns, hamlets, gardens. He wants to build the longest barge, invite more foreigners to settle the empty lands. Bring the greatest happiness to the greatest numbers.

There is no stopping us, Katinka.

We have the strength. The wisdom. The courage.

This is the Russian century.

Russia can never be shoved aside. By anyone.

This is what we bestow on those who come after us.

We give them strength.

We give them dreams.

Only then can we die in peace.

Potemkin's voice is bright with exultation. It rises and falls like a priestly chant. His eye flames with the visions he delights in.

Believe me, Katinka. I've seen the future.

They'll bless us.

We have won already.

She, too, feels victory in her bones, though her confidence does not come clad in mystic visions. It is born out of careful calculations of gains and losses. Of strong nerves and a steady hand.

Usurpers can be lured into complacency and vanquished. An enemy can be outwaited and outfoxed.

A grandson, fresh and unspoiled like a swath of a new fabric, can replace an imperfect son.

"We *are* the children of Providence," Potemkin declares every time he arrives from the south with stories of blossoming orchards, rivers teeming with fish. Abundance is reflected in new deeds, land charts, statutes. Drawings of new towns, columns of numbers.

Russia is getting richer. A lot may yet have to be done, but a lot has been done already. Where only fear once ruled, order has prevailed. Where poverty and superstition paralyzed the will, the light of reason shines on new schools, houses, hospitals.

Fat, thriving, flourishing, robust are the adjectives she uses: for fields, herds of cattle, immigrants from Bavaria, Baden, Hesse, and the Rhineland she has invited to Russia to settle.

Solid. New. Statues, pavilions, bridges, apartments, palaces, gardens.

Swarm is a noun she likes to roll with her tongue, the orgy of abundance.

Augment is a favorite verb.

On the grand scale, when all accounts are added up, losses subtracted, her ledgers are a thing to behold.

Potemkin comes and goes. His visits are a disruption, welcome and yet exasperating. He claims time and space. In her study and in her boudoir. Sometimes they make love — more a gesture of possession than lust — but mostly they confess to the messiness of their days.

The candlelight is kind to their aging bodies, picks up the glow of flesh, not the wrinkles. According to the gossip their spies collect in the salons and the streets, they are insatiable. Catherine throws her doors open and calls in one guard after another to service her. Sends back the ones who cannot please her fast enough. Potemkin's women loll on ottomans dressed as odalisques, awaiting his arrival. He keeps ancient vases filled with precious stones for them to dip their perfumed hands in. He has made porcelain casts of his engorged penis and gives them as souvenirs to cast-off lovers.

"Are you really that vulgar, Grishenka?"

"Would it surprise you if I were?" He winks and grins with such childish pleasure that she laughs.

They finish each other's thoughts. She insists he should wear thicker furs and coats for the winter. He thinks she works too hard. She still hasn't learned ruthlessness in assessing people's qualities. Gets tempted by potential where she should demand proof of past performance. "I'll look for another secretary," he promises. "Have I not found Lanskoy for you?"

Sasha Lanskoy is her Favorite. *Sasha is, as you have promised, a gobbler of poetry, history, philosophy, and art,* she writes in a letter to Potemkin. *Keen on acquiring a limitless knowledge of what is of highest quality in human endeavors. Cheerful, honest, and very sweet.*

She calls him Sashenka.

Her first gift to him was a gilded copy of Algarotti's *Newtonianism for Ladies,* a promise to explain not just the nature of light and colors but a proof that an open mind can examine and refute the stale evidence of the past.

Levitsky, who has been commissioned to paint him, complains that Sashenka won't stand still long enough. "He bounces, Your Majesty, upsetting the august proportions I'm trying to render."

The painting, now finished, annoys her, though she doesn't quite know what is the most irritating. Her own bust right over Sashenka's left arm? The marble face with empty eyes and a double chin? The ample folds of Sashenka's breeches? The engorged knot of a tassel near his groin? The handle of his sword standing erect? But Levitsky wouldn't dare to insinuate, would he?

"A splendid portrait," Sashenka has exclaimed. Since he is entranced, she has no heart to voice her misgivings.

Monsieur Alexander is also fascinated by Sashenka's portrait. At seven, her eldest grandson is chatty and fearless. Constantly seeking her hand, turning his face up to her as he asks his endless questions.

"Is he your husband, Graman?"

"No."

"Why is he wearing a wig?"

"It is fashionable."

"Why does he want to be fashionable?"

"Because he wants other people to respect him."

"Am I fashionable?"

"Yes."

"Even though I do not have a wig?"

"A little boy doesn't need a wig."

"Do you love him?"

"Yes."

"More than you love me?"

"What nonsense you speak! You are my little chevalier, my prince. No one else is like you."

Summer is a traitor and a thief. It tempts with warmth, but it harbors poison.

On Wednesday afternoon, Sashenka Lanskoy swallows hard and winces. "The pain in my throat won't go away," he tells her. "It'll be the death of me."

"Another falsehood," she says, trying to cheer her lover. She picks up a handkerchief and makes him spit the words out into it. "There," she says, throwing the wet handkerchief out of the window. It flutters in the air before a gust of wind carries it somewhere into the Tsarskoye Selo gardens. "Ill humor is a vice," she reminds him. "You are twenty-six. We still have time to grow old together, though I'll be at my dotage well before you."

His face is oval, his cheeks clean shaven, free from rouge. Sashenka Lanskoy prefers simple bob wigs and hair powder with orris-root, which smells of violets. "You help me think," he has told her once. "And you give me food for thought," she retorted.

"All I need is a bit of rest," he concedes with a smile. "I might even sleep," he adds, though this would be rare, for — like her — he finds it hard to sleep during the day. Their bodies are well attuned. They both like to wake up early. They both fall asleep as soon as their cheeks touch the pillow.

Sashenka goes to his room to rest and she settles in the Gallery with her book. She is reading Lord Chesterfield's letters to his son. Filled with excellent advice. Worth keeping in mind for Alexander. Her grandson is ready to learn the importance of good handwriting. Or to be given the first lessons in eloquence properly tailored to different audiences. How would you tell this story to your teacher? Your little brother? Your servant?

Sashenka returns an hour later, revived by sleep, joking at his own fears. His eyes are tawny, like a lion's. Strangely piercing in a pale face.

"Enough of this service to the Empire! Let's go for a walk, Katinka," Sashenka urges, offering her his arm. This eagerness is what she loves in him. He has put on his white coat, embroidered with silver and red birds of paradise. Her gift to him. One of many.

They stroll around the pond, past the small obelisk where her late dogs are buried. Not all of them, only the most beloved. Sir Tom, so fond of nipping the heels of visitors who moved too fast for his liking. Lady Tomasina, who'd leap into the air at the mere sight of a squirrel.

They talk.

Of the flamepoint embroidery she has become particularly fond of, for the rich colors remind her of peacock feathers. Of another shipment of engraved gems on their way from Hamburg, her gift to him. Of Sashenka's progress with intaglio carvings. She thinks his precision and dexterity astounding, but he is not satisfied. "I've tried carving a heron," he confesses with a sheepish grin, "but I think it looks more like a duck."

By the time they are back in the palace, he doesn't want the day to end. "Just one quick game of reversis, Katinka," he insists. "I really want to win."

She makes sure he does. "Look," she says, showing him her last card, the trump queen of spades. "I've been utterly defeated."

"Tomorrow we'll play again," he says and reaches for a glass of raspberry kvass. He flinches as he swallows.

Only then does she notice that his eyes are glassy with fever. "Go to your room, Sashenka," she says. "Rest."

He obeys, though reluctantly. By the door he stoops to pick up some invisible speck from the floor. Turns back and hesitates before leaving. An hour later — prompted by the memory of his bone-white face — she sends a page running to his room to check on him. The boy returns immediately.

"Monsieur Lanskoy," he reports, "has just sent for Doctor Rogerson."

She sits by his bed and watches him. Sashenka's eyes are closed but his eyelids twitch sometimes. He is sweating from the summer heat and the fever. The maids have dipped sheets in cold water and hung them in the room. From the garden comes the scented breeze. Birds squabble and sing.

"Sleep," she murmurs, wiping Sashenka's forehead with a towel dipped in ice water.

She thinks of what her father once told her. That in the forest, as long as the birds sing, a wanderer knows that there is no wolf or bear close by.

On Friday, Sobolevsky, the second doctor she has summoned, brings cooked figs with him, soft enough to swallow without pain.

This is the only food Sashenka eats, but he drinks tea and kvass and weak ale.

The doctors are hopeful. He is young. He is strong. He has an excellent constitution. Faithful Vishka, who has just come from the Winter Palace, where she was overseeing the fumigation of the Imperial Bedroom, reminds her that in July the year before, a horse kicked Sashenka Lanskoy so badly that his chest was bruised and he was spitting blood, but a week later he was riding again.

There is solace in such words.

By Saturday, both doctors stress that Sashenka is calmer. This is a good sign, they say. The fever is diminishing.

At midday, there is this odd bout of hiccups that won't pass, and a purple rash appears on Sashenka's body, but he is alert and even sits upright in his bed. "Bring me my gemstones," he tells his valet.

Catherine is worried, but she is not frightened. Since Sashenka complains of being too hot, Vishka has been ordered to find him a cooler room. She recommends a small room on the ground floor, in the west wing. "It may be far away from your bedroom, madame," she says, "but it is well shaded by the old tree."

The room has not been used for a while. It smells of mice, but Vishka promises that the maids will scrub the floors with scalding water mixed with vinegar and scent it with perfume.

On Sunday, the room is ready and Sashenka is strong enough to walk there himself. He approves of the red ottoman and the velvet-covered puff to rest his feet on. And the encrusted armoire for his nightshirts. And the rosewood side table with a copy of Lucretius bound in morocco leather.

"You've thought of everything, Katinka," he says. His voice is hoarse. "Now I'll get well."

But then at night, hot and humid, Vishka wakes her up. "Please, Majesty," she says, breathless. "Come fast."

When Catherine rushes into his room,

239

Sashenka doesn't recognize her. "I have to go," he insists in an angry voice. "Why are the horses not harnessed yet? Who told you to be so slow?"

"It's me," she says, repressing the flicker of terror he would have seen on her features. "Katinka."

He doesn't hear. His body tenses, his hands thrash blindly as if he were drowning.

She wipes his forehead with a towel dipped in ice water, soothes him with promises that all will be as he wishes. His horses are on their way. The grooms are bringing them to the courtyard. They are outside already. "Can't you hear the bells?" she asks. "I can."

For a moment he seems to have understood her, for he says, "Those are not my horses."

He falls back on the pillows. His hair, cropped short, is slick with sweat.

When she holds a sliver of ice to his lips, he sucks on it greedily.

She wishes to stay with him through the night, but Rogerson forbids it. "The contagion resides in the air," the doctor says. "It's too dangerous, madame."

A young, strong body, Catherine repeats to herself. *Surely he will recover.*

She hardly sleeps that night. With Vishka at her heels, she walks through the corridors of the Tsarskoye Selo. She stops by paintings, holds a candle up, making sure she looks only at those where life triumphs. Lovers united, a pilgrim returned home, a vase with blooming flowers, a warrior returning from battle with a garland over his neck.

By Tuesday, Sashenka is dead.

"Never!" she screams when Vishka asks her to name the day for the funeral.

For seventeen days and nights she stays in her room. She doesn't dress. She doesn't wash. She receives no one but Vishka, who sighs but doesn't complain of having to serve as a chambermaid and merely casts quick, worried looks at yet another plate of untouched food.

Her eyes are sore from tears and rubbing, the skin underneath puffy. In the mirror, she examines the furrowed flesh of her neck, the thinning hair, the odd-looking flaps of skin that have grown on her shoulders and under her breasts. If she pulls on them, they bleed.

She has ordered Sashenka's belongings to be brought to her. His engraved gems, his books, his wig, his dress uniform, which she tries to put on but, finding it too tight, places on her pillow instead. It smells of nothing but pepper, a smell that makes her sneeze.

In Algarotti's book, she notes, half of the pages have never been cut.

On the eighteenth night, she goes to the room where Sashenka's embalmed body lies in its coffin. The body she refuses to have buried.

"Leave," she tells the mourners. They don't dare to disobey her.

The coffin, lined with white satin, is surrounded by candles. Her eyes slide, slowly, from Sashenka's black jackboots to the red jacket, the silver oak leaves embroidered on the collar. Finally, she forces herself to look at his face. "So calm," Vishka has said.

No, not calm, Catherine thinks. *Defeated. Cheated out of life that should've been his. And mine.*

Hair coiffed in an elaborate pouf is curled over his ears. Powdered with the wrong powder. Lavender, not orris. Someone has placed two gold coins on Sashenka's eyes. Between his fingers is a passport to the other world signed by the priest. She wants to remove the coins, and the passport, but the effort seems enormous. Besides, she doesn't want to touch Sashenka now. She wants to remember his skin warm with life.

So she sits there, on a low chair, watching him. Asking: "Why did you leave me?"

There are no answers on her lover's still face. He is oblivious of her desire, her sorrow, her pain. As if his lips never caressed her, never sought to give her pleasure. Shy, she has heard him described. *Not with me,* she thinks. *With me he couldn't be shy.*

Each breath that leaves her chest robs her of some small part of him.

■ ■ ■ ■

"I've come as soon as the news reached me," Potemkin says. Sunburn has left a reddened smudge across his forehead. There is a trace of soot on his chin. Catherine clasps the hand he has extended toward her. The strong, hard hand of a soldier.

He is still wearing his heavy traveling clothes, splashed with mud. His boots leave dark, wet imprints on the carpet. He has ridden here all the way from Kremenchuk in seven days, more than a thousand miles, forced his way into her bedroom, taken one look at her, and said: "*Matushka,* I won't let you follow him."

She wants to cry, but her tears are gone.

"Come," Grisha says.

She lets him lead her, because she cannot think of doing anything else. They descend the stairs, pass the main hall, walk into the gardens. She is dimly aware of eyes watching her. Through the keyholes, from behind the corners. Frightened, worried looks.

In the dusk, wet trees take on shadowy, spectral hues. By the time they reach the reed-rimmed pond, her skirt has soaked up so much water it clings to her like another layer of skin. She stumbles on gravel sleek with rain, but Potemkin holds her arm too tightly to let her fall. Water lilies are taking over the pond and should be trimmed. Why does she have to tell the gardeners what they should pay attention to?

Standing here in the garden, she sees that the palace windows flicker like fireflies. The servants are lighting candles. Somewhere from the pond comes the fetid smell of rot.

Has she been vain? Greedy for flattery? Been obstinate? Inattentive? Suspicious? Jealous?

"Keep walking," Potemkin says. "Don't stop."

"Where are we going?" she asks him.

"Nowhere," Grisha answers.

"Then why?"

"Because we have to move."

"Why?"

"Because if we ever stop, we die."

"Maybe I want to die."

"No."

She stops, in defiance, but he pushes her on. Forces her to keep walking until she is too tired to go farther. Only then does he relent. "I won't let you follow him," he repeats.

She rests her head on the crook of his neck. His lips touch hers. His tongue parts her teeth, dives inside her. It is acrid and bitter.

She begins to talk. Father is gone, and Mother. Both died far away, unseen. Panin, always stirring her son's mind into disobedience, was struck down by apoplexy. Grigory

244

Orlov lost to madness. Drooling in a wheelchair, not even a spark of recognition in his deadened eyes when he looked at her. As if there were no difference between his Katinka and a piece of flotsam.

"Children of Providence, Grishenka? Are we still blessed?"

Potemkin doesn't answer, but his arms hold her tight. The thought flashes that as long as she can still lose herself in his embrace, she'll find the strength to keep on walking.

Her galleys are moored near Kaniv. She is on her way to inspect the Crimea. Her next stop is Kaydaki, where the Austrian Emperor is already waiting for her.

The dream of the thousand and one nights, she calls this voyage. The year of 1787 is the year of her victory tour, her triumphant inspection of the newly conquered lands. Potemkin, her Prince of Tauride, is laying it all at her feet, fertile fields carved out of steppes, new towns and ports, new trade routes, new fleet of ships, new peoples of the Empire dressed in their colorful garbs.

"Didn't I tell you, Katinka?" he says and grins. "Wasn't I right?"

They are the best of partners. Their thoughts travel the same roads. No one but he understands why conquests matter. Others speak of riches to be had. Imagine themselves lording it over old rivals. Avenge ancient humiliations. Potemkin says: "Remember the Middle Kingdom? The Chinese Emperor called back his big ships and locked them away. Who remembers him now? The moment you stop growing, you begin to wilt and die."

Russians are not sailors ready to conquer distant lands or trade in fragrant spices. So Russia must grow outward, expand at her core. Elizabeth's wars were glorious but brought Russia no land.

Hers have.

Peter the Great went north. Catherine moved west and south.

The imperial barges bustle with activity. Courtiers prepare for ceremonial duties. Servants rush about with platters of food, fresh linen, jugs of wine. Painters with easels scurry about in search for the vantage point to capture the most important scenes of the day. When the journey to the Crimea is over, the drawings will be transformed into paintings, sculptures, or porcelain figurines to adorn her dining tables or mantelpieces.

Potemkin has thought of everything. *Dnieper*, the gold and scarlet imperial galley, contains the Imperial Bedroom, an audience chamber, and a study furnished with a beautiful mahogany writing desk. An orchestra plays soft music for her whenever she wishes. At every stop, Prince Potemkin, with a roguish sparkle in his good eye, conjures up a garden. Potted trees and shrubs, clumps of blooming flowers, and carpets of luscious moss are laid on the steppe. One day a path might lead to a fountain; another, to a bubbling spring. A bench can stand in plain view or be hidden behind junipers. "You can force a flower to bloom!" Catherine says and laughs.

"You and me, *matushka*. We are invincible."

Not a moment is wasted in idleness. Triumphant arches and garlands of flowers at each stop are reminders of her imperial duties: to hear a liturgy, host a ball, receive a local representation. That is the purpose of this sumptuous journey. To listen to her people. In every town, she questions the bishops, the landowners, the merchants. What would make your lives easier? More prosperous? What could I, your Empress, do to be of use?

"Why come so far to see nothing?" Mister Redcoat, her latest Favorite, sulks. "It's as if we never left the court." His predecessor tried to badmouth Grishenka and was dismissed. Let's not recall at what cost.

Mister Redcoat's real name is Alexander Matveyevich Mamonov, but how can she call a lover of hers Alexander? Or its diminutive *Sashenka*?

"I travel not to see places but people," she tells him. "Places I can learn about from maps and descriptions."

Mister Redcoat lowers his head. She is still

sure that his young mind could be improved, molded into a finer shape.

"My visits may be short, but I give my people means to approach me," she continues. "Those who might be tempted to abuse my authority take note and fear that I might discover their negligence and their injustices."

Mister Redcoat lets out his breath. His fingertips drum a fast beat on the tabletop. There is a yellow stain on his collar and black under his fingernails. Vishka will have to remind him of the virtue of cleanliness.

Kaniv is a Polish town, the property of Stanislav's nephew. A few days before, in Russian Kiev, visiting Polish grandees ate her food, drank her wine, and spun their big and small intrigues. Of their king of twenty-two years they spoke with irritation. Complained of Stanislav's constant whinings about ancient virtues now vanished, of his melancholy musings. Poland's losses are always their fault, never his.

Who supports him? Poets? Painters he commissions? Sculptors he employs to build statues of once triumphant Polish Kings? The weakness of character is a sea in which virtues and talents drown.

Twenty-nine years ago Stanislav was her beloved, but the past is a distant and foreign land. Her Russia is expanding. His Poland is shrinking. She made him king. His choice was to be her staunch ally or an adversary. He isn't much of either.

A king once made can be unmade; Catherine knows that better than anyone.

The moment Stanislav climbs on board the imperial galley, the courtiers flock about him, curious and excited, eager for every scrap they can weigh and measure. The meeting of onetime lovers, after twenty-eight years. Everything shall be recorded, passed on, gossiped about. First words, first gestures. Her smile, his smile. Or their absence.

The court speaks of nothing else, Catherine's valet assures her. Bets have been made. Predictions float. Will she shed a tear? Will he? Even Queenie and Vishka get caught in this ghastly foolishness, fretting over which adornments would suit their mistress best. A feather with a single diamond? A string of black pearls? A fichu to cover Her Majesty's neck? "Why would I wish to cover my wrinkles?" Catherine asks them. "I've lived for fifty-eight years. Would you wish me to be ashamed of it?"

Why is everyone trying to push her back into sentiments long dead? Because she is a woman? In love with flattery? Ignorant of the interest of her empire?

The imperial gifts are all lined up: For Stanislav, St. Andrew's order and a gold medal with her image on one side and Peter

I's statute on the other. For the women of his family, the order of St. Catherine and imperial portraits in diamond-studded frames. There are also more substantial tokens of her favor. Annuities, gifts of jewels.

The Russian Empress is no miser.

"Count Poniatowski," the footman announces, using his family name, as Stanislav enters her audience chamber. His gait is somewhat stiff, but graceful. He wears ivory-colored silk.

Not "the King of Poland"?

Is she supposed to take it as a sign of his modesty? A desire to avoid royal etiquette? Or is it a clever bid to her sentiments? Will he also call her Sophie? Or bring back the memory of the daughter they once had?

Her gaze sweeps over the King's face. Fifty-five, and his younger self still lingers in his brown eyes, in the finely sculptured jaw, the dimples in his now rouged cheeks. Upright, lithe, and still smoothly handsome, although, after a closer scrutiny, a tad worn out. No blemishes, though, no redness around the nose. Repnin wrote her: *Not even a glass of wine with dinner, which in Poland is being read as a reproach, not a virtue.*

Around them scraping, shuffling of feet, breaths withheld. Potemkin has asked with this curious grin of his: *Not even a tinge of regret, Katinka? Didn't you tell me that he was* loving and beloved?

To Stanislav's myopic eyes she must seem a blur. When he is close enough to discern her features, he tugs at the edge of his jacket, adjusts the lace ruffles. The gesture has something desperate about it, as if he has suddenly decided he has put on the wrong clothes. The jacket is fitted tight over his slim figure, its edges thick with silver embroidery. *Like a crust,* Catherine thinks. *Or a shield.*

Potemkin has said: "Be fair, Katinka. Admit it: The Polish crown *was* a fatal gift."

Stanislav bows and lifts his head. His eyes sweep over her face, her arms, her expanded waist. *Too swiftly,* Catherine thinks. *Were his lips always so narrow?*

"We welcome the King of Poland at our court," she says and extends her hand. Stanislav takes it tenderly and kisses it, with a reverence afforded to a Holy Relic. His own hand feels limp. Have *his* spies not warned him she values firm grips?

How they all gawk. Queenie has folded her plump hands, as if lost in prayer. Prince Potemkin gallantly points the way. Mister Redcoat screws his eyes up toward the ceiling. Her Favorite's rudeness, oddly enough, pleases her. Childlike, she thinks it. A little amusing. Like her grandsons' antics.

She makes a gesture toward her study. There is no point in delaying the inevitable. "Shall we retire, monsieur?" she asks.

251

■ ■ ■ ■

Once inside, she heads for the ottoman, annoyed by the heavy thump with which her body settles. She motions to her guest to take the armchair opposite. Silence grows. If it is allowed to last any longer, it will become menacing.

She inquires about his uncles, his sisters, brothers, cousins. Is the Palace on the Water finished to his satisfaction? Does he know a good painter capable of architectural accuracy? To paint St. Petersburg. A city needs to be well portrayed.

His family is well. His nephew is the apple of his eye. A young man of great promise. But perhaps the Empress noted it herself, having met him in Kaniv?

She does recall the young man. Not too handsome, and somewhat stiff, but pleasant enough.

"Yes," Catherine answers. "You have all reasons to be proud of him."

Stanislav knows an excellent painter. Bellotto, a Venetian. As soon as he gets back to Warsaw, he will make sure she receives a sample of the man's work. What pleasure it will give him!

Pleasantries. She is already anticipating Potemkin's questions. *You were right,* she will say. *It was not too awkward. I did have good taste in men, even when I was young.*

Foolish to forget that everything comes with a price.

Stanislav's hand dives into his breast pocket. He extracts a wad of pages, places it on his knees.

"Please, madame, would you consider my proposal?"

Hands make sweeping gestures, the laced cuffs flutter. Stanislav's speech has been well rehearsed: Russia will fight the Turks again. It is inevitable, and then Poland can be of help. He offers her twenty thousand troops, armed and disciplined. She will have to pay for it, but still it will be an investment. Wise and profitable. The Ottoman Porte, conquered, will yield rich territory. He sees Poland's borders extended, touching the Black Sea. Strong Poland will be a buffer between Russia and Prussia. "A granary and a boulevard for our joint armies."

He gathers up the papers and holds them out to her. "This modest memorandum," he says, "is an outline of my proposal."

It always amuses her how highly people think of themselves.

A king who cannot even control his own subjects wants an army, and he wants her to pay for it. As if she hasn't given him enough already! And what has she got in return? First a bloody rebellion. Then constant petitions and intrigues. She would've preferred bluntness. Acknowledgment that in Warsaw — among the constantly warring factions — without his special influence in St. Petersburg, he is nothing.

Poland, divided, is an unmanned fortress. Why spoil what is working in Russia's favor? Let warring factions undermine one another. It's all that simple.

"It's a very sound proposal, but I need time to examine it." She takes the papers from his hand, noting its tremor. She rises. "My courtiers are all impatient to meet you. Prince Potemkin tells me that you've prepared a splendid evening ball in my honor. I hope the Prince has warned you that I won't stay very long. These days I always retire at ten."

He jumps to his feet. And then he says it: "I've waited for this moment twenty-eight years."

She flinches. But he doesn't stop.

A flood of words. A torrent.

How he worried about her when Elizabeth died. How he lay awake at night tormented by rumors of assassins. Torn and soothed by memories of their happiness. Of their child he was not even allowed to mourn. No one else has ever ruled his heart like Catherine has.

With a flick of his hand, he opens the cover of his pocket watch. Her own young face looks at her from the inside flap. He recalls the time when they sneaked out of the palace to be alone. They got into a sleigh, buried themselves in furs. One moment she was in his arms, another she was thrown off the speeding sleigh. Into the snow. Struck her head on a stone. He thought she was dead. He prayed to the Almighty. He offered his life and his happiness for hers. And then she opened her eyes. And she kissed him. How does one forget such moments?

"I once asked you not to make me King but to call me to your side. I still wish you would," he says and pauses, as if still considering the word he is about to say. *"Sophie."*

Her heart quickens. She considers what she has just heard.

You made me King, so support me now? You have no right to expect anything in return? You have no right to change?

Anger is not easy to hide. It lingers. It drags out images from the past, long hoped left behind. Floorboards shaking under her feet, a glass pane shattering into splinters. A mattress on the floor, soaked with her sweat. Peter, sucking at his pipe, looking at her with contempt. Mother asking: "Have you already forgotten who you are?"

"It's time to join the rest," Catherine tells him.

Queenie and Vishka, who went to the Polish ball, declare it magnificent. The Polish King, Queenie says, must have spent a fortune on the decorations alone. On the main

255

table there was a beautiful display made entirely of sugar. A sleigh with two figures inside was making its way through the sugar dunes toward a magnificent sugar garden. There were paths leading to intricate caves lit from the inside. There was a triumphant arch. And an obelisk. And a hermit's hut, beside which a flock of sheep was grazing.

"*Matushka,* spit on Mister Redcoat," Potemkin says. "The faithless wretch doesn't deserve you."

Her servants have trampled the grass and spread a cloth in the shade of the young birch trees. They wiped the plates, cups, saucers from the everyday service and unpacked the provisions. Melon cubes on a bed of crushed ice, peach halves wrapped in leaves. Slices of bread smeared with freshly churned butter, *bliny* with caviar, and bottles of cold kvass. On double-layered plates lie pink paper cornets with grapes and small cakes hidden inside.

At the end of an outing at the edge of the woods, a summer treat awaited. Folded iron furniture is comfortable enough, though the legs of her armchair wobble as they dig into the moist earth. The sun rays glitter through the young branches and throw little balls of light upon the white cloth. Dogs lie in the shadow of the carriage that has brought them there, panting; some lick the grease off the carriage wheels.

Captain Platon Alexandrovich Zubov, lean and trim in his steel-colored dress uniform, has taken the seat opposite her. They are still strangers, although his lips have caressed her nipples, his clean-shaven cheek rested against her thigh as he kneeled before her, desperate to know if he has pleased her enough.

All is still before them, weaknesses unveiled, desires confessed. None of it is certain. She might still send him back, in spite of his youthful charm and twinkling black eyes. She needs solitude. To find herself, after so many losses.

The handsome Captain picks a paper cornet and peeks inside. His fingers deftly extract the grapes, one by one, and pop them into his mouth. His tongue is stained deep red. Queenie laughs when she tells her how the Captain memorizes maxims from books to impress her: *Do not waste time on empty activities. Abandon an opinion if it is refuted. Only the ignorant believe they know everything.*

Her grandchildren — Alexander, Constantine, Alexandrine, Yelena, and Maria — play at a distance. Alexander, who will turn twelve in December, wishes to build a summerhouse from sticks and leafy branches. But as soon as the first elements of the structure are raised, his younger brother, Constantine, declares their endeavor stupid. Why build a house in a place they will soon have to leave?

She recalls holding Constantine the day he was born: crying, creased, his unfocused eyes shying away from the light.

"What shall we do, then?" Alexander asks, his voice throbbing with hurt. The boys strive for supremacy at all times, so why does her grandson now prefer to sound offended rather than to command?

"Let's go to Crimea," Constantine decides. With a few adjustments, a row of folded chairs becomes an imperial barge that goes up and down the imaginary waves of the Dnieper River in reenactment of their grandmother's grand journey to inspect her conquered lands. Maria, chubby and quite ugly at three, chortling with glee, sways in Alexandrine's arms. Alexander hands her a field glass made from a roll of paper and tells her to admire the rapids. "I can only see trees," Maria announces with utter seriousness, "and I can see Graman."

"You have to pretend we are far away from here," Constantine yells, yanking the field glass from her hands. "You are spoiling everything, you dunce!"

Maria bursts into tears.

"See what you have done?" Alexandrine says accusingly, as Constantine jumps out of the imaginary boat. He has a horsewhip in his hands and lashes at the grass, the trees, at anything that he imagines stands in his way.

It is July of 1789, the year she has turned

sixty. A tumultuous time, she calls it in her letters. In the last months, she has been betrayed by one lover, and now she is courted again.

"I've tried to warn you of his duplicity, but you wouldn't listen," Potemkin told her.

Queenie has denounced the departed Mister Redcoat as a deranged fool who will soon be pining for what he has lost. Captain Zubov, the lover who has come courting, has a far more pleasing disposition. With this one, there will be no more sulking, no more accusations. "Why does a breakup hurt so much, though?" Catherine has asked Queenie. But Queenie's explanations are always predictable. "Because Your Majesty is too good. Too forgiving."

Betrayal is a loss. Losses hurt.

Under my own nose, she thinks, with a pang as sharp as if she has just learned of Mister Redcoat's tryst with her lady-in-waiting. Told of fruit from her table he has been sending to his mistress. Shown the room where the two rendezvoused. "Right after he'd stormed out of Your Majesty's bedroom. Having accused Your Majesty of neglecting him!"

"May I, Your Majesty?" Captain Zubov asks. He holds the platter of melon chunks before him, like an offering.

She shakes her head, but her handsome Captain insists. She picks a small piece and puts it in her mouth. The red flesh melts on her tongue. It is ice cold and very sweet.

She looks in the direction of the children. With Constantine gone, Alexandrine and Yelena are whispering something to each other, their heads touching. Maria is rubbing her eyes with her pudgy fingers. Alexander is standing alone, his arms folded, his eyes on the ground. With his right foot he is kicking a tuft of grass.

A game, Catherine thinks. *We should all play some game.*

Blindman's buff is one blunder after another. Constantine refuses to play. Maria retreats into her nurse's arms after tripping and falling on her face. When he is blindfolded, Alexander waves his hands and takes a few perfunctory steps without trying to touch anyone.

Captain Zubov asks to speak. He is not just a Captain in Her Imperial Majesty's army, he announces, he is a famous magician.

Alexandrine and Yelena turn toward him as he extracts a crimson handkerchief from his breast pocket and with elaborate effort pushes it inside his folded palm. "One, two," he counts, "three," and opens his palm to show that it is empty.

Yelena gasps with glee.

They are gathering around him now. Maria has left her nurse's arms and is holding Alexandrine's hand. Constantine is leaning

260

forward to see better. The handkerchief has appeared again and is showing up in most unexpected places. Behind Maria's ear. In Alexandrine's hair, in the folds of Yelena's gown. Each appearance is greeted with screams of ecstatic laughter.

Even Alexander has joined them and is standing beside his brother.

The handkerchief is lying abandoned now, for the Captain has asked Yelena to choose a card. She settles on the queen of spades, and the queen of spades appears on top of the deck.

"A diamond," Maria decrees. Constantine rolls his eyes but doesn't interrupt when Alexandrine explains that Maria has to choose a number or a figure, not just a suit.

"How old are you?" Alexandrine asks Maria, who puts up her plump hand showing three extended fingers.

"Three of diamonds, then," Alexandrine tells the Captain, who shuffles the cards deftly and then, after a moment of suspense, draws one card for each letter of Maria's name. When he reaches the second *a*, the card he uncovers is the three of diamonds.

Catherine, too, joins the applause. But the show is not over yet.

"Look," Constantine cries.

One of the cards leaves the deck and hovers in the air as if hesitating where to turn. Captain Zubov makes first a quizzical face and then a happy one, for the card is clearly leading him toward her.

Catherine extends her hand to touch the card, but before she manages to do it, Captain Zubov catches it in midair and tosses it from one hand to the other. The card turns around as it floats back and forth.

Her grandchildren are bewitched. Maria stands with her mouth open. Alexandrine and Yelena applaud. Constantine demands to examine the card. "How does he do it?" he asks Alexander, who shrugs in response.

Ensnared in the hilarity of the moment, Catherine extends her hand again. Captain Zubov places the card on her open palm. His black eyes dance with joy. His skin has such a lovely olive hue to it. On his upper lip, a dark shadow marks the outline of where his mustache would be if he let it grow.

He places the card on her palm and then the card lifts up.

She laughs. The card floats down and settles on her palm. She tries to touch it with her finger, but the card lifts again. This time the Captain catches the card in midair and puts it back on top of the deck. He makes a gesture of surrender. His palms are empty. He can be searched but he has to warn everyone that he is very ticklish. To prove it, he shakes his whole body like a dog out of water.

Maria giggles.

Constantine settles himself beside Captain Zubov and pesters him with incessant questions. How old was he when he started riding his horse? Can he climb a tree to the very top? Can he swim across the Neva?

Platon Alexandrovich Zubov, Catherine thinks. Such a long and heavy name for someone who has made her laugh again. Black hair, black eyes. It comes to her, then, her nickname for him. Le Noiraud.

"Will you tell me how you do it?" Constantine's voice is tingling with eagerness.

Le Noiraud bends toward him and whispers loud enough for her to hear: "Only one person in the whole world can get the secret out of me."

What comes next happens all at once. The folding table rocks, the cornets fall from the layered plate, the grapes spill out and roll among the dishes. The melon platter falls to the ground at her feet. Red stains appear on her lilac gown and when she steps forward she feels something soft and moist yielding under her satin shoe. The footmen rush toward them, picking up the fruit, the platter, pieces of broken china. The dogs begin to bark.

"I didn't do it," Constantine cries, for all eyes are on him.

It takes her a moment to acknowledge what, obviously, is the truth. But it is hard, for she has missed the moment Alexander

263

extended his hand and pushed the folding
table. By the time she turns toward him, her
oldest grandson is no longer by her side. It is
Platon Zubov who silently directs her eyes to
the diminishing figure running toward the
woods.

"No," she says when Queenie asks her
permission to go after Alexander. "The boy is
in the mood for a quarrel. He will come back
when he is ready to apologize."

Alexander returns half an hour later, when
all evidence of his outburst has been cleared.
He is limping. His face is scratched, his
clothes wet and dirtied with mud. The nurses
and Queenie fuss over him, and he lets them
wash the muddy stains off his cheeks.

When he does approach her, Catherine
waves everyone away.

"But why you, my Monsieur Alexander?"
she asks when he has whispered his apology.
"Can you explain to me the reason?"

His eyes fill up with tears. He shakes his
head.

She is still seething with incomprehension
when she hears a galloping horse. Dogs are
barking again. The grooms run toward the
rider, who dismounts quickly. She recognizes
the bearlike frame of Count Bezborodko —
her trusted secretary — who hurries toward
her.

The news must be important. He wouldn't

have interrupted her otherwise.

"News from Paris," Bezborodko gasps, handing her the dispatch. His glove is torn at the base of his thumb; his stockings have slid all the way to his heels. There is a sleek stream of sweat flowing down his forehead. His horse neighs and stomps the ground. The dogs are still barking. "The mob is in the streets."

She is still not sure why the news of a rioting Parisian mob could not wait for her return. And then she hears: "The Bastille fell, Your Majesty. This is just the beginning."

There have been victories and quarrels. In St. Petersburg, Potemkin bangs doors, tramples her carpets with muddy boots, screams and bangs his fist on her desk. What are these storms about? He wants her to negotiate with England; she refuses. He urges caution; she wants to call their bluff. He rages. She has colics and spasms. "Go after him," she orders Zotov when Grishenka leaves cursing her and slamming the doors after him. "Make sure he is all right."

We always quarrel about power, not love.

His ill-wishers poison her mind. No bounds, no shame. His mistresses are getting more greedy, knowing he'll think nothing of sending his messenger across the country to fetch a swanskin fan or a pair of silk stockings. All five of his nieces (to make a harem of his own family!) swim in riches. While the peacock clock he ordered for his Empress in London has been paid for by the state funds. And while he keeps an apartment in town with shelves on every wall, each packed with banknotes.

Evidence?

Plentiful. Ironclad. Letters, orders, confessions. There is always someone willing to testify to the sins of the mighty. Sloth, negligence, greed, vanity, lust for any woman who takes his fancy.

In the end, Potemkin always prevails. Turkish fortresses fall. The steppes turn into fields. Towns raise where only grass grew. The Prussians who plot against him are thwarted. "I don't hide my passions, *matushka,* but if I take, I give back tenfold. What is mine is always yours."

The ill-wishers scurry away. Until the next time.

The last party Potemkin gave for her was the most splendid. As if he knew nothing must be allowed to surpass this memory.

It was a rainy St. Petersburg day, and yet the Tauride Palace blinded her with radiance. Rows upon rows of torches illuminated the colonnade; light spilled from opened doors. The courtyard teemed with onlookers, craning their necks, pushing for a better view. Children perched on their parents' shoulders, waved their hands. *Why so many people?* Catherine thought. *He knows I don't like crowds.*

"Long live the Empress!" someone cried, and she acknowledged the answering roar from the crowd with a wave of her hand. The people cheered.

She saw Potemkin as soon as she alighted. Her one-eyed giant in his scarlet tailcoat, a gold-and-black lace cloak tossed over his shoulders. The diamonds sewn onto his coat and cloak glittered and sparkled as he began walking toward her through two lines of footmen. His head was bare, his bejeweled hat perched on a pillow his adjutant carried behind him.

"Too heavy for his head? Is Prince Potemkin perchance trying to discover how many diamonds one man can wear all at once?" These were Le Noiraud's words, oozing with jealousy and envy. Platon Alexandrovich Zubov, the latest of her Favorites, does not take well to another's glory.

"Enough," she silenced him. He rolled his eyes and sighed, but obeyed.

When Potemkin approached her and kneeled, she raised him to his feet. He took her hand, ready to lead her inside, but then, suddenly, the human wave moved forward. Someone screamed in pain. A wooden barrier fell. A burly man, shoved forward by some invisible hands, barely avoided crashing into her.

A revolution? she wondered, terrified. *Here, in Russia? Like in France?*

For a moment, she did think that this might be the end. That the crowd would trample them all. She read so many Parisian reports that the mind furnished her with vivid images. Men and women pulled out of carriages, thrown to the pavement with force that shattered bones and skulls. The enemies of the revolution bludgeoned, torn to pieces, their heads paraded on pikes. Street dogs feasting on their bloody remains.

Potemkin had seen the flash of fear in her eyes. "It's nothing, Katinka," he whispered.

It was nothing. Some foolish servant had missed the cue and opened the stalls with free food too early. Her people didn't want to kill or maim. Her people wished to stuff their pockets with treats far more than watch the Empress walk by.

She hadn't always been that easily frightened. Once she used to think crowds credulous, easy to sway the way she wished them to go.

"Come, beloved *matushka*. Three thousand guests are waiting for you."

Potemkin led her toward the palace. Inside, in the Colonnade Hall, stood her whole family, dressed in their finest. Paul and his wife, Maria, flanked by Alexander and Constantine. Her granddaughters, in white frilly frocks, their cheeks flushed with excitement.

The fiery brightness came from fifty massive chandeliers, each with dozens of burning candles, more than twenty thousand, she was told. And then there were more torches, their light reflected by mirrored walls, by crystal pendants, by gilded walls and columns.

Behind the Colonnade Hall, the Tauride winter garden spread, exuding waves of moist, fragrant warmth. Hyacinths and orange blossoms. Roses and lilies. Blooming peonies beside snowdrops, a subtle hint that nature's laws can be suspended, that some alliances can be forced. Lamps were hidden in clusters of mock grapes, pears, and pineapples. Silver and scarlet fishes swam in glass globes. The cupola was painted like a sky, with white fluffy clouds over Prussian blue. Paths and little hillocks led to statues of goddesses.

A temple to her stood in the garden center, with a statue placed on a diamond-studded pyramid. Underneath it, a placard: *To the Mother of the Motherland and my Benefactress.*

What an enchanted evening it was! Beautiful children dancing a quadrille, dressed in costumes of blue and pink and sparkling with jewels. Monsieur Alexander dancing a minuet with Alexandrine. Both so graceful, so light! And then, as darkness fell, Potemkin took them all into the Gobelin Room, where the tapestries told the story of Esther and where a life-size gold elephant stood, covered in emeralds and rubies. Once she took her seat, the tapestries rose up as if by magic, for her Prince had turned the Gobelin Room into a theater. There were two comedies, a ballet, and then the most splendid procession of all the peoples of the Empire. "Look, Graman," Alexander screamed in excitement. "The captured Ottoman pashas from Ismail are here!"

Fete superb, she thought. *This is how we conduct ourselves in St. Petersburg. In the midst of trouble and war and the menaces of dictators. Europe, take note!*

"Don't say a word yet, Katinka," her Prince whispered in her ear when she turned to praise him. He led her back to the winter garden, to the statue of herself as goddess, where he again fell to his knees. And then he gave a sign, and from among the shrubberies a man's resonant voice began to recite, *Grom pobedy, razdavaysya!*

Triumph's thunder louder, higher!
Russian pride is running high!
Russia's glory sparkles brighter!
We have humbled Moslem might.

Hail to you for this, o Catherine —
Gentle mother to us all!

Only when she wiped tears from Grisha's eyes, when she embraced him and assured him that no joy could ever match this evening as long as she lived, did the orchestra begin to play.

The grand ball began. She didn't dance.

She was too tired and her legs hurt. But she played cards with Maria Fyodorovna for a while, ignoring her son's forced smiles, too thin a cover for Paul's disappointments. Watched the children dance for her again. Sat at her table, which was covered in gold, illuminated by a ball of white-and-blue glass, when Potemkin stood behind her chair and served her until she insisted he sit down beside her.

They didn't have to talk to know their thoughts. The coded dispatches to Berlin and London would be filled with sneers at Russian extravagance and insufferable pride. What garish displays of Asian taste! What waste and arrogance! What unbridled lust! But the monarchs of Europe are not fooled. They will know: Russia, united, disciplined, and fearless, is the power to be reckoned with.

At two A.M., when she protested she could no longer keep her eyes open, Potemkin finally let her go. But not before her victorious Prince, the conqueror of the Crimea, gave his orchestra another sign and intoned the mournful aria he had composed for her: *The only thing that matters in the world is you.*

■ ■ ■ ■

Goodbye, my friend, I kiss you, was the note she sent after Grisha when he departed to the south soon after that night. It was Zotov who told her how that morning after the fete, even after the last guests left, Potemkin wouldn't lie down. How he lingered among the remains of his party, ate from abandoned dishes the servants had not yet cleared, dipped his fingers in the wine and sucked on them. And then, with the sun high in the skies, he wrote the letter she has read and reread so many times:

Alexander, the firstborn of the nestling eagles, is already fledged. Soon, after spreading his wings, he will soar over Russia, and it will reveal itself to him as the most expansive of maps . . . expanded borders, armies, fleets, and cities that have multiplied . . . a populated steppe . . . such will be the beautiful sight before him, and we shall have the pleasure of seeing in him a Prince who possesses the qualities of an angel, meekness, a pleasing appearance, a majestic bearing. He will awaken in everyone love for him and gratitude toward you for his education that has rendered nothing but gifts to Russia.

■ ■ ■ ■

There is no shame in loving her grandson. Of seeing him triumph over his father.

Patience has never been Grigory Orlov's virtue.

"No restraints," she has told Alexei. "No dousing with ice-cold water. No locked doors, no more bleedings. No blows. No discipline. Do nothing that displeases him. Let him be."

Zotov has been given orders to admit Prince Orlov to her chambers at all times. "In all manner of dress," she has said, and so Grigory Orlov might appear in his dressing gown, or in the odd assortment of uniform pieces, as if he tried to remember which parts of his wardrobe went with what.

It hurts to watch him in this state. Empty eyes, locked on some scraps of the past that might, at an unexpected moment, break into a lucid memory. He is only five years younger than she is. No longer a lover, but in the end, a friend.

A friend who has not run away from her or betrayed her as others did. Or accused her of ingratitude.

His brothers try to guard him. But he is Grigory Orlov, reckless and clever and impossible to tie down. A moment of inattention, and once again he is climbing down the wall of the Gatchina house, mounting his stallion, riding to St. Petersburg, appearing abruptly clad in his stained undergarments, arms outstretched, mumbling his rapture. "Do they love you here, Katinka? Do they care for you? Are you not hungry? Are you not thirsty?"

Why is she letting this deranged Count roam the palace? Exposing himself. Chasing chambermaids. Scaring her grandchildren. Foreign Ambassadors have countless anecdotes to report now. "To Russia's shame," the courtiers whisper into her ear.

When she replies that she is not ashamed of showing compassion for a man who had once been her companion, they change their arguments.

Grigory Orlov is still very strong. He can still bend a horseshoe. A fire poker. They have seen him wield a birch tree trunk like a saber. At Gatchina, he tore a window from its frame. Jumped into a waterfall from a bridge and almost drowned.

He might mistake her for someone else, some figment of his deranged mind. Shatter her skull. Or push her down the stairs.

"No," she says. "He may not know who I am, but he'll never harm me."

She believes it.

Once when she is alone, reading in her study, Grigory Orlov walks in and tiptoes toward her. His wig, its pigtail torn off, is crawling with lice. He speaks in an urgent whisper. "Come, Katinka," he says. "Right now. We must hurry."

"Where do you want us to go?" she asks gently.

"On a pilgrimage, Katinka. We must walk all the way. We must pray."

"Why?"

He gives her a long, ardent look. There is no confusion in it, only sorrow.

"To repent for what we've done!"

When has the game changed so abruptly?

She is still sending requests: *Do try to end matters with the Turks soon; warn them that if they do not accept our terms now, we shall be quite free to make our conditions even more onerous. Remind them that one works with what is, not what might be.*

Calculations consume her thoughts. Thrilling calculations that come after battles. Dispatches flying back and forth. Hints gleaned from deciphered letters, threats exchanged, old alliances flaunted and new ones sought. A political brawl they both relish, which will — so soon — deliver another glorious victory. The Turks might be reluctant to admit defeat, but the stark truth always trumps the illusions of grandeur.

I don't have strength, *matushka.* I am

extremely ill. I am worn out, as God is my witness.

She is in Tsarskoye Selo when she reads these words. With Le Noiraud, who is absorbed in a new telescope, training it at distant figures in the gardens below. Exclaiming his delight at spotting Alexandrine skipping while her governess, Miss Williams, was stifling a yawn.

"Your granddaughter is a beauty already, Katinka. Look how she lifts her skirts!"

She folds the letter, and unfolds it again, as if Potemkin's troubling words could vanish. It is September. Her gardeners are in the midst of planting shrubs and preparing new beds. The newest seed register includes new varieties of asters, phlox, mallows, and chrysanthemums.

She sits down at her escritoire right away and pens a letter urging caution: *Take your medicine, Grishenka. Rest. Stop eating so much. Let me know how you feel. Tell your doctors to write a report for me.*

It calms her, somewhat, to write these words. If she were with him, she would send all his women away, lower the blinds, and insist on a lot of sleep. But Potemkin's women are a vain, selfish lot. All they care about is their own pleasure.

It isn't jealousy that dictates these thoughts. It is instinct. The gift of always knowing what others truly want, of not being fooled by ap-

276

pearances. Of foreseeing dangers during the times of calm.

The letter that comes next contains reports on negotiations. They are going well, though Potemkin cannot give her details. He doesn't trust the codes or the messengers. Turkish spies are everywhere. Catherine will have to trust his judgment, let him make decisions. He is her most loyal and most grateful subject.

I am better, he also writes. *The danger has passed, but I remain very weak.*

If another bout comes, I shall not have the strength to endure it.

He is better, she thinks with relief. *There will be no other bout.*

"The Prince is working too hard," she tells Le Noiraud, who — she notes with satisfaction — has written his own letter to Potemkin. Not the most graceful or heartfelt, but straightforward. *We are all awaiting news of Your Highness's speedy recovery.*

For an instant, a smile plays on Le Noiraud's lips, but it dies as quickly as it is conceived. Now her lover's forehead is creased with concern. Not just for the Prince, he says, but for her. Hasn't she been ailing lately? The sore throat, the cough, the return of the colic, the swelling feet? She, too, is working too hard, forgetting her own comfort.

Forgetting that he is waiting for her company every night.

His eyes, soft with love, hold a tinge of unease. They have not lain together in weeks. Not for the lack of his eagerness. Or trips to the rooms she had furnished for moments like these. But images of lusty nymphs cavorting with satyrs, or wine corks in the shape of bare buttocks, evoke a mere tingle where once fire raged.

"Yes," she admits, perhaps too quickly. "I forget to think of myself. It is kind of you to worry."

Le Noiraud waves his hand. He wishes no praise. It is merely his concern for her wellbeing that prompts his words.

The child, she thinks of him. *The child may be awkward, selfish at times, but he cares for me.*

The dispatches from the south grow shorter. One contains a list of ailments: fever, headache, paroxysms that refuse to go away. But then another assures her that sweating has brought relief. And in the letter after that, Potemkin worries that the oared fleet is late and the river might freeze before it arrives. Isn't that a sign that he is getting his strength back?

She sends him a silk dressing gown. Green, with golden trim, embroidered with peacocks, to remind him of his gifts for her. Urges him

278

to leave matters of state alone for a while. Her thoughts are waging their own battle of hope against fear: Aren't many soldiers falling ill there, in the camps, but they are not dying? Isn't he strong? He is only fifty-two.

But why is he not writing himself? Why is Popov, his servant, taking down his words? Why is Potemkin's signature barely legible?

Beloved *matushka,* not seeing you makes it even harder for me to live.

Matushka, oh, how sick I am. I have no more strength to endure my torments. I don't know what's become of me.

My only salvation is to leave.

Later, in Tsarskoye Selo, Sashenka Branicka gives her the account of his final hours.

"My *voslublennyi* uncle," she sobs, "ordered his Cossacks to take him away from Jassy to his beloved Nikolaev. 'Will you come with me?' he asked, and I promised I would never leave him. And he smiled when I said this . . . He couldn't walk on his own, so Popov carried him down to the carriage. The fog was so dense when we departed that we couldn't see much . . . When we stopped for the night, I was still hopeful. The doctors observed that his color had improved. That his pulse was still strong."

The girl's beauty is still fresh in spite of her thirty-seven years and four children. To think that once she thought her provincial.

The two women have locked themselves in the silver salon, with its mirrored balcony doors reflecting their black-clad figures. Catherine's bulky and short, Sashenka's slim and graceful.

It is the end of October; darkness comes early.

"I sat by his bedside until dawn," his niece continues. "He was troubled by much coughing. He couldn't sleep at all. He'd doze off for a few moments, then wake up. As if someone was chasing him. But in the morning, he seemed better."

How can it hurt so much? To hear of his last hours?

"We left for Nikolaev in much haste, but we were not fast enough. He knew the end was coming. 'Popov,' he ordered. 'Stop the carriage. I don't want to die inside this cage.' He insisted he wanted to lie down on the grass, so his Cossacks spread a carpet on the ground. Popov carried him out of the carriage. He was still wearing his new green dressing gown. And he was holding Your Majesty's letters in his hand. He couldn't read them anymore, but he kissed every one of them. And then he just . . . stopped breathing."

Once Potemkin had written her that only

death would end his service to his Empress and Russia. He kept his word.

She places her hand on Sashenka's cheek, tucks the loose strand of hair behind her ears. Grishenka's favorite niece begs to be excused for her disheveled state, wonders how she can go on living. She refuses to meet with anyone at court. Her carriage is waiting in the courtyard. All she wants now is to go back to Belaya Tserkov, her Ukrainian estate, where she can cherish her uncle's memory undisturbed.

"Is Branicka gone, Katinka? Already?" Le Noiraud asks when their paths cross later that day. His gaze slips from her reddened eyes to her hands clasping and unclasping, her fingernails, bitten to the quick.

She is still hoping he won't say it. Hold the reins of his jealousy, let her go on with her mourning.

But Le Noiraud's shapely lips are already moving. His tongue moistens them in preparation for the venom that she will try and fail to ignore.

"I hear Branicka has taken the coffer with all his jewels. 'It's my share,' she said. 'My uncle wanted me to have them.' But if this were so, why couldn't she wait until the coffer was opened in your presence, Katinka? Why wouldn't she trust you to honor his will?"

She stares at Platon's handsome face. There is something in him that she cannot explain, this determination to continue, even if everything about her warns him not to.

"All I want to do," he says, blinking, "is to guard your interests, Katinka. Be of use to you. You are too forgiving."

She refuses to dwell on the shortcomings of a boy who doesn't yet know how to be a man. But when her ministers ask whom to send to Jassy to take over Potemkin's duties, she doesn't hesitate. "Bezborodko," she says.

■ ■ ■ ■

PART III
NOVEMBER 5, 1796

■ ■ ■ ■

9:40 A.M.

Hands — strong, capable hands — try to lift her from the floor, but her body has become unmovable. She has grown. Become like the ancient boulder from Karelia she chose for her statue of Peter the Great. Massive, solid, covered with ancient moss.

They told her a boulder like this cannot be moved. Let alone hauled through miles of forests and marshes. Too heavy, too big, they said. It will drown in the sea. In the Neva.

They were wrong.

They were wrong about many things.

"We cannot call anyone else. No one else must know. All together, now —"

"Careful!"

"Adrian Moseyevich, you are pulling too hard. It is not helping. We have to do it all together."

"Put the mattress on the floor. Right now! What are you waiting for?"

285

"On the floor, I said, by the bed!"

"Here?"

"No, more to the left! Away from the drafts."

Thoughts like careless children scatter away, playing blindman's buff. There is relief in being lifted from the floor, carried to her own bedroom.

She is heavy.

She can hear heaving breaths, grunts, words of caution. "Not like this . . . turn around . . . lower . . . through the door . . . watch for the dress . . . don't trip."

"For God's sake. Pull her skirts down!"

"Wipe the blood."

"No one can come in. Not without my permission. If anyone asks, say the Empress needs to rest."

"May God have mercy on us all!"

"What shall become of us now?"

"There is no blood . . . No injury."

"Has Majesty hit her head?"

"Fainted, perhaps?"

"Wipe it, fast!"

In frozen faces, eyes fill with fear. Someone is gasping for air. What are they all thinking? Are they mourning her death already? "I thought at first a thief had broken in," Queenie informs someone with pressing insistence. "The papers were scattered everywhere, the cup was lying on the floor, broken, the clock was knocked off the mantel."

A hand is pressing a mirror to her lips.
Too hard.
Her heart lurches forward, stumbles, pounds. A maddened fly buzzes about her ear, insistent, vile, set on its business. How do maggots breed?
Vishka says with serene joy: "Her Majesty is alive. Her face is warm."
Queenie insists: "Let Her Majesty breathe. Do not crowd her. Step back." In her voice a warning. Not a word shall leave this room. A temporary weakness can be explained. A fall. A slip on the floor. Her Majesty is not as steady on her feet as she used to be.
They do step back, away from her bed. Feet shuffle. Gasps recede. Catherine closes her eyes.
Before thoughts begin to make sense again, one smothers her with terror. What if she lost her mind? Became raving mad? Like Grigory Orlov, not knowing who he was in the end. Staring ahead without seeing, saliva dripping down his chin.
But the fear does not stay. Her thoughts are lucid enough. It is just her body that has taken leave of her will.

9:45 A.M.
Someone must have opened the window. The

287

air that sneaks inside is cold and fragrant with wood smoke.

Everyone is bending over her. Zotov is placing a screen beside the mattress, propping it with chairs.

Why have you put me on the floor? she wants to ask, but can't. Other questions crowd in her head. The papers on her desk are important. The latest version of the partition treaty she hasn't yet finished annotating. A letter to the Swedish King she has drafted and wanted Bezborodko to comment on before she works on it some more. Papers that should be hidden from prying eyes. Will Gribovsky know not to archive them? To lock them in her desk drawer and keep the key?

A clock chimes. One soft chime means a quarter of an hour has passed.

"There is always hope." Rogerson answers someone's question. "Greater when the constitution is strong, when there is the will to recover."

How did she miss the moment of her doctor's arrival? His hands are clammy; his short-cropped hair is wet with melting snow. Bending over her, he says something about slippery roads, people falling over on sidewalks, his sleigh having trouble passing by the Admiralty.

That's where the feral dogs gather, she thinks. Without masters, the beasts keep their own counsel. Stake their boundaries, fight with those who try to invade their territory. Spend their days scavenging or hunting. Lick their wounds. Mate. Raise puppies.

She has refused all requests to have them rounded up and shot.

"Apoplexy." Rogerson's crooked teeth are blackened by tobacco. "Blood has risen into Her Majesty's head. Its force has burst some vein open. Give me my bag . . . lancet . . . sharpie . . ."

Vishka, who only a moment before rejoiced that her mistress was alive, is now standing motionless beside the screen, blocking the light. Queenie is not moving, either. But somehow a bag appears in Rogerson's hands, the lock snaps open.

"Quick!" The sharp edge of a lancet is gleaming in his hand. "Hold the arm . . . press harder."

He doesn't say anything more, but he has cut her veins so many times that Catherine could say it for him: *Blood thickens. Bloodletting will take the pressure off. Humors have to be balanced.*

"Should we send for Count Bezborodko?" Zotov asks. "Or will Her Majesty come 'round soon?"

"Yes," Rogerson says. "I mean, I cannot tell."

There is uneasiness in his voice; she hears it. But Rogerson has always been a man of little faith.

That Queenie is sobbing she can understand. But Vishka?

Her headache has diminished already. It
will soon go away completely. She will make
it go away. Pain has afflicted her before. She
thinks of horses who follow their trainer's
every move. A step behind, always behind,
always attuned to the smallest change of direction.

Her doctor mutters: "I'll try everything in
my powers. The rest is in God's hands."

Poor Rogerson, who cannot even heal a flea
bite, announcing his incompetence. Why has
she tolerated him for so long?

The law forbids anyone to speak of the
Empress's death, or even to think of it. But a
thought cannot be stopped.

Who in this room is mourning her already?
Who is rejoicing? And why?

A hard iron ring is pressing on her forehead.
Like the metal band that holds the barrel
together. Sleep beckons, but she refuses to
yield.

9:48 A.M.
Her lips are parched with thirst. Her servants
are talking among themselves, as if she were
not there, a black crow fallen down a soot-
smeared chimney. "Her Majesty this . . . Her
Majesty that . . . too much work . . . too little
rest . . . that terrible, terrible shock . . . He
should be proud of himself now . . . the

290

scoundrel . . ."

Why is no one giving her water to drink? What is more important for them than their Queen's comfort?

The furs with which she is covered give off a whiff of bergamot and jasmine. Dead animals give up their warmth willingly. Generous of what is — to them — no longer of use.

Oh, the hunt, pinning down her prey. The pursuit that brings the true thrill. The possibilities of evasion that needed to be foreseen and thwarted. Unexpected turns. A frozen moment of fright that could — if withstood — save a partridge from the hunter's eye. Though not from the keen noses of hounds.

I didn't think you of all women would change, Sophie.

Stanislav, loving and beloved. Once. Long time ago. Why should she care? What in nature remains as it always was?

Are you the same man you once were?

9:50 A.M.

Two flintlock pistols. She used to keep them at hand, cleaned after each shot. Ivory-stocked, with her initials on the handle. What happened to them?

There is so much babbling, muttering, moaning around her. The palace is in flux. Ripples go through all the rooms, corridors. She feels them, as a queen bee must feel the

291

movements of all her workers and soldiers and builders.

When Father died, Elizabeth forbade her to wear mourning for a man who was not king. Mother died in Paris. Alone. In poverty, harassed by debtors. Her last letters were so dull, as if written by a schoolgirl with nothing to say. *The day is fair . . . less rain than last year . . . but more than the year before.*

A throne is a lonely place. Friendship flees from monarchs. Catherine has been warned about that. Varvara's last letter came from Warsaw. *To the hands of the Empress only.* To the Empress — this should be added — who planned to do so much for her old friend and her daughter. Saw them at her side, in splendor. Made the mistake of imagining their joy, or — why deny it — their gratitude.

I wish to begin with a small borrowing from Monsieur Voltaire, knowing how highly Your Majesty holds him in her esteem. I've reached the time in my life when I long for a simple life. Like the old man at the end of *Candide,* I wish to cultivate my garden.

The Voltairian plague, Catherine thinks, is spreading like black fungus on her roses. Can't those who wish to desert her think of other excuses? Admit to selfishness, perhaps? Or even plain fear that they are not good enough? Why claim that happiness is found only among carrots and cabbages?

I beg Your Majesty to free me from the Imperial Service. My daughter and I will cherish the memories of our Russia until we die.

Don't speak ill of the dead, they say.

Elizabeth's deathbed swam with blood. Screams silenced prayers. Thrashing hands were blind. Even a Holy Icon was not safe. "I've waited for this day for so long," Catherine thought then. Recalling her injuries and humiliations.

Her empty belly. Her stolen son.

The spying on her person, the poking and sniffing about her body, the curses, the slaps, the jeering mockery of the imperial questions: *So you have already made your plans, Catherine? You think you have outwitted me?*

You are a hypocrite, Catherine. A dissembler. A thief and a usurper.

You've sworn on the Holy Icon to make your son a Tsar. It's Paul's crown you are wearing on your head.

He knows that! He has always known!

A dying woman's voice fades and falters. Death takes away everything. The living have the last word.

10:00 A.M.

Her hands stretch across the mattress. Her legs are spread wide, and no tightening of muscles will bring them back. Her lips are still parched. Why can't they see it?

"Still too much blood in the brain," Rogerson explains to someone whose figure melts into the shadows.

The brain, the body. Scaling skin, muscles probed with cold, sweaty fingers. The body that has betrayed her. Risen against her and refuses to obey. Not the first time.

"Open the window!"

"Don't. The draft will make Her Majesty worse."

"Her Majesty is blinking."

"Her Majesty cannot hear you."

"Her Majesty's eyes are moving."

She can hear. In the distance, the dog whines and someone shoos it away. And even with eyes half opened she can see their useless gestures, feel their petrifying fear.

Vishka, who is squatting beside the mattress, whispers: "I've tried to fetch Platon Alexandrovich. But when I told him Your Majesty has taken ill, he just covered his head in his arms and mumbled something I couldn't understand."

In Vishka's voice derision is mixed up with compassion. She never liked the Imperial Favorite much, but she doesn't wish his downfall.

You've taken care of me for so long, Vishka. And — unlike so many others — you've never left me.

"Platon Alexandrovich thinks it's all his fault!"

There is no puzzle in this. Platon has angered her. No wonder he is afraid. Catherine hasn't forgiven him yet.

Will she?

Perhaps.

When she is ready.

Not yet.

Vishka stops talking and moves aside. Is Rogerson back with his cures? Always the same. *Chew some rhubarb, madame, have a gentle vomit.*

10:05 A.M.

There is tingling against the soles of her feet. Ticklish — playful, almost. But then the skin begins to heat up and chafe. Blisters must be forming on her skin.

What is Rogerson doing to her?

Hasn't he hurt her enough already?

Her eyes are opened just a slit. If she opened them wider, would she see what the doctor was up to? But her eyelids are made of lead. The inside of her mouth tastes like tarnished brass. In her ears she hears the peal of tiny silver bells. There is a cold, wet spot underneath her. Has she relieved herself without knowing? When?

The sharp welt of pain on her arm means that another vein is opened. Blood barely seeps out, dark and thick, Rogerson announces. His tone is brisk. Almost a bark of impatience.

"Is it very bad?" someone wants to know. "Will this bleeding help?"

"There is no way of telling," the doctor replies, and she hears the dull thump of something falling on the carpeted floor.

Her court women and her doctor. Well-meaning but, in the end, useless. She should've known not to expect too much from them.

"Your Majesty! Can you hear me?"

Is that Bezborodko's voice? Her capable minister, a man who knows her thoughts and her will. Bezborodko will calm their feverish minds. Bezborodko will fetch her grandson. He will know there is no time to waste.

A thought pierces her. If she had to escape from this room, it would not be possible. Fire would consume her. A collapsed beam would bury her. A pillow pressed hard would suffocate her. A dagger would slide under her rib and out again.

Count Bezborodko is kneeling beside her mattress, his face gray with unease. His eyes are taxing her, assessing what is still possible, what can be preserved and what has to go.

They don't miss much, the sharp eyes of this fox.

Get Alexander here, she tries to say. *He has to know I have fallen. Give him no choice. If he isn't pressed, he will start thinking too much, weighing sentiments against duty. The young grow wiser when it is too late.*

"Can Your Majesty see me? Give me a sign?"

I'm looking at you! You know what to do. Isn't it enough?

Bezborodko is frowning. His hand slides over the contours of his beard. Does he doubt her grandson will obey her will? Forget his duty?

Fetch Alexander. Now. Tell him. Everything.

She imagines her grandson bent with pain at the thought of what has happened to her. But this is not the time for pain. This is the time for action. Sometimes one must go through the motions and think later.

It's like fighting the Hydra. One slain head sprouts two others. One has to burn the stumps with fire, faster than they grow back. And bury the immortal one, the one that cannot be destroyed, under a giant rock and hope it won't ever escape.

I've done that, Catherine thinks.

"Has Her Majesty said anything? Has Her Majesty called me? Opened her eyes?"

The face of the young man bending over her is exquisitely gracious. The curved dome of the forehead is alabaster white. Black eyebrows frame almond-shaped eyes.

The man clasps her hand like a child frightened by the dark.

"Katinka," he sobs in her ear. "Please forgive me."

Forgive you for what?

Her body remembers him. Her nipples, her loins recall his slow, languid kisses. The touch of his silky skin, his warm tongue used to bring tremors of pleasure.

Long time ago.

His name is Platon.

I know you, Catherine thinks. *I know your name.*

Fear oozes out of Platon's black eyes, pours off his white skin. His hands cling to hers. His fingers are cold. Hard. *Bony,* she thinks. *Does he not eat enough?*

Somewhere in his cave Endymion sleeps, the beautiful lover of Selene, the goddess of the moon. He sleeps so that he won't ever have to grow old.

For a moment, she sees a throng of faces surrounding them. None are familiar.

There are whispers, too. A torrent of them.

She is old and you are young, they torment.

298

She is ugly and you are beautiful. She is power-ful and you are nothing. Her toy, her amuse-ment, her distraction. Now that she is leaving, you, too, will be gone. But unlike her, you will pay for our disappointment, for our fawning over you. For everything we had to suffer in your presence, for all the praises you drank from our lips. We have betrayed ourselves for you, and now you will pay for our humiliation.

"What will become of me, Katinka?" her moon lover whispers. "If you leave me, Paul will have me killed."

Hands smooth her hair, wipe her lips. Hands drag Platon away from her bed. His wailing protests seep inside her hurting body. Travel down her veins into her heart, into her liver, her spleen.

Her muscles tighten.

There is a slight tingling in her limbs. Her heart thumps. For a moment it seems pos-sible that she can lift herself out of bed. She spies a tree with a broken branch, bleeding sap. She reaches toward it with her hand. *Push, Your Highness,* she hears a woman's voice. *Push again, slowly this time. Listen to me. You have to do what I tell you. Now!*

"Her Majesty is trying to say something. Can't you see? Her Majesty's lips are mov-ing. She's looking at me."

10:15 A.M.

The glow of light coming from the window means that it is morning. The room seems odd only because she is lying on the floor. Her big, canopied bed is right behind her. She is in St. Petersburg, in the Winter Palace.

I should be working now. Why am I not in my study?

Something has struck her down. An assassin's blow? Did someone dare after all? Who? That French revolutionary Bezborodko warned her about? Some deluded Pole bent on revenge? Or a Turk or Cossack?

Success breeds enemies. Weeds out false friends.

Does friendship flee from Sovereigns or do Sovereigns flee from friendship?

10:25 A.M.

A howl pushes itself into her thoughts. It is coming from outside. Someone behind the door is desperately pleading to be let in.

Alexander?

"Who was Hector's mother?" she remembers asking him once. "What song did the sirens sing? Which gods aid Hercules?"

Her grandson rattles off his answers with assurance. "And now, Monsieur Alexander," she says, "repeat the same line with more authority. The insipid softness of a gentle fool doesn't suit you."

10:30 A.M.

Hands at her armpits are pulling her up to let her lie more comfortably. The pillows under her head are soft, filled with goose down. Her head sinks into them with gratitude.

The new position feels cool, like fresh *banya* water Potemkin poured over her hot, sweating body. But her tongue feels swollen, encrusted with bitter, leaden taste. Rogerson is poking at her ribs, feeling for her pulse. His gestures feel flicking and nervous. Is he worried by her thumping heart?

She should be paying heed to what is happening, but something shimmering catches her eye. She tightens the muscles on her face and her eyelids lift just a crack, enough to discern a small mirror Rogerson is holding in front of her face. Stones in the frame reflect a cascade of dazzling lights, a chain flashes gold. The face in the mirror is swollen and red.

Is this me?

Mouth open, saliva dripping down my chin?

This is all Rogerson's doing. She never trusted doctors. She was right.

301

A stupid old man.

Murderer.

Fool.

Whose side are you on? Mine or my son's, who wants me in my grave. Who wants old women clad in black to weep and wail for me.

"Look. There! Look at the mirror! Her Majesty is breathing again."

12:00 P.M.

The cannons blast at the Fortress of Peter and Paul. This is where Elizabeth lies buried. And Peter the Great.

The windows shake, panes rattle. Crows scatter into the sky, shrieking their loud protests. If they are so wise, why do they mind what always comes?

Count Bezborodko is issuing orders. No one to leave the palace. No one to come in. No one to leave the city, no messengers, dispatches. All visitors to the palace are to be told the Empress is busy with political matters that cannot be postponed. They are to wait for summons. In silence.

He is not Potemkin, but he will do. Most equal to business at hand. A purse of silver is sometimes better than ingots of gold — ready cash to riches that cannot be used. Fortune needs to be nudged along. When her speech comes back, she will have a perfect gift for her minister. A compass ring set with diamonds. With an inscription: *In recognition of the fact that you always remember the direction of your journey.*

"Let me in. What is happening?"

Could it be Alexander? Outside the door? But why this pleading voice? A Tsar doesn't plead, Alexander. A Tsar walks in where he wants to be. Who would dare stop him?

"Her Majesty is resting now, Your Highness. She cannot be disturbed."

12:10 P.M.

Grishenka, she whispers, and Potemkin comes back before her, older than she remembers him and ravaged. There are broken veins on the skin of his nose and under his puffed eyes. A frizz of red hair hangs over his forehead.

"What are you doing, Katinka?" he screams.

She doesn't understand why Grishenka is so upset. Why he forces her to sit down in an armchair, why he hollers for her maid.

Kneeling, he takes her swollen foot in his hand. Her toenails have grown so thick and full of unsightly ridges that it takes special pliers to trim them, but Grishenka pays no attention to them. He has lifted her right foot up and wipes it with a handkerchief.

The handkerchief is stained with blood.

"Have you not felt anything, Katinka?" he asks.

She shakes her head.

"How is that possible?"

She doesn't know what he is talking about until he shows her a shard of glass he has extracted from the sole of her foot. The night before, she knocked a carafe off a side table. The evening maid swept the floor but missed a piece of glass.

"I didn't see it," she says.

In Grishenka's good eye, she sees fear. Not because she hadn't noticed a piece of glass lying on a carpet, but because she stepped right on it, and did not feel it lodge in her foot.

Because she kept on walking.

3:00 P.M.

The dream she has fallen into is sticky, broken into shreds. It makes no sense, yields no order. A well, filled with water, a kangaroo boxing with its small front paws, a bird pecking at the windowpane, infuriated by some phantom reflection that refuses to yield.

The well, rimmed with stones, is covered with soft, dense moss. There is a fable about a well and frogs, a fable her grandchildren could never resist. Two frogs whose marsh homes have dried out are considering jumping down a well. "Wait," the wiser one says. "Suppose this one dries out like the marsh. How would we get out?"

■ ■ ■ ■

She comes around to Constantine's jarring voice. "We've been on a sleigh ride. With Alexander. The footman told us to hurry back. Wouldn't tell us why. Just hurry, he said. And then they wouldn't let us in."

Her younger grandson demands the account of the morning. Gribovsky obliges with the story of the door they had to force open, the limp imperial body sprawled by the commode. The six footmen who lifted it from the floor. The laborious procession to the bedroom. The fearful premonitions and predictable protestations: How could we have known? No one else must learn of this.

"Why is the Empress still lying on the floor?" Constantine screams. "Is this how you want my father to find her?"

Paul is on his way?
Where is Alexander?

Constantine's words lash the servants into action. In a flurry that follows, she is lifted up and placed on the bed. It is a better place. Higher. Above her, on the underside of the canopy, there is a portrait of Minerva woven of silk. The goddess reposing, her helmet cocked, the rest of her armor cast aside.

Constantine is wearing his Horse Guard

dress uniform, a white wool tailcoat with red cuffs. In the Winter Palace, the choice of regimental colors is never insignificant. Horse Guards is the imperial regiment, which is enough for her son to hate it. The white tailcoat is a declaration, a pledge of allegiance.

Constantine settles heavily beside her. He fidgets. He struggles for words. Candlelight softens the harsh edges of his face. He wants to summon the seriousness that would carry him through this moment. He will stand by his brother.

She makes another effort to speak — useless, like all the others. She thinks of the winter market. Carcasses of pigs, cows, sheep, oxen standing on stiff, frozen legs. Constantine's eyelashes flutter when he looks down at her, but then he averts his eyes as if her humiliation is an embarrassment he doesn't want to witness.

"Your Highness." The chaplain's voice is reedy. "It is time. May we begin?"

The wind is moaning in the chimney. Constantine nods and stands up. Zotov hands him a glass of water, which he empties in one gulp. He is still frowning, and she feels a rush of pity for her younger grandson. Pity for a child lashed by desires, torn apart by passions he cannot control.

Her head aches. Someone is fumbling with the fireplace, flinging logs into the hearth. Sparks are flying up the chimney; cinders are leaping out of the grate. For a moment the room is brighter, but then it darkens again.

Constantine has loosened the collar of his jacket. His cheeks are flushed. *He must have drunk vodka,* she thinks, *not water.*

I am the living bread . . . If anyone eats of this bread, he will live forever.

The liquid that seeps out of her mouth is very bitter. Breathing is so slow.

The chaplain crosses himself.

O Physician and Helper of them that are suffering, O Redeemer and Savior of them that are in affliction . . . have mercy on her who has grievously sinned, and deliver her, O Christ, from her iniquities, that she may glorify Thy divine power.

Constantine is chewing something nervously. There is a nick on his chin, a line of dry blood. "They are on their way," he says. "All of them. Papa. Maman. My sisters."

He does not mention Alexander.

For a moment Catherine is terrified that something terrible has happened. What if the French assassin chose him for his target? What if Alexander is lying somewhere, his skull cracked open, blood seeping into the soil? Unable to take on what he has promised.

She holds a memory of Constantine, thrashing like the Devil. Trampling the flowers. Her beautiful tulips the gardeners tended with such care. Red and white petals bruised, broken, and Constantine standing amid the debris, tearing the green stems with his teeth. Screaming. "Look at me! Look at *me!*"

A child jealous of the flowers.

She doesn't want to look at him now. Through the gathering darkness she can make out some long, wavy smudges right above him. Is it a trick of the shadows? The wavy lines multiply and thicken. When they finally straighten, they are like bars of an enormous cage.

3:05 P.M.
The line of her life is not broken yet.

A woman of sixty-seven can have an attack of apoplexy and recover. It may leave scars, but she will learn to live with them. If she cannot walk, she will be wheeled. If she cannot speak, she will write.

I still have time, Catherine thinks. *I'll hear thunder; I'll see lightning.*

Hail may flatten the tulips in the garden, but a rainbow will still appear.

Pain will go away, or I'll live with it.

Through the veil of her eyelashes she sees the mirror again, pressed against her lips. In it a wrinkled face, lips twisted in a rigid grimace, slowly disappears behind a moist, foggy film.

This is my breath, she thinks. *I'm alive.*

3:40 P.M.

Le Noiraud hunches his shoulders, lets out his breath. Gingerly, as if she were a porcelain doll, he touches her arm, the one that lies on top of the blanket with which Zotov has covered her. The skin on his knuckles is reddish, frozen once in a winter long gone, unable to return to the pale waxy whiteness that is his pride.

Tears flow down her lover's rouged cheeks. He wipes them with the back of his hand. Then he wipes it on the lapel of his jacket. Ivory white, now stained with rouge.

I gave you this jacket.

Her nostrils discern the smell of burnt paper. Tin flecks of ash have stuck to his hair, his sideburns.

What have you burnt? Your accounts, ledgers, lists of the gifts I've given you? My words? My orders?

There is a stir at the door, a shuffle; an angry voice insists on something.

Le Noiraud's hands are trembling. His eyes dart to the door and back to her.

Fear doesn't become him.

"You are not dying, Katinka," he mutters. "They are all wrong."

The memory that comes is of an afternoon in Tsarskoye Selo, right after the lover's hour.

The Gallery is bathed in dappled sunlight. The black iron chairs are set in a circle; the hot fragrant tea is sweetened with Astrakhan honey, the same the cook has poured on cucumber slices. Platon is sitting beside her, resplendent in his silver-trimmed ensemble, a hint of black stubble on his chin.

Mulling over the memories of her pleasure?

Paul and Maria Fyodorovna have just joined them. On their scrubbed faces she can read the resolution to be agreeable, not to give the slightest offense. Paul declares the most recent renovations a vast improvement. "Less glitter, more elegance," he says approvingly, seeing Elizabeth's gilding gone, replaced by discreet Wedgwood braids. So much for the loyalty of a snatched child. The living Empress trumps the dead one.

Her daughter-in-law dutifully admires the statues in the Gallery. Demosthenes and Cicero, so thoughtful and beautifully serene, she exclaims. "No wonder the boys love playing here so much. I just hope they don't cause any damage."

The princes of the realm are not truant boys. They are never unsupervised. Ever since they were born, she, their grandmother, made sure of that. No matter how hard it is for her daughter-in-law to accept it, important lessons are best learned through play.

She won't say it, though. No need to spoil a pleasant afternoon.

The conversation moves on to a painting she has just bought. A bunch of tulips arranged in a crystal vase, their white petals streaked with yellow and pink. One of the petals has fallen off already onto the lace-trimmed tablecloth. A dewdrop glitters on it. A *vanitas* painting, the dealer called it, portraying the transience of life. In the background, on the same tablecloth, one can discern the shapes of an hourglass and a crumbled piece of bread.

Le Noiraud shifts in his chair. There is a twinkle in his eyes, a promise of mischief to liven up what he considers a boring moment. From his chest pocket he extracts Holberg's *Moral Thoughts*. He has taken to opening the book seemingly at random, though Catherine knows he has marked the passages with pieces of ribbon, for different occasions. Red for a warning on some human frailty. Yellow for a clever and cynical twist. Green for a hopeful turn of thought.

You are happy if you imagine yourself happy, he reads aloud.

"Is that what you do?" she asks, smacking him playfully with her fan. "Just imagine yourself happy?"

Philosophy and wit may not be Le Noiraud's strong suits, but he will manage. He will extricate himself with his usual charm. Some flowery declaration will make her laugh.

She can already see a twinkle in her lover's eye.

But this is not what happens next, on that dappled afternoon, with the busts of ancient sages looking at them with their marble eyes.

Paul, her pug-nosed son, is flapping his arms, a big marsh bird gathering his strength. "I fully agree with Platon Alexandrovich!" he declares.

Le Noiraud leans back in his chair. His long legs stretch forward, his hands fold behind his neck. "Have I said something stupid?" he asks.

Is this what Le Noiraud remembers now? Is this what is sending shots of terror down his spine?

4:05 P.M.
The screen has been moved closer. It now stretches at the foot of the bed, blocking the curious glances of those who pass by. Someone has thought of her comfort. *Alexander,* she thinks. He must have ordered the screen. Her gratitude is so profound that it chokes her. In small gestures like this lies true greatness.

Her valiant knight, her warrior, her heir.

From behind the screen comes Count Bezborodko's wheedling voice; the Vice-Chancellor is placating someone. "Your Highness," she hears, "my profound and unwavering devotion."

Alexander — for it surely must be her grandson's figure looming in the misty blur — is wearing Preobrazhensky greens with red facings. The uniform she herself wore on the day of the coup.

Alexander, her true child, her prince, looks stricken.

I'm afraid, his face says.

Fear has to be conquered, Alexander, locked deep inside. Away from the face.
Fear melts the will.

4:08 P.M.
"Is the Empress in much pain, doctor?" Alexander asks. He is no longer sitting beside her. This is why his voice comes to her muted.

"I cannot tell, Your Highness," Rogerson answers. He opens his hands like a child showing he has washed them well.

"Can we still hope?"

"There is always hope, Your Highness, for there is no end to God's mercy," the doctor says.

Why is Rogerson not looking at her? Why is he talking as if she were no longer here? As if life was a secret from which she has been excluded? *Durak,* she thinks. *A fool.* To him she is already a vessel filled with bile, blood, humors, secretions. Of rot, of excrement, of sour vomit.

313

This, too, has happened before.

That night when she gave birth. A womb, not a woman.

The past is threatening to snag her again, suck her into its darkness. Beside her, on the side table, there is a small mirror in a silver frame, one of the few things from Zerbst she managed to keep. It was a present from her beloved governess, Babette. Babette, who had cried so bitterly that winter when the news came of the approaching journey. "To Berlin" was all she was allowed to tell her. Russia was still a secret, her fate there unknown. "But you cannot come with me. I'll write to you, I promise. Tell you everything I see and hear."

The look in Babette's eyes is what she recalls. The hurt, the pain, the disappointment all rolled into one.

"I'll be back in a few weeks."

All lies.

All necessary.

Is this how friendships break? With one look? Or in silence?

Queenie is dipping a cloth in a basin and wiping her lips.

The cloth is not wrung properly; drops of water roll down her neck, onto her shoulder, and sink into the mattress. The sensation is not unpleasant.

Poor dear Queenie. Fidgeting. Unable to

be still, her gaze bewildered.

How have our lives become so tangled?

She remembers Queenie's arrival at court, the days long gone when she was still merely Anna Stepanovna Protasova, the Orlovs' ugly cousin, an old maid of thirty-four. There has been some awkwardness of introductions, some misgivings about having the Orlovs' spy about her person, but they have all melted in time.

Queenie's fingers plump the pillows, adjust the folds of the blanket. Strong, warm fingers of a loving soul. Delicate. Soothing.

Touching her.

Somewhere, far away, a dog howls in pain, filling her with sorrow so heavy her chest feels crushed. As if there were no boundary between her body and that pain.

4:10 P.M.

A lanky man with a pug nose approaches the foot of her bed.

He is my son. His name is Paul. I don't like him.

Her son has installed himself in a small room off the Imperial Bedroom, where she used to keep her most beloved books. The room has no other door, and everyone who goes in or out has to pass by her bed. The servants hurry with furniture: the writing table, the armchairs, the daybed.

Pages in bright red livery hover by the door, ready to run errands and carry messages. Their gazes slide away from her bed. Have they abandoned her already? Or are they still placing bets on the shape the future might take?

Paul, his face stiff like a mask, turns to his wife, who is sobbing loudly. "The Empress of Russia is dying! May God Almighty guide us in our time of trouble!"

4:15 P.M.

A rustle of a skirt, a flash of white lace. A hand places blossoms on her pillow. A cloud of white blooms.

"Can you hear me, Graman? It's me, Alexandrine. Please, Graman, look at me."

A fresh and simple smell, sweet almond mixed with rose petals.

The child bends and kisses her hand, which is not at all required. Then she places another kiss, this time on her cheek. A delicate, warm caress, a brush of a butterfly wing.

Her granddaughter is wearing an unbecoming gown of stiff brown taffeta. Her hair is pulled away from her face, tied in the back.

There is a memory in which Alexandrine, still a baby, stumbles away from her nurse's arms straight into the Tsarskoye Selo pond, trips, and falls. By the time the nurse lifts her up, the child's face has become livid, spat-

316

tered with mud. The stem of a water lily clings to her granddaughter's cheek. For a terrifying moment, she thinks the girl is dead. But then, Alexandrine gasps and begins to scream.

Her granddaughter is alive. Merely frightened by what she cannot, yet, comprehend.

4:20 P.M.
"I won't let you go, Katinka.
Wake up! Remember what happened before the fall!
Think!"

Last night was filled with merriment. Catherine wore her necklace of thirty black pearls. She wanted Count Cobenzl, the Austrian Ambassador, to see them. Alexandrine was there, too. Twiddling the hem of her sleeve in her slim white fingers, one slightly stained with ink.

They all watched a French comedy at the Hermitage Theater. About scheming servants and bumbling lovers reunited at the end. "On this earth," the Empress told her actors when they approached and bowed to her, "night descends over each life. But in my theater, the sun always returns and shines upon our days."

Is this when Alexandrine hunched her thin shoulders and burst into sobs?

"We are the children of Providence," Potemkin whispers. "All will be well. There is still time. This is not the end. Didn't I tell you, Katinka?"

"You did."

"So you believe me now."

"Yes."

And she knows he is right, for her muscles move. Her fingers close on something soft and warm.

They all rush to her bed. Alexander, Rogerson, Constantine, Zotov. They trip over themselves, in a rush to see what makes Queenie scream with such joy, such abandon.

"God have mercy!" Catherine hears. "*Gospody pomyluy!* Her Majesty has just pressed my hand!"

Think harder. Concentrate.

The biggest whore in Europe, they call her. Wanton. Full of filth. The Empress of Russia holding her skirts up, spreading her legs from Constantinople to Warsaw, sucking in whole armies.

Insatiable.

The English draw her seated on the throne decorated with two-headed eagles, wrapped in ermine-trimmed robes. Having gorged on the Ottoman Porte, she is spitting out

318

crescent-shaped scraps from her toothless mouth. The French depict her tearing Poland off the map of Europe with her bloodied fangs. Or holding out an empty cup to be filled with the semen milked from defeated men.

If they do it, it is virtue. If I do it, it's a sin.

They are ambitious. She is hungry for glory.
They are skillful. She is crafty.
They inspire others to great efforts. She is letting others do the work and seizing the credit.
They are valiant kings, conquerors, heroes. She is the Medusa, the vampire, the harridan. An ugly witch, eager to copulate with the Devil himself.
There is no reasoning with slander. It breeds like vermin. It scurries in shady corners, spoils all it touches. Smuggled in the folds of travelers' coats, between pages of books, in the double bottoms of trunks, it delivers its venom straight to the heart.
Her enemies, her ill-wishers — irked that the upstart Russia they used to dismiss has to be reckoned with or even feared — want her to forget that nations are like merchants, forming and breaking alliances according to the rules of costs and profits.
Empires need to grow or die.

■ ■ ■ ■

But something went terribly wrong, Grishenka. Why? You know why. You remember. Go to the beginning. Think of everything that has happened.

On that August morning, she gets out of bed slowly, for her right leg is swollen and heavy.

Pani, her Italian greyhound, is up, ready to assume her self-imposed duties. A cold, wet nose sniffs at the odors left by the night, examines their wordless exposés.

"Good girl, Pani," she murmurs, patting the dog's head.

The bedroom maids have laid out her simple morning clothes, a loose white satin gown, a crepe bonnet, a pair of soft bearskin slippers. She dresses quickly, anxious not to waste time. Later, Queenie and the maids will have enough time to fuss with her looks. And be more careful. On the back of her head she can still feel the slight burning in the spot where, yesterday, the curling iron came too close to the skin.

The Imperial Study is the adjacent room. Beside a pile of stiff folders tied with ribbons, a pot of steaming coffee is waiting on a silver tray. She walks there slowly, trying not to lean on the bad leg too much, Pani at her side.

The summer of 1796 has been tedious, hot

and humid. In Tsarskoye Selo, the gardeners have despaired over the black spots on the rosebushes. Daily spraying with fermented compost tea has not helped. In bed after rose bed, leaves have yellowed, withered, and died. Here in St. Petersburg, it is the young birch trees in the Summer Garden that do poorly. The roots, the gardeners say, wrap around the trunk, choking off nourishment.

But the summer is almost over. And what is gone should not be dwelled on. The Empire is not run on regrets.

Among the papers on her desk is another in a series of handwriting exercises she has requested. Her eldest granddaughter, Alexandrine, is in dire need of practice. As it is, her hand might do for a truant boy, but not for Russia's Grand Duchess about to get married.

In this sample, unlike in the previous one, the lines are even, though the letters are still too small, too hesitant:

Ashes were already falling, not as yet very thickly. I looked round: a dense black cloud was coming up behind us, spreading over the earth like a flood. "Let us leave the road while we can still see," I said, "or we shall be knocked down and trampled underfoot in the dark by the crowd behind." We had scarcely sat down to rest when darkness fell, not the dark of a moonless or cloudy night, but as if the lamp had been put out in a closed room.

Catherine makes quick notes on the margin for Miss Williams, the imperial governess. More attention should be paid to the choice of fragments Alexandrine copies. Why give the child *The Fall of Pompeii* when a love poem would've been more appropriate?

The clock chimes seven. In the antechamber, her ministers must be gathering already, but Count Alexander Andreyevich Bezborodko, her chief minister, has still not arrived for the morning briefing.

It is not like him to be late.

They go a long way back, Bezborodko and she, companions of many journeys. People like that are becoming rare around her. Death is a cruel gleaner. So is desertion in the name of righteous indignation. So are friendships abandoned for silly reasons. Accusations of betrayal when none was intended.

Pani is chasing her tail. Growling, whirling around, faster and faster, snapping her teeth. What happens in a dog's head at moments like that? Is play merely a rehearsal for a hunt? Or is it the sheer exuberance of joy, the animal life force that propels Pani to exert herself until exhaustion wins?

The word *pani* is Polish. It means madame. Catherine came up with the name as her little revenge on a tedious guest. Harmless, really. In every litter there is a puppy like this. Overly eager to please, longing to be touched and petted, the tiny tongue licking everything within reach. A Polish princess who was staying at the Winter Palace just when the puppy was born was like that, too. Cringing. Always hungry for attention. Always trying to get herself noticed. What a pleasure it was to chastise the puppy in the woman's presence. "Show a little restraint, Pani. Don't pee yourself with excitement at my sight, Pani." Not that the hint was ever taken!

"That's enough, Pani! Lie down!"

Pani freezes in mid-chase and gives her mistress a puzzled look. As if, for a brief moment, she is unsure what was expected of her. But dogs are undisputed masters of the art of pleasing. The tail, abandoned, curls downward, and Pani saunters toward her favorite resting spot. Right beside her mistress's legs.

Palace wisdom holds dogs to be faithful and cats false and sneaky. Cats moan and screech on the roof at night. Or, worse, they wail like abandoned babies. Or like a witch in heat. The maids recall the village stories of witches turning themselves into cats to drink the cows dry, or to stifle a child in its cradle.

Such are ignorance's murky limits, unlit by the sunshine of reason.

She takes one more sip of coffee. Black, for this is still morning, though later she will indulge herself with a smudge of cream. She is aware of a tightness in her chest. It takes her a moment to recognize it for what it is. The grip of tenderness and joy. Soon, the first of her granddaughters will be married.

Her attendants' voices float from the antechamber. Queenie and Vishka are talking about Le Noiraud.

"Alexander the Great slept with a copy of *The Iliad* under his pillow."

"Not everyone is Alexander the Great. Let's agree on that!"

"We want more than we can chew. We want it now."

"Few men know how to become a personage of distinction. Didn't I tell you that before?"

Their exchange is predictable, yet another eruption of petty jealousy, the fare of the inner chambers. Scorn for the Imperial Favorite is the only topic on which Vishka and Queenie fully agree. Vishka trusts no one, so this doesn't come as a surprise. Queenie, who has thus far approved of Platon Zubov, must have now changed her mind. Hence her list of Le Noiraud's most outrageous sins:

He holds a levee like a French king. Arrives in his dressing gown, has everyone stand in silence and watch him being dressed and coiffed, while those who haven't bribed his valets sufficiently crowd outside. He spends too much time at empty chatter with his gossipy sister. He thinks Pygmalion is a great Greek philosopher. He has acquired a field glass and, at the time when he is supposed to be reading, he has it trained on the maids' quarters.

Clever Queenie sweetens venom with laughter. But her stories are all carefully chosen. It's Le Noiraud's family aspirations that Queenie questions now. Platon's sister has just sent back a length of satin, claiming it was too dull and too plain. Others may think it insignificant, but Queenie has a knack for the underside of stories. For hasn't Grand Duchess Elizabeth just bought some of the same swath for Alexander Palace in Tsarskoye Selo? Is it merely a coincidence, Queenie wonders aloud. Or does Prince Zubov's sister desire to outshine someone far more important than she is?

Vishka laughs. It is no news to her that everyone's life, when examined close enough, is utterly and brutally banal.

Everyone's.

The energetic rap on the door sounds like a drumbeat. Pani raises her head and gives her mistress a reassuring look. Actions that are repeated do not merit canine vigilance.

"The Swedes have arrived, Your Majesty," Bezborodko announces, as he rushes in, the buttons of his jacket undone, begging forgiveness for his tardiness. "I waited for the latest reports. I knew Your Majesty would have questions."

There is a hint of jasmine about him, not quite drowned by musk and snuff. "We possess a soft spot for actresses," Queenie, who keeps the tally of all court liaisons, says. "A well-turned ankle drives us insane."

"Catch your breath first, Alexander Andreyevich," Catherine says, smiling. "Sit down. I still haven't finished with my morning work."

Nodding with gratitude, the Count takes his usual seat with flourish, in spite of his bulk. Pearls of sweat glisten under the rim of his wig. He may not have slept at all, judging by the red-rimmed eyes and the sagging skin under them.

Pani greets Alexander Andreyevich with an elaborate dance of wiggles, leaps, and tail wagging that ends only when he lets her rest her front paws on his big, bearlike chest.

"How could I've forgotten my beauty," he murmurs, extracting a piece of blood sausage from a black lacquered box he carries in his pocket. "You can have it, Pani, but only if Her Majesty permits."

"Her Majesty has no objections," she mutters, without lifting her eyes from the report on Jewish religious laws she had requested. Until Russia's borders moved eastward, the Empire had no Jews. Now many thousands have become her subjects.

She can hear Pani devour the treat and sniff for more. "Have some dignity, Pani," the Count scolds. "You'll get what you deserve!"

Before she puts the quill away, she adds one last comment, requesting a full description of *kahal* courts. Gribovsky, her secretary, needs to be reminded that a summary doesn't mean omissions of basic facts.

Bezborodko's portfolio of gold-leaf leather looks imposing, but most likely her minister won't even open it. Like Potemkin, he can quote whole documents after reading them once. He never takes notes, confident that even hours later he'll be able to dictate her directives to his secretary without a single distortion.

Pani, the creature of habit, whimpers again and is promptly rewarded with another piece of blood sausage. The silly dog almost chokes as she greedily devours the treat.

"When did they arrive?"

"Well past midnight, Majesty," Alexander Andreyevich says, taking out a white handkerchief from his breast pocket. He pats his forehead first, before wiping his greasy fingers, one by one, and folding the handkerchief into a neat square. "On account of the aurora borealis, which the Swedish King insisted on admiring for two full hours. Oblivious of what a rare and exquisite Rus-

sian jewel awaits him here. And what hospitality."

Bezborodko, a wise flatterer, uses soft colors
and a delicate pencil. He will not besmear
the picture he wishes to adorn with a coarse
brush and a great deal of whitewash. Like a
skillful doctor, he proportions his doses to
the constitution of his patient. He knows
when hints work best and when to be direct.
Platon should stop sulking at him and take
note.

"The King, Gustav Adolf, his uncle, the
Regent, twenty-three courtiers, and over a
hundred servants," the Count continues.
"They are all at the Swedish mission. The
young King woke up at dawn, read the Bible
for one hour before requesting a simple
breakfast of buttered bread and strong coffee."

"Handsome?" Catherine asks.

"Exceedingly," Bezborodko replies, twisting
his full, red lips into a bemused grin.

"Come, come, Alexander Andreyevich," she
says indulgently. "Out with it. Quickly."

Bezborodko raises his index finger and
declares in a solemn voice: "*The Lord said,
give and it shall be given to you. Weeping may
endure for the night but joy comes in the morning. Destiny is God's will* . . . Such are the
pearls of Swedish wisdom."

His Swedish Majesty, God bless his sweet

youth, claims the privilege of uttering all thoughts that please him. So far these moral maxims please him the most. The result not so much of an overly religious disposition, perhaps, as the dire lack of a more worthy occupation. Gustav Adolf is a kind of unfinished man of the world, affable but still timid and wavering.

His uncle, the Regent, believes he can control him.

"I know it on good authority that the Regent of Sweden is weak, pleasure loving, and credulous," her minister continues. "Especially awed by anything that smacks of mystery and supernatural powers. In Stockholm, he visits Mademoiselle Arfvidsson, the same clairvoyant who claims to have predicted the late King's assassination."

"Weak?" Catherine probes. "Or cunning?"

Bezborodko nods. He, too, agrees that the Regent is capable of annoying but clever ruses to raise the stakes and force Russia's hand. Gustav Adolf's engagement with Princess Louise of Mecklenburg was such an idea. The necessity to break the current ties is now being used as a bargaining position. The Mecklenburgs themselves are of no consequence. Too weak to afford even a sulk. But the Swedes stand to pocket a fortune for the change of royal sentiments.

"I've taken the liberty of assuring Mademoiselle Arfvidsson's favorable prophecy."

Bezborodko's voice rises with a theatrical glee. "For a hundred rubles, both coffee grounds and tarot cards foretold Gustav Adolf's betrothal at the end of a long journey and delivered a few good omens for the linked future of Sweden and Russia." When he smiles, his whole face lights up, his eyes sparkle. The small gap between his two front teeth gives him an impish air.

Absolute perfection, she, the Empress, likes to remind her two grandsons, is unattainable, but some people manage to arrive pretty near it. Here in front of her is a perfect courtier. A trifler with triflers, serious with the serious, always in tune with those who pipe, and yet underneath it all, a man of steel, sharp like the Damascus blade.

They talk for a while longer about matters closer at hand.

In the Fortress of Peter and Paul, the Polish prisoners have been issued another set of interrogation booklets. Since the last round yielded little but grandiose statements about the trampled rights of their beloved Motherland, this time questions have been replaced by direct instructions: List names of those who aided you in your rebellion; supplied you with weapons, food, money; and printed your manifestos. Their leader, Kościuszko — kept under surveillance in a comfortable room in the Commandant's house — is attended by the best surgeon. His wounds are healing well. The rumors, most likely started by Americans, have no basis in reality. There is not the slightest danger of amputation.

"In a few more months, Your Majesty," her minister assures her, "the Polish cauldron will stop bubbling over."

She nods in agreement.

Bezborodko requests permission to depart. His reports will come — as they always do — with the morning dispatches.

"Go!"

The Count is already at the door when he pauses, as if he has just remembered something. "I've taken one more liberty on Your Majesty's behalf. In Sweden there is a custom of placing freshly cut pine branches on the floor before visitors arrive, to make the air smell sweet. Two days ago, I sent a cartload of pine branches to the Swedish mission."

A self-satisfied grin blossoms on Bezborodko's sensuous lips. "The King, I'm told, has been touched by Your Majesty's thoughtful hospitality. To tears."

Of all of her granddaughters, Alexandrine is the prettiest, with clear blue eyes, her hair falling in honeyed coils. She has the fluid grace of a ballerina. It is easy to forget that she was such an ugly baby, with a tuft of hair that wouldn't fall off or grow.

"It's best to let nature take its course," Queenie counseled. In all matters of love, her servant thinks herself an expert. Claims dreams that predict betrayals. Visions that foretell unexpected encounters, reveal hidden passions, trysts cleverly concealed. Queenie spots love bites and hands passing sweet notes. Gifts too lavish or intimate to be innocuous. To her undying satisfaction, Queenie foresaw Mister Redcoat's treachery. Only in her own case does Queenie blunder. "Why would I wish a husband, madame?" she once asked. "To order me around? Tell me what I cannot do?"

In the blue drawing room, Alexandrine's eyes dart to the ceiling, to the painted figures of Truth and Wisdom surrounded by a rosy-cheeked brood of plump children. For the last few weeks, Miss Williams has been assigning readings from Swedish history and geography. A few stories of the Vikings, and then, to capitalize on Alexandrine's love for animals, a great deal about elk, reindeer, and the habits of seals.

By the window stand two giant pots in which blooming lemon trees display their yellow fruit against green, shiny foliage. Lemons, the gardeners tell the Empress, are rare plants: They can bloom and bear fruit at the same time.

The blue drawing room is close enough to St. George's Hall for the music of the peacock clock to reach them. The elaborate golden clock was Potemkin's gift, and an endless source of fascination for all her grand-children. Alexandrine and her brothers loved to sneak into the Hall to watch the owl, peacock, and cockerel perform their little dance numbers. The cockerel was Constantine's favorite, which didn't stop him from sticking his finger into its beak and damaging it.

"I always liked the owl best." Alexandrine laughs, jerking her head like an automaton and flapping her hands, a pretty accurate imitation of a machine that must have delighted her brothers once. "Even though it was in a cage."

Alexander favored the peacock, for it was the biggest of them all. "And," Alexandrine adds, her right hand making a graceful half-circle in the air, "it bowed so grandly and spread its tail. It's so amusing now, Graman, but we used to imagine we could shrink and go to live with them."

Her granddaughter is speaking too fast, forgetting the importance of enunciation. There is still so much she has to learn.

The court, Queenie assures her, is all excitement and joy. Everyone says Grand Duchess Alexandrine deserves all happiness available to us on this earth. Though, once she leaves for Sweden, the dear child will be sorely missed. The servants are already speculating on who will be going with her. Our Russian seamstress? The preserve maker?

The pastry cook? The chocolatier?

"Remember how you always chose Gustav Adolf's portrait?" Catherine interrupts Alexandrine's chatter, patting the ottoman seat beside her. "Every time I showed it to you?"

"Yes, Graman."

Alexandrine sits down gingerly, her gaiety subsiding as abruptly as it erupted, her cheeks now crimson with embarrassment. Her pink satin gown is decorated with white ribbons. The only jewels she wears are a single string of pearls. There is a faint smell of singed hair around her. The hairdresser should be more careful with his curling iron.

That had been their favorite game, a grandmother showing her eldest granddaughter portraits of eligible men sent by foreign courts, together with letters that detailed the advantages of a possible union. The sizes of kingdoms, strengths of alliances, the luster of connections and lineage. "Whom do you like best of all, Alexandrine?" she'd ask, and Alexandrine, dimples in her plump cheeks, would always point shyly at the Swedish heir to the throne.

"You'll see him soon," Catherine says now. "In his Swedish flesh and blood. Are you happy that he has come?"

Her granddaughter's eyes seek the comfort of the Anatolian carpet with its octagonal patterns of elephant's feet. "Yes, Graman. Only . . ."

"Only what, my dear?"

There is silence, uncomfortable and painful. Alexandrine is struggling with herself, knowing it is too late to hide a thought already announced. Where is it coming from, Catherine thinks, in all her grandchildren? This strain of timorous submission? Even Alexander has it, though he at least tries to hide it, knowing how it vexes her. He who had never been coddled or swaddled when he was a baby. Taught not to fear the dark. Allowed to explore whatever took his fancy. His questions were never ridiculed, always patiently answered.

"Isn't . . . the King . . . already engaged?"

"But he is not married, is he?" Catherine answers lightly. There is no need to tell Alexandrine more than that. All the child needs is to be comforted. A few words will do, a clear line of reasoning:

"The King doesn't care for Princess Louise, Alexandrine."

"How do you know that, Graman?"

"He has made no attempt to even meet her. And he has come hundreds of miles to see you."

Alexandrine's eyes blink. "Why would the King even like me?" she wonders.

So far Miss Williams has made little progress in teaching Alexandrine how to overcome her fears. Although the day before, in her diary, the child wrote how she had made herself stand on a Gatchina bridge, the small wooden one in the park, over a waterfall. For a count of twenty-five breaths. With water roaring underneath. The bridge she always used to run over as fast as she could. *Why would it collapse just when I stood there?* she wrote. *Was I that important? Or was my fear a veil that covered my lack of true humility before God?*

Catherine puts her arm around her granddaughter, pulls her closer. The child's cheek rests on her bosom. "Because you are beautiful and sweet and graceful, my darling. And very, very important."

Alexandrine's body is soft, pliant. Trembling now, for the child is sobbing.

Let her cry. Hasn't she herself always cried with much ease? From joy and pain. Frustration and the heady whirl of success. Tears are a cure, a release. Better than words. Better than Grandmother's assurances. Tears will be more plentiful once Alexandrine is in Stockholm. Without her brothers and sisters. Without her Graman to come to in moments of doubt.

When the sobbing subsides, she lifts her granddaughter's face up. "Spit," she orders, presenting a handkerchief. Alexandrine obeys with a shy giggle. This, too, is an old childhood ritual. Wetting a handkerchief with saliva to wipe a stricken face. Her brothers would always poke their tongues out, or make monkey faces.

They both laugh at the memory.

"How are the Gatchina roses this summer, Alexandrine?" she asks. "Have you painted any?"

"The pink ones. I've found a beautiful rosebush near the bridge."

There is an imprint on Alexandrine's cheek where she had pressed it to her grandmother's gown. Acorns and oak leaves woven from gold thread.

"The little wooden bridge over the water-fall?"

Alexandrine pauses for a moment before she nods and whispers, "Yes, Graman. That's the one. How did you guess?"

When Alexandrine leaves, Catherine rings for Queenie.

Her maid knows her habits well, for she comes in with a bowl of birdseed and a cane. The cane is sturdy, made of ebony, with an ivory handle set in silver, its end carved into a lion's head. "Venetian design," Le Noiraud calls it, with an air of authority that she neither questions nor confirms.

Before opening the window, Queenie insists on wrapping a thick woolen shawl around her mistress's shoulders. Everything is dangerous now — a chill, a sudden gust of the wind, an exertion she wouldn't have given a second thought before.

The Empress submits herself patiently to Queenie's fussing.

"Are you sure, madame, that you can manage?" Queenie's breath smells of chocolate.

"Quite sure. Open the window now."

We wear down until we cannot wear down anymore. Then we fall apart.

Alexander comes at midday. Her grandson wears a green morning jacket, her recent gift, sleeves embroidered with Russian two-headed eagles. Her handsome Monsieur Alexander, his smile a mere suggestion of merriment, so like her father's.

"I've got something for you, Graman," he mutters as he brushes his lips against her cheek. When he was little, he used to lick it, eager for the taste of her face creams. Almond was his favorite. Or was it orange blossom?

She runs her hand through her grandson's thick hair. She loves its reddish tint, but he demands it be called auburn. *Redheads,* he insists, *unlike me, are impulsive and unreliable.*

"What is it, dear?"

Alexander takes a sheet of paper out of his pocket, unfolds it, and places it on her desk.

"Please, Graman, read."

Catherine has weakened her eyesight in the service of the Empire. Her spectacles are no longer enough. She needs her magnifying glass to be able to read handwriting this fine.

Alexander settles on a chair beside her.

There is a whiff of snuff about him, of horses, and of wet leather. In spite of what she has heard of his new friend's beneficial influence, he has been to Gatchina again.

> To my sister, for her amusement on such an important occasion.
> A Queen of Hearts.
> A play in one act.

She glances at her grandson before resuming. He has spread the fingers of his left hand and pretends to examine the gold of his signet ring. His right hand is clenched into a fist.

> A voice of a young woman singing offstage:

> Oh tender heart,
> how cruel you are,
> how much you wish of me . . .

> Enter a young man in a riding habit. Upon hearing the singing he declares: "They tell me that good voices only go with plain faces. That to be fair, and sing well, is the privilege of angels."

Alexander turns his face away as she reads. Embarrassed or upset? Alexandrine has always been his favorite sister. Once, when he got it in his head to live on a deserted island, she was the only one he invited to come along with him. "You'll have to leave Maman and Papa. And Graman. And your dog. Will you do that?" "Yes," Alexandrine replied instantly. "I will."

Enter an elderly man richly dressed. The woman's voice fades away as if in fright. The man rubs his hands and mutters: "My Drina, my beloved. I must tell her of my devotion to her."

Catherine reads on, quickly. The play is short, an interlude more than a drama. Alexander knows her tastes well. The rich lover is spurned; young passion triumphs. In the final scene, the bride sweeps in, radiant and happy, to a chorus of well-wishers.

"Excellent," she says and watches the faint smile grow, blossom with relief. "Would you like it staged, Alexander? For the wedding? You could do it yourself if you wish. At the Hermitage, like you used to."

"I don't know," he says.

He is tempted, though. She can see it in his eyes. The anticipation of choosing the right actress, virginal and sweet-looking, her lips delivering his lines.

"How has Alexandrine been lately?" she asks.

"Anxious. Happy. Scared. Happy again. Constantine teases her. When she plays with her dog, he says she will smell like one."

"That rascal!"

"He calls the King her intended. She says he is not. She says the King is already engaged to the Princess of Mecklenburg. 'So why has he come?' Constantine asks. 'And why do you blush?' "

Alexander laughs as he reports on the bickerings of his siblings. "I've come to guard you, Graman," he told her, when he was not yet five. Brandishing his wooden sword, he pointed at the guards by her door. "Now, please, you can send them all away! I will protect you!"

Her leg aches. Rogerson advises more blistering. To draw the humors out, bring forth what is hidden. Her skin is raw already, covered with bleeding sores. Why would another blister be of any help? But this is not a question her doctor is able to answer, so, in his usual way, he pretends to be shocked by it.

Alexander is looking at her with troubled pensiveness. A child in the woods, not sure of his way, still looking for clues. To a nineteen-year-old, the world is full of extremes. A silent hour with his wife is enough reason for despair. His new Polish friend's confidences might trouble him, too. Her eldest grandson, her true heir, has yet to learn that not all loves last forever and that, in the end, most friendships flee from Sovereigns.

"You haven't finished yet, Graman," he

says, pointing at the page in her hands, reading the final lines aloud:

> May the chaste desire that enchants her
>   breast,
> Enlarge itself from day to day,
> That she may bear many fruits of love!

"It's beautiful, Alexander," she says, though she knows the play is a mere pretext for her grandson's presence. His searching glance is a hint, a plea.

"I'm told that the Swedish King is a serious young cheerful man with a good heart," she remarks, keeping her voice and carefree.

Alexandrine will do well as the Queen of Sweden. There are many advantages to this union. An important northern ally secured. The threat of future wars averted. Russia and Sweden united. But no need to dwell on what Alexander knows already. For he also knows the first disappointments of marriage. The waning of desire, the impatience with too many expectations. His wife's hot, bitter tears.

He is still looking at her with the silent plea in his eyes. Her silly boy won't ask the question he has come to ask.

"Alexandrine doesn't have to marry Gustav Adolf, if he doesn't please her." She answers the unasked question herself. "She knows. We've had a little talk already, your sister and I, and I told her that."

Alexander's eyes brighten.

"Really, Graman?" he asks, unable to hide his delight, like the child he still is. "You mean it?"

"I mean it."

"It's all fine, then."

"It's all fine."

This is what Alexander wishes to hear, for he plants a firm kiss on her cheek and stands up. For a moment he leans on her, as though forgetting how big he is.

"Remember how you wanted to guard my room, Alexander?" she asks.

"I wonder what happened to that sword," he says, chuckling. "I really liked it."

"Constantine broke it. He was jealous."

There is a memory of a child rigid with fury. Of a scream that carried through the palace corridors. Catherine chases the memory away.

"Yes, I remember now," Alexander says, shaking his head.

And then he is gone.

Each spurt of the Empire's growth brings a cascade of escalating problems. Expanding borders doesn't just mean ordering new maps. Old laws that come with acquired lands have to be integrated with Russia's code or abolished, new administrative units approved, new taxes established.

This is all in a day's work: Decide if all

Poles who call themselves nobles are worthy of their rank? What about those who own half a village or a few cows, and have no written proofs of their noble status? What about the Jews, who, under the Polish rule, have kept their own laws and customs? Now that they are Russian subjects, should they be allowed to settle anywhere in the Empire? Or be kept in the areas where people are accustomed to their presence?

At the newly drawn eastern border, the Prussians are proposing swaps. They might be ready to concede Warsaw for gains in the north.

"You are not listening to me." Le Noiraud looks at her with reproach.

The winter garden where they sit is a few steps down the corridor from the Imperial Study. In August, the garden lacks the charm it exudes as an escape from the frozen world during the winter months. Still, a small stream bubbles happily and meanders past laurel and myrtle trees, past the shrubbery, where wild hens nest. There are monkeys here, too, and rabbits, white guinea pigs, some free, some on leashes.

Birds fly free in her paradise, pecking at the seeds scattered for them among the flowers. Only big birds are tethered. An eagle, a stork, and a crane. Now, in the summer, she allows them to be taken outside, into the open space covered by a fine mesh so they cannot fly away.

"What are you thinking about?" Le Noiraud asks, a little petulantly.

"Our Swedish guests."

Gustav Adolf and his uncle have ventured outside the Swedish mission, alone, dressed in the plain attire of merchants. In Bezborodko's latest report, the Regent called St. Petersburg a bad imitation of European capitals. "Have you noticed," he told the King, "how travelers who should write about the beauty of Russian palaces always end up listing the numbers of their corridors, rooms, and staircases? As if they have been contracted to clean them!" The young King, bless him, had replied that he didn't like forming his opinions based on other people's impressions. That he wished to learn more of the Russian ways.

This is more or less what she tells her lover, although, of course, without mentioning Bezborodko. Not that it is of any help.

It's not hard to chart the routes Le Noiraud's thoughts traverse. To follow the convoluted route of jealousy and unease that makes him ask: "Is it Bezborodko again? Is he telling you lies about me?" His fingers are tugging on the embroidered hem of his waistcoat, loosening the gold thread. He curls his shoulders as if to shield himself. A subtle gesture, but the one she always notes.

Le Noiraud, her handsome, brooding falcon. His face looks so serene, so patrician, with his high forehead, his Roman nose. The white skin, eyes still filled with pensive sweetness, though now fear darts across them. Most people are so ugly. Men especially. Pudgy, with oniony skin, dead crusty matter in its folds. The tufts of hair sticking out of their ears.

"Nobody is telling me lies about you," she answers, knowing how seldom words soothe him.

Le Noiraud's forehead creases. His hand covers hers, his fingers pressing. Jealousy tortures him. Fanciful conjectures that would've flattered her once.

"What is Mister More-Perfect-Than-Thou telling you about me now?" Le Noiraud insists, his voice brittle and plaintive. For years, the two men have played a subtle game of slights. A bow too cursory, a sneer observed, a wink. A swift retreat to avoid each other's proximity. Nothing specific either of them can be reproached with. "I hold His Highness in most sincere and profound respect," Bezborodko answers each time she brings up the subject. For his part, Platon is still convinced her minister was behind her refusal to let him fight in the Polish campaign, no matter how many times she assured him, "Why can't you believe that I wanted you safe, with me!"

"That he holds you in most sincere and profound respect," she says now.

"Hypocrite!"

She sighs. She doesn't wish to be dismissive of Le Noiraud's fears, but other matters worry her more. Like Vishka's remark that Constantine's bride, Anna Fyodorovna, spends far too much time with Alexander's wife. Perhaps Anna Fyodorovna is lonely. In a few short months, the girl has changed her religion, her country, and her family. Her mother and sisters have left for Coburg, and she might never see them again. One can understand loneliness. And the consequence of too much solitude, the insecurity that amplifies all whispers and makes it seem they are all about your own shortcomings. Though — if it persists — Alexander would have to be told that such behavior is not reflecting well on his young wife. Anna will — one day — be the Empress of Russia. She must set an example for all Grand Duchesses.

"Is everything all right, Katinka?" Le Noiraud whispers. He is covering her hand with kisses that once brought a rush of heat to her cheeks and throat, but now merely tickle. This is what he wants most of all. The elation his own power over her pleasure once brought.

Her lover is still so young. At twenty-seven, one doesn't understand that desire withers. One hasn't sampled the ashen taste of age.

Butterflies flutter around them. Some are as big as rose blooms. With curious patterns on their wings. They feed on pieces of sweet melon the garden servants leave on plates.

Catherine doesn't want him hurting. All is as well as it could be. No one will replace him. No one can.

It is hard to know what tugs at her heart more. The brash playfulness of his touch? The stillness of his head on her lap, relinquished, fragile, utterly hers? Le Noiraud will do anything to hold on to the importance her attention gives him. Beat his chest, crown himself with thorns. In his room he keeps a pistol oiled and ready. "If you order me to go, I'll blow my brains out," he vows.

"Remember how you showed the children your card tricks in the meadow?" she asks. "I've never seen Constantine so awed by anything. And he was not the only one!"

The flare of hope in his splendid black eyes tells her that she has won.

The three of them curtsy. They wring their hands. Alexandrine, who has walked in first, has bloodshot eyes and a puffy red nose. Her sisters, Yelena, who is twelve, and Maria, who is ten, trail after her.

It is Alexandrine who speaks. They were strolling in the garden. Her dog was chasing a rabbit. She called after him. *Bolik, Bolik.*

He didn't hear her.

He didn't turn back.

He didn't come home that night, as the gardener said he would.

"We've searched everywhere," Yelena adds with a dark note of satisfaction. This child relishes bad news, as if misfortunes prove some deeply held conviction she cannot otherwise reveal. Maria nods with grave energy; there's a smudge of soot across her cheek.

"I've called and called, Graman," Alexandrine repeats. "But Bolik hasn't come back."

Three pairs of eyes are fixed on her now. She is the Empress. She can put things right, send servants to search for Bolik. When they were younger her grandchildren were ready to believe that she had a flying carpet and an invisible cloak that let her go anywhere and hear everything that was said.

Bolik is a white Bolognese. His hair is a mass of white, wooly ringlets. A smart little dog who never caused trouble. Why would he suddenly bolt and not come back?

The gardener, her granddaughters tell her, has seen Bolik by the garden gate. He tried to corner him, but Bolik was too fast.

"As if a devil chased him." Yelena repeats the gardener's words slowly, weighing their significance. Last year, after their sister Olga died, Yelena started demanding stories of ghosts and witches. The silly maids obliged with tales of black cauldrons in which poisons

349

brew and of pale specters that haunt the empty palace corridors at night. "Possessed," the maids said of Olga, who could not stop eating before she died. "As if her stomach turned into a bottomless pit."

"Bolik always came running to me when I called," Alexandrine reminds her.

"We'll find him," Catherine says and promises a rescue team. She warns Alexandrine that red eyes will not make her look pretty for the Hermitage ball she has planned for tomorrow.

She doesn't mention the Swedish King.

Alexandrine pulls on her braids, a flighty, nervous gesture that mars her serenity. Yelena makes a circle with her foot, tracing the shapes of the mosaic floor. Maria is poking her finger inside her nose. The three of them slouch, and as she studies their appearance she sees the stained cuffs, ink-stained fingers, fingernails bitten to the quick. So much for trusting their mother and governesses to raise them properly.

She has not interfered with the upbringing of her granddaughters. The boys were enough of a responsibility. Her daughter-in-law should have been able to handle the girls. But now she wishes she had been more vigilant. Paul's wife is too lenient, too trustful of their good inclinations.

"When I was a girl," she tells her granddaughters, "I would not be allowed to slouch.

Or pick my nose like a milkmaid."

Maria hides her hands behind her. She is a sturdy child, stronger than her sisters. Her face has a rosy hue, as if she spent her days roaming in the garden like a peasant. Yelena straightens instantly and smooths her dress. It is a lovely Indian muslin dress, buttercup yellow, with an embroidered hem. Much nicer than Alexandrine's pink robe.

"Please, Graman," Alexandrine manages to say before her voice breaks into a sob.

"Hush, my dear," Catherine says. "No more tears."

Silently she curses Bolik, the ungrateful creature. She thinks of the feral dogs that roam the embankment. Palace dogs do not fare well against street mongrels. Bolik might be nothing more by now than bloodied scraps of white fur, a chewed-up bone.

She rings for Zotov and instructs him to start looking for the dog. Her valet nods gravely as Yelena and Maria recount the particulars of Bolik's escape. Alexandrine is the only one silent.

"I promise." Zotov's quiet, capable voice rings in the air, as he escorts the girls outside. "We'll find him."

When the girls leave, she finds it hard to concentrate on her work. Where is it coming from, this unchildlike sadness in Alexandrine's eyes? This stubborn insistence to give alms to the pilgrims herself, oblivious of the grimy hands covered in sores, the stench of the soiled rags on their rotting feet? The conviction that if she omits her morning prayers some misfortune will strike?

"You do this because you are stupid," Constantine once said, to which Alexandrine replied: "There is the need for stupid people in the world."

Even the closed windows of the Winter Palace cannot keep away the cries and shouts, the noises of the city. Dogs howl, merchants praise their wares. In St. Petersburg, one is never far away from the crowds. Millionnaya Street gets choked with attendants and hangers-on. Carriages get stuck, drivers curse one another's incompetence and lack of skills. Horses, frightened by sudden movements, bite and kick. This city is never still and never silent.

Beside her, Doctor Rogerson is expounding on his favorite topic.

"By nature, Your Highness, women are by far more amorous than men. Conjugal embraces please them more. Such is the composition of a female body. A sign of vital forces, of animal magnetism at work." Human society, he also says, has mostly failed to make allowances for this abundance of female energy.

Catherine braces herself for a lecture. Men

352

like to instruct her how to remedy all problems. One more imperial ukase, Your Highness! A few stern orders! Wiser men than Rogerson believe that ruling a nation is as easy as writing a few sentences peppered with exclamation marks.

But Rogerson is in a humbler mood today, resigned to inform, not offer solutions.

He tells her about static electricity, which he calls "yet another proof of life's vital force." He describes an experiment in which a woman's finger sent pricking shoots accompanied by a crackling noise.

Her doctor's lectures are far more useful than his potions and bleedings. To prepare for them, he pores over books in the Imperial Library and carries on correspondence with English doctors. He is smart this way. He knows the Empress judges a conversation by the amount of information she learns from it. There is no cure for curiosity, she likes to say.

"It's a terrible waste." Rogerson shakes his head as he comes up with medical examples of harm caused by suffocating what is natural. Clogged passages of life force cause the eruption of boils. Diminish efficiency in other faculties. Disrupt sleep, cause dryness in the mouth and *passages intimes*. What is not used either withers or gets irritated. Great ills come from both in the end.

Rogerson looks up, seeking her gaze as his

hands busy themselves with her sore leg.

The sores do not heal. The edges of the wounds redden and exert yellowish pus. The dressings need to be changed daily. The swelling never goes away. Is this why impatience sets in? The need to point out the limitations of medical knowledge?

"Why am I growing heavier?" She interrupts Rogerson's musings. "I've never eaten much. I've never drunk more than you, monsieur, have advised. What is happening in the depth of my flesh?"

Doctor Rogerson's chin bears the nicks of a dull razor or a careless barber. Vishka reports that he is sending money back to Scotland. A cousin on his mother's side is searching for an estate there. A few years ago, she thought that her Scottish doctor would make a decent husband for Queenie. Until Bezborodko pointed to a sentence in Rogerson's letter to his Edinburgh friend: *The Empress wishes me to court a woman whose interests clearly lie elsewhere.*

Her doctor is convinced oxygen is the culprit. "Pneumatic chemistry, Your Majesty," he answers. "The respiratory tract takes oxygen from the body and mixes it with the carbon from food." Normally this carbon should be expelled, he explains, but in some organisms, the process has been obstructed. The cure is introducing more oxygen into the system.

"How?" she asks.

"By breathing treated air, madame."

"Why should I believe you?"

"A wise question, Your Majesty. Your Majesty knows more than I do of the limitations of the human mind."

Rogerson is a smart courtier. He doesn't tell her to believe in his theories. He claims a scientific mind: *Until it is proven otherwise, I shall assume this to be plausible.*

With deliberate movements, Rogerson unpacks his case. A lancet for cutting the vein on her leg, the bowl for her blood. He places them carefully on a clean linen napkin, making sure the lancet is positioned just so. Medicine is not above borrowing from magic tricks.

Abracadabra?

Mankind enjoys deceiving itself?

"May I, madame?" he asks, before removing her slippers and scrutinizing her toes. One of them attracts his attention. He fishes for a magnifying glass.

"Cure by treated air." She returns to the conversation. "How is that achieved?"

His eyes still fixed on her toe, Rogerson describes a chamber from which air is either pumped out or in with bellows, installed to increase or decrease pressure. According to Boyle's Law, as the pressure increases, the gas volume is reduced. He reminds her of an experiment she has seen before: a ticking clock placed in a glass tube. After the air is pumped out of the tube, the ticking of the clock is seen but not heard.

"Doctor Beddos, madame," he says, finally putting the magnifying glass aside, "is the one who proposes this English cure."

Catherine finds herself listening closely. The elastic properties of air have always intrigued her. Matter that can be shaped, molded. "But wouldn't it be dangerous?" she asks, recalling a court demonstration her grandsons' tutor had arranged once. "I've seen how quickly a vacuum brings on a dove's death."

Doctor Beddos, her court doctor assures her, is not creating a vacuum in his chambers but merely adjusting the pressure of the air. But when she asks, in all seriousness, "Should I try it then? Shall I send for Doctor Beddos?" Rogerson advises her not to waste her money and precious time. "Doctor Beddos, madame," he says, "is so enormously fat that he is called a walking featherbed."

The lancet has a carved ivory handle.

The doctor is so fast with the cut that she misses the moment when the edge of the lancet slashes her skin. "Only two ounces, madame," he says. "Moderation is the best policy."

It is when her leg is bandaged that she asks: "I've lost all pleasure of desire. Is there anything you can do to bring it back?"

Rogerson frowns. "Is this a recent development, madame?"

A confession is called for. An admission of another loss. Harder to bear than she has ever expected. No, it is not recent. It came about in ebbs and flows. Now even these have ceased and she has shriveled inside, dried up. It is as if some careless maid scrubbed her skin too hard with ashes. Nothing can evoke the old sweet pleasures. Even in Tsarskoye Selo, in the love rooms she has furnished with such great care, her body defies her. Nymphs and satyrs can couple all they want. Sculptures can open up to reveal the thrills of passion. Books can depict the tugs of desire, but in her nothing stirs but memories of what has once been.

"Why?" she asks her doctor.

But Rogerson never has answers that satisfy. All he can speak of is her womb shrinking, one humor that needs boosting at the expense of another.

From his array of tonics he picks three bottles with white labels: *Teriac Farook. Tribulus Terrestris. Ginger and Epimedium Extract.*

She is to drink thirty drops of each, with water, three times a day.

If this won't work, he will get a fresh supply of salep, restorative marmalade made with Satyrion roots. And the eryngo candy he has brought with him from his last trip home.

"Any news about Bolik?" Catherine asks

Queenie.

"Not a sight of him." Queenie shuffles to the window to air the room after the doctor's visit. She eyes the tonic bottles Rogerson has lined up from the tallest down with suspicion. Just breathing these, her maid claims, gives her a headache.

"Is Alexandrine still crying?"

"All the time. Nose red. Eyes swollen. Nails bitten."

This is not welcome news. Not now when Alexandrine must look her best.

Alexandrine is Queenie's favorite among the Grand Duchesses, so what she says next is even more troubling. "The sweet child has asked me about Xenia again."

Blessed Xenia is the source of many stories, old and new. A reckless husband's sudden death, without time to repent his sins, makes his young wife put on his Preobrazhensky coat, green with scarlet facings, and give up all her earthly possessions to roam the streets of St. Petersburg in penance for his sins. Now an old woman, her hair long, gray, and matted, Xenia walks barefoot summer or winter, through snow and mud, streets and fields, not minding the sharp pebbles or harvest stubble. When Xenia tells people to go home to cook *bliny,* someone in the family is going to die. Xenia performs miracles. Mothers follow her, begging her to bless their children. "Blessed Xenia can see the future," Alexandrine insists.

For Alexandrine, Blessed Xenia is a forbidden subject. It hasn't always been so, but it is now, after too many requests to be allowed to see the madwoman. Some souls have to be protected against themselves. For their own good.

"The young mind, Your Majesty, is impressionable." Queenie offers her consolations. "Soon enough other concerns will prevail." But in her voice there is doubt. Queenie has been at court far too long to dismiss the dangers of innocence. Or the desire for sainthood that leads to renunciations. More dangerous, indeed, than others, for fortified by faith.

It isn't hard to see why Alexandrine is captivated by Xenia's tale. Sudden death is what her granddaughter fears. A bolt from above. An unexpected summons to the hereafter. An account of her days. Explanations of all actions.

The summons her poor sister Olga received.

In a child still so young, pain and fear grow deep roots. Especially if her confessor does nothing to stop them. *When I was Alexandrine's age,* Catherine thinks, *it was life that excited me, not saintly deprivations. My fears were not of the hereafter but of this world.*

Sophie of Anhalt-Zerbst was not born a Grand Duchess of All the Russias. Sophie of

Anhalt-Zerbst could have ended her life in some forsaken castle, in a freezing turret, ruling over cabbage fields and herds of cattle.

Insignificant, forgotten.

Alone.

At her request, it is beaming Le Noiraud, the dark blue ribbon of the Order of the White Eagle across his chest, who escorts the Swedish guests to the Diamond Room. *Are you happy now?* Catherine thinks, as Platon's eyes dart toward the glass cases where the crown jewels glitter on red velvet. A hint to the guests to do the same. Which they don't.

At seventeen, the King of Sweden is indeed exceedingly handsome, in the smooth, crisp way of the young. A tall, graceful prince with a pale, drawn face, long hair brushing his shoulders, clad in black velvet, he approaches her with remarkable dignity.

"Dear Count! We all welcome you to Russia!"

She calls him Count, for Gustav Adolf IV of Sweden is traveling incognito. For the Russian trip, the King calls himself the Count of Haga. His uncle, who stands right beside him, barely reaching his nephew's shoulder — the Regent until the King's majority — chose the name of the Count of Wasa.

Catherine is sitting in her gilded armchair carved with double-headed eagles. She is rouged and powdered, clad in cloth of gold, flashing with precious stones. Her gown is heavy and stiff like armor. Drops of perspiration gather on her back into a stream that rolls down her spine. It is an early afternoon, hot, in spite of open windows and a breeze from the Neva.

The Empress has ordered Platon to bring the Swedish visitors here through Raphael's Loggias. The gallery is Quarenghi's masterpiece, but her own idea, copied from the Raphael Bible in the Vatican Palace. Frescoes depicting scenes from the Creation to the Last Supper, set in the borders of stucco, among the bustle of flowers, fruits, and birds, have been called an art school for all Europe. The scenes are both peaceful and serene. Raphael, like her, preferred happy endings. Only the images of the Last Supper hint at death and resurrection.

The guests have also passed by the Hermitage library, where the walls are covered with the finest Romanov portraits. Platon was to make sure the King stopped by the likeness of Alexandrine, at seven, wearing a Russian *kokoshnik* and looking particularly sweet and virginal.

"Your Imperial Majesty!" A pair of burning brown eyes rise to meet hers. Gustav Adolf bends to kiss her hand.

"I cannot allow this," Catherine says, smiling. "I cannot forget that the Count of Haga is a King."

361

The King bows again with an easy grace. "If Your Majesty will not give me permission to kiss her hand as Empress, at least allow it as a lady to whom I owe so much respect and admiration." He speaks in perfect, elegant French. His pleasure at being in the presence of a Russian Sovereign is an honor he will not soon forget. It is a yardstick he will measure all future honors against and is sure to find them wanting.

The sun streams through open curtains, lighting up the squares on the intricate mosaic floor, bouncing off the gilt vases on the marble mantel.

The King's hands are white and very soft. Could he rein in a horse? Stop it from bolting?

After a moment of hesitation, Le Noiraud puffs up his chest and positions himself right beside her. The King and the Regent no longer pay any attention to him, which will be reason enough for sulking.

The King does not mention God or Destiny, but — is it modesty or caution? — he doesn't inquire about Alexandrine, either. Instead, he recounts praises of the Winter Palace he has heard from his late father. No descriptions, however, could ever do justice to what he has now had the privilege to observe with his own eyes. He has paid attention to Raphael's Loggias. "What a pleasure it must be," he exclaims, "to possess what the greedy Vatican considers its own unique treasure."

The Regent bobs his head at his nephew's praise. Pudgy and pasty, Catherine thinks him, like an underbaked dinner roll.

"The choice of subject matter in particular," the King continues. "What pleasure to see art that draws a human mind so deeply into the beauty of spiritual transformations!"

These words are followed by a straightforward, earnest gaze. This man will not cringe. Or irritate her with incessant flattery.

From behind the Diamond Room doors come the impatient noises of the court awaiting the first glimpse of the guests. The voices rise and fall, hushed only to break out into a hum of pretended indifference. But before she proceeds to the reception hall, she points to the glass cases and the giant ruby in her scepter. "The size of a hen's egg," she says with an impish smile. "I only mention this because Your Majesty's late father presented it to me during his last visit here. He had no son yet, and I had no granddaughters, but it was his wish then that our houses might be connected one day."

Is it a blush she sees on Gustav Adolf's cheeks?

"But I have to make a confession before we proceed any further," the Empress continues. "My eldest granddaughter, Alexandrine, has had a misfortune of losing her beloved dog.

So you must forgive her if she seems distracted and sad. It's not on your account, though I'm afraid that you might have been an unwitting cause of the unfortunate occurrence."

"Me, Your Majesty?"

"My granddaughter blames herself for letting the dog run away. Her mind has been too much occupied by today's ball, which, as you know, we are giving in your honor. The child has been weeping all day."

"A sign of a tender heart," the King replies.

She claps her hands, and the doors of the Diamond Room open wide. She turns toward the King, who promptly positions himself at her side, forcing Platon to move back. She leans on Gustav Adolf's arm and stands up. Her steps are slow but deliberate; she ignores the pain.

Platon glances at himself in the silver-framed mirror. Quickly, as if he needed reassurance that he is still here.

In the Audience Room the courtiers are waiting. As Catherine passes by, all eyes are on her, gauging the amount of her attention, the measure of how far they have climbed or fallen. Have they merited a full greeting? A mere inclination of her head? Or just a consoling smile? After she has passed, they will jostle, push away those who have lost, take the precious inches of their space, watchful for those wishing to unseat them.

And so the parade begins, in full glittering splendor. Her swarming family, lined up. Son: pug-nosed Paul, in his Preobrazhensky uniform, stiff at attention. Daughter-in-law: Maria Fyodorovna, flat-faced, wide-bottomed, still weak from the last pregnancy, leaning on Paul's arm. Never mind them. Beauty may have skipped one generation, but it has certainly favored her grandchildren. On their right, dashing Alexander with his Elizabeth. On their left, Constantine with his Anna. Behind them, Alexander's new friend, Prince Adam, his embroidered jacket the hue of ripe plums. It's of him that Bezborodko says "possibly too serious." As if reading and talking about books with Alexander can be construed as a fault.

And the girls! Three granddaughters, grouped together, their fresh faces like the first blush of spring. Alexandrine is in the middle. A chain of roses crowns her forehead. On her chest, pinned, her grandmother's portrait, its frame glittering with diamond lights. The white muslin of her underdress is enlivened by the sumptuous pink gown, trimmed with gold lace. Her hands are folded on her chest; her eyes are cast down. A fairy virgin princess awaiting her fate.

The King bows with a flourish in front of the Grand Duchesses. He cannot take his gaze away. Louise of Mecklenburg is not going to be betrothed much longer.

Alexandrine lifts her chin slightly. Her quick, furtive look deserves an approving smile of encouragement. The King says something to Alexandrine, then pauses to hear her response. He should move on, but he doesn't, coming up with more questions. Alexandrine must be answering them to his satisfaction, for he makes no effort to leave her. In the end, Alexander intervenes, indicating the line of courtiers awaiting their introductions, with the always-too-eager Madame Lebrun pushing herself forward. The King bows again and folds his hands, begging for forgiveness. Alexandrine smiles and nods her understanding of royal obligations.

The charms of coyness are as powerful as the brilliancy of wit.

"He's ours," Catherine whispers triumphantly into Le Noiraud's ear as he leads her to her comfortable ottoman, from which she will watch the evening unfold. "Smitten already."

When she asked Alexander to play host, her grandson had flinched, as if pricked by a pin a seamstress overlooked in the folds of his shirt. "Won't Papa mind terribly if I do?" he had asked. But now Alexander is all charm, Elizabeth at his side, radiant in ivory-white satin. The dress is laced too tightly, though. Elizabeth should think of motherhood, not vanity. Which is as bad as the excessive melancholy she confesses in her letters home: *Each pang of sorrow is like a drop of ink falling into a glass of water, turning something that used to be clear into dirty gray.*

Gustav Adolf glides from one cluster of courtiers to another. From her vantage point Catherine follows his nods, his elegant steps. There is no shyness in his gestures, no hesitation. Naked, he must be marble-like and solid. With a slight pang of regret she has to admit that even Alexander and Constantine, her two strapping grandsons, pale beside him.

The Prussian Ambassador, in black velvet, approaches to pay his respects and — no doubt — gauge her latest thoughts on the Polish partition treaty, which she'll thwart: The Prussians always wish for more than their share. But there is no need, for he merely offers praises for her granddaughter's charms. "Grand Duchess Alexandrine has managed," he gushes, "to shine, among such condensation of beauty."

Beside her, Platon sits silent, his fingers toying with the ribbon across his chest. A deep frown creases his impeccably sculptured forehead. Le Noiraud is piqued because the Prussian Ambassador has addressed him as *Mon Prince,* a slight he will neither forget nor forgive. Prince Zubov, according to the Prussian Ambassador, does not deserve to be called *Mon Seigneur* or *Votre Altesse,* because his title was too recently acquired.

Across the ballroom, her son stands, gawking, an emptiness around him like a magic circle no one but his wife and children dare to cross. Her eyes quickly slide over Paul's lanky frame, his small head that looks as if it will wobble off his shoulders the moment he moves too quickly.

There has always been something wrong about Paul. As a boy, he was never still, pushing ahead of everybody else. Rushing to the table before meals were ready. Eating too fast, finishing before others barely started, and then complaining how slow they were. Talking incessantly. Arguing when it was no longer necessary. Stubborn. Wanting things his own way or not wanting them at all. "Impatience is a common flaw of extreme youth. His Highness will outgrow it," his tutor assured her, but she knew better. Impatience was like a cancer of the spirit. It would grow and poison all that it touched.

Paul makes her think of a cuckoo. Not of the echoing calls said to predict the number of years one has on this earth, but of how it lays its egg in another bird's nest. Of how the cuckoo chick grows bigger than the duped parents and still demands to be fed. Not that she believes the rumors that the child she gave birth to had been snatched and another placed in its stead, that Paul is Elizabeth Petrovna's bastard. Simpler explanations suffice. The overheated nursery, the careless and ignorant nurses who filled her young son's head with nonsense. Stories of *bogatyri* who leaped through mountains and slew monster nightingales or of clever peasants who outwitted sly merchants and married princesses of the realm. Or that she, his mother, could make herself invisible and thus will always know what he says.

The nurses must have thought little of such teasing; a good-natured joke of no consequence, the stuff of their own childhoods. But her son was not a sturdy peasant boy who would laugh at such nonsense. Her son screamed in terror at the sight of her.

Paul's gaze acknowledges hers, but he will not approach her again. They've already exchanged their customary greetings. *Dear son. Beloved mother.* No need for anything else. She'll not spoil the bubbly feeling of pleasure. She'll watch the young dance. Lithe bodies hopping about, still capable of such exertions. Alexander holding his head high, his dance steps perfectly assured. Elizabeth beside him, her shining hair adorned with black pearls. Anna Fyodorovna, perfectly content as she skips over the ballroom floor, Constantine holding her by the tips of her fingers.

Fans flutter like butterflies' wings. Skirts swell and rustle. Feet mark time. The scents of orange flowers and jasmine mingle with musk and snuff.

When the music stops, she can hear the clink of coins thrown on the card table next door. And the thumping of the billiard cues, sending the wooden balls on their way.

Having fulfilled his duty of court introductions, the Swedish King is not leaving Alexandrine's side.

Alexandrine Pavlovna, the future Queen of Sweden, is still panting after the dance. The King has taken off his soft velvet cap and plays with its jeweled trim. For a moment, brief and fleeting, Alexandrine touches it, too, then withdraws her finger quickly, as if in fright. He talks and the child listens, her eyes fixed on the tips of her satin slippers. But she is not entirely silent, for at times the King laughs heartily in response to her words. The two young lovers are given wide berth. No one wishes to interrupt what has been so eagerly anticipated.

The Regent has been watching the young lovers, too. Now, defeated, he approaches the imperial ottoman. He clears his throat. "Some actions seem preordained, Your Majesty," he says. "Impossible to resist. Like flood. Like winter snow."

"Seem?" Catherine asks. She doesn't care to remind this ugly, balding man that she was not the one to break her end of the bargain with this Mecklenburg charade, which will now have to be undone.

The Regent mutters something about ill-wishers betting on the wrong horse, unleashing a torrent when they merely desired a sip of water. He will not be remembered in Russia for the precision of his metaphors, but what he is trying to express merits attention. When he speaks of "important events, the implications of which are still not fully understood," he means Russia's latest acquisitions. He is saying that the partition of Poland has not gone down well in Sweden. Russia is getting bigger, and Europe is afraid. Which country will she swallow next?

"Negotiations are still required," the Regent says in a hoarse whisper. He seems convinced that vagueness carries more clout with her than straightforward admissions. "A variety of approaches might have to be suggested. Safeguards considered, mutually agreed upon."

The music resumes. Alexandrine tips her sweet face up toward the King's. She is saying something, and he watches her with rapture. Then he clasps his fingers to his lips, as if her granddaughter managed to astonish him even more than he thought possible.

A surge of magnanimity overwhelms Catherine. She will not gloat.

"I've heard much praise of the King's palace," she tells the Regent, opening her swanskin fan, rimmed with black feathers. "It is just outside Stockholm, isn't it? Where the air is good?"

371

The Regent, not pleased to change the subject but not ready to insist, confirms the validity of her praises. The air is indeed excellent. The grounds spacious. The Swedish royal palace is comfortable and well thought out. The library is particularly charming, with paintings copied from Herculaneum on the walls. A Gothic altar serves as a stove. And there is a Chinese temple in the gardens. Right next to a Greek temple. No one can accuse Sweden of not knowing that chinoiserie is de rigueur.

"And how many rooms does it have?" Catherine asks. "I always find exact numbers important. Don't you agree?"

Well before midnight, the Empress retires to her inner rooms. The young should be left alone. Her presence can easily become a hindrance, and she doesn't wish to spoil their joy. She remembers the days of her own youth only too well. Mother's cutting admonitions still ring in her memory.

Le Noiraud is the only one who accompanies her, his lips curved in a painful grimace. All evening, Platon has made no attempt to dance with anyone, although Princess Dolgoruka tried to coax him into a polonaise. He stayed faithfully at his Empress's side, amusing her with his witticisms: "It's sometimes necessary to play the fool in order to avoid being deceived by cunning men." Or trusting the diverting power of gossip: The Regent's wife is in love with a fat Frenchwoman. Prince Adam — "Why does he stick to Alexander like a burr to a dog's tail, Katinka?" — has Ambassador Repnin's eyes and Repnin's chin, but his mother's Roman nose.

Alone with her, Le Noiraud is no longer able to hide his fury.

He has been humiliated. He has been slighted. Not just the Prussian Ambassador but even that Swedish runt, the Regent, has addressed him as *Mon Prince.*

Anger makes him taller, chisels his features. He pulls at his chemise, ripping off buttons that roll under the bed. Mother-of-pearl, set in gold. Vishka will have to retrieve them in the morning.

"Keep your voice down," she says impatiently. She doesn't think the little Regent could manage to bribe anyone close to her, but she believes in caution. She wants to rest, not relive another imagined slight. Her leg is tugging at her again, pulsating on the threshold of pain.

Le Noiraud perches at the edge of her bed. Dark curls show through the opening in his chemise. "Katinka," he says, and his voice breaks. He throws his arms around her to kiss her, but she turns her head abruptly and his lips land on her cheek.

He blinks, startled, suddenly close to tears.

It's his fragility that tugs at her heart. *Without me,* she thinks, *he'll perish.*

Settling beside Le Noiraud, she puts her hand on his. It is late. Even with the windows closed and curtains drawn, the sounds of the ball filter through to her bedroom. Laughter, the staccato of dancing feet. It'll be hard to fall asleep, and she has work to do in the morning.

"Madame Lebrun was quite taken with the shape of your lips," she recalls. "Or was it the patrician line of your forehead?"

Platon's hand still quivers under hers, but he is smiling already, her flighty butterfly, so easily satisfied with even a tiny victory. He rests his head on her lap.

"Would you let her paint you, Katinka? If I asked you?"

"And would that please you?" She closes her eyes. She longs for darkness. Snuffed candles. The sound of Platon's feet as he climbs the stairs to his own rooms upstairs.

"Yes."

"Then I will."

"When?"

"As soon as Alexandrine leaves for Stockholm."

"Promise."

"I promise."

The aftermath of victory: Stanislav August Poniatowski, the King of Poland, is in Grodno

374

on her orders. In the last months, horse riding has become his all-consuming passion. The landscape around Grodno apparently invites dreaming. The silver ribbon of the Niemen River enchants.

Prince Repnin, who is in charge of the royal prisoner, warns that Stanislav is writing his memoirs. *Confessions,* he calls them, in the manner of that detestable Rousseau.

The Empress doesn't need warnings. The Polish King's archivist is one of her best spies.

The King's letters are opened and read, his papers copied. All visitors coming or leaving the Grodno palace, family and friends included, are thoroughly searched, their movements recorded and timed. Catherine knows to whom Stanislav has written in cipher, begging for a condemnation of Poland's dissolution. She knows who has — so far — evaded an answer and who has complied and why. She knows that Stanislav frets over his "secret" wife's fainting spells. She also knows who steals bottles of claret from his cellars and how much perfectly good lace is claimed to be damaged in the wash and is then sold in the town.

The Confessions, so far, dwell on the time of their first meeting, forty-one years ago now. He a Polish Count visiting St. Petersburg, she a Grand Duchess with an uncertain future. *Sophie,* he calls her . . . *her shining black hair . . . her lips begging for a kiss . . .*

such was my lover, the mistress of my fate . . .
to whom I gave all of myself . . . offering what
no one else has possessed . . .

He knows she is reading these words. What does he want her to remember? Old promises? Old dreams?

The Empress has no patience for dreamers.

As the guillotines fell and Parisian gutters were overflowing with the blood of his betters, Robespierre was dreaming of his Republic of Virtue. Of free people, gentle and filled with wisdom, walking its streets. Of garlanded girls in flowery robes gliding through colonnades of white marble. Of all sins eradicated, a world without jealousy, hypocrisy, superstition.

Dreamers are not harmless. They drag suffering in their wake.

She scans the list of the King's expenses: food, salaries, candles, wine cellar, sweets and coffee, stables, and fuel. When Repnin suggested she double the King's "pocket money," she agreed. On the enclosed ledgers, she can see Stanislav's signature acknowledging three thousand ducats per month: *Stanislav August Rex.*

I've been generous, Catherine thinks.

He signed an act of abdication. She didn't force it. It was a straightforward choice. Cling to symbols and grand gestures and go bankrupt. Or surrender and your debts shall be paid and you and your family kept in comfort. But her generosity has not sufficed, for Stanislav floods her with petitions. Can so-and-so's sequestered estate be freed? Confiscated lands returned? A penalty for anti-Russian actions reduced? A Russian pension granted? The newest Russian subjects cling to a conviction that their onetime King still has influence in St. Petersburg. And he, the wretched dreamer he has always been, believes that, too.

I made you King, she answers him in her thoughts, *and what have you done? Let yourself be ruled by anyone who stomped his feet and screamed at you! Allowed the revolutionary fever to consume your people! Tried to scheme against me with the Ottoman Porte and France!*

She goes through the sheaf of papers with growing impatience. The tedious and mundane obscure what might be important.

For instance: At six each morning, the King's chamberlain brings him a cup of thick bouillon. It is made fresh every day, the cook locking the kitchen door as he prepares it.

Is the King afraid he might be poisoned?

Every day, Stanislav goes for a ride. Lososna is his favorite destination. Once there, he always alights and crosses the bridge to the other side of the Niemen River.

For what reason?

Why are these questions not asked until she

377

asks them? How many times does she have to stress the importance of vigilance? Is Bezborodko the only one she can fully trust?

She takes a fresh sheet of paper, dips her quill, and, in her reply to Repnin, asks for an investigation. Not too obvious or crude. No direct questions. *Observe and draw conclusions.*

And then she adds: *Since the act of abdication, Stanislav August is a* former *King. We wish this fact reflected in all future correspondence.*

"Prince Repnin tries his best, Your Majesty," Alexander Andreyevich replies when she shares her indignation with him at the morning briefing. "In his own cautious way."

She takes it for what it is. A reminder that a perfect courtier does not reveal his feelings to anyone. So she stops herself from quoting another of Repnin's revelations that suspicious-looking men have appeared in Grodno. *Wearing round hats, Your Majesty, which signals revolutionary inclinations.*

Pani, having devoured her blood sausage, settles underneath the desk and tries to lick her mistress's leg. Her snout roots underneath the clothes; her tongue pushes against the raw skin.

"Now, about Gustav Adolf, madame," Bezborodko begins, rubbing his hands.

The King spent another morning traversing the city on foot with his uncle, refusing all offers of carriages or horses. In the streets, much merriment has been made of the dress of the Swedes, their short coats, cloaks, and round hats.

The two have been to the Academy, admired the wax figure of Peter the Great, the pair of shoes he made with his own hands, and a pair of stockings he mended. They admired her manuscript of the Code of Laws. The King wished to know how many of these laws had been implemented. Then nodded when told that wise Sovereigns have to exercise patience in such matters, for there is a difference between writing on paper and writing on human skin.

Her minister delivers his report with a flickering smile of pleasure, from memory, without opening his folder, which — as she well knows — will confirm his accuracy word for word. "In short, Majesty, we are making excellent progress. It is openly said that most of the King's attendants are already counting the largesse associated with a royal wedding."

Other developments are far less welcome.

The French, having brutally murdered their King and Queen, have announced their unalterable will to fight for the liberation of all Europe. At least for now, this means invading Italy. This is worrisome in spite of the dismissing snipes about the sorry state of the

French troops. If the French troops are as ill-shod, hungry, and dressed in rags as they are said to be, the Austrians should've defeated them long ago.

"Venetians are terrified, Your Majesty," her minister concludes, "scrambling for support. But who will fight for them now?"

Pani, who senses the end of any visit, wags her tail and stretches her slim, agile body, her long, graceful neck. There are thick drops of pus in Pani's eyes. Queenie must have forgotten to rinse them with a chamomile infusion. Catherine feels a tweak of annoyance.

The smells that waft into the room, the scents of drying leaves and wood smoke, are no longer those of summer. The warm months are so fleetingly brief. It is only the Russian winter that drags on.

"One more thing, Your Majesty," Bezborodko says, having already asked permission to leave. "Grand Duke Constantine . . ." He pauses, a pained smile on his face.

"What has he done this time? And how much will it cost me?"

It turns out that Constantine loaded a cannon with live rats and fired them at a wall. Inside the Marble Palace. Ruining the fresh wallpaper she had ordered from Milan. Frightening his wife senseless.

Why? Why do the young disdain what is offered to them? Where does it come from, this need to spoil all that is good? To waste away the hours? To destroy rather than build?

Anger churns in her, even as her minister offers his consolations. The excuses are almost the same he has used when reporting on the escalating debts and Orlov-style gallivanting of her younger son, Alexei.

"Most young men need to blow off steam, Your Majesty. I was also quite reckless at his age."

"Give me your hand, Katinka," Le Noiraud insists.

She extends her right hand and he holds it between his palms and rubs it until she feels her blood quicken. Then he pulls at each of her fingers, to loosen the joints. His own hands are warm and dry. His skin soft. "You don't spare yourself," he says. "I protest."

"Is your sister keeping well?" she asks.

Le Noiraud's eyes, almond-shaped and so beautifully framed in black, look at her with childlike amazement. Is the Empress clairvoyant? Can she read his mind? He was just about to speak to her of his sister.

Her lover places her right hand back on her lap and takes hold of her left one. His gestures are slow and languid.

"I hate the summer here," he says. "We shouldn't have left Tsarskoye Selo so early."

His sister's dacha is his only escape in the city. He was visiting her only yesterday.

381

Lambro-Cazzioni was there, too. "You must remember him," he says. "He has served as Admiral under Prince Potemkin. A Greek."

She doesn't remember.

"I've known him for some time now," her lover continues, "but it takes a woman to discover a man's hidden virtues."

Catherine closes her eyes. Le Noiraud's fingers linger at the swollen knuckle of her left hand. His voice still carries in it some of the amazement of yesterday's discovery. "So incredibly propitious," he says.

It was Le Noiraud's sister who found out that the former Admiral is also a healer. She had this skin lesion on her arm for some time, and the Admiral noticed it fester. He begged to be allowed to treat it. His remedy was simple. He learned it at sea, from an old Greek sailor. Daily baths in cold seawater. No blistering, no bleedings. After a week of treatments, his sister's wound was completely healed.

"Will you let him see your leg, Katinka?" Le Noiraud asks, kissing her hand. "If I beg you to?"

She shakes her head. She doesn't have time to waste with some quack who — like all of them — will beg for a pension.

But Le Noiraud insists. He folds his hands as if in prayer. He whispers, "You promised me to take care of yourself. It won't take long. He is waiting outside. Do it for me. I beg you."

He has changed in the last few months. The air of unease around him has thickened. His liveliness has faded.

You were not sure about him, Potemkin, she thinks, *but look. He doesn't just think of himself. He is concerned with my health. He worries about me.*

"Not a medical man, per se, Your Highness," Lambro-Cazzioni says in his halting French. "Which allows me to claim that I've inflicted less harm on mankind than others."

In spite of her misgivings, he pleases her with his rugged looks, his military airs. Keeps himself straight, moves with precision. His hands are well kept, with fingernails clean and trimmed. And he makes no attempt to ingratiate himself by mentioning Grishenka's past favors.

"You may have a look, monsieur," she says.

Lambro-Cazzioni kneels on the floor and expertly removes Rogerson's bindings. Exposed, the leg looks worse than she remembers it. The skin has a bluish hue, the lesions are secreting bloody pus.

The Admiral sniffs at the bindings. He smears the tip of his finger with the bloody discharge and touches it with the tip of his tongue.

"Sweet blood, Your Majesty," he declares.

"What does that mean?"

The explanation he offers — there is too much sugar in her blood — makes little sense. Unlike Queenie, Catherine doesn't crave sweets. Rogerson has prescribed one glass of sweet Malaga wine a day to calm her down and strengthen her constitution. She doesn't even sweeten her coffee.

The Admiral listens intently. "It's not always what we eat, Your Majesty. The body has its own mysterious ways."

The word *mysterious* makes her flinch. Perhaps she has been too hasty in her decision to admit the man. What will he speak of next? The power of ancient incantations? Or a witch hiding a ball of hair and bones under her bed?

"Mysteries are merely problems yet unsolved," she retorts in a terse voice.

The Admiral must have sensed her displeasure, for he straightens. "The Greeks have many faults, Your Majesty, but we have been around long enough to gather some undisputed wisdom."

Smallpox is his proof. Long before British doctors discovered the miracle of inoculation, Greek and Turkish peasants knew of ways that protected their children.

"You may try your cure," she decides, in spite of her misgivings, and watches his ruddy face beam.

"The seawater needs to be very cold, Your Majesty," the Admiral explains, as a servant enters with two basins.

The water will be cold. Chunks of ice still float in it.

He places the empty basin on the floor and rests her leg in it. With a small tumbler, he draws the cold seawater from another basin and dribbles it over her skin.

Catherine closes her eyes. The water still smells of the sea, bringing memories of her childhood pleasures. A run along the Baltic beach, a blackened log covered with seaweed, her bare feet splashing in the shallow waves. Babette's voice reminding her of the bounty that comes from the sea. Fish, sea salts, amber.

"How does that feel, madame?" the Admiral asks.

"Better," she says. The leg, numbed with the cold, has yielded. "If this continues, perhaps I'll make another tour of the Crimea. Would you advise it, monsieur?"

"Excellent idea," the Admiral says, clucking his tongue. "With Your Majesty's permission," he adds, "I'll come every morning with fresh seawater. So that Your Majesty can continue her work in the service of the Empire, undisturbed."

In the meantime, he advises against binding and blistering. She should expose the leg to the air whenever she can. Let the skin breathe, let the lesions dry. No matter what mighty Rogerson will come up with to discredit him.

Which he will try.

An hour later, the leg is still free from pain. When Rogerson's arrival is announced, she sends Queenie to tell him his ministrations are not required.

" 'Not ever,' he asked, 'or not today?' " Queenie relates the exchange. "So I said, 'not today.' So he asked 'Why?' and I said I have no way of telling what Her Majesty thinks, but that Your Majesty must have her reasons. And he looked as if he had just swallowed a toad."

Nothing cheers Queenie up like a small act of revenge.

The King, Queenie announces, was particularly impressed by the elegant structures of the Russian bridges. He was also charmed by the dancers on Vasilevsky Island. And amazed by the friendliness of people in the streets. Queenie, whose waist must have gained another few inches in the last week alone, is nearly jumping for joy. "What a kind and considerate young man he is," she says. "And his uncle bears himself like a true *boyar.*"

Bezborodko's reports are less starry-eyed. The Regent didn't like the Bronze Horseman. His arguments: The giant sacred rock brought from Karelia to the bank of the Neva with such effort was twenty-one feet high, forty long, and covered in thick moss. Once it was cleaned, hewed, and polished, it was no longer a giant sacred boulder but just a big rock. Peter the Great, who was to survey the great Empire from its heights, can merely peep into the first floor of the neighboring houses like a second-rate bronze spy.

The court dress Queenie helps her put on replaces her loose morning one. Queenie pats dabs of almond cream onto her mistress's cheeks. Smears her temples with oil of verbena, filling the room with its faint citrus scent. Her chatting will stop if not encouraged with questions. A tacit agreement they arrived at years ago, comfortable like the loose gowns, the kidskin slippers. It suits them both.

"Has Bolik returned?"

"Not yet."

"How is Alexandrine taking it?"

"The sweet lamb is trying not to cry, madame. She had her painting lesson."

"What is she painting?"

"A birch grove."

"Good enough to show to the King?"

"It's not finished yet."

"Then we shall wait."

Queenie shuffles through the room, gathering the remnants of the afternoon chores, the silver bowl in which the ice has almost melted, the towels, the jars of creams.

"Are you sure, madame, that you can manage?" She echoes her old question as she fetches the cane. Although it is hard to see of what help Queenie could be if her mistress faltered. Thankfully, only a short corridor separates the Imperial Bedroom from the study. And Catherine's bad leg is still free from pain.

"Quite sure."

The gray goose quills are tempting. It would please her to write to her old friend Grimm, describe her plans to replace the remaining rectangular flower beds at Tsarskoye Selo with the natural look that she so much prefers. But Queenie is already presenting the list of visitors awaiting admission. Twenty names at least, a whole afternoon wasted. Chambers's name, thank goodness, is first on the list. The imperial architect's report of the Chinese Village he is constructing in Tsarskoye Selo is long overdue.

Queenie has left her post for a moment, drawn by some jingling noise in the antechamber, another palace drama unfolding.

It's always like this at court, this realm of self-absorption. To be noticed is part of the game. Thus, everything is an outrage, a scandal, an offense, a spite of cosmic proportions. Some armchair traveler to Russia claims that Grigory Orlov has been strangled by his brothers? Or that Prince Potemkin poisoned Sashenka Lanskoy out of jealousy? Or that he himself had been poisoned by To-fana water? By Platon Zubov, perhaps? Bring it all to the Empress. Lay it at her feet as proof of vigilance or foresightedness. Expect praise and reward. And always, always, mind how much Catherine has given to others.

What happened to free spirits, weightless, untethered? The company of the brave? Larger vistas, beyond the confines of these gilded rooms?

Queenie returns to announce that two of the imperial maids-of-honor are waiting to be admitted. They have a request to make. "Important, Your Majesty," Queenie says, clearly well rewarded for her eloquence on their behalf.

Another tale of desire and delay, ambitions thwarted, merits overlooked? A favor granted deemed too obscure, declared a backwater of the courtly possibilities?

"Let Monsieur Chambers in first," the Empress decides.

Queenie gives her a hurt look. Her faithful friend, fat and panting after the smallest effort. What was the ditty Platon has come up with?

This ugly maid whose belly goes
at least a step before her nose.

"Your Majesty," Chambers says, bowing low to kiss her hand. "Here is what I propose."

He is a tall, shapely man, her architect. Fond of his fine clothes. Jeweled buckles on his shoes, lace ruffles, white silk stockings. The gleam of gold pleases him, and the smoothness of velvet. But today he has dressed in haste, for Catherine spots a button undone, the white smudge of powder on his shoulders.

The drawings he unfolds are beautifully executed on parchment paper.

She marvels at the neatness of lines. In her Chinese Village, there will be houses, bridges with fretwork railings, a vermilion-colored pagoda, and an observatory. Chambers plunges into praises of single-braced palings, the importance of symmetry. He shows her sketches of temples and garden pavilions to which many paths lead. He extolls the virtues of garden seats tempting at the end of a long walk, offering respite to the visitor. Of pleasure rooms, palisades, and intricate latticework. Octagons, he says. Painted panels. Patterns that mix Chinese and Gothic designs.

What a pleasure to see an idea take shape!

"Elevations and lacquered wood are a happy mixture, madame," Chambers continues, his voice lit with passion. "The Chinese gardeners plant without any order of disposition of parts. They have a different sense of beauty. Asymmetrical."

Why does it have to be so rare, Catherine thinks, *a moment like this one?* Hearing something both new and intriguing. She should have made such conversations into a commandment, an imperial ukase: *Thou shalt not bore thy Sovereign.*

"They are called *sharawaggis* of China," Chambers continues. "A Chinese word to describe the quality of being surprising through graceful disorder."

Travelers who have passed by her court on their way from China have told her of an Imperial Palace that sprawls over an area that could easily contain a city, of its ornaments, which attract not so much by the costliness of materials as the breathtaking intricacy of work.

Women there, the travelers have said, live in seclusion. Many wives vie for a husband's eye and design ways of keeping his attention. By any means. One imperial concubine smothered her own son to cast suspicion on the Emperor's first wife. She succeeded, for who could conceive of a mother sacrificing her own child? A memory of Paul snorting his displeasure over something long forgotten comes as she bends over the blueprints.

"I beg Your Majesty to take a closer look." Chambers prances as he speaks, bobs his head like a bird in search of worms. He has sketched a handsome pagoda with dragons. With bells in their mouths! His drawings, he stresses, are not the amusing parodies of Chinese buildings that other architects ply, but sincere imitations of style, characteristics.

Free but accurate. Not a particular building, he continues eagerly, but the spirit of many. He wants her to notice the pleasing disorder of the grounds around them.

"Garden design should differ from nature," Chambers says, "like a heroic poem differs from prose. Nature cannot give pleasure without assistance from art."

It'll cost, she thinks, when the architect leaves, happy that his expanding budget has again been approved. But anything of importance and beauty has its price. Chinoiserie is in fashion everywhere now. Russia cannot be backward. She doesn't want to hear that she fancies the less important, the second-rate.

Queenie comes back but doesn't mention the maids-of-honor and their quest. They must have resigned themselves to their fate for the time being. Small mercy, but sweet! But her servant has other annoying news.

The parlor where she likes to read in the afternoon is swarming with flies.

The chambermaids left the windows open, Queenie explains. She is flustered with annoyance. Incompetence, laziness, lack of foresight always make her rage. In Queenie's world, these are major crimes.

"I want to see it," Catherine says. It must be the lightness in her leg that prompts her to go into the parlor. *Swarming* is an exaggeration, but the flies are there. Buzzy, circling the room, annoyingly close.

Called to the rescue, Zotov paces the room. He scorns rolled newspapers or slippers in favor of fly flaps he makes himself from stiff sugar paper and a wooden stick. He is swift and graceful. He can swat a fly in mid-flight, though most get trapped by the closed window, buzzing against the invisible barrier that has now cut them off from where they've come.

Enraged, Queenie leaves to scold the offending chambermaids, who will walk about with long faces for hours, trying to draw everyone's attention to the injustice of their fate.

One more swat and the last of the unwelcome guests is lying lifeless on the floor. Zotov picks them all up and wraps them in his checkered handkerchief.

"Your Majesty can now read in peace," he announces.

In this palace, where death has so ruthlessly thinned the ranks, Zotov's is another comforting face. He was born at the palace, a son of a valet, and has never lived anywhere else. At the time of the coup, Catherine recalls, he was no older than ten. She remembers him walking behind his father, carrying her fan, absorbed by the utter seriousness of his task.

"I've seen a cat in the garden that looked like Pushok," she tells him. "The same white fur, the same kink in the tail. But isn't Pushok long dead?"

"Dead and buried," Zotov confirms. "When Mistress was still with us."

They talk about the descendants of Elizabeth's favorite cats, Pushok, Murka, and Bronya, stalking the cellars and back stairs, taking up residence in the attic when the imperial dogs moved into the palace.

"Packs of cats," Zotov says. "Colonies."

They eat what they can forage. They shy away from people.

Zotov gives her a cautious look, gauging the level of her interest in his stories. He will stop the moment he discerns the slightest impatience. A perfect servant. Alert. Irreplaceable.

She nods to encourage the words to flow.

It amuses her to hear that unseen wars are being waged in her palace. Cats from the cellar fight those from the attic. Woe to anyone who strays outside of their territory and is not fast enough. In the wine cellars, the cupbearer pages often come across the wounded. If they don't make it, their rotting corpses will betray their last hiding spot.

The palace servants, Zotov reminds her, have long memories. They recall the times when imperial cats wore velvet coats and feasted on roasted chicken breasts. "How the mighty have fallen," they say now, as the cats dart away at their sight. The boys chase them. Cats not swift enough end up with their tails set on fire. Or have their heads pushed into a sack, left to run in all directions blindfolded.

Zotov pauses for a brief moment, considering the wisdom of telling her more, and decides against it.

Catherine is grateful. She doesn't want to hear of eyes plucked out, or skins torn out of a live cat to cure some ailment. "I've something for you," she says. "Madame Lievens swears Alexandrine is growing every night. She is taller in the morning by an inch."

The Grand Duchesses are given a new pair of shoes each week, sixteen dozen pairs of gloves a year. They have plentiful supplies of powder, patches, ribbons, combs, and silk hoops. For the summer, each is provided with three flowered coats, three plain or striped silk dresses, and one nightgown. Madame General Lievens, the chief governess of all the Grand Duchesses of the Imperial Household, had been ordered to prepare a trunkful of clothes to be given away.

"Take your daughters to her today," she tells Zotov. "Let each choose a new outfit."

Lucretius is what she settles on for this day's reading: procreant atoms to which no rest is allowed, for their movement through the depth of space is incessant. Some of them collide and bounce far apart, others recoil. Entangled by their own shapes, they make a rock or the bulk of iron.

Power attracts its opposite. What cannot be diminished through force will be slowly chipped away.

"Atoms in the void?" Potemkin would've groaned. "Why don't you pick up Plato instead, Katinka? Read of a beautiful young body that turns our thoughts toward perfection."

But they won't let her enjoy her musings and her solitude for too long.

"Your Majesty," Vishka whispers, exposing her blackened teeth, crowding in her mouth like beggars at Easter. Her hair has grayed in the last months, and thinned. The baggy skin under her eyes gives her a bewildered look. Her second lady's maid has an uneasy look about her, but the determination in her eyes is proof that, at least in her mind, the matter is important enough. While Queenie is sprawling, taking more and more space, Vishka is shrinking.

The book closes with a soft thud.

If Vishka is here, it must be time to go over the upcoming move to the Tauride Palace. *His* palace, Catherine still calls it in her mind. Prince Potemkin's. Grishenka's. She had bought it for him and then from him — so that he could pay his debts — and gave it to him again. Now it's once again hers, her preferred summer residence in St. Petersburg, where no cannon salutes announce her comings and goings. Where petitioners are not admitted and empty court talk doesn't have to be suffered.

Vishka has a whole list of matters awaiting her decision. Grand Duke Alexander is asking for permission to invite Prince Adam, and if permission be granted, he would like to house his friend in the Blue Suite. Alexandrine is begging to be allowed to return to the Winter Palace for the night, on account of Bolik, who might show up. The Tauride steward is reporting that all is ready to receive Her Imperial Majesty, but begs permission to hire an animal trainer. The kangaroos, the King of England's sumptuous gift, are causing a small sensation. A special observation platform has already been built near their cages, but the experience of watching these splendid beasts would be enhanced if a trainer could orchestrate a clever show of their boxing skills.

"There is one more matter Your Majesty might wish to know about," Vishka says when all is decided. (Prince Adam can stay, Alexandrine cannot keep going to and fro between two palaces, and the Tauride gardens shall not be turned into a circus!) Unlike Queenie, who believes herself an expert on love and finer feelings, Vishka delights in reporting petty sins, a valet who steals her ribbons to frequent tea taverns or gin shops, a maid who wraps herself in the imperial shawl when she thinks herself alone.

"Is it about Alexandrine?" Catherine asks.

"No, madame," Vishka demurs, hesitating. As if, after forty years of service, she still does not quite trust her mistress's benevolence.

One has to be patient with old servants. Coax the truth out of them slowly, without putting words in their mouths. There is such a brief moment before what is worth hearing turns into what they think would please you. Gestures work better than words. A squeezed hand, a smoothed cheek, followed by a look into their eyes, a promise of attention.

But this time the cause of Vishka's agitation is Grand Duke Constantine, married only this February, with much pomp and expense. Vishka walked past the Marble Palace, where the young couple live. The windows were open, and she heard screams. "Like a cat skinned alive," Vishka gasps.

Has she ever heard a skinned cat?

Constantine, for whom she, the Empress, once wished the splendors of the Byzantine Empire, who was to restore the light of Orthodoxy to the darkened East, lead the Russian troops to Constantinople, defeat the Turks, and bring home the golden fleece to Russia, is a disappointment. Drunken evenings at taverns, smashed furniture, debts unpaid, creditors threatened with a thrashing have not ended in spite of numerous promises.

Casting an envious eye in the direction of

398

the abandoned book, she calms her maid. Constantine is an unpolished bear. He has always been one, since he was a child. Even then his teachers complained that he was doing things in fits and starts. Translating Plutarch from Greek one moment, only to run away to shoot birds as soon as his tutor turned his back. No wonder he is impatient with his wife.

Vishka persists. At the Marble Palace, Grand Duke Constantine allows no one to enter his private study. If the smell coming out of it becomes offensive, Grand Duke burns a purifying cartridge there. The maids beg to be allowed to clean the room, but they are told to stay away. The walls of the main salon are stained with red wine. The portraits in the Gallery are riddled with bullet holes. Two have had their eyes cut out. The carpets in the bedroom are torn to shreds. "And now Grand Duchess Anna Fyodorovna is crying all the time," Vishka adds slyly. "She won't say why, Your Majesty."

Anna Fyodorovna, to be truthful, is not the brightest of God's creatures. A pretty face, yes, but her movements are awkward and her education has been neglected. Seven months in Russia and her Russian has barely improved.

There have been other reports already. Queenie has mentioned how the Princess reads French novels by the cartload and weeps over the travails of imaginary lovers. What is it that Anna expects? Flowery declarations of her husband's passion? Adoring looks? Staring at the moon? Platon has summed it best: "She has the wit of a sheep. All she sees is her own misery."

"Tell me everything," she tells Vishka with a sigh.

Anna Fyodorovna is complaining that her husband is ignoring her. Constantine is complaining that his wife is always sulking.

More troubling is that Anna Fyodorovna and Alexander's wife persist with their mutual visits in spite of having been warned of Her Majesty's disapproval. And lately the visits have become clandestine. More than once, servants have been bribed to take Anna through the back stairs, her face covered with a veil. Elizabeth, who should've refused such subterfuge, takes part in it. The two have been heard whispering together in German.

Oh, well, the Empress thinks. *Silly girls cling to each other.*

"This will pass, Vishka."

"This isn't right, Your Majesty," Vishka insists. "Grand Duchess Elizabeth has such a tender heart. It is so easy to burden her with troubles she should be spared."

Faithful Vishka, the juggler of hints and suggestions. What her maid is really saying is that Elizabeth should concentrate on getting with child. And that she should be more mindful of her position at court. Place herself above her sister-in-law, keep her distance. Elizabeth, who one day will become the Emperor's consort, should watch whose confidences she receives, whose whispers she heeds.

It is still summer, but outside, migrating birds are already gathering in fluttering crowds. From the meshed section of the winter garden comes the jittery commotion of her flock. Swallows, turtledoves, and orioles are nervously flitting from one branch to another.

Catherine is not looking forward to winter, to fur-lined boots, heavy pelisses. To stuffy rooms scented with hot vinegar and mint. Her aching bones have not yet soaked up enough of the warmth of the sun.

"This is why Constantine is angry with his wife," Vishka continues, oblivious to the chattering birds. "Our high-and-mighty Princess doesn't know when to stop. She expects attention, but how much does *she* give?"

Mercifully, Vishka doesn't expect answers to these questions. Satisfied with the results of her confession, she concedes that matters are perhaps not all that bleak.

"That they quarrel," Catherine says, "is a good sign. It means they are not indifferent to each other."

Over the next weeks, many balls and festive

suppers will be given in honor of the Swedish King. The first will take place at the Tauride Palace. "Wouldn't the Winter Palace be more convenient?" Le Noiraud has asked already. "One story, no stairs," Catherine has replied. "Much easier on everyone's knees." *I have to lie to this beautiful child. You know that, Grishenka,* she thinks, and — in her mind — her Prince of Tauride chuckles at these words in reply.

After the news of Potemkin's death arrived, she came to the Tauride Palace every day, even if for just a few stolen moments. It seemed to her that Grishenka might appear from behind the marble column, his dead eye half closed, his hair wet, for he had just doused it under a pump.

Le Noiraud's beauty astonishes her every time her eyes rest on him — here in the corridors of the Tauride Palace, or on the gilded sofas in her inner rooms, where he likes to lounge dressed in his glittering velvets, smelling of musk and sandalwood, his feet buried in a deep soft carpet, his hooded eyes resting on the old paintings of faraway landscapes.

Now Le Noiraud has shoved aside Zotov and Queenie, who trot a few steps behind them, and pushes her rolling chair along the main Gallery, entertaining her with his descriptions of the visiting Swedes. The *Re-*

gent, he mimics, minces his steps as he walks, as if he were trying to negotiate his way across a freshly washed floor without wetting his shoes.

The King appears in his monologue, too: Gustav Adolf does *not* approve of levity. Gustav Adolf prefers *serious* discussions to gallant *talk.*

"How serious?" Catherine asks.

"Oh, you know," Le Noiraud replies airily. "The nature of man. The limits of reason."

"That serious," she teases.

It is a credit to Platon that he hasn't mentioned Potemkin at all. "No need to be jealous of the dead," she has told him more than once, but Le Noiraud cannot help himself. His complaints about the Tauride Palace are veiled in concern. He doesn't like it because here his rooms are too far away from hers. The canal smells of rot. Unlike the free-flowing Neva, it gets clogged with debris. He mentions miasmas, putrid vapors, irritated lungs.

The palace teems with running feet and the vile tempers of servants in a hurry. The footmen are hanging the last of the chandelier crystals. Maids polish the doorknobs and hunt for smudges on the glass panes. Tables are swathed in white cloths and decorated with garlands of flowers and ribbons. From the garden come the sounds of the orchestra practicing a contredanse.

The servants bow when her small entourage passes, but they do not abandon their chores. Across the main hall, her old housekeeper, Madame Bolyanska, is chastising a maid over something, her nagging voice rising over the melee.

Bolik is still missing. This very morning, Alexandrine asked Miss Williams if God is testing her with this loss. Then she wanted to know how it is possible to feel happy and miserable at the same time.

The rolling chair is a constant reminder of defeat. Even in this palace where there are no stairs to impede her, Catherine cannot walk farther than the length of a room. Memory pricks her: images of Empress Elizabeth Petrovna panting after just a few steps, her flushed cheeks, swollen feet, flesh spilling out of her slippers. What would she have said seeing her now? "Destiny sniffs after you like a bloodhound, Catherine"? There would be a sneer on her lips, too, and a taxing, sour look at Platon. "Wearing old gloves till we can get new ones"?

In the last years, Catherine has ordered some changes to the palace — added a theater and a chapel — but most of the rooms, Picture Hall, the Tapestry Sitting Room, the Chinese Hall, are the way Potemkin left them. She has not touched their old bedrooms. Both have narrow beds, plain wallpaper, and square tables made of birch wood, but there are differences. In hers — the larger of the two — goats and shepherds roam on the ceiling and there is an antechamber that she uses as a meeting room. His is a monk's cell: A giant cross hangs on the wall; a threadbare carpet covers the floor. So far, Platon has not asked for permission to sleep there. She will never allow it, but it is better to leave such things unsaid.

The bedroom still carries the faint smell of burnt vinegar from a fumigation pastille, in spite of Queenie's assurances that it has been thoroughly aired. Catherine leaves the rolling chair at the threshold. She has added only a bookshelf and a proper writing table.

Le Noiraud casts a curious eye over the bookshelf, his finger tracing the slim volumes she has brought here from her library. No murderous French instigations disguised as philosophy, she tells her lover. "This is my favorite," she says, pointing at the four volumes of *Solitude Considered, with Respect to Its Influence upon the Mind and the Heart*. She tells Le Noiraud that the author, Monsieur Zimmerman, is a physician to his Britannic Majesty at Hanover. She doesn't tell him that she considers hiring a German to replace Rogerson.

"Does he advocate solitude, then?" Le Noiraud asks, his head cocked like that of a curious bird or an eager puppy. He knows full well she won't resist explanations. "Wants us to become hermits? Connect with wild beasts?"

"Oh, no," she protests. "All he says is that under peaceful shades of solitude, the mind regenerates, faculties acquire new force."

Le Noiraud blinks and shakes his head in protest. "I don't wish for solitude," he mutters. "I wish to be with *you.*"

She smiles at him.

Alone, she looks through the window at the leaden sky. The rain is not welcome, for it will stop the guests from walking in the garden. It would be much better to give the young an excuse for moonlit walks.

Oh, well. Not all can be controlled. Better to concentrate on what can be.

On her writing table lie the dispositions for the evening. The sequence of dances, seating arrangements for the chief table and the card games. Le Noiraud will sit beside her, together with Lev Naryshkin. They will keep her laughing while the young ones dance. Outside, the fireworks will display Catherine's wheel and shooting stars so that wishes can be made. She checks the selections of flowers, wine, and brandy, the choice of china. The plates from the Green Frog service, the most suitable for bucolic thoughts. Gilded cups always look good in candlelight. The table centerpieces will display the porcelain figures from her collection of the peoples of Russia. A few chosen ones should be placed around the figurine of her, the Empress, seated on the throne.

In spite of all these efforts, she knows, the ball will not equal the ones Grishenka used to give. Without him, splendor is a shadowy word.

For months after the news from Jassy arrived, Potemkin was everywhere, in the people he once loved, in the places he inhabited, in the objects he touched. His presence was evoked by a book with gnawed edges, for she could never stop him from chewing on anything he held in his hands, or by a broken china basket lovingly glued together in penance for a bout of anger. Catherine kept waking up to the memory of seeing him standing over her, his face gray in the semidarkness, his giant body hunched. Gazing at her for a long time and then, soundlessly, making the sign of the cross over her head.

Now, five years later, she remembers him only the way he was on that last day she saw him. In his riding boots, the black patch over his bad eye. Stumbling as he entered her room. *He's younger than I am,* she kept telling herself, seeing how ill he looked. *He will bury me.*

Only here can she still, sometimes, recapture the richness of the past. Only here, at an

407

odd moment like this one, in this small bedroom or in his sprawling winter garden where he once lavishly planted oleanders and bougainvillea, she may feel Grishenka's presence at her side.

Beloved *matushka,* not seeing you makes it even harder for me to live . . .

Le Noiraud, whom Queenie must have fetched, uncorks a bottle with reviving salts and places it under her nose. The acrid smell of ammonia makes her gag. She swats at it, as if it were an annoying fly.

Le Noiraud wraps his arms around her. "You've been thinking of him again," her lover murmurs. There is nothing but concern in his voice.

She nods.

"Cry, Katinka," he coaxes in his silky voice. "Cry."

It feels good to admit to grief. To let tears flow and then have them wiped off her cheeks gently. To see her own reflection flickering in Le Noiraud's eyes.

In the end, work is always the best remedy.

She reaches for Bezborodko's latest report on Alexander's Polish friend, Adam, with whom her grandson has been spending so much time lately. The two have been seen in animated conversations at the embankment.

408

They have also ridden to the countryside around Tsarskoye Selo, where they spent whole days rambling through the fields and meadows. Seven times in August alone.

Shooting birds?

Talking, Bezborodko writes in his report. *Of Rousseau, American democracy, and food.*

Prince Adam has come to St. Petersburg at her orders. His family, the Czartoryskis, have foolishly backed Kościuszko's rebellion and had their estates sequestered as a result. When they begged her forgiveness, the Empress wrote: Send your son to Russia first.

The Czartoryskis are an old Polish family. Their lines are ancient, their connections by blood or marriage impeccable. And their ambitions are vast. Now — with the new borders — they have become Russian subjects. Defeat always breeds resentment.

The Czartoryskis, her minister assures her, are fast learners. They've accepted what is plain to see. From now on, power comes only from the Imperial Court.

Perhaps.

It's true that Prince Adam no longer resembles the wary guest he had been when he arrived. Polite, oh, yes, but also stiff and aloof. Now, the Dolgorukis find him charming, the Vorontzovs praise his wit and elegance. And, of course, Maria Fyodorovna considers Adam the crème de la crème. Though her daughter-in-law's gushings have to be taken with a grain of salt. One of the Czartoryski girls married Maria's brother.

So what have Alexander and Adam been talking about on all these long walks?

The spy's report is not very illuminating here. The two wanderers dismissed the servants. Carried their own gear. Testimonies of a few peasants at whose huts the two sought refreshments are brief: The grand gentlemen delighted in black bread, sour cream, and especially fresh kvass straight from the root cellar.

Conclusions?

The report is clear here. Disadvantages of this friendship: Grand Duke Alexander has a tender heart and is prone to idealistic flights of fancy. What sort of Polish nonsense might Prince Adam try to impart to a future Tsar? There is also jealousy at court, for the imperial grandson has not chosen a Russian prince of blood as his companion.

Advantages? For a future Russian Tsar, an influential Polish friend is a valuable asset. Especially one who possesses a fine, well-educated mind, one in whose company Alexander won't be drawn into youthful mischief. Books have already been checked out of the Imperial Library: Rousseau. Tacitus. Plutarch. Cicero. Only the night before, her spies tell her, the two discussed the American principles of government for hours.

If such animated exchanges of ideas continue, Alexander might stop sneaking out of the palace to take part in his father's Gatchina parades. A few signs point to it already. Alexander's Gatchina uniform is still in his bedroom in a locked drawer, but he has not had it brushed for a full week.

So I advise patience, coupled with caution, Bezborodko concludes. *Especially since nowadays, the young find confessions irresistible.*

Bezborodko is right. At court, little can be hidden away. And what is concealed, sooner or later, will be trusted to a letter, or the pages of some diary. Patience has always been Catherine's friend.

Her eyes return to Bezborodko's summary of Alexander and Adam's nightlong discussion. How they first decided on a question to be resolved: What saved the American Revolution from the excesses of the French debacle? Alexander favored fate and the will of the people. Adam argued for the vastness of American territory and the lack of traditional structures.

Her son Paul is a dismal failure, an embarrassment she doesn't deserve, but her grandson is her most precious reward. Her smart, wise, handsome grandson, whose mind she has been shaping since the day he was born. A promise so splendidly fulfilled.

Her Monsieur Alexander.

Her flesh and blood.

For she can see herself in him.

He is Russia's future.

She is still absorbed in these thoughts when, from outside the room, muffled sobs interrupt.

"Grand Duchess Anna Fyodorovna is begging to be received," Queenie says, a wry smile on her plump face. "On her knees."

Queenie smells of pastries. Plums, berries, and melted butter. She must have been to the kitchens again, unable to resist the bubbling pots and sweet froth of fresh fillings.

"Now?" Catherine asks, casting a look at her desk.

The sobs do not diminish.

"Anna Fyodorovna insists," Queenie says. "I told her to come back tomorrow, but she won't listen. She is not herself, Your Majesty."

"Let her in, then," she says and sighs. If Anna is sent away now, she'll go to Elizabeth or Alexandrine with her woes. Spoil their mood.

Queenie opens the door. Constantine's bride rushes in. Her black hair has been hastily pinned up; red ribbons flutter behind her. The sleeves of her white morning dress are stained with soot. Was she trying to start a fire? In August? There are livid circles under her hazel eyes, and she clasps her hands and presses them to her small chest, tugging at the folds of her fichu.

412

A sweetly pretty girl, petite. *Piquant,* someone described her. When she first arrived in
Russia, her face was all life and mirth. Now
it's tearstained.

"Your Majesty," she mutters, placing a
respectful kiss on Catherine's hand.

"Whatever is the matter, Anna?"

Anna does not answer.

"Sit down, my child," Catherine says, handing her a handkerchief. Instead of wiping her
eyes, the girl rubs at them as if trying to erase
a stubborn stain. These eyes used to be her
best feature. They seemed bold and eloquent,
suggesting a certain hardiness that could have
served the girl well. But Anna shows little
toughness now.

"I'm so sorry, Your Majesty! Please help
me!"

"What are you sorry about? Have you done
something wrong?"

"Oh, no," the girl exclaims. Being sorry was
just an expression she has assumed would
please the Empress. Her hands, unclasped,
have settled over her belly. Is she *enceinte,*
perhaps? Beating Elizabeth to it!

But Anna Fyodorovna does not have the
startled expression of an expectant mother.

One does not wish for these confidences. It
would suit Catherine to stay away from the
sordid details of her grandson's marriage. To
be spared intercessions and tears. She recalls
the time of Anna's arrival in Russia, the fetes,

413

the soirees, the incessant escapades through the chambers of the Winter Palace to see the imperial jewels, or the grand chandeliers in the ballroom. One would hope that the little goose had been warned what an imperial marriage entails.

So why is she, the Empress and their grandmother, being treated to some sordid scene of family drama?

"There is no good way to say what you have come to say, Anna." Her voice is as flat and curt as she can make it without sounding angry. "So just say it."

The girl hesitates. "Your Imperial Majesty has been so kind to me . . ."

Married for four months already. Time for her to realize the limitations of childish dreams. Put aside her silly novels.

"Well, then, my dear child," she says. She thinks: *You are wasting my time, taking minutes I need for matters far graver than a bride who expects a great deal of happiness where merely some is possible.*

"My husband doesn't love me," Anna blurts out.

So the little Princess has seen some of her dreams shattered. *God dealt you a decent enough hand, Princess,* she wants to say, *but you have to play it well.* Instead, she asks: "Why do you say that?"

"He is often despondent."

"Why does that bother you? His disposition is as it has always been."

"He says odd things."

"What things?"

"That he wishes to run away and live among the soldiers. That he will dig himself a hole in the ground and live there."

"Does he say it often?"

"Yes. And he sometimes leaves for the whole night and does not reveal to me why. Or where he goes."

"And why do you need to know his every step?"

There is more and more hesitation in Anna's eyes. A silly girl, forgetting how little she has brought into this marriage. Why do people need the reminders of their insignificance? Why, when left to their own devices, do they dream up countless other destinies for themselves? Her spies report that Anna is not unwilling to respond to the advances of handsome courtiers. Was that what Constantine noticed? And is this why she is trying to discredit him?

"Your Beloved Majesty, I beg you," Anna whimpers.

There is more. Constantine has told his wife that he married her only to stop Grandmaman from scolding.

"But this is just childish nonsense!" Catherine exclaims. "You don't know him as well as I do. You must've upset him with something.

He is rash in his anger. But he has a good heart and he'll grow to love you."

Anna drops her head, stares at the floor.

This is what it comes to. Anna Fyodorovna wants to be reassured.

"I've been like you," she tells Constantine's bride. "I came here to marry a stranger. My husband was not in love with me at first. I had to make him love me. I had to find my own place at court.

"As a Grand Duchess, I had to make myself useful to him. Share his interests. Help him with chores he considered tedious. I learned everything that was important to him. I won his trust."

Anna Fyodorovna is staring at the floor, not daring to interrupt. Perhaps some of this story will penetrate her foolish dreams. Perhaps it will be enough.

But it's not. The little Princess is shaking her head, pulling up the sleeves of her gown to reveal bruises, blue and yellow, on her arms. Then she opens the morning gown and lowers the chemise. The skin of her breast is mottled with welts.

There is a moment of silence. Time to consider what is possible, what can be said, and what needs to be merely hinted at.

"Have you spoken to anyone about this, Anna?" Catherine asks, carefully.

Her grandson's bride shakes her head, but is this the whole truth? The rambling letters she writes to her mother are mostly filled with trivial details. Has she managed to send others, ones her spies didn't intercept? Or perhaps these seemingly innocuous words she uses are part of a cipher? Though what would Maman do now but advise her daughter to be patient, speak of duty and marital obligations?

"I'm glad you have been silent about it," she tells the girl. "That you have protected the innocence of others."

Anna sobs now, a wailing sob of despair, a telling sign that some hints have been passed on, some confessions have been made.

"You are a clever girl," Catherine continues. Her voice is harder now. There is no good way to say what she has to say. "I can forbid him to touch you. Is this what you want? To become an estranged wife a few months after the wedding? He is second to the throne, you know."

If you want the balls, the dances, the glamour of the court, there are sacrifices to be made. You have to be silent. You have to be loyal to me. You have to find a way to cope. Get pregnant, give him a son, and take a lover. Let your husband have his pleasures, and take care of yours. This is how most people live. In this country and in others.

"Do you want to go back to your mother?"

Anna Fyodorovna considers these words in silence. It's hard to tell where her thoughts go. Pleasures or pains of being a Grand Duchess? Or does Anna still believe that she, her Empress, can change her husband's ways? That she can save Anna from more pain?

She extends her hand and tucks a loose lock back under Anna's ribboned cap. "How are the contredanse lessons progressing, my dear?" she asks. "Elizabeth tells me that you are more graceful than she is. Tonight I want to see you dance."

The Tauride Palace, polished, buffed, tidied, and decorated with garlands of flowers and fresh pine boughs, is thronged with guests. Queenie reports that everyone admires the porcelain figures of the Russian peoples and the clever ways the refreshments have been arranged. Sturgeon mousse in the shapes of giant fish with cucumber slices as scales. Vodka bottles encased in blocks of ice, in which frozen white rosebuds appear to float. "The cook won't tell anyone how he does it," Queenie complains.

The Swedish King's eyes pretend to slide off the riches he sees, but it is an act. Before he paid his reverences — referring to St. Petersburg as the magnificent Venice of the North — he stopped by Grishenka's collection of old icons and whispered something to his uncle.

The ball in honor of the Swedish visitors is a fitting scene for young passion. The floors are gleaming with wax to make dancing easier. The gowns are sumptuous; the jewels flash in candlelight. *Nature is our teacher,* she thinks. *Display the colors, get noticed, entice. We are all dancing the same dance.*

From her ballroom podium, Catherine watches Gustav Adolf approach Alexandrine. Her granddaughter wears pink satin; a gauze fichu hides her slim shoulders. Ringlets fall on her neck. Her eyes are bright and shining whenever she looks up, but she is shy and mostly stares at the floor.

Dear child. So much is still before her. The sweetness of the first kiss. The stirrings of desire, the ecstasy of release. *Take it all, my love,* Catherine thinks. *Drink as much as you can, for it vanishes so fast.* Desire is nature's blessing. When it leaves, decay takes over. Rot and pain. Emptiness and grief.

Alexander is casting a gloomy eye at the Swedish King. Jealous, Catherine thinks, with the jealousy of an elder brother. Adam is tugging his sleeve, pointing at the orchestra, which is settling at the raised podium. In a deft imitation of a butterfly whirl, one of the contredanse figures, his long arm rests behind an imaginary lady's back.

Alexander nods and laughs.

Paul has just arrived from Gatchina and is strutting toward her, always a reluctant guest, suspicious of everything around him. The Empress hears his loud snorts. The rasping sound, though familiar, is ever more annoying. Even breathing doesn't come easy to this awkward son of hers.

He's wearing the Preobrazhensky greens, a concession to her, Catherine knows. He prefers the tight-fitting blue Prussian uniform. At Gatchina, Paul calls her Imperial Guards spoilt and ignorant of proper military discipline. Unlike Imperial Field Marshal Suvorov, her son believes in the power of powdered wigs and polished buttons. It comes from inside him, this insatiable love of muskets, cannons, uniforms, bugles, and horses. The desire to see his soldiers move in unison, like wheels in some giant machine. The Prussian drill, the goose step, the tight-fitting blue uniforms. Suvorov may have beaten the Turks and the Poles, but her son still believes that Russians are not good enough to lick his Frederick's boots.

They exchange greetings. Catherine asks about his health; Paul tells her about his wife's plans to remodel this or that Gatchina room.

On the ballroom floor, a dance has just ended. Alexandrine bows gracefully and lets the Swedish King lead her back to her governess, both showing the unmistakable symmetry of attraction. Their heads tilt toward each other's.

"Is Alexandrine not too young, perhaps?" Paul asks. "Wouldn't it be prudent to prolong the engagement for at least a year?"

"Why?" Catherine asks bluntly.

Paul blinks. His pug nose twitches, and he rubs it with his knuckle. "My wife and I were thinking —"

"What does Maria Fyodorovna object to?" she interrupts. "Does she know, perhaps, of other illustrious prospects I'm not aware of?"

"No other prospects," her son stammers in response. Then he changes the subject. The Gatchina gardens have been particularly lush this year. The roses thrived.

That, too, annoys her. How quickly he gives up. How does he think he might rule Russia? By deferring to anyone who is louder than he is?

Her son is still speaking, but she no longer listens.

Faithful, observant Vishka hovers, always ready to rescue her mistress. One gesture is enough for her to rush toward them with a worried expression on her wrinkled face.

"May I have a word, Your Majesty?" she asks.

The Grand Duke of Russia, the heir to the throne, lets himself be sent away like a schoolboy.

The Swedes, Vishka reports, are standing in the hall, awed by the presents they have received from the Empress, arguing about the best way to express their gratitude.

"Excellent." Catherine nods when Vishka stops to catch her breath. "Now get me Constantine. I need to speak to him."

From the corner of her eye, she can see Paul bend over Maria Fyodorovna, who is shaking her head in disbelief. When his wife asks him something, he shrugs his lanky shoulders and stalks away in a huff.

Pride, the Empress thinks, another failing of the weak.

Her younger grandson approaches, sweaty from dancing, his broad face brightened with a grin that reveals a set of strong teeth, the military recruiters' dream. He is not as handsome as Alexander, but — like his older brother — the heir presumptive to the Russian throne takes after his mother. There is no hint of Paul's pug nose or lanky limbs.

A memory flashes in her mind. The children brought in by the nurses to report on the activities of the day and to say good night. The two boys must have been breeched already, for she recalls Constantine standing behind Alexander, tugging at his trousers. She remembers how their faces shone, how their arms closed around her neck, how sweet their little bodies smelled.

"I need the Marble Palace, Constantine," she tells him now. "I want to put Kościuszko there." She explains to her grandson that the defeated leader of the last Polish insurrection is ailing and needs more comfort than his current lodgings at the Fortress of Peter and Paul can provide. "In the meantime, you and your wife can live with me at the Winter Palace."

She wants him to think she is confiding in him out of pressing necessity. He shouldn't suspect his wife of confessing her sorrows.

"Some will envy you this proximity to my person," she continues. "I know it won't go to your head, but I'm not as sure of your young wife, so I'll have to ask you to be vigilant."

Anna Fyodorovna, she explains, is flighty and a bit vain. She is apt to take the move in the wrong way, as a sign of her superiority. "I shall expect to see her at my side daily, not to elevate her above her sisters-in-law but to give her more polish, more restraint. She needs my help to be groomed. More than I thought she would."

Constantine grunts. "She is also mean, Graman! And silly. You should hear what she sometimes says!"

She lets this pass. She doesn't want him to dwell on his wife's shortcomings. Kościuszko is a much better topic. Constantine, too, needs a lesson in governance.

Kościuszko is a rabble-rouser, worse than Pugachev and his Cossack rebels have ever

423

been. If she hadn't stopped him, she would've had another French Revolution on her hands. Nobles swinging from the lanterns. A guillotine in Warsaw. Serfs slashing their masters' throats.

Kościuszko rouses emotions abroad, anti-Russian sentiments. Indignation and sanctimonious protests have to be weathered. But some complaints can be disarmed, neutralized, turned into an advantage. She is angry at the rebel general, but she will treat him with kid gloves. "As you no doubt understand, Constantine," she adds.

Her grandson nods, pleased to be taken into her confidence.

"Appearances matter," she reminds him. She doesn't wish to be accused of perfidy and cruelty. Most of all she doesn't want Kościuszko to become a hero, give him claims to martyrdom in a Russian prison. The Marble Palace will be a perfect place for him. He will enjoy full comforts, and yet he'll be able to see the Fortress from his windows. A sight that will remind him of his defeat. There are other advantages of this move. The Polish prisoners in the Fortress will envy him. There will be accusations of collaboration. Hints of favors, perhaps even betrayals. "I don't have to explain to you, Constantine," she adds, "how this will be to Russia's advantage."

Her grandson gives her a bright look. He rubs his hands. Big, wide hands covered with reddish hair. His fingernails are filthy, but she refrains from pointing out the virtues of cleanliness.

"No, Graman," Constantine says, his voice rising with excitement. "You don't have to explain it at all."

By the marble pillar, Count Bezborodko is talking with the Austrian Ambassador. The Empress gestures for him to approach her, but to her surprise it is the tedious Madame Lebrun who — having assumed the sign was meant for her — bows deeply and rushes toward the throne.

"I'll get rid of her," Le Noiraud offers with pleasing eagerness. As soon as Constantine went back to the dance, Platon appeared at her side. Unlike her grandsons, he always knows where he wants to be.

"No need," she says, as Lebrun approaches with a blissful smile on her rouged face, two white ostrich feathers bobbing over her elaborate coiffure. "It would be too cruel."

"Your Imperial Majesty looks like Minerva Triumphant," Madame Lebrun declares as she bends to kiss the imperial hand, praising "the incomparable interplay of deep blues and warm ocher" of the imperial mantilla. She is again smitten with Platon's patrician profile, especially the fine line of his high forehead. "*Votre Altesse* must have some distinguished Greek ancestors," she gushes.

Madame Lebrun is a painter. She came to St. Petersburg a year ago, armed with stellar letters of recommendation, and made it universally known that her portrait of Marie Antoinette had been declared brilliant in every court of Europe. This claim and the few portraits of the Imperial Family she has been allowed to paint have secured her commissions from the best Russian houses.

There has been adventure in Madame Lebrun's past, which she will recount in excruciating detail if allowed. An escape by coach from Paris to Lyon and over the Alps to Italy dressed as a working woman, accompanied only by her daughter and the child's governess. All out of fear of being dragged to the guillotine as Marie Antoinette's most loyal friend.

"My beloved Queen, may her pure, tortured soul rest in peace," she says now, wiping an imaginary tear from her eye, "came to me in a dream last night. Eating galettes filled with almond cream. Happier than she has ever been on this earth."

Every French exile in Russia has been a dear friend of Marie Antoinette's. Just as every Pole who comes to St. Petersburg begging for favors assures Catherine that only the few deluded hotheads she now keeps in prison participated in the failed insurrection. Everyone else in Poland always wished for the Russian rule. And every one of them has lost cartloads of silver dishes, stacks of priceless tapestries and paintings, and a superb wine cellar if even one Russian soldier happened to set foot on his estate.

Madame Lebrun casts quick, birdlike glances around to check how many eyes have noticed her elevation. She bows and gasps as she describes her efforts to do justice to her exquisite models. "The muse can be so hard to entice. Frequently I have to put the palette aside to lie down with wet sheets across my eyes and simply wait."

Madame believes in the power of constant chatter and adoring phrases. Everyone she has ever painted possesses incomparable charm, angelic sweetness, or extreme graciousness that are almost impossible to capture in paint.

They have not been off to a good start. Alexandrine and Yelena sat for their portrait first, and she, their grandmother, found the result disappointing. Madame Lebrun captured some of the girls' freshness and vitality, but there is something wooden in the painting, too.

Platon, gratified by having been addressed as *Votre Altesse,* asks Madame who her lucky model is now.

"Princess Dolgoruka," Madame replies. "But if I could count on Mon Seigneur's powers of persuasion, I would allow myself much higher hopes."

Here it comes, Catherine thinks, *the inevitable request.* And sure enough, after another elaborate bow that makes the ostrich feathers tremble, Madame Lebrun expresses her ardent hope that the Empress of All the Russias might, one happy day, grant a poor French exile the ultimate favor. "To paint Your Imperial Majesty's divine countenance."

"Perhaps in a few months," Catherine replies. "When I have more time to pose."

The fan in Madame's hand flutters frantically. Her lips part in a beatific smile. "Oh, Your Majesty," Lebrun gushes, eager to see victory even in a vague promise. "This indeed is the happiest day of my life."

She catches sight of her grandson at the open window, staring into the smoky darkness. Alexander does not move, apparently impervious to the growing merriment of the room, the laughter, the swaying tones of the polonaise.

She would have liked to see his face, but it is turned away from her, and she can only imagine it. Pinched with apprehension, intense. Poor Monsieur Alexander, always wishing to turn back the clock and retreat to his boyhood. The best time of his life, she thinks, not without pride. Her gift to him, to all her grandchildren. The time of wonder tempered by reason. The time of wholesome joy and worthy pursuits.

You cannot be a child forever, Alexander, she could tell him, but won't.

It is getting late. The rain has stopped and the night is starry. On the canal, small boats float, bathed in lantern light. Curious passengers look toward the Tauride Palace, eager to catch the glimpses of the glittering ball. "How many people are there, Graman, who have never seen me and whom I shall never see?" Monsieur Alexander asked her once. What an inquisitive child he was. So thoughtful, and so very, very clever.

The ball unfolds in its own predictable way. Hardly a moment passes before someone comes to kiss her hand and exchange a few words. At the end of the evening her hand is swollen.

Prince Adam is leading Elizabeth in a minuet, each of his gliding steps precise, like the movements in a Genevan clock. Through her lorgnette, she watches the Prince's lean face, set in grim concentration. What is the matter with today's youth? Why are they prone to these serious moods?

To her relief she notes that Alexander leaves his solitary post and joins the dancers with true joy on his face. *A fine open countenance,* one of the recent visitors to the court described him in his letter. *Well spoken of by everybody.*

He is dancing now with Alexandrine, holding her hand by the tips of her fingers, making her circle around him. Vishka should be reminded to send the dance master a nice gift. There should be enough snuffboxes left from the last order. With her profile carved in ivory. The dance master may not deserve the most sumptuous ones, but one set with smaller diamonds will do.

Alexandrine, her golden hair elaborately braided and adorned with roses and forget-me-nots, looks older than her fourteen years. Bolik, the fugitive, has not been forgotten. There has been a sighting by the Admiralty that sent her granddaughter into a frenzy, but the ungrateful beast managed to elude the palace grooms.

After the minuets, the orchestra begins to play a polonaise. Prince Adam must have noticed the imperial gaze, for he is bowing to her, his gloved hand on his chest. Is she the only one who notices how Elizabeth's presence brings color to his cheeks?

Gustav Adolf is dancing with Alexandrine again, having intercepted her hand from Alexander. The child is meekly submitting herself to this tyranny. They form a most enchanting pair, two slim, young bodies gliding across the ballroom floor.

The King has made it widely known that the Russian imperial hospitality has quite overwhelmed him. He is touched not only by the magnificent entertainment he has experienced, but by the small, precious gestures of thoughtfulness. Especially the pine branches sent to the Swedish mission to make his room smell of fresh pine needles.

Alexandrine, her face a lovely rosy hue, is making a small circle around the King. When they are married, Catherine will make sure that in winter Alexandrine receives the finest caviar from Astrakhan and her favorite *varenikis*. In the summer months, she decides, she will send her granddaughter Russian silk and china, and a good supply of diamond-studded snuffboxes to give away, mere baubles but priceless enticements to win loyalty.

Alexandrine will need many good friends at the Swedish court.

The ball will continue well past midnight. After the dances end, the young men will go to the adjacent room. They'll wrestle, take burning candles out of water with their mouths. Such simple amusements will do them good. Alexander is excellent in them. So is Constantine. The Swedish King will have to try hard to beat his future brothers-in-law.

"Find out what they are talking about," she orders Le Noiraud, for Gustav Adolf has approached Alexander and the two of them have moved to the side of the ballroom.

As soon as the Favorite is gone, Alexandrine rushes to her side, asking breathlessly: "Did you watch me dance, Graman?"

"Yes," she says, jokingly. "You were so

clumsy."

"I wasn't," Alexandrine says. "Everybody said so."

"Everybody? Or just one person?" Catherine teases. "What has this person told you, besides praising your dancing skills?"

"That I have the most melodious voice. That I'm the most beautiful of all the young women . . ." Alexandrine prattles her delight. What a pleasure to see her so alive with joy. There has been no talk recently of Blessed Xenia and other martyrs or brides of Christ. If it weren't for Bolik, the child's happiness would be complete.

"How I envy you that you will soon see Stockholm," she tells Alexandrine. "I hear it is a very handsome city."

"But Graman," Alexandrine protests. "The King hasn't said anything of inviting me there."

What lovely teeth this child has, small and even. Like little pearls. A blessed Princess, who will be — Catherine knows it — so happy. Whose life will be peaceful and long. She can see her granddaughter surrounded by children, beside a husband who adores her. The vision is so powerful that she squeezes her eyes shut.

"Are you feeling unwell, Graman?" the child asks anxiously.

"I'm feeling very happy tonight, my dear," she replies and clasps her granddaughter's hand. The small, shapely hand of a young woman, a hand she will so soon give away.

Le Noiraud is back from his errand, waiting for her permission to approach.

"Go now," she says to Alexandrine. "You mustn't leave your suitor alone for too long. There are many beautiful princesses here eager to steal him."

"This is *not* true," Alexandrine protests, just as she used to only a few years ago when told: "Oh, you've just missed a unicorn. Hurry, hurry, it is still in the garden. If you run, you can still see him."

Platon tells her that the Swedish King and Alexander were speaking about the Russian *banya.* "Is it like the ones in Finland?" the King wanted to know. In Sweden, he told Alexander, they used to have *bastu.* It wasted firewood; it made morals loose. The venereal diseases spread through them like wildfire. He quoted the Swedish doctors who warn that such baths bring convulsions, loss of vision, tumors. This is why, he said, they did away with this custom. "Nothing makes the body as clean as a good sweat," Alexander said to that. "And the women?" the King asked. "Do they go to these Russian *banyas,* too? Doesn't the steam disfigure their bodies? Make their skins brown and shriveled?" In reply, Alexander offered to take the King with him to the palace *banya.* "You will feel like a River God," he promised.

433

"And what did the King say to that?" Catherine asks Platon.

"That he will try the baths at the Tsarskoye Selo. As soon as he has a chance to go there."

The big ballroom clock chimes eleven. It's an old clock, not always reliable. "Why keep it?" Le Noiraud complains, but Catherine refuses to have it replaced, for it remembers the youth of Peter the Great. She has always loved antiquities, but now old things are doubly precious to her. They have withstood dangers and the vicissitudes of chance.

Today was a good day. She has used her time well. At the Winter Palace, Anna Fyodorovna will be obliged to present herself in court dresses every morning. There will be no more bruises. Gustav Adolf is again dancing with Alexandrine, and even when he doesn't, he cannot keep his eyes away from her.

She can rest now.

"I shall let the young play," she tells her lover. "You may stay if you wish."

Platon directs his cautious gaze toward the place where his brother, Valerian, leans on the marble pillar, surrounded by the prettiest maids-of-honor. Ever since his return from the Polish campaign, Valerian's every appearance at court creates a small sensation. He is more handsome than Platon, big-shouldered and more manly. His missing leg only adds to his appeal. A Russian hero can claim his spoils.

Poor Le Noiraud, so painfully aware of anyone's advantages in the game of passion. If only he could give her pleasure, as he used to, when her body could still feel desire. If he could make her melt in his arms, under his tongue. If he knew she waited for his touch.

Rogerson's tonics give her nothing but gas. Or a bitter taste in her mouth that won't go away. Inside her there is nothing but the ashen memory of what was once a delight.

In the palace yard, the servants have sprinkled the cobblestones with water. They are sweeping up the debris of the ball: torn handkerchiefs, crumpled ribbons, horse dung, spilled oats and sawdust, pieces of broken glass. The willow brooms swish. Baskets are filled and carted away. In the distance, someone is sharpening tools. She hears the soft rumble of metal grinding against a whetting stone.

Vishka has reported fifteen lost jewels and one twisted ankle. There is evidence of trysts on the library ottoman, the billiard table, and the servants' stairs. A drunken guest has climbed into the kangaroo cage and put a hat on one of the beasts. "It was a round hat, too," a symbol of revolutionary sentiments, Vishka declared with a sour grimace.

Revolutionary sentiments remind the Empress of the Polish prisoners, a constant source of irritation. Potemkin may have been right when he argued against partitioning Poland. "Keep the country weak, but alive," he insisted. "Let them quarrel among themselves; then they won't unite against us."

Sometimes all of it is too much to bear.

On top of it, money is flowing far too freely. The water supply system in the Tsarskoye Selo is in dire need of repairs. The estimate is for 68,193 rubles.

The secretary responsible for the royal residences, Peter Turchaninov, presents her with his proposal for new furnishings of the Chinese pagodas. The cost is more than twenty-five thousand rubles.

"Why so much?" Catherine asks.

Turchaninov, a little man who bows and scrapes incessantly, is mortified. "Quality is expensive, Your Highness," he mutters, stealing a careful look at her face, checking how much patience she still has for him. His cringing makes her long to slap him.

Among the proposed costs, the most expensive items are Holy Icons, leather armchairs, new dressing tables and chests of drawers. Fringes and tassels double the cost of the draperies.

"We can do without those," she decides, as Turchaninov bows again. "And no one will notice."

Turchaninov is not pleased, but he will never scrape up enough courage to try to influence her judgment. His thoughts are like ants in the unknown territories, probing the air, checking where it is safe to venture.

Other costs can be at least halved, the Empress tells him. Holy Icons must be the smallest that can be found. Imitations painted by serf artists would do. No mirror should cost more than twenty-five rubles. She doesn't need armchairs. Black leather chairs will do just fine. There must be enough old dressing tables, chests of drawers, and wash-basins in the attic. "Also," she adds, "when you furnish new guest rooms, use the furniture we already have. Borrow pieces from the rooms and return them when they are no longer needed."

Turchaninov seems to have shrunk even more, almost dwarfed by the papers on which he scribbles his corrections. What is he thinking? That the Tsarina of Russia is losing her mind? How can she spend hundreds of thousands on palaces for others and begrudge herself a bit of luxury? What does this tell the foreigners who come to observe how the Russian Emperors live?

The foreigners. An ever-present chorus of critics. Their words are the mirrors Russians see themselves in.

Turchaninov has finished his scribblings and looks down at his boots. There is something he wants to say. He has an ominous grimace on his face, as if he possessed advance knowledge of a disaster. What will he tell her? That cattle no longer breed? That bread dough no longer rises?

Turchaninov is not wearing a wig, and his hair is smeared thick with pomade. *If he walks in the sun,* Catherine thinks, *it will melt and stream down his neck.* The image of her secretary with rivulets of pomade streaming down his neck strikes her as immensely funny. But she manages to stifle merriment.

"Do tell me what is on your mind," she says and waits.

Her request unleashes a flood of words.

It is Paul. As soon as the Swedish King accepted his invitation to Gatchina, her son ordered the old trees cut down. Every single one of them. Massive oaks that remembered the time of Peter the Great, all carted away by the serfs.

Why?

To make room for a military parade!

"I just thought Your Majesty should know," Turchaninov adds mournfully. "Trees take such a long, long time to grow."

Queenie, who comes in as soon as Turchaninov leaves, is panting with exertion.

She has merely unfolded the towels and spread them on the bedroom carpet, but even this seems too much for her growing bulk. "She buys these marzipan pigs," Vishka grumbles. "Puts them on her nightstand like decorations. Then, every time she wakes up, she eats one."

The Admiral is already waiting in the antechamber with a bowl of his seawater.

"Get some rest," Catherine tells Queenie, "and send him in."

Admiral Lambro-Cazzioni walks in, asks her how she slept, places the bowl on the towels Queenie has spread, and begins pouring seawater over her sore legs. Cupful after cupful.

Her feet look terrible. Her toenails are thick and yellowed; the skin is livid and covered with festering lesions. In spite of the Admiral's promises, the seawater baths have not stopped the bleeding.

Even though the cold water brings some relief, it lasts only a moment. As soon as the flow stops, the pain returns.

The Admiral knows the imperial habits by now. He doesn't try to linger longer than necessary or draw her into a conversation. He hasn't yet asked for any favors, either. Perhaps this is why she still lets him attend to her, even though she is losing faith in his cure.

The Admiral's unruly hair resembles a bird's nest. His forehead is riddled with wrinkles; his temples sport fans of crow's-feet. Yet there is something joyful about the old man. And he does try so hard to make her feel better.

"A Turkish pasha says to his doctor: 'It hurts me when I press my foot. And when I press my arm. And when I press my ribs. Tell me what is wrong with me.' So the doctor examines the pasha for a long time and finally says: 'Your Highness has broken your royal finger!' "

As soon as Catherine bursts out laughing, the Admiral scoops up his porcelain basin and leaves. Queenie is already motioning for the maids to take the towels away.

The wooden pandora sent from the Imperial Wardrobe for her inspection this morning is modeling a loose satin gown, embroidered with golden oak leaves and acorns along the trim. The green cloth and red facings are the Preobrazhensky colors, mirroring her dashing uniform from the days of the coup.

The actual uniform hasn't fit her for a long time, but Vishka assures her that it is well preserved, laid in a cedar chest, sprinkled with pepper. Awaiting some glorious placement, no doubt.

At Kunstkamera, perhaps? Beside Peter the Great's stuffed horse?

The pandora doll's polished wooden face has no eyes, no lips, and no ears. There is something disturbing about it, some stubborn memory of regret.

"Will this do?" Queenie asks, having reported that the imperial seamstresses are in the frenzy of preparations. "The Grand

Duchess will have the most sumptuous wardrobe."

The word should be *trousseau,* but
Queenie, whose eyes glitter with joy at the
very mention of Alexandrine, will not tempt
fate.

"It'll do very well," Catherine decides.

Platon's little monkey is shivering in his arms.
A cheeky fellow, fond of grabbing the wigs of
courtiers and throwing them on the floor. Or
pinching the hands that try to pet it. Vishka
swears that the little beast is fond of defecat-
ing on the floor and then smearing its fingers
in the filth.

Outside of her Tauride window, frogs croak.
She should order Zotov to take her to the
park in her rolling chair. Some fresh air might
do her good.

Le Noiraud sets the monkey on one of the
armchairs and ties its leash. The beast settles
down immediately, resigned, and curls up for
a sleep.

"Look," he says, and extracts a piece of vellum paper from his breast pocket.

A certain Colonel Uspensky came to him
this very morning, asking for admittance. "An
elderly officer I didn't recognize," Le Noiraud
says as she unfolds what turns out to be a
petition. "Not a courtier. Not someone who
has sat in the antechamber waiting for a
chance. Someone whose account should be

trusted." In his voice, she can hear his tension. This story is not innocuous. It is aimed at someone.

Catherine puts on her spectacles and begins to read. Colonel Uspensky certainly doesn't know how to present his case. He goes on too long about his past achievements. He was with Prince Potemkin at the storming of Ismail. He fought in both Turkish wars. *I have lived through the enemy's capture. I have made my peace with death, though my sacrifice was not accepted.*

Only by the middle of the next page does it become clear that Uspensky is writing on his son's behalf. A son who had no opportunity to serve his Motherland. A son who was foolish or unlucky enough to be drafted into a Gatchina unit.

At the mention of Gatchina, Catherine's impatience evaporates.

My son doesn't know I'm writing this, but I can no longer stay silent. He is all I have. His honor is my honor.

The son, Captain Dmitri Vladimirovich Uspensky, has been imprisoned and stripped of his rank. Called a disgrace to his family and a traitor to his command. The father's questions on the nature of this transgression have remained unanswered.

442

Refused permission to see my son's commander, I traveled to the Gatchina Village. I was stopped at the gate and demanded to declare my business. Having been warned by well-wishers, I disguised myself as a merchant and was able to present various tools for smithing.

As I was let in, the hour of my arrival was recorded. I was told to leave Gatchina before dusk and denied permission to visit any houses or accept any hospitality.

I sold my wares quickly, but my questions if anyone heard about my son's crime were met with averted eyes and silence. I left in despair, but by the Lord's grace, a few *versts* outside the village I saw a young lad on foot. Since he looked tired and thirsty, I offered him a ride in my carriage. Having accepted my offer, he confirmed that he was indeed a resident of Gatchina permitted to spend two nights away on his business. I invited him to partake of refreshments at a roadside tavern, where he soon became talkative. After some coaxing, he told me that the Gatchina soldiers are punished for every deviation from the rules, which change often and without notice. The lad swore that the Grand Duke himself observes his troops from the palace balcony with a spying glass, and nothing escapes his attention.

I have learned that my son, Your Most

Esteemed Highness, has been beaten and deprived of his rank, because his pigtail was half an inch too long.

Le Noiraud is watching her. There is hope in his eyes and also a sly shadow of satisfaction. He lacks the skills to hide what he has sense enough not to say. Her son, Paul, never a shining genius of this court, is a petty and vindictive tyrant.

She has always believed that a court is the best test of character. Rich soil where men can grow and flourish. Or whither and rot.

"You've done well to bring this to me," she tells him.

Dinner is served the way she likes it. Plain food. Boiled beef. Fish soup. Cucumbers with honey. And in the center of the table, the dish she always requests: potatoes. Today they are served in two ways: boiled, mashed, topped with melted butter; and fried with lard into crisp squares.

Potato plants are much better than grains at staving off hunger. Easier to cultivate, more nutritious, resistant to many of the diseases grains succumb to. This is not her opinion but a simple truth, scientifically backed. And yet in spite of her efforts, Russians are not convinced.

The mandrake family, they used to tell her. The plants of the dark, of poison. Now they no longer call potatoes poisonous, or Devil's food. But they still ask how food dug out from dirt could be superior to grains that ripen under the sun? And why were potatoes not mentioned in the Bible? Peasants still spit when they look at the misshapen bulbous roots. Why not keep them for the hogs and other beasts? they ask.

She has a plot of potatoes in all her kitchen gardens. She insists the bulbs must be served at all court functions, to set an example. But it is not the rich and powerful who need potatoes, but the poor. Why does it have to be so hard to bring progress? Why are human minds such stubborn creatures of habit? And why do those who least can afford it resist the most?

At this small family dinner, Alexander sits at her right. Elizabeth is beside him, attentive in a wifely fashion. Then Constantine with Anna, who is particularly quiet today. Apparently she is now sorry she had to leave the Marble Palace. "So soon?" she asked when the footmen came to pack her things.

On her left is Le Noiraud, pecking at his food like a bird. A few morsels of beef. A spoonful of mashed potatoes. Queenie is convinced he is worried about his digestion. He has been eating sprigs of mint and parsley, chewing rhubarb, and drinking sienna tea.

Alexandrine has come with Madame Lievens. The chief governess of the imperial princesses is not looking her best today. Summer heat makes her pant. Sweat has made a ragged trail on her rouged cheek.

The talk at the table is of the Swedish guests. Their tact and consideration. Madame Lievens declares them most generous in their admiration. The King in particular praises everything he sees.

"When are you going to Gatchina again, Alexander?" Catherine asks her grandson.

"Tomorrow," Alexander replies. He throws her a cautious look, probing the possibility of her displeasure. It is hard to hide her feelings from Alexander. But she manages to make her next words sound casual.

"Your presence will bring your parents a great pleasure," she says. "It will take your mother's mind off the baby. I hear that she distresses herself over nothing."

Nicholas, the newest Romanov arrival, is big and healthy. The wet nurses laugh that he sucks their milk like a giant leech. His face is plain but wholesome, like his mother's. And his disposition is so sunny! There is no unnecessary crying, no fuss when none is required.

"After dinner, Alexander," she tells her grandson, "I want you to come with me to my study. There is something I need your advice on."

Alexander takes a quick sip of water before he nods.

The rest of the dinner proceeds with usual hilarity. Alexandrine is teased about the handsome Swedish King. Anna frets about a delayed shipment of bonnets. Elizabeth takes Alexandrine's hand and the two promise to go off to the garden as soon as their presence is not required. Catherine need not have worried about these tête-à-têtes. They talk of such trivial matters, her two princesses. They fret over invisible blemishes on their skin. The difficulty of contredanse. The need to rest before evening entertainments. Their conversations can last for hours like that.

Is this why Alexander is tired of his wife? He has been brought up on conversations that satiate curiosity, bring satisfaction. Elizabeth, like Anna, adores stories of star-crossed lovers, fiery confessions of passion and longing. Alexander's wife makes excellent progress in Russian, she is smart, but there is little passion in anything she attempts, and even less purpose. As if, in the end, it were all the same, a conversation with a scholar or empty gossip with her sisters-in-law.

Elizabeth won't keep Alexander's attention for very long if she continues like this, the Empress thinks. She will have to drink pain and disappointment. Unless children come and give her days meaning.

Alexander follows her to the study, casting his eyes about as if he expected someone to be there.

She arranges her lips into the most motherly of smiles. "I've received this only yesterday," she tells him, handing her grandson Colonel Uspensky's letter.

Alexander reads carefully, lips pursed. The letter is accompanied with a report confirming Uspensky's reputation and the validity of his request. Young Uspensky has indeed been given a beating and imprisoned for the length of his pigtail.

Her grandson's jaw is squared; his hands tremble slightly.

"Please, Alexander," Catherine asks softly. "Perhaps you could use your influence at Gatchina to help a man who deserves help. If I make a request, it will be misconstrued as interference. Will you do it for me?"

Alexander nods and she watches him leave, the letter folded quickly and slipped into his breast pocket.

"Do you think our little Olga ever comes back to watch us?" Alexandrine asked her once.

Saint Olga, Olga Prekrasna, Olga the Beautiful. Saint Olga of ancient Russ who avenged her husband's death, who set fire to the houses of her enemies by sending them doves with burning scraps of paper tied to their feet.

"No, Alexandrine," Catherine replied. "The dead don't come back."

What does Alexandrine remember? A room filled with candles, a small coffin set on brocade and velvet. The air heavy with the scent of mint, chamomile, and the sweet, heady *ladan,* the herbs of the dead. A child's head topped with a ribboned cap on a pink satin cushion trimmed with lace. Her lips almost white and paper thin. "Too good for this world," someone mutters.

Olga Pavlovna, Alexandrine's little sister, is dead. The baby had such wide shoulders when she was born, it took two full days for her to come out of her mother's womb. "Another girl for me to marry off," Catherine had thought then.

For weeks before Olga died, the girl could not stop eating. As soon as one meal was finished, she would scream for another. Hard-boiled eggs, thick slices of buttered bread, pieces of smoked herring. Sorrel soup, beets, roasted potatoes, greasy *lardons.*

"More," she screamed, insatiable in her hunger, as soon as a plate was taken away from her. "More," she screamed when her nurses protested that she had had enough.

They tried to distract her with stories of sacred birds. Sirin, kangan alkonost, fabulous birds of paradise, wise birds with women's faces that could calm the sea and enchant those who heard their song.

But Olga shut her ears. Then the fever came. Sweaty, persistent. Glassy eyes, crimson cheeks. Head thrashing on the pillow, cries of pain. Day after day, hours of racking pain. So cruel that death came as a release.

Grieving, too, is insatiable, Catherine thinks. Like woodworms, it burrows greedily through what seems solid to the careless eye. It leaves corridors of pain in its path. It weakens a structure.

Other losses carry with them the seed of possibility. Riches lost can be regained. Ambitions thwarted can find other outlets. But the dead cannot come back to life. Grief is always with you.

These thoughts are interrupted by a soft tap on the door to her reading room. It is Queenie, whispering that Madame Lebrun has been waiting all afternoon and begs to be admitted. Claims to have some very, very important news.

"I keep refusing, Your Majesty, but she insists," Queenie declares, her plump hands folded together in a pleading gesture. Has she just collected another hefty bribe?

"All right, then," Catherine says. "I'll see her, but tell her I have little time."

A faint scent of turpentine hovers around Madame Lebrun in spite of a lavish dosing with sandalwood.

"Your Imperial Highness! Once again you have been most generous to me!" Madame

Lebrun curtsies and bends to kiss the imperial hand, muttering something about angelic sweetness. She has not been in the Tauride Palace before, and now casts greedy glances at the paintings on the walls.

Angelic sweetness or not, to make sure her impatience is perceived, the Empress clears her throat.

Madame Lebrun takes the hint. Grand Duchess Maria Fyodorovna, she begins, permitted her to attempt another painting of Grand Duchess Alexandrine. "This time, Your Majesty, I'm painting the Grand Duchess alone. In a muslin dress. It is a secret for now. A most precious gift for her father."

"If it is to be a secret gift," Catherine teases her unwelcome visitor, "is it wise to tell me about it?"

Madame Lebrun protests, folding her hands like a squirrel begging for nuts. Secrecy was never, ever meant to include the Empress of Russia. And now the portrait, although not finished, is at the center of an unexpected but wondrous occurrence.

"What occurrence?"

"It's the Swedish King, Your Majesty," Madame gushes. The weak ray of sunshine plays over the pearls in her hair. "The young man of incomparable charm, if I may say so. And extreme graciousness." This fine young monarch came by her studio yesterday, interrupting his daily walk through the city. Which

451

he considers unrivaled in its charm.

"Indeed?" Catherine asks, aware that her voice has betrayed her interest and that now Madame Lebrun will milk it for all it's worth.

"Indeed, Your Majesty. A most remarkable young man. Keenly interested in art."

Catherine resigns herself to hearing how the Swedish monarch has praised Madame's talent. How Madame has queried him about the details of the famous coronation portrait of his father she has never had a chance to admire herself. And how the charming young King personally invited Madame to Stockholm to view this amazing work of pure inspiration. "Your Majesty must have heard of it, I'm sure."

Finally, the story reaches its intended conclusion.

"The King, Your Majesty, asked to see what I was working on. How could I refuse? Oh, how I wish Your Majesty would see with what rapture he perceived your granddaughter's divine countenance."

Is that all?

It is not all. Madame Lebrun knows how to stretch her moment. Glowing, she allows herself the pleasure to sketch the scene as it has transpired. The King dressed in black, his long hair gently falling on his shoulders. The velvet hat he is clutching in his hands. The hand raised, making its way to his heart, then the hat falling from his hands, to the floor.

And then the words: "She has captured my heart. I cannot leave Russia until I'm assured she'll become my wife."

What joy to see a wish fulfilled, carefully laid plans come to fruition! For her darling girl, there will be no more melancholy musings, only the pleasures of a good marriage. For Russia, a long-wished-for alliance. Sweden will be back in the Russian fold.

At a moment like this, even Madame's gabbling can be endured.

When Madame Lebrun finally leaves, Catherine takes a quill and snaps the inkwell open. On the top of the page she writes: *Two main conditions to be met before the engagement between Alexandrine and Gustav Adolf can take place.*

Then she takes a ruler and draws an even line underneath it, making sure the line ends just on the margins. Then she continues:

A complete severance of the ties with the Princess of Mecklenburg.

An assurance in writing that Alexandrine will have all she requires to practice her Orthodox faith.

Both conditions she considers self-evident, but in matters of importance it never hurts to be straightforward. No new engagement is possible without breaking the current one.

And a Russian Grand Duchess is not a petty Prussian princess marrying an emperor. Religion is her tie with Russia, a tie to be nurtured and encouraged, not broken.

She rings for her secretary. Gribovsky enters at once, in his usual dark gray ensemble, which is getting too tight. Like Queenie, he cannot resist the palace treats.

She orders Gribovsky to develop the two points into a one-paragraph statement, with ample space beneath for the King's signature, so she can have it on her person at all times.

August is almost gone.

It is with regret that she decides to return to the Winter Palace, to the avalanche of papers. For a few days only, she tells herself, knowing this won't be so. Whatever time government business doesn't claim will be devoured by preparations for the betrothal. She will soon be pestered for decisions. Will St. George's Hall do for the ceremony? What decorations should be prepared? In what colors? The wardrobe headmistress is already asking for an audience. Zotov has mentioned that the peacock clock is stuttering when the owl enters. Will there be enough time to dismantle the whole mechanism and clean it?

As if nothing can be decided without her.

Alexandrine, however, is relieved to be back at the Winter Palace. Bolik's still missing, though the sightings of him never stop.

Perhaps — though one shouldn't be too cynical — because every such sighting assures a reward. Alexandrine's chambermaids must be instructed to fold jasmine petals into her undergarments. This will surround the child with a lovely fragrant vapor, a far more delicate scent than perfume.

"What do you think, Pani?"

Pani wags her tail in agreement, oblivious to the change of residence. As soon as her green velvet pillow is placed on a floor, she settles on it with her customary delight. And as soon as Bezborodko presents his greasy morning offering, all is fine in the dog's world.

Now that Alexandrine's engagement is on its way to completion; the issue of succession becomes pressing. Catherine has postponed the matter long enough. Too much has been on her mind. And — this, too, is best acknowledged — she dreads the unpleasantness of it all.

But there is no advantage in keeping her decision secret. Not any longer.

An official announcement will clear the air. Alexander must get used to the thought of taking his father's place. Start taking part in Council meetings, watching and learning.

When?

September will likely all be taken by the betrothal. October by Alexandrine's departure to Sweden.

"November?" Count Bezborodko suggests. "On the Grand Duke's name day?"

This, the Empress decides, is an excellent suggestion.

Her leg is getting worse. By the end of the day, it turns into a phantom limb, unusable but still tormented by waves of throbbing pain. The open sores in between her toes ooze bloody pus. A shooting pain travels along the shin up her hip.

She won't admit it, though, not yet. Rogerson, Queenie tells her, is denouncing Lambro-Cazzioni everywhere as a dangerous quack who has turned Her Majesty's head with his sorcery. As if he were selling her the tears of John the Baptist! Silly Rogerson, with his mounting gambling debts, afraid she will sack him and send him back to his gloomy Scotland moors. How tedious, human vanities. How predictable.

Her hand hurts, too. Not while she writes, but as soon as she lifts the quill off the page. Sometimes the pain returns during the day in most unexpected moments. When she opens a snuffbox, or lifts something, no matter how light.

Her body is giving in. Worn in service to the Empire. Thirty-four years taking their toll.

Old age takes us by surprise. Is it because it is the only stage of life from which there is no escape, no return? No one can ever look back at old age from a distance.

Years do not make sages, she likes to observe, just old men and women unsure of where they are going. This is why she wants to surround herself with the young. Effervescent, pliable, moldable. The future of the human race. In their souls there is still color.

Before dusk falls, from the Hermitage window she catches a glimpse of a well-dressed woman on the Moyka bridge walking with a companion, a girl in a gray bonnet. The girl is saying something; the woman — her mother perhaps — shakes her head and raises her hand in exasperation. The girl lifts her hands and covers her ears. Is she being scolded for some petty misdemeanor?

A moment later, when she looks again, the two have reconciled and walk arm in arm, the girl leaning toward the mother, lost in some story.

Varvara Nikolayevna?

Darya?

The absurdity of this thought amuses her. The woman who walks away is much too young, and much more graceful than Varvara ever was. The girl limps slightly as she walks, which, too, is wrong.

And yet . . .

The memory that comes is of the sharp and

angry moment of Varvara's leaving. A misunderstanding. An undeserved accusation. Grand expectations that always anticipate more than can be granted. Recriminations spreading like the black fungus on her roses.

Like the heir of Candide, I wish to cultivate my garden.

The boundary between friendship and betrayal is a thin one. It has to do with entrancement and expectations.

You have not been the only one, she tells Varvara in her thoughts. *But you were the first one to leave me. Refused to take what was offered to you with generosity and gratitude. For reasons you never even tried to explain.*

She has hardened herself for this moment.

Being a Tsar, she'll tell Alexander, *may often seem like a burden. But in the right hands, power is the only means of assuring the happiness of the greatest number.*

In the right hands, she will repeat.

One has to safeguard the good that has already been done.

Sometimes a son must step over his father.

"This is my true kingdom," she tells Alexander, pointing to the books in her library.

Rows of volumes are arranged according to the subject matter, author, and language. The books from Diderot's collection stand out,

458

with their elaborate lettering on soft brown calfskin. She herself has always preferred simple leather bindings. Not too much gold tooling, no jewel-encrusted edges, for it is the content that matters, not the covers.

Only the other day, between the well-worn pages of her Montesquieu, she found a yellowing letter in a childish hand: *We are well. We hope you are well, too. I kiss your hands and feet and your little finger. Your little grandson Alexander.*

"Can I see the medals, Graman?" Alexander asks with his old, childish eagerness. He pulls out the shallow drawers one by one, exclaiming at each new discovery. "Oh, I remember this one," he says, holding the Victory at Chesme to the light.

All her life Catherine has always collected something. Paintings, porcelain, china figurines, cameos, books. The archive shelves are piled with old herbaria, boxes with shells and fossils. Rocks from the frozen fields of Siberia. Twisted roots shaped like human limbs.

Passions long gone, she thinks, as she watches her grandson dive into her old treasures. Not empty memories of the past, but evidence that she has lived and loved. That she didn't pass by what caught her fancy. This is why she is keeping it all. As proof.

She has settled in her library chair by the

window. Her bad leg is resting on a velvet footstool. It hurts, at times far more than it used to before the water treatment began. "You've visited Gatchina again," she says.

Alexander, bent over an open drawer, pauses before turning toward her. It is not a question, so it does not require an answer, so he is silent.

"Are your parents as well as they look?" she continues. "I had so little time to talk to them at the Tauride ball."

"Quite well," Alexander answers, straightening. "Though Maman is wearing herself out, for she checks on the baby far too often."

He has left the drawer open.

The Empress motions to her grandson to take the chair beside her. Alexander sits and immediately squints, for he is right in the line of the setting sun. His eyes are bloodshot from lack of sleep. But when she tells him to move the chair to the right, he protests that it's not worth the fuss. The sun will go down in a few moments. He will not be bothered by it for long.

She lets him talk of his baby brother, the latest family addition, whose education she is already planning, even though — with two older brothers — his chances for the throne are slim. *Big Nicholas,* Alexander says fondly. Always hungry, wearing the wet nurses out. But never crying without a good reason.

"I've heard that the trees are gone from the

front Gatchina courtyard," she says when he pauses.

"Are they?" Alexander says, blinking in genuine astonishment.

How does one *not* notice a line of old trees gone? Cut not because of disease, but so that these ridiculous Gatchina regiments have more space for their endless parades. Ruled "without dissipation, lassitude, and leniency," as her son likes to say, implying that hers are ruled by all three. In Paul's world, uniforms, cracking heels, jingling sword chains, and spurs trump old, shade-giving trees.

"All gone, I hear. Oaks, too. Let's not talk about it, though," she continues. "I wanted to ask you about that poor Captain Uspensky. His father has petitioned Platon Alexandrovich again."

At the sound of Le Noiraud's name, Alexander winces. No love is lost between these two, which is not a surprise, for Alexander has never liked any of her Favorites. But if she were to pay heed to all instances of childish jealousy, she would be entirely paralyzed. And entirely alone.

"But Papa already pardoned Captain Uspensky!" Alexander flashes her a bright smile of triumph. He is happy to narrate what has happened. Captain Uspensky was summoned, and Alexander was allowed to question him in person. "As long as I wished, Graman," Alexander stresses. "Without anyone present." The Captain confessed to negligence in taking care of his uniform and his hair. He begged forgiveness for letting his commander down. "It was not just the length of his pigtail," her grandson adds quickly, anticipating her sneer. "And it wasn't his first offense."

"I'm very pleased you have resolved the matter with such speed." She decides not to point out that the hapless Captain may have been instructed in what to say in front of the eager young Grand Duke.

"But I didn't do anything," Alexander protests. "Papa pardoned him before I even mentioned the man. Papa was right, too. He merely had to set an example. Discipline is important, isn't it, Graman?"

She doesn't answer. The library clock chimes. Enough time has passed already. "There is something else I wish to talk to you about, Alexander, something of enormous importance." She takes a deep breath: "Being a Tsar —"

He doesn't let her finish. "No, Graman, please!"

The words she has decided on fly away, unsaid. This is just as well, for it pleases her that Alexander knows or has guessed what she wishes to say. Foresight bodes well for a future Tsar.

"It'll kill Papa . . . He'll never forgive me."

Alexander's face proclaims emotions like a

462·

manifesto pasted on city gates. He is cringing at the thought of his father's wrath. Of being yelled at, accused of betrayal. Or pushing his father to his grave. No, that's not what Paul would say. He will say: *Why not tie a stone around my neck and throw me into the Neva? Why not jump for joy as I gasp for my last breath?*

Dear Monsieur Alexander with his soft heart. Forgetting how pleasing one will always hurt others.

"What nonsense you speak, child," she chides softly, ignoring the crimson hue of her grandson's cheeks.

It's never easy to hurt someone we love. But she has made up her mind.

"When I die, Alexander, you — not your father — will succeed me. I am not asking you to agree. I just want you to know."

Blunt, perhaps, but this is the time to state her decision, not to give the reasons for it. To soften the moment, she puts her arm around him. She feels him stiffen.

"We are talking of the distant future. I'm not ready to die just yet, Alexander."

He listens, nodding, though still frowning. No matter. Monsieur Alexander will accept his destiny. He always has.

"We shall speak about it again, later. When Alexandrine is gone to Stockholm, perhaps," she says. His reddish hair is thick, springy

463

under her fingers. Like fleece.

"Yes, Graman."

"Just remember, you are not responsible for what your father thinks or does. You are only responsible for yourself."

Alexander is looking at her with his blue eyes in which she can see the brown speckles. The Anhalt-Zerbst eyes, her father's legacy. "You are right, Graman. I promise I'll remember your words."

Surrender? Already?

But it is no surrender. Her words didn't convince him. She can see it in his face, in the quiver of his jaw. He has merely lost enough ground to decide he needs reinforcements. Withdraw, pretend to agree. For now.

Not a bad strategy, when you think of it, even if it won't work.

She hoped that after a few days of not being admitted to her side Rogerson would be less sure of himself, less judgmental. She was wrong.

"In Scotland, people believe that a horsehair thrown into the water will turn into an eel," her doctor mutters as he scrutinizes her leg with a magnifying glass, clucking at a new patch of reddened skin that has appeared overnight.

"The pain has diminished, though," she insists.

Rogerson pokes the reddened spot with his

finger as if he has not heard her. There is a deep frown on his forehead as he puts the magnifying glass away. "And that rubbing the skin with eel oil makes one see fairies."

The Empress lets her court doctor grumble. He will not admit any improvement that does not come from his own treatments. To him, Lambro-Cazzioni is an ignorant quack.

"In Greece," Rogerson continues, "everyone is a doctor."

He advises stopping the seawater baths right away, before they can do real harm. He advises returning to a regime of blisterings and purgings of the body from accumulated poison.

"No," she says, covering her sore leg with her petticoat before he has time to wrap it in his bindings.

Rogerson gives her a hurt look. *You are Empress,* his eyes say. *You will do what you want.* He gathers his instruments into the leather bag, slowly, placing each one meticulously in its place.

She doesn't want Rogerson to leave in anger. He has been the court doctor for almost twenty years. The secrets of her body are open to him. Secretions, rashes, swellings, and love bites. So far, he has been discreet. He watches over her as well as he can. She is still alive.

"Why would poisons cause my leg to swell?"

she asks. "Wouldn't they affect my stomach first?"

Her doctor's desire to instruct is stronger than his jealousy and wounded pride.

"The stomach and intestines, irritated by poison, sympathize with the integumentary system, which includes the skin. This is what causes inflammation. It's like one eye becoming infected from another."

He takes a piece of paper from his pocket and draws a system of connected vessels that fill up when water is poured at one end. This is what is happening in her body. Nothing is truly separated. Everything touches on something else.

She lets him talk until the last notes of irritation melt in his voice, and only then promises to rethink his recommendations. He bows deeply as he leaves.

"Nothing I did not anticipate," she tells her minister as she recounts her conversation with Alexander. *It takes time to harden up,* she thinks. *There are some drawbacks of a happy childhood. No one breathes down your neck.*

"May I make a suggestion, madame," Bezborodko offers, with a quick furtive shake of his head. He gives her a sheet of paper. A greasy mark where his thumb has been is a trace of Pani's treat.

It is a letter from Maria Fyodorovna, addressed to her grandson. Short, without adornments or flowery preambles. It assures Alexander that his acceptance of the throne over his father's head is not only wise but unavoidable. *You will save our beloved country,* it reads. *You will fulfill your destiny and earn your mother's most heartfelt blessing.*

Clever!

She understands Bezborodko's scheme immediately. Pat, maybe, but precisely what will soothe Alexander's misgivings, ease his troubled conscience. Sweeten the bitterness of what he — the young Prince of the realm — so foolishly considers a terrible betrayal.

Bezborodko is not Grishenka; no one can be. But he is close enough.

As soon as the Count leaves, she takes a clean page from the pile Queenie has placed in front of her and writes a plan of action:

1. First thing tomorrow I will send for Maria Fyodorovna. Ask her to come alone, for I need her advice.
2. I will let her prattle about the baby. I will not interrupt her.
3. I will tell her that the Swedes have asked about her Chinese pavilion, of which they have heard even in Stockholm. Tell her how pleased Gustav Adolf will be to see the Gatchina gardens. Then I will ask if she has engraved any stones lately, for I have

a great need for unique and personal gifts from the Imperial Family.

4. I will congratulate her on Alexandrine's deportment. Tell her how pleased I am with the way she has brought up her daughter. We shall speak of the arrangements for the trip to Stockholm.

5. I will tell her how highly Alexander thinks of her.

6. I will mention Paul's rages. Mention my motherly concern over them.

7. Coffee should be served with apple puffs and macaroons. Maybe linzer torte, too.

8. Silence until she has eaten.

9. I will explain what she has to do. Why she needs to write a letter to Alexander to assure him of her support, and then I will hand her the draft and ask her to copy it in her own hand before she signs it.

Maria Fyodorovna arrives when the clock in the corner shows fifteen minutes past three. Her hands are pudgy. Her face is round. She has armed herself with excuses. The baby was choking and squinting its eyes. The wet nurse was terrified. "I hope, dear Mother, you haven't waited for me long," she says.

"You are not late, my child," she says. The many faces of Maria Fyodorovna, reflected in

the ornate mirrors of the silver salon, loosen
and break into a smile.

They sit on the sofa, beside each other.

"Nicholas is perfectly healthy." Maria Fyodorovna continues her report from the nursery. "He is bigger than Alexander was at his
age. Bigger even than Constantine."

The servants bring in trays of refreshments.
The coffee is served with warmed cream and
sugar. Latticed with dough strips, the linzer
torte is filled with raspberry and red currant
jam and sprinkled generously with sliced
almonds. It smells of lemon zest and butter.

"Linzer torte," Maria exclaims, clasping her
hands just like Alexandrine. "I haven't had it
for so long. Was it in Berlin? Or in Vienna?"

She, the Empress, doesn't answer. Or point
out that it makes no difference now when
Maria had linzer torte last.

Maria eyes the thick slice of torte with
delight before digging her fork into it. She is
a slow eater. "Chew your food well," she tells
all her children. They still laugh about it when
they are alone.

But these are all minor irritations. They can
be endured.

The afternoon unfolds as she has planned
it. Maria, given so many reasons for pride, is
beaming. Gustav Adolf has praised her Pavlovsk gardens? Liked her engraved cameo
stones? She will present the King with a
choice collection of her latest efforts when he

comes to Gatchina. They are all looking forward to this visit.

"One more piece of torte?"

"I really shouldn't. But if Maman insists . . ."

"I do insist."

Maria is so predictable. She won't change a subject on her own accord. She cannot bear silence, and will fill it with endless prattle. She won't ask why she has been summoned, though it's clear that she assumes it is because of Alexandrine and Gustav Adolf.

And so they talk of Alexandrine, a topic they fully agree on. How handsome the young couple look together, so straight, so graceful. How well mannered Alexandrine is. They fret about her first months in Stockholm. The child will miss them all so much! There is no escaping loneliness, even with the best of husbands. It takes time to build a new life. Get used to a new palace. New servants. New customs. Swedish is a difficult language.

Alexandrine will be watched. Every mistake she makes will be noted. Would it be wise to ask Princess Dashkova to accompany her? The Princess is waiting for such a request, of course. Most eager to get herself back into her Empress's good graces. There are advantages. The Princess has been a family friend for so long. She will offer advice and comforting words. With her sharp eyes that never, ever miss a slight. Real or imagined.

They laugh in unison.

The mirrors reflect two figures seated on the apple-green sofa. Close enough, but not too close. Just so they can see each other face-to-face. On this quiet afternoon of warm confidences, of shared concerns. Dear old Queenie's cravings. Pani's festering eyes.

That Bolik! Why did the ungrateful rascal run away? And right now! It would have been such a comfort for the dear child to have that dog with her. Is it true that there have been sightings of him? By the Admiralty? But that Bolik ran away each time? Or maybe it wasn't Bolik at all?

He was such a sweet puppy. So curious and yet so fearful. Scared of mops and tin buckets. Must have been frightened out of his wits by some scullery maid to run away like that.

Finally the last smear of the torte has been scraped away with the side of the fork. The plate is back on the serving table, another piece declined.

"One more thing, my dear," Catherine says. In the mirror, her daughter-in-law's bulky figure freezes.

With Maria, there is no point in hinting. Her daughter-in-law is not really stupid, but she must have decided long ago not to make any guesses, no matter how straightforward and obvious they seem, and this decision has served her well enough.

If only she, the Empress, could order her

daughter-in-law to choose her son over her husband! But this cannot be done. She must argue her case. And so she swallows her pride and talks to Maria Fyodorovna as if she were explaining her policy to Bezborodko.

"My son, I regret to say, is not fit to rule Russia. You know it as well as I do."

What takes place at Gatchina is the best example, Catherine continues. Paul is unpredictable, easily influenced, irresponsible. He believes in ruling by fear. He desires blind obedience at all cost. Criticizes her, his mother and Empress, for doing away with kneeling in front of her.

He will turn all Russia into the kind of military settlement Gatchina has become.

Maria lowers her eyes, her only shield.

"There is no need to dwell on more reasons," the Empress continues sternly. "They are too painful to all concerned."

Maria's hands clench.

"Alexander will succeed me after I die," the Empress says. "But I want it announced soon. He needs to tackle responsibilities that will prepare him for the throne. It won't be easy for him. It is not easy for anyone. This is why he needs our support in these difficult moments."

She pauses and waits for her daughter-in-law to look at her, but Maria doesn't lift her head. She is breathing fast but not crying, which is a good sign.

Catherine continues her explanations. "Alexander tortures himself with guilt. He doesn't want to hurt his father's feelings."

Another pause, the last one before the final punch.

"Alexander, my dear Maria, needs his dear mother's support. He needs to know that his mother will take his side. Will prepare his father for what must happen. Soften his disappointment. Make his father see that nothing that truly matters to him will change. That he can have his Gatchina army the way he wants it. Run Gatchina the way he always has."

The letter is in her hands. A simple but heartfelt letter of assurance, a mother telling her son she understands he is forced to accept the burden of power for the good of Russia and that she offers him her blessing and her prayers.

"Please, my dear Maria," the Empress says. "Read this. Talk to me if you wish anything changed. If you trust my judgment, copy it in your own hand and sign it. Bring it to me and I'll lock it in my private coffer. I'll give it to Alexander myself."

She says: When the time comes. She says: A secret between the two of us for now. My utter trust in you. Our common love for our Prince.

Maria takes the letter in her hand as if it were a bone-china cup from Sèvres, so

473

delicate and thin that it might break when her fingers close on it. Glances over the sentences quickly, lips moving as if in prayer.

Hasn't enough been said? What else does the foolish woman want to hear?

"Alexander needs words in his mother's hand that he can read when doubts assail him. His mother, whom he loves and whose judgment he trusts. His mother, who, when his grandmother dies, will be the one all imperial wives and daughters will come to for advice and support."

Maria lifts her face.

But instead of Bezborodko's shrewd, competent eyes, two deep pools of watery blue stare at her with terror.

"Then Grand Duke Paul asked the Swedish King if he agreed that Pavlovsk was but a shadow of Gatchina," Queenie says, shaking her head. "In Maria Fyodorovna's presence!"

This is Paul's idea of diplomacy, to ask his prospective son-in-law to criticize Maria Fyodorovna's pride and joy.

"And did he?"

"He said both were equally beautiful." Queenie laughs.

She has braided three kerchiefs together and wrapped them over her head. Blue, red, and yellow. There is something cheerful and girlish about this combination of colors. Quite attractive, even on Queenie, with her

474

hairy upper lip and chubby cheeks.

Told to sit down, Queenie settles on the ottoman. Rests her bulky body on the embroidered cushions, every one of them adorned with a bird. Her plump elbow is stuck right into the beak of a big blue parrot.

Queenie has brought news from Gatchina.

She heard it from a young maid-of-honor in Maria Fyodorovna's entourage. The latest of Queenie's many protégées, spotted at some country estate or other, lured to St. Petersburg with promises of imperial favors and a husband. Thus this is all gossip, but it would be unwise to dismiss it. Something about Queenie attracts confessions. Women come to her. With broken hearts, empty pockets, troubling dreams. Even Maria Fyodorovna has sought her advice. Over trifles, but still.

"The Swedish visit," Queenie continues, "went quite well, considering."

Considering what, Queenie?

Queenie frowns. Pensive now, she strives to deliver what she has heard, free of her own conjectures. Facts only. Not what you think happened but what you either saw or heard. Old lessons, only the best of spies remember.

The linzer torte may be remembered fondly, but after Maria Fyodorovna's return to Gatchina, there has been considerable unpleasantness. On account of her evasive answers to her husband's questions.

What questions precisely, Queenie? the

475

Empress thinks, but won't interrupt. It will only delay what's most important. Queenie is not known for her conciseness, but for her sixth sense, which lets her hear what others don't.

Paul, as might have been expected, wanted to know what his wife talked about with Maman.

Everyone at court, it seems, is capable of imitating Paul's voice: high and shrill, sentences delivered with petulance. Queenie's imitation of Paul interrogating his wife is uncanny:

The two of you only talked about Alexandrine?

And about Katya Dashkova, who will be asked to go with her. If we agree.

She asked you if we agree?

She did.

Really! So why are you avoiding my eyes?

There would've been more, Queenie announces, her plump chest heaving. Only then the guests arrived.

Right before noon. Seven carriages. The Swedish King, the Regent, the Swedish Ambassador, a few other grandees. No ladies, which made it awkward for Maria Fyodorovna.

A lot of military talk ensued: Paul's kind of talk, which did not involve battles and campaigns but a lecture on how the length of a pigtail and deft application of hair powder are not frills — as some Russian command-

476

ers maintain — but proof of discipline. There was an inevitable parade with demonstrations of bayonet attacks. A show of Prussian military drill.

How predictable her son is! How unable to move away from the ruts of his feeble mind! Is there anything, ever, he can surprise her with?

Well, she thinks a few moments later: *One needs to be careful what one wishes for.*

Queenie, flustered, perfectly aware of the effect her words are causing, is describing this scene:

In the great Gatchina dining room, with its carved ceiling and walls covered with paintings of famous battles, Paul presides over the table. He has drunk too much, which happens often, though this time the wine is making him not merely reckless and spiteful, but sentimental. Or maybe, incorrigible Queenie observes, it is not just the wine but the thought of Alexandrine's anticipated nuptials and the presence of the man who will so soon take her to his bed. A moment a father might dread, Queenie suggests.

Any father.

To continue: Paul talks quite a bit. Too much, is a more apt description. Hardly allowing anyone a word edgewise. Recalling Alexandrine when she was growing up. For his eldest daughter — he wishes to warn his illustrious guest — was not always as sweet

477

as she is now.

It's tempting to get caught in Queenie's story. The memories of Alexandrine slipping rotten plums into Constantine's riding boots. Or drawing cat's paw prints on the wall in her bedroom. With her own sooty fingers! Hiding her hands behind her back and claiming she didn't know who might've done it!

Tempting to laugh with Queenie, too. Laugh and forget the passage of time.

But this is not why Queenie is here, allowed to loll about on the ottoman.

"What happened next?"

Queenie grows serious. The dinner, she says, ended. All the ladies present — at Maria Fyodorovna's signal — stood up and left.

Right outside the dining room door, in the melee of voices that followed the ladies' departure, Queenie's protégée heard the name: *Kościuszko.* And then, in the utter silence the word brought upon the Swedes, Paul Petrovich, who thinks himself a Prince worthy of the Russian throne, called the Polish rebel, his mother's prisoner, "a valiant general I greatly admire."

"I couldn't believe my ears," Queenie says, shaking her head and wrinkling her nose. "But it's not a name one mistakes easily, madame."

Like flies to carrion, the Empress thinks the following morning, sorting through the daily flow of petitions from her new Polish subjects, hoping to feed on the mishaps of their compatriots.

Conquests move more than borders. A crushed rebellion reshuffles real estate. Those who supported it lose, those who opposed it stand to gain a reward. Each estate confiscated becomes the object of someone's desire. A motivation for a sincere report. A cause for a confession. A reason to plead.

Enemies turn into friends, friends into enemies. But Alexander doesn't have to know that yet. For now, she makes sure he has little idle time. No more visits to Gatchina, no long discussions with Adam on the nature of American democracy or some other youthful folly. Every morning, she sends for her grandson to join her in her study. With a cautious character, such as Alexander's, slow steps work best. He will not even notice how, after a few weeks, he is drawn into more and more projects.

"I'm considering sending Princess Dashkova with Alexandrine to Stockholm," she tells her grandson. "What do you think?"

The court is readying for the engagement ceremony. Joyful preparations, filled with laughter and frenzied flutter. Alexandrine is being fitted for an engagement gown of white satin embroidered with silver rosebuds. Her sister Maria is jealous and wonders when she, too, will be betrothed. "Does the King of

Sweden have a brother?" she wants to know.

"Isn't Princess Dashkova ill?" Alexander asks. "And hasn't she angered you over something?"

"Dashkova did anger me," Catherine answers. For him, her clever heir, she has nothing but patience. "She allowed the publication of books that shouldn't have been published." Dashkova is the head of the Russian Academy. She should know that vigilance matters. Foresee what might stir up sedition.

Should she be more blunt? Spell it out? Remind Alexander how the French King and Queen rode wooden carts to their deaths, the mob cursing them and all monarchs? How bodies of aristocrats swayed from the Parisian lanterns, or were torn to bloody scraps? Was that a good time to publish a Russian play in which a rebel chastises a Tsar? Or one in which the author instructs the Empress how to rule Russia? Calling her blind! A dupe of scheming courtiers!

No need. Being too forceful doesn't work with Alexander. It's best to let him reach his own conclusions.

"Is it really that important to censor such thoughts?" he asks. "What is gained from pushing them underground?"

She gives him a nod of approval. When she was designing Alexander's education, some things were of the utmost importance. Such as teaching him to question what he was taught. And the ability to assume various dictions. Restate the plot of an Aesop's fable in a simple style. Then in a grandiose style. Write a letter as if you were Achilles right before dying.

"Inform me, but do not humiliate me," she continues her explanation. "If you think something doesn't work well under my rule, come to me directly and tell me what needs to be reformed and why. You know me well, Alexander. I've always listened to reason. But Russia is not ready for instigators, announcing their threadbare ideas from street corners."

Alexander's gaze slides over her desk and rests on her amber inkwell, its copper tint matching his hair. Yes, it is easy for a young heart to take sides. Simplify what is complex. Forget that a future Sovereign cannot mistake his own wishes for those of his country's. But it is a grandmother's duty to watch over her grandson. Warn him when he is erring in his judgment. Point out the pitfalls he cannot yet see.

"Words are not innocuous, Alexander. Thoughts expressed aloud can make men bold. Especially thoughts that promise easy solutions."

Alexander frowns and leans backward as if to push her words away. Has she been too forceful again? But her grandson is no weakling.

"What is wrong in giving people the right to express their thoughts, Graman? Like they do in America."

"Americans harbor many delusions, Alexander. They, too, will learn that there is no point in consulting the ignorant. What is the purpose of giving voice to those whose vision is limited and filled with their crippled, wishful, unenlightened thoughts?"

"And what about respecting the dignity of the human nature?"

"But the human is an animal, Alexander. Animal instinct is not to live in peace, but to hoard and pillage. Why allow it for the sake of noble ideals? What is the point in noble failure?

"Besides, Russia is not a new country, like America. Russia is more like France, and you cannot advocate for what is happening there."

In this argument, she is winning. She can see it in her grandson's slumping shoulders, his slight nod.

"Remember Pugachev, Alexander. You may say it was twenty years ago. You were not even born then, but you have to remember that blood was spilled. It happened once. It can happen again. These 'wise and suffering' peasants can again turn into a bloodthirsty mob. Hang me and you from the nearest lantern."

Her voice flows, soars. She is on safe grounds. "It is better for a Tsar to be thought intolerant and cruel than to allow another such tragedy."

She smiles, satisfied with her own words. This is how she imagined him to be when he was still a teething baby. Coming to her for advice. Listening to her arguments. Coming up with his own, to counter her, if necessary. Forging his own opinions. Finding his own way.

Sometimes a dream takes many years to come to fruition. But how sweet the time when it does.

What plans she has for him! For the next few years! Daily conferences like this one will continue, become more and more serious. He will watch her make decisions. Question her advisers. Analyze their reports, but always draw his own conclusions. Alexander will learn fast. When he is not with her, Bezborodko will watch over him. Tutor him in the art of managing the imperial business.

But serious matters will have to wait for the official announcement of succession. Now it is wiser to show Alexander a list of gifts Alexandrine will take with her to Sweden. A list carefully constructed, she points out, to reflect Russia's achievements. Porcelain from the Imperial Porcelain Manufactory, silver from Tula, stockings small enough to be hidden in a walnut shell, from silk harvested in the Crimea.

"Our Alexandrine will hold her head high

483

at the Swedish court," she says with a chuckle of triumph.

Alexander catches her excitement. He, too, has ideas to contribute. He knows of a serf painter who has rendered the Winter Palace so skillfully that every crack in the wall is there. A painting like this would be a wonderful gift for his sister. Alexandrine could look at it every time she feels homesick.

They work together, side by side.

When it is time for Alexander to leave, she opens the drawer of her bureau and takes out an embroidered satin sachet. Inside it is a snuffbox: on its top, a cameo of a bee leaving the hive to pollinate a fruit branch.

"This is for you, Alexander," Catherine tells him. "I want it to remind you of me every time you hold it. And to remember these words: *What's the point of being disgusted when you can repair what disgusts you?*"

The Swedish accounts are in disorder, Bezborodko's report claims. The Regent is keeping false accounts in order to confuse his enemies, but often cannot distinguish which are the true ones himself. *An Augean stable, and I see no Hercules yet!*

Gustav Adolf, so far, is utterly oblivious of his uncle's disguise skills.

Seated across from her in the Imperial Study, the King describes his visit to

Gatchina. The young man's elated, agitated manner has made Pani desert her velvet cushion and watch him intently.

"The games, madame, were most intriguing," the King says. He was particularly taken by the memory game Maria Fyodorovna proposed. Take a quick glance at a tray with many objects on it, and then try to recall as many of them as possible. A favorite game, she claimed, of all her children.

"How did you do, monsieur," the Empress asks, "in this game?"

"Not as well as Maria Fyodorovna herself," the King confesses. "But I had no practice."

Pani, having decided that he is no threat, rests her narrow gray paw on his lap, expecting a treat or at least a pat on her head. The King stiffens slightly. He is not a dog lover.

"I wish I had brothers," the King continues. "Or sisters," he adds with the wistfulness of a child who has spent too much time among adults.

"Loneliness does not have to be endured," Catherine says and watches him nod with eagerness.

The awaited moment has arrived. The Swedish King is ready to declare his love for Alexandrine. She can see it in his widened eyes and flushed cheeks.

"Before you say anything, monsieur," she interposes, "I need to make some things very clear."

Gustav Adolf gives her a startled look, as if she caught him stuffing his pockets with the imperial silver. But she does not put him at ease. She wants his full attention.

"My granddaughter has a pure soul. She may have been raised at court, but this child cannot conceive of malice or intrigue. She needs to be protected from all harm."

At these words the King's face relaxes visibly. He believes himself on solid ground. His brown eyes moisten, and his voice softens. "I wouldn't let anyone harm her."

"That I don't doubt, monsieur," she tells him. "But you cannot be always at her side. You, too, have enemies. The masked man who murdered your father could not have acted alone. Besides your affection and goodwill, Alexandrine needs her family and her position in her new country."

"I have no intention of denying her that," Gustav Adolf protests. "I can assure —"

"Please," she interrupts. "Let me say what I have to say and let me be plain. You, monsieur, are Lutheran. My granddaughter is Russian Orthodox. Have you considered the issue of faith?"

The King gives her a startled, incredulous look. What did he think she would talk to him about? His father's intimate inclinations? His frolicking with Baron Munck?

"Doesn't a wife," Gustav Adolf asks in

reply, "always take on the husband's religion?"

"Russian nobles are forbidden to leave the Orthodox Church. If a Russian Grand Duchess ever abandoned her faith, she would cut herself off from her family and from Russia. And then she would be alone."

The Empress pauses, letting him assess the consequences of her words. She would have liked to watch his face, but the Swedish King has lowered his head. All she can see is the straight line of his skin where his shiny hair parts before it falls along his cheeks. She hopes he is thinking beyond love and faith, calculating his own advantages, thinking of the future. What use would Alexandrine be to him without her influence in St. Petersburg?

"If you seek my permission to marry my granddaughter, I'll give it, under the condition that in Sweden she will be allowed to worship the way she does here. Do not reply to me right now, monsieur. I intend to depart for Tsarskoye Selo for a few days. Think about what I've said. If this is impossible, make the most of your visit, and when I come back you will leave without resuming this conversation. But if you stay, I'll know you've accepted this condition."

The King raises his head. His face is pale but composed. He thanks her for her straightforward manner, which he values tremendously. And then, his body slumping, a punctured balloon deflated, he leaves the room.

At the door, Gustav Adolf gives her one more look, as if still incredulous that he had heard her right.

He bows.

The doors close, and she is alone again. Pani returns to her cushion, circling it a few times before settling to her midday nap.

Poor Gustav Adolf, not yet a true King, and already torn between what he desires and what he can have. Is she truly asking for that much, though? Haven't dogmas always been disputed? Wine or blood? Flesh or wafer? One God in three spirits or three gods in one? A song of love and suffering or wrath and damnation?

Isn't religion only an imperfect human view of what is ultimately unknowable? Doesn't it change with time? With circumstances? Where were the Lutherans before Martin Luther? Calvinists before Calvin?

Isn't it best to accept that there are some things we will never know and busy ourselves with what we can change?

And then she wonders what has happened to the cane she had given Gustav Adolf's father (cousin Gu, she called him) when he came to St. Petersburg for the first time, in 1783. He was her first cousin, on her mother's side. The cane's knob was made of a single diamond worth sixty thousand rubles.

■ ■ ■ ■

As soon as Gustav Adolf leaves, Le Noiraud comes into her study. His black eyes are rimmed with red.

Vishka reports that he has ordered one of his pages to watch for the King's visits. She also informs her that the Favorite cannot sleep. "We are quite unsure of ourselves," she remarks with a sour smile. "A pinch of jealousy might've done us some real good."

Le Noiraud does not take a seat, but walks about the room. A distinct blend of musk and almond oil trails his every step. Too strong, but this is not a good moment to point out such a trifle.

He stops by the mantel as if to admire the Chinese vase, then the porcelain figures she has placed in a row: an onion seller, a fisherman, a cobbler. Old gifts from the Prussian King she still finds endearing. The onion woman, Grishenka always maintained, looks like a witch.

Platon's restlessness and silence are meant to make her ask for reasons. So does the studied pose he assumes by the fireplace, with his elbow resting on the marble. He knows this shows his handsome figure to the advantage. The cloud in his eyes darkens.

"Has Gustav Adolf proposed?" he finally blurts out, defeated.

"Almost," Catherine replies.

"What happened?"

"I don't want him to rush. Young favor is warm but not durable . . ."

Le Noiraud nods with cheerful eagerness, a pupil who knows how to please his teacher. "Then it has to be snatched and improved."

When she laughs, he saunters to her side and kneels beside her. His head feels heavy on her lap, for he presses it with desperation. Are these sobs or laughter she hears?

She lifts his head. Rouge is smeared on his wet face.

"What's the matter with my silly boy?"

The warmth in her voice melts him. "I'm nothing, Katinka," he mutters. "They laugh at me."

She doesn't have to ask whose indifference is the cause of Le Noiraud's despair. There are many ladders of rank, some more obvious than others. Alexander Andreyevich Bezborodko is the culprit. Grishenka called him a genius and a friend, but in Platon's eyes what matters most is Bezborodko's indifference to him. The imperial minister does not consider the Imperial Favorite a worthy opponent.

"I'm of no use to you. You don't need me. Nothing I do is even worth noting. I bring you news, and you dismiss it . . . Give me a chance, Katinka," he says. "Let me do something worthy. Like my brother has done."

490

It is better not to let Platon dwell on Valerian's recent conquests. The brothers barely speak ever since Platon decided Valerian was trying to take his place at her side.

"Anything that will let me prove my worth," Platon continues. He fixes his eyes on hers, pleading with his whole body. The sweet memory that crosses her mind is singed with regret.

If she could still feel anything when he made love to her, none of this would have mattered.

"Please, Katinka. I beg you."

The pain in his voice is real. It makes her heart melt.

"I'll think about it, *Votre Altesse,*" she promises, and sees him smile. "Now, go away," she adds. "I have work to do."

"What is this smell?" Vishka asks when she enters with another pot of hot coffee half an hour later. "May I open the window?" she asks and tries, in vain, to stifle a sneeze.

Platon's heavy perfume permeates her study, in spite of Vishka's airing, but unlike Vishka, Alexander Andreyevich Bezborodko makes no mention of the scent when he arrives to deliver his reports.

The Swedes have been taken to Tsarskoye Selo. Gushed over the hanging garden, the splendor of the amber room. Gustav Adolf

491

wondered if he could re-create the Golden Enfilade at his palace. Not as long and as sumptuous, he said, but enough of it "to create a resemblance to this incomparable interior."

"He didn't mention for whom?" the Empress asks, beaming with pleasure.

"Implied, not stated bluntly, Your Highness," Alexander Andreyevich answers. "We should start talking about drafting the engagement contract."

"I've been considering asking Prince Zubov to do it," she says and waits. With her minister, directness is the best policy. He deserves it, and he can handle it. "Prince Zubov doesn't know it yet," she adds. "You, Alexander Andreyevich, should concentrate on the matter of succession."

"As Your Majesty wishes."

There is no surprise in Bezborodko's eyes. A perfect courtier knows she can read silence as well as words: *It is Your Majesty's decision. I wouldn't have made it, but the matter does not warrant an objection. This is a simple negotiation of a contract agreed upon in principle already. What can go wrong?*

So the matter is closed.

In one of the paintings in the Winter Palace bedroom, Sarah, old and shrewd-looking, brings Hagar to Abraham. The patriarch, his torso bared, is sitting in bed, staring at Hagar's rosy and glowing skin. The girl averts her eyes, but her anticipation of her deflowering is visible.

How easy, one might think, to foresee the future. Two women. One young and fertile, the other old and believing herself barren, desperate for the young woman's womb.

But it is withered Sarah's son who will inherit his father's kingdom. And beautiful Hagar will be left in the desert, her child an outcast.

Catherine likes to study Sarah's face in the painting. What is the old woman thinking as she leads the beautiful slave to her husband's bed? That youth and beauty do not last? That wisdom is a far better bet?

"Different parts of the body are more prone to certain diseases, Your Majesty," Rogerson says. "Breasts and testicles are the seat of cancer. Legs carry our weight and are thus prone to bone and skin fatigue."

He cannot hide his pleasure at the evidence that her leg is not improving. In two places, the skin between her toes has begun to blacken. So has the ball of her foot, after a pebble got into her shoe and she did not feel it. Her thickened, hard nails are now surrounded by a layer of yellowed skin, which Rogerson presses with his finger. There is a grimace of triumph on his face. Valuable time has been lost. Damage now has to be undone.

Drastic measures must be considered.

"How drastic?" she asks.

"It is too early to say, Your Highness."

"How drastic?" she repeats angrily. Why do people insist on hiding the truth from her?

"I might have to amputate the toe, madame," Rogerson answers. "But only if it doesn't improve," he adds hastily.

The word *amputate* is terrifying. It conjures up the surgeon's saw cutting through a living bone. Muscles sliced open with a lancet. Veins tied up and cauterized. There is searing pain and a fountain of blood. Soldiers who lose limbs at war are young and strong, but even Valerian, who wears his wooden leg like a badge of honor, wakes up at night screaming.

The doctor avoids blaming the Empress directly, but he cannot resist exposing Lambro-Cazzioni's cure for what it is. Trickery. Unproven wishful thinking. A triumph of persuasion over knowledge and experience.

A quack, he implies, will remain a quack.

She lets her doctor lecture her, though her mind wanders from fear to resentment. Rogerson claims great authority, he uses Latin terms and fancy words, but under his care her legs didn't fare any better.

"Perhaps it won't have to come to that, Your Majesty," Rogerson continues. "There is no point in fearing what is not here yet."

Bleedings will have to resume, and purgings. The ulcers will have to be cauterized.

She will also have to take five grains of James's powder every morning, together with two grains of calomel.

"James's powder?" she asks. "Don't you always say that it is good for fevers?"

"And the rheumatic affliction," Rogerson states, his voice firm, secure in his victory. "Because it contains antimony, madame, known to reduce inflammation of tissue."

Catherine nods, resigned. The specter of an amputation is enough to make her agree to submit to Rogerson's treatment. Vishka will be trusted with telling Lambro-Cazzioni not to come again in the mornings. A suitable gift should soften the Admiral's disappointment. Something he can use at court gatherings, impress others with. A jeweled snuffbox with an appropriate naval scene? The victory at Chesme would be best. At least two dozen of them must still be available from the last shipment.

"As little walking as possible, madame," he advises. "We don't want unnecessary pressure on the bones and ligaments. And it's best not to dwell too much on the source of aggravation. The mind is a healer, but it can also irritate the noxious matter. Cheerful disposition is critical. Distractions do work."

Rogerson, Vishka tells her, has rejected his cousin's proposed purchase of an English estate because it was not grand enough. *In Russia,* he has written, *I have learned to aim higher.* Profits come not just from his hefty fees but also from selling his tonics.

"Countess Betskoy has left St. Petersburg. She will not attend her daughter's coming-out ball," he remarks, as he gathers his instruments.

Her legs, bound tight, seem even more lifeless. Her lips are parched in spite of all the water she has drunk. Why would she care about Countess Betskoy?

"Her goiter has grown considerably in the last months. It is now too big to be covered with ruffles and fichu." Rogerson bows. "The Countess decided that the sight would endanger her daughter's chances for a good marriage."

The Empress doesn't say anything.

Le Noiraud enters in his embroidered dressing gown, enveloped in the woody, earthy smell of expensive musk. He brings her a basket of fresh apples. An offering of the fall.

There is a frown on his high forehead. The beauty of his face softens her heart. He is still so young, so impossible to warn against the vagaries of fortune.

The apples he has brought her are red and shiny.

She won't tell him that she still prefers cherries, won't remind him how Potemkin always sent her a bowl of them. Not in the summer, when they were plentiful, but on the first day of the New Year, when he brought them at great expense from some southern orchard and rushed them to the capital in a heated carriage.

"Let me, Katinka," Le Noiraud says. Slowly, with a silver pocketknife, he pares an apple in one continuous peel, until it falls softly on the carpet. A red ribbon he leaves for the servants to pick up.

She should chasten him. Tell him this is not the way to earn the servants' loyalty, though he won't understand her objections. He frowns whenever she does anything out of such scruples. Lights her own fire in the morning, or inquires after the stoker's children. Remembers names of her maids, their parents, their siblings. "Not that much of an effort," she explained to him. "And it goes further than the most costly gift."

Le Noiraud thinks such gestures charming, divinely good of her. But he doesn't believe her calculations.

Now he cuts the peeled apple into two halves, removes the pits, and hands her one half. He makes a tired joke on how it should be her tempting him with an apple, but she smiles nevertheless. It pleases her to see him so lively.

"A man in London," he tells her, "invented a machine not bigger than a toothpick case that is capable of destroying a whole building."

"How?" she asks.

"Reduces it to ashes."

"You speak in riddles, Platon. Who is making such a claim?"

"I don't know his name," he confesses. "But he is a famous inventor. I can find out if you wish me to."

"It's not that important."

Le Noiraud gives her a pained look and turns his face away from her. It is a studied gesture, meant to be noticed.

"What is it?" she asks. "What have I said that has hurt you?"

"Nothing."

She will have to pry it out of him, the price of whatever misdemeanor she has committed. He will deny a few times, then beg her pardon for being too forthright. The very thought of these rituals irks her. Why can't people say what they mean? "I need to know what bothers you. Without it, how can I know what you really think?"

Le Noiraud confesses that it is the Admiral's dismissal. Why did she have to send him away? Didn't she say that the seawater baths were making her feel better? Why did she stop them? Is it because it was his sister's idea?

"Who told you that?" she asks.

"My valet heard rumors."

"Your valet needs to concentrate on the state of your wardrobe," she retorts.

Catherine feels anger rise, a surge that

quickens her heart, but just then Le Noiraud falls to his knees. The Admiral is not that important. If he knew that his stupid cure wasn't helping, he would have thrown him out of the palace himself. "On his face. Into the gutter," he gushes.

"Make me useful, Katinka," Le Noiraud blurts out. "Send me where I can do something that matters. You tell me I have talents. Abilities. What are my tasks, though? Such as anyone could accomplish! I'll be twenty-nine soon. I want to prove how much I can do for you. Days drag so much when I find my occupations are mere trivial amusements."

"Not quite that trivial," she protests.

"You know what I mean. I know how to be helpful in small things. But this is not all I want." She hears the rattle of self-pity in his voice.

"All right," she says. "Prepare the betrothal contract. Negotiate the final wording of the clauses. Morkov will help you."

"Is that all?" Le Noiraud asks sullenly. "Is this Bezborodko's idea? Is this what he thinks I'm only good for?"

"No," she says, still patient. "It's mine. But I expect no apology. I like my apples too much to make you sulk."

On his face, disappointment and amusement wrestle.

She takes the apple from his hand. She doesn't want to hurt him. Or belittle him.

She shouldn't have mentioned Morkov. She should've let him choose his own advisers, but it is too late for that.

"I agree that it is not the most difficult of tasks," she continues, watching the frown on Platon's forehead deepen. She concedes that the conditions have been agreed upon in principle. But it is always the final wording of documents that is of the essence. This is what she entrusts him with.

Something in her words soothes him. He does not rise from his knees, but he does look up. His eyes brighten with some thought she will not inquire about. And then he buries his face in her lap. She can feel his hot breath penetrate through the dressing gown. He moves his head gently, nestling into her.

She lets him hold on to her, burrow deeper. Nothing inside her stirs in response. It is as if her blood stopped short of flowing into the extremities of her body.

"I always disappoint you, Katinka," Le Noiraud murmurs.

"You don't."

He lifts his head. There is fear in his eyes. Fear she kisses away, until he smiles.

Only later, much later, when the apples are all eaten and they have watched the Neva from the palace window — the illuminated barges on which merry crowds explode with laughter and Gypsy songs — only then does she allow herself a few reminders:

"*Fortirer in re:* Give up no point. Accept no lessening of conditions until necessity forces you to. And even then, give in inch by inch, disputing them as you go on.

"But at the same time remember to gain his confidence. *Suaviter in modo.* Engage his heart. And when you have it, then impose on his understanding.

"Do not confuse your opponent with your enemy. Remember that the manner is as important as the matter."

He listens.

He nods. He caresses her hand, kisses each finger, traces the palm of her hand with his lips.

He promises to remember each and every word of her advice.

And then he tells her that when the Swedish negotiations are over, he will conquer China for her. "I swear, Katinka. You'll have real pagodas for your gardens. Trees you have not seen before in your whole life. Flowers that will astonish everyone who visits. Birds of unimaginable colors."

She laughs. "How will you do all this?"

He will march an army through the interior of Russia. He has already charted the route, past the Ural Mountains. The Chinese will never expect an attack from the north. "Valerian agrees," he says, and only when he brings up his brother's name does it occur to her that this is not a lover's teasing. Her beautiful

501

Le Noiraud is deadly serious.

He wants to be like Potemkin. A Viceroy. A conqueror.

"If Valerian agrees," she says, trying to suppress the slightest sign of laughter, "then I'll consider it."

This is when, for a brief unsettling moment, she feels as if an iron hoop has encircled her chest, making her fight for breath. A bright flash coming from somewhere inside her makes her eyes blink. Her lips quiver. There is a slight tingling in the tips of her right hand.

She forces herself to take a deeper breath. Then another.

It's nothing, she thinks. *It'll go away.*

It does.

It is still hard to believe her eyes. Has Bezborodko opened his folder? Taken a sheet of paper from it? Could it be that time makes a dent even in his infallible memory?

She is going to jest about this, but something in his countenance stops her.

"These pages have been found hidden under a floorboard in Prince Adam's room," Bezborodko says. "I would like to read them to Your Majesty in their entirety."

There have been moments in our past conversations when the Grand Duke stopped in mid-sentence and hesitated as if wishing to say something before changing his mind. There have been hints: "We are not always trusted, my dear Adam, we are being pushed where we do not wish to go." Once, when we found ourselves ignorant of some aspect of the American principles of government, he exclaimed, "If only La Harpe were here, he would instruct us well! He knew how to inspire a young mind! We are blind like moles without him!" With tears in his eyes the Grand Duke confessed to me how much he missed his Swiss tutor. On another occasion, as we were watching the antics of kangaroos in the Tauride garden, the Grand Duke expressed a wish to buy a small estate, somewhere in Switzerland, where he could live with his wife as a private citizen and cultivate his garden. "For I have resolved to rid myself, in the future, of my burden," he said.

I didn't say anything then.

Ardent hope is not the best of advisers. My countrymen have learned this painful lesson well.

Yesterday the Grand Duke wished to see me alone. "Let's not waste such a gorgeous day sitting inside," he said when I came to his room, proposing a stroll in the gardens.

We walked briskly through the park, which, although rather small, has been cleverly designed in the English style with meandering paths, dense shrubbery, and unexpected clearings. When we were away from the palace his voice turned into an urgent whisper. "Please don't stop, no matter what I say to you now. Please continue walking at the same pace, without looking at me more than you always do."

I nodded my agreement.

"For some time now I've been awaiting the moment when I can unveil my true thoughts before you," he said. "I don't want you to equate me with those who surround me. I'm not in agreement with this court."

I kept my pace; I didn't look at him.

"I think it cruel and wrong to take what is not ours. To see greed disguised as policy, to watch shameless flatterers receive the estates robbed from those far more worthy only because they dared to defend their own country from destruction!

"I've noticed that you've been cautious around me, that you don't dare say the words that you carry in your heart. You don't have to be.

"I want you to know how often my wishes were for Kościuszko and his insurrection against our Russian troops. I want to assure you of my great admiration for this noble man and to tell you that I have been deeply saddened by his defeat."

He spoke fast, as if we had only this short time in the world when all that is of true importance can be said. He spoke, and I could not believe the words I heard were truly coming from the lips of a Grand Duke who will one day sit upon the Russian throne.

"How often I wished I could sneak into Kościuszko's prison cell! Shake his hand and tell him of my admiration for his character, his courage in opposing tyranny. Assure him that my heart is on the side of his unfortunate compatriots who cannot speak up for their country if they don't want to lose their freedom and their fortune."

I became conscious of a new note of bitterness in the Grand Duke's voice. He paused, and for a moment the flow of his confession — for this is what it truly was — broke. Deep emotions were fighting for their supremacy: "I'm not entirely trusted . . . I'm continuously being honored by concerns . . . my sentiments are dismissed as childish and transient."

How I wished to stop walking and hold his hand, assure him of my joy at hearing such noble words, but I remained true to my promise and let my legs carry me forward.

"As I'm honest with you, I'm hoping you will soon trust me enough to be honest with me. Believe me when I say that I respect your feelings, share your sorrow and your pain. Out of everyone at this loathsome court only my wife shares my way of thinking. She, too, cringes at the thought of

505

injustice. Anyone else would've betrayed me."

The Grand Duke of Russia stopped at this moment and briefly touched my arm.

"Will you honor me with your full confidence and trust?" he asked me. "As I have just trusted you?"

I nodded my agreement, too moved to express my joy. A Tsarevich brought up in hatred of all that is Polish, surrounded by flattery and dreams of absolute power, has emerged with his soul unscathed! What other proofs do I need to believe that the rule of tyranny has no future? That the end of injustice is near!

There is a painting of the Annunciation in the Imperial Bedroom that she likes to examine. It amazes her how little a skillful painter needs to achieve an effect of sumptuousness. The pearls on the fringe of Mary's robe are but a dollop of gray, each touched with a tiny spot of white, yet so perfect in tone that from even a step away each drop of paint becomes a jewel.

There is a lesson in this. Eyes are easily fooled. One doesn't need to provide all details — just a hint is enough. Everything else can be completed from memory or desire.

Stretched on her bed, she listens as Le Noiraud assures her that the negotiations with the Swedes are proceeding well. He and Morkov have drafted all the clauses. They are meeting with the Swedes tomorrow, to discuss the final wording.

This is Russia's time. Her Russia, which has shown Europe its true mettle. This is the time of acquisitions and tough bargains. Compared to the Ottoman Porte and Poland, the Swedish one has been longest in the making. And the Regent is still trying to approach the French. All of this will stop once Alexandrine is their Queen.

"Tomorrow?" she asks.

"Right after breakfast," Le Noiraud replies.

She looks at the clock. "Show me what you've prepared so far," she says. The tone of her voice is a mistake, she realizes, as soon as the words leave her lips. Platon is not Bezborodko. For him, the negotiations are not government business but a chance to prove himself, to assert his usefulness. She should have been more indirect, milder, more encouraging.

"Do you not trust me even that much, Katinka? Or is Bezborodko whispering to you again?" The hurt in his voice singes her.

"I don't discuss you with anyone," she replies, hoping this will do, at least for now.

Le Noiraud nods but doesn't look at her. What will come next, if she doesn't stop this silliness, is sulky silence, his ultimate weapon. She should let him be, her young lover. *Be more indulgent,* she tells herself. *He wishes to impress you.*

This is the time for a compromise. She won't ask to see the draft, but she cannot entirely abstain from offering her warning. "The Regent is the one you have to watch," she says. "In spite of all his promises, he is the one who will try to come up with obstacles."

"I watch him. I know."

"All right, then."

A small victory, and yet what pleasure it gives Platon. He opens his arms and embraces her, his face bright like the North Star. "It shall all be the way you want it, Katinka," he murmurs. Alexandrine, the Queen of Sweden. Her husband's beloved. At her side, her Orthodox confessor and priests whispering advice. Swedish policy slowly adjusting to further and aid Russian interests.

For a moment, he does look like a triumphant warrior, on a mountaintop surveying the slain enemies strewn on the field. The bloodied banners, the groans of the dying. The shouts of his own troops, who worship him.

For he who is beloved of women wishes men to love him.

For a moment, she remembers Potemkin, the two of them giggling over their triumphs over Mustafa's defeat. Counting the fallen fortresses. Discounting the Turkish threats.

The children of Providence. Charting the carefully chosen steps that nudge fortune along.

There is still some pleasure in the warm, moist kisses, the cuddles of young arms. The look of adoration that holds her above all other women. The pride in a young man's eyes that she, his Empress, has chosen him from among so many others.

Le Noiraud leaves, beaming. When the doors close, his voice comes to her from the anteroom, chastising someone's slowness, urging someone else into action.

Soothed by her lover's happiness, Catherine allows herself to think of the dead. Not for long, but long enough to hear their warnings.

Don't be too foolish, Katinka, Grishenka chastises her. *He is vain. He thinks too highly of himself.*

Does he love you enough, matushka? Sasha Lanskoy's voice echoes. *Is he even capable of love?*

But aren't the dead always jealous of the living?

What I cannot change, I undermine, she thinks as Prince Adam is announced.

The gilded doors open, and Alexander's friend walks in with an air of studied concern, a mask of his unease.

Prince Adam has come here because she

has willed it. Made his sojourn at the Russian court a condition of her future benevolence toward his family after their foolish support of the uprising. The Czartoryski estates have only been sequestered, not confiscated, but the old Prince Czartoryski has taken her decision for what it was, a warning. Give me one more reason for Russia's displeasure and a mighty family shall fall. If you wish me to forgive you and reverse my order, let your heir see what Russia truly is, let him watch and learn.

This is what she thought then. Was it a mistake?

For it also might be argued that this friendship — with all its youthful follies — is a good thing. An heir of a grand Polish family is bound to a Russian heir to the throne. Ties forged so early might last a long time. Survive the change of circumstances. A gamble? Yes. But if it succeeds, ties that strong cannot be bought or legislated.

Prince Adam bows with a polished grace. There are dark circles under his eyes, evidence of a sleepless night. Another long talk with Alexander? Do the young ever sleep?

"I wish to tell you how grateful I am for your influence over the Grand Duke," she says.

At the mention of Alexander's name, Prince Adam's face stiffens. If he hopes to cover his thoughts, his mask is a porous one.

"My grandson tells me wonderful things of your summer walks," the Empress continues. "Exertion paired with stimulating conversations is the best medicine."

"Getting to know His Imperial Highness has been an honor," the Prince says.

"You've been with us a whole year. And I have heard nothing but good about your conduct. You, monsieur, are a reader, which I respect more than anything. You care about ideas. You want to learn what you do not know. Your mother should be proud of such a son!"

Prince Adam raises his blue-gray eyes. There is a flicker in them. Of amusement? Of fear? Is he worried the Russian Empress is trying to entrap him?

"But this is not why I summoned you," Catherine continues with a benevolent smile. "I want to ask for your help." She does not say "in return for the favor of my forgiveness your family requests." There is no need for such vulgar bluntness.

"How can I be of service, Your Majesty?"

"I'm worried about Alexander."

His face stiffens again. He is really too predictable.

"What I want to say," she continues, "I must say in utter confidence. Not a word must ever be revealed of this conversation. We are both people of reason. I won't make you kneel and swear secrecy on the Virgin

511

Mary. But I will ask for your word of honor."

He nods, whispers his agreement.

Now that she has his word of honor, backed up with a hammering heart, she begins: "There is no good way to say it, so let me be straightforward. My grandson Alexander will succeed me. Over his father. I won't dwell on my reasons. You are an intelligent young man, and you've seen enough. It'll be better for Russia. Which includes you and your family, for Russia is your homeland now."

She pauses. On Prince Adam's face a whole constellation changes. It is not often that one sees so much joyful hope fighting to burst out from under a mask of caution.

The words flow off her lips, each a jewel. "Alexander understands. His reasoning mind accepts my arguments, but his heart is troubled. He dreads causing pain, crushing his father's hopes."

Prince Adam nods his head vigorously. What did he write in his diary? *What other proofs do I need to believe that the rule of tyranny has no future, that the end of injustice is near!*

"Do not mention it first," she continues, "but should my grandson seek your advice in however roundabout a way, put his mind at ease. Tell him how important it is for a country to be ruled with the wisdom and courage he possesses. Tell him that a son's

512

duty to his father is not greater than a Grand Duke's duty to his Motherland."

She speaks for a while longer. On friendship and its duties. On the need to offer support when it is necessary. "I know you agree with my assessment of my grandson's virtues. His mind and his heart."

Another nod, a smile appearing and folding into seriousness. Her young guest needs time to collect his thoughts, hide the excess of his joy.

"Your Imperial Majesty can count on my help," he says solemnly, as if taking the vows of a monk.

"You have my gratitude," Catherine says.

All that is left now is a wave of her hand. A smile. A few words of excuse. She has no more time. The Empire is a hard taskmaster.

The Prince bows and walks toward the door with the springy step of a youth whose prayers have been answered.

Later the same day, she tackles the growing flood of papers. Treaties, petitions, lists of titles to approve. All demanding amendments, suggestions, requests for more thorough investigations. Arrows appear on the margins; her comments grow longer, more elaborate. Her fingers are stained with ink. She has gone through a whole bunch of quills.

Conjectures need to be separated from facts. Ledgers of advantages and disadvantages made. This, too, awaits Alexander, who needs to get over his youthful enthusiasm for rebels. Should she start him on it now? With the simplest of tasks?

With a Grodno report, a confiscated letter. Addressed to His Majesty Stanislav August, the King of Poland.

For Your Majesty's eyes only.

The handwriting is clear enough, but the letters are very small, making the reading difficult.

I'm hoping that this letter will find Your Majesty in good health, in spite of the trying circumstances and uncertainty of the last tragic months. It is really an apology, as Your Majesty will discover in due course, but before I reveal the reason for this act of contrition, I must explain the circumstances that proceeded it.

My name is Darya. I am Varvara Nikolayevna's daughter. I hope that Your Majesty still remembers us, for I carry fond memories of those days, which seem to me more a beautiful dream than reality.

My own daughters, when they were little, begged me to tell them of the time when I played in the corridors of the Winter Palace with the Grand Duke Paul. They loved to hear that I once sat on the lap of the

Empress of Russia and listened to her stories. But I haven't talked of these times for many years now. The circumstances we live in have not made such memories welcome.

My dearest mama died in peace, almost two years to the day after my stepfather died. Not a day passes without me thinking of her, but I'm trying to remember her the way she was, not the way she became in the last months of her life.

Your Majesty will be pleased to know that my mother's life has been happy. She and my stepfather ran a small but prosperous bookstore in Kraków. They were a devoted couple, and Mama never spoke of our years in St. Petersburg. Even to me it often seemed impossible that a bookseller's wife, in her gray unadorned dresses and sensible shoes, was once Countess Malikina.

It was right after my stepfather's funeral that I first realized something was odd about her. She would be talking with me about my daughters, and I would see her eyes wander, as if the subject did not interest her. Then, suddenly, she would rush to another room, where I would find her rummaging through drawers. "I've forgotten where I've put my spectacles," she would exclaim. Or "I just wanted to make sure I haven't lost my keys." I would help her locate what she was looking for, but this did not stop her for long, and soon she would rush off again.

I took this unease to be the result of grief after losing a husband who was her true friend, and I hoped that, in time and with God's assistance, she would find consolation in me and my family. But she refused to go with me, so I left her in Kraków, promising to visit soon. When I did, a month later, she took me aside and in a whisper informed me that the servants were stealing from her.

"What is missing?" I asked, but she just stared at me suspiciously.

"Why do you need to know?" she asked.

"I want to help you find it," I replied.

"They all say that," she told me. "But I'm not such a fool to believe them."

The servants swore they didn't touch anything they were not supposed to touch, and knowing their devotion to my mother, I believed them. Indeed, it was one of the maids who showed me that Mama hid silver spoons under her own pillow, having wrapped them in an old stocking first.

There were many more such troubling incidents, and, after Mama came back from a walk trailed by urchins who taunted her for speaking Russian to them, I took my mother into my own house. The move upset her greatly at first. She could not get used to the layout of the rooms and would find herself lost on her way from her bedroom to the parlor. Or she would ask me what happened to the service door in her room, and when I explained that we never had service doors she made a funny face and winked at me. Then she began wandering through the house and the outbuildings at night. Once a maid found her with one of the barn cats asleep on her lap. "I've found the Empress's cat," she said.

My elder daughter, who was fourteen at the time, came to me one day and said that Grandmamma called her Catherine. "But I'm Barbara," she said. Mama looked at her as if my daughter had lost her mind. "No, you are not," she said, quite cross with her.

The same conversation was repeated a few times, and since protests made Mama only more puzzled and upset, I told my daughter not to correct her. For weeks after that, Mama would pull my daughter into her room, ostensibly to tell her something. "Secrets," she said, but they were all warnings. Someone was trying to hurt her, she had to be careful, she had to watch out. "But who is trying to hurt me, Grandmamma?" my daughter asked. "They," my mother would whisper. "They" were listening at the door. "They" were watching them both through the keyhole. "They" knew of everything. "Run away, Catherine," she would cry. "Run, before it is too late. Run, before they steal your soul."

It broke my heart to see Mama the way she was. The doctors were of no help and only weakened her with excessive bleedings. My beloved mother — and I shudder even now as I write these words — was rapidly losing her mind. Soon she no longer recognized my husband, my children, or me. She talked to herself, ceaseless monologues in Russian, in which I discerned scraps of conversations and pleadings to the ghosts that haunted her troubled mind. "Go to her, please. She is alone. She is hurting. Tell her I've not left her. Tell her I'm coming."

In the end it was anxiety that killed her. She would still smile brightly at me when I walked into her room in the morning. She would let me wash her and dress her, but soon she would grow uneasy, shuddering at each sound. When she was in her room she wanted to go outside. When she was outside she would stop the servants and beg them to take her home. Once I heard her scream in her room most horribly. When I rushed in, I found her sobbing, rocking a small pillow as if it were a newborn baby. It was one such attack that brought forth the fever that carried her away.

In a way I was glad that Mama was spared the knowledge of the tragic events of the last year. She knew nothing of the lost insurrection and the final partition. But Your

Majesty has a much more profound grasp of these sad events than I do, so I will limit myself to the true reason for my letter.

When Our Lord in His Mercy had taken Mama to His side, I went back to the Kraków house to clear her things. She had an old cedar chest under her bed that I remembered from St. Petersburg. There were many things in it that I expected to find. The old white muslin dress that was once my grandmother's, now failing at the seams. A piece of amber with two bees in it. My late papa's letters tied with a ribbon. My own drawings and those of my daughters, all dated and neatly sorted.

I also found other odd and messy pages in Mama's own handwriting, reminders to herself, they turned out to be, as if she were trying to record what was the most important to her. *I have a daughter, Darya, and two granddaughters: Barbara and Aniela. Masha, my Russian servant who came with me from St. Petersburg, is dead. I buried her in Warsaw, near my baby brother.*

It was among these odd pages that I found two notes in Your Majesty's handwriting that I wish to return. I have no idea how they came into my mother's possession. They are addressed "To my Sophie, to be delivered into her own hands." The seal is broken, so they have been read, and I do not know why my mother did not deliver them. Or maybe she did but was asked to dispose of them and kept them for some reason of her own.

She has taken the answers to these questions with her to her grave, and if she sinned, she will take her penance in the other world, so it is not for me to judge her. All I wish to say is that at some point she must have puzzled over them herself, for on one of these notes I found scribbled in her handwriting: Who is Sophie? I don't know her.

There is more, but Catherine puts the letter down. Her hands tremble, her eyes itch.

Varvara Nikolayevna is dead.

Goodbye, my friend, she thinks.

But it is the prickly thoughts that pain her most. Varvara, in a light blue gown, walking swiftly down the palace corridor, holding Darya's hand. A swirl of blue and white. A peal of laughter that promises a few precious, carefree minutes. Stopping to pick up a kitten, whisper something into its ear.

When did it go wrong?

I beg Your Majesty to free me from the Imperial Service.

"Not all friends take kindly to advancement," Vishka said when Varvara's letter arrived, so long ago now. "Many find it easier to pity than to admire."

Fond memories . . . when I played in the corridors of the Winter Palace with the Grand Duke Paul . . . What does a child remember, so many years after?

A sickly boy, fussy, colicky, and so easily terrified?

On September 11, the day of the engagement, chaos rules. Messengers race back and forth, pages announce the most recent arrivals. "Everyone wants to see Your Majesty," Queenie grumbles, fending off requests for an audience.

Even in her study the Empress can hear the frantic pace of the preparations. Carriages roll into the palace yard, servants shout orders to delivery boys. Alexandrine's engagement may be a private ceremony, but the capital city is swirling with excitement. People are already gathering outside the Winter Palace, hoping for a sight of the Swedish visitors.

Defeated, she pushes the unread reports aside and rings for Zotov to help her to the rolling chair.

In her dressing room, the maids, the hairdresser, and the wardrobe seamstress are waiting. The imperial gown is laid out, ivory white *robe ronde* embroidered with heavy gold thread. Her jewelry keeper is holding a black velvet cushion with necklaces and earrings for her to choose from. The air smells of orange blossoms, almonds, and a whole array of lesser scents emanating from open jars of pomades, creams, and powders.

It will take the small army of servants at least two hours to get her ready for the evening.

Queenie and Vishka are looking flustered already. Miss Williams has been asking what to do, for Alexandrine is refusing the slightest touch of rouge on her cheeks. And Maria Fyodorovna has sent her page with a request for some silver lace, for hers got torn in the carriage. "Will Your Majesty take a look at these samples, please?"

"Splendor is hard work," Catherine tells Zotov, as he helps her out of her rolling chair and mutters his toneless "Indeed, madame."

The wardrobe seamstress is dispatched with enough silver lace to replace the whole hem of Maria Fyodorovna's dress. Miss Williams is told to let Alexandrine decide what the child wants on her big day.

It is four o'clock when she hears Le Noiraud's angry whisper. "He wants to discuss it with Your Majesty personally," Queenie reports.

Her face is smeared with a mixture of mashed cucumbers and honey; her eyes are covered with chamomile compresses. The wardrobe maid who has been brushing her hair moves aside.

"The King? What does he want to discuss?"

she asks, removing the compresses from her eyes.

"This is what I asked, too," Le Noiraud replies. His fingers tap the back of her chair. He mentions *dogged stupidity that defies reason.* Then *deviousness he cannot understand.*

Slowly she is able to put together Le Noiraud's account of the last four hours, though it still makes little sense. Plenipotentiaries met to sign the treaty. At first all seemed in order, until Le Noiraud could not find the page with the article that secured Alexandrine's freedom to keep her religion. "The King has taken it," the Swedes answered when he asked why it was missing. "His Majesty wants to discuss it personally with the Empress."

"Now?" Catherine asks. "Why didn't he wish to discuss it yesterday?"

Le Noiraud doesn't answer her question. "I told them it was too late for discussion," he says. "So they want to sign the treaty without it for now."

The unease in his voice alerts her. There must be more to this story. Has he been too trusting? Too eager to do well?

I'll get it out of him later, she decides. Her guests are beginning to arrive. Her hair has to be curled, coiffed, and powdered. She is only half dressed, and the stomacher is far too tight. The seamstress needs to loosen it without upsetting the line of the *robe ronde.*

"If we sign the treaty without the article now, it'll be too late to insert it afterward," she tells him. "Which is exactly what they are hoping for."

He should've known that much without being told, but she waves this thought away. "It's a ploy," she continues. "They are trying to find out how much can be snatched at the last moment. We must stand firm."

Relief shines in Le Noiraud's eyes. Before she has the time to stop him, he kisses her on her cheek and gasps. His lips are now smudged with the cucumber mixture.

At six o'clock, when the Empress's toilette is almost finished, Queenie announces that Alexandrine would like to present herself for her grandmother's inspection.

The Empress nods her agreement, but when the doors open, it is Count Morkov who rushes in, apologizing for his intrusion.

"Necessary, however, madame," he pants. "For we are at a loss."

Can nothing go right these days? she thinks. *What else should I get ready for? Shortages of snow in Siberia? Another ship carrying my purchases sinking to the bottom of the sea?*

Queenie casts her mistress a worried look. Vishka stops the seamstress, who has just spotted something amiss with the *robe ronde* and approaches her, a row of pins between her lips. "Out, all of you! Quick!" she tells the servants.

Count Morkov wastes no words. The last two hours brought no progress in the negotiations. The Swedes insist that the clause on religion must be discussed.

"Now?" She asks Morkov the same question she has asked Le Noiraud. "Why didn't the King wish to talk about it yesterday?"

Morkov gives her a bewildered look. "But madame," he says. "The King didn't have that clause yesterday."

For a moment, the world stops, and then twirls madly, in some incomprehensible romp. Blood rises to her brain. Tiny bells ring in her ears, a whole distant chorus of them.

"It happened," she hears Morkov's voice, "on Platon Alexandrovich's insistence. To avoid the unnecessary arguments, he said. He assured us that Your Highness approved. Only when we noticed that the clause was missing . . ."

Her heart thrashes like a cornered beast. She has the urge to tear off the *robe ronde*, the stomacher, free herself from stays, the chemise. Morkov's words fade and surge. "Platon Alexandrovich ordered . . . Platon Alexandrovich demanded . . ." With a courtier's sixth sense, he has already gauged the true depth of her rage and is on the lookout for spoils. One courtier is down, another can climb up. The more unexpected a fall, the sweeter.

The thought crackles, bright like lightning, jolting her back into control. She has made a mistake. Not the first one, and not the last. A mistake that she needs to correct the best she can.

Her heart is slowing. She must be looking calmer, for she can discern growing disappointment in Morkov's eyes. Whatever he was hoping for no longer seems as certain.

"Write down what I tell you," she orders, and dictates to Morkov a short paragraph of intent. *I . . . Gustavus Adolfus . . . formally promise . . . assure for my future wife . . . the complete freedom of worship . . .*

"Go back to the King," she tells the Count. "Get him to sign this for now. Tell him we'll work out the exact wording of the contract after the betrothal."

This is a compromise. She is not happy with it, but she has no choice. Le Noiraud has been foolish, to say the least, but the Empress is also annoyed at the Swedish King. A puppy baring his milk teeth. She has been clear enough in her wishes, hasn't she? What is he truly objecting to? Is he hoping he can corner her with his sulking?

In the antechamber, Maria Fyodorovna is telling Alexandrine to hold herself straight. A bit too late for motherly admonitions, but her daughter-in-law has always been slow.

They all come in. Her granddaughters and

526

their mother, a cluster of excitement and expectations. Hands wave, handkerchiefs wick away tears.

Alexandrine shimmers in a white satin gown, embroidered with silver butterflies fluttering over flowery twigs. A muslin fichu covers parts of her neck. By the end of September, she will be on her way to Stockholm.

"Graman!" the child cries, throwing her arms around her grandmother's neck.

"Let me look at you," she says.

Alexandrine lets her hands drop and swirls to show the graceful sweep of her gown. "Chin up," Yelena whispers, and her sister obeys.

"Remember what to do after the blessing, Alexandrine?" Maria Fyodorovna asks. "Remember to count to six before you make another step?" They have been rehearsing the lines and movements all morning, but it is one thing to practice and another to remember everything when the whole court is watching.

Alexandrine rolls her eyes and smiles. Of course she knows. A few days only and the child has grown.

There will be an official blessing with the Holy Icon of Our Lady of Kazan right after the betrothal, but now there is still time for a few private moments. First of all, she, the Empress, announces her wish to adorn her granddaughter with a proper gift of jewels.

527

One of the pages brings the jewels on a plump, velvet cushion. An amethyst necklace, matching earrings, and a clasp for Alexandrine's hair, which the hairdresser has loosely pinned up, leaving golden ringlets on the nape of her neck.

She places the necklace around her granddaughter's throat. The purple stones are set in white gold and framed with diamonds. Her hands must be trembling slightly, for she fumbles with the clasp.

"He'll faint when he sees you," she whispers in her granddaughter's ear. "But don't tell this to your maman."

Alexandrine giggles, her cheeks crimson. How young eyes glitter, even without belladonna! How precious youth is. And how brief.

Doors open again to admit the rest of the Romanovs, who flow in with cheerful smiles. Three generations of the Imperial Family. Her son and his wife, her grandsons with theirs, and her granddaughters. Even baby Nicholas is here, bundled up, asleep in the wet nurse's arms.

Reverences are paid. Compliments exchanged. The imperial gown is declared exquisite; the ivory satin is of the most luxurious sheen, the embroidery reminiscent of most ornate mosaics. "Your Majesty will outshine us all," Elizabeth, Alexander's wife, says with a gasp.

She, the Empress, gives Alexander a quick assessing glance. Bezborodko has told her that her grandson didn't sleep much last night. Walked across his bedroom back and forth. Broke into a sob he tried to muffle. Wrote for a long time, then burned all the pages and scattered the ashes from his window. Alexander is hurting, but pain cannot always be avoided. It will pass. The decision he has made will make him stronger. He is still young, though. Still soft. She'll have to be tender with him for now.

Maria Fyodorovna rushes to embrace Alexandrine and to admire the amethysts.

Paul clears his throat, then retrieves a folded page from his breast pocket. "Since there will be no time for it later," he says.

Her son has prepared a speech, which he now reads with excruciating slowness. Alexandrine is admonished to be virtuous and faithful to her future husband, to defer to him in all matters. To remember her womanly duties, keep the purity of her thoughts and the chastity of her deeds.

Catherine wonders who has written it for him, for the words flow far too smoothly to be Paul's. Maria Fyodorovna? It does have a touch of her gushing sentimentality.

Alexander embraces his sister and whispers something in her ear. She nods and hugs him back. Constantine pinches her cheek and makes her laugh. Yelena places a quick kiss on her sister's lips. "I can't believe you will really leave us," she weeps. Maria asks if she could go to Stockholm, too. "Just until Christmas," she says. "Graman . . . please . . . may I?"

"You?" Constantine teases. "You don't even know how to curtsy!"

"I do!"

Paul has put his hands on Alexandrine's shoulders and is repeating the same admonitions he has just read. "Remember, my dear daughter, a woman's place. *Never* contradict your husband in anything."

Even the tone of his voice annoys her. *How is it that there is nothing of me in him?* Catherine wonders, brushing away the memories of her husband's grunts, the gropings of clammy hands, these few suffocating moments before his sweaty body would slide away from her. The queasy smell of bedsheets, stained with vodka and his stink, for Peter refused *banyas* with a vehemence that bordered on rage. "I won't submit to these monstrous customs. You always do what these Russians want! You've become like them, Sophie! I won't."

Could Paul be Peter's son after all? For he has none of Serge Saltykov's looks. None of his seductive charm. Could it be that a child does not resemble either parent? Or were those rumors right? Did Elizabeth replace her baby with another? One of her own bastards, perhaps?

Paul finishes his admonishments and then makes a step toward her, then another. Does he know she is thinking of him? He must, for his skin reddens, his pug nose lifts in a pathetic attempt to make him look somewhat bigger. She should let him come up to her, exchange a few polite inquiries, but, suddenly, this is too much of an effort. It is so much easier to talk to the young. It is their exuberance, their hopeful trust, that she craves now.

"I wish to speak with Alexandrine alone," she says.

Paul hesitates. Before he can consider his next move, she takes Alexandrine's hand in hers and leads her granddaughter away to her dressing room.

Alexandrine approaches the mirror, eager to admire her new jewels. "Such a beautiful hue, Graman," she exclaims. But then she turns and asks with a childish lisp: "From where I sit, will I see the peacock clock?"

"You will. Why not let the maid rouge your cheeks, *cherie*?" she asks. The child's face looks wan.

"This is how the Lord has meant me to look, Graman."

"The Lord has meant you to look as pretty as you can, my silly girl," she says and opens a box of rouge. "Just a tiny bit of color," she continues as she dabs the rouge on Alexandrine's smooth skin. "See," she says, pointing

531

at the reflection in the mirror. "So much better, isn't it?"

The melting wax of the candles that light St. George's Hall mingles with the heavy scents of perfume. It is an imposing hall, the ceiling supported by white, gray, pale red, and blue marble columns. The throne is elevated above the floor. She is wearing her crown, meticulously polished after Vishka spilled wax on it from her candle. A heavy ermine mantle is draped over her shoulders, a scepter is firm in her hand. Above her is a canopy with the two-headed Russian eagle; behind her a shield with her initials — C II, Catherine the Second, the Empress of All the Russias. Along the walls the Imperial Guards stand at attention, their blue coats faced with blood-red.

Lev Naryshkin is whispering something to the Austrian Ambassador, who nods vigorously, stifling a laugh.

Paul sits on her right, Alexander on her left. At her feet, on a low stool, is Alexandrine, her slender hands clasped. "Will you keep looking for Bolik, Graman?" the child has asked. "Even when I am in Stockholm?"

And yet angry thoughts hover, furious, distracting. Is there no one around her with any sense anymore? No one she can rely on with even the simplest of tasks? "Do you not trust me even that much?" Le Noiraud wanted to know.

The betrothal ceremony will begin in a few minutes. The Archbishop will deliver his blessing. She will make her speech, the parents will bless the young couple, and then — finally — much-awaited respite. As soon as the reception begins, she'll ask Bezborodko to take over the negotiations. She wants no more delays, no more surprises.

The peacock clock begins to move. At her feet, Alexandrine leans forward for a better look.

What a child she still is, Catherine thinks, but then she, too, gets ensnared in the spectacle.

First the little bells on the owl's cage sound their warning. Then the owl, the golden peacock, and the cockerel begin their solemn dances. The bird of wisdom, the bird of unity between what is and what has perished, and the bird of resurrection. "You'll always think of me when you look at it," Grishenka said when he first showed her the clock fifteen years ago. Grinning with pride, a magician displaying his newest illusion. Only he is no longer here and no magic can bring him back.

The birds freeze when their dance is finished.

It is seven o'clock.

On her right, Paul is thrusting his chest forward, drawing the air through his nostrils with a faint whistling sound. Her son, who

533

still thinks himself her heir. Those who aspire to the throne should struggle for it among themselves first. In the animal kingdom, the young fight for their place. The mother has only that much milk in her teats. The strongest are the ones to live.

She doesn't think it cruel. It is part of nature. It serves a purpose. She has made these calculations before and she knows the pitfalls of easy mercy. The happiness of the greatest number is what matters in the end.

Time thickens, becomes heavy. At her feet, the child closes her eyes. Alexandrine, her sweet Princess, motionless, as if waiting were a game of hide-and-seek and she had already found her place and was determined not to move. How will she survive in a foreign court? Still unaware that innocence flies in the face of nature's laws. It spells submission. It spells weakness.

The blessing she, her grandmother, has prepared is short but elegant. *May you always be safe and true to the virtues of your upbringing. For you are our beloved child, the ray of sunshine in this house, our joy and our hope.*

The Swedish King has still not arrived. Neither has Le Noiraud. How long does it take to scribble a few signatures?

The ceremony, once it begins, will be tedious and long. Two hours, if she adds all the necessary toasts, speeches, and congratulations. The stomacher is still too tight, in spite of the seamstress's efforts. It digs into her body. There will be red welts when she finally removes it. The weight of the scepter makes her elbow sink into the arm of the throne. And she can feel the spot where the hairdresser clumsily burnt her scalp with the curling iron.

Alexandrine and Alexander exchange glances. Alexandrine flashes her brother a shy smile. Her first granddaughter to be married. Two more to go. Thank goodness Nicholas is a boy.

Prince Adam, Bezborodko has told her, has dispatched a letter to his father, granting old Prince Czartoryski full powers of attorney over the family estate, to be administered as he sees fit until his death.

The doors should open any moment now.

To break the boredom of waiting, Lev Naryshkin amuses everyone with his antics.

"If I were a princess who is about to go to Sweden, I would take with me a fox stole, a bear blanket, a pelisse, a snuffbox, a carriage wheel, a bucket of water, a cat, a fish."

Even Alexandrine chuckles.

"Why a fish?"

"To have something in the bucket."

"But why a fish in the bucket?"

"To take it out of the water and then put it back in again."

"But why?"

535

"To remember what the water is for."

Alexander twists in his seat, as if trying to catch a glimpse of someone. Dolgoruka with her wild Tartar eyes? Or Golovin's big-breasted daughter? He is not looking at his wife much these days. There are remedies for that, but one should not suggest them too early. Monsieur Alexander will make his own discoveries, learn what is worth the effort and what could be endured. Queenie is right. Elizabeth should've given Alexander a son by now. She wouldn't cling to her husband so much if she had a baby to think about.

"What is taking them so long?" Paul asks, snorting like a sow.

"Are you in such a hurry?" Catherine snaps, but instantly regrets the sharpness of her words, for Alexandrine hunches her shoulders as if readying herself for a blow.

"Is anything wrong, Graman?" the child asks.

She can hear it already, in the rising whispers, the sudden pauses in conversations; eyes are turned to the closed doors, willing them to swing open.

She runs through the possibilities in her mind. Le Noiraud, knowing she must be furious at him, is desperately trying to redeem himself, wrangle some impossible and now superfluous victory. Just let Gustav Adolf sign the paragraph of intent! Forget your annoying ambitions for a moment. There'll be plenty of time for that later!

Her eyes rest briefly on her chief minister, who is escorting Princess Dolgoruka toward the window, where the crowd is thinner, and where the Princess can better display her charms. Should she send Bezborodko to the negotiating room? He would be delighted to set things right, show the young how much skill they still lack. This is a fleeting temptation, though. She is too seasoned to surrender to impatience. She will never reveal her hand too early. If the Swedes became aware Platon has overstepped his authority, it'll be used against her in the end. It always is.

The chimes? Already? The owl stirs again. The flowers, which are in fact small hammers, move, producing a sequence of soft tones.

She remembers being a child, frightened to see the hands of a clock turned back. Thinking that the world would collapse into endless repetitions of what has already been. Now that she is older, she wishes it were true. What she would give to relive what has already passed! To know the betrayer before he betrayed.

Eight o'clock.

The delay, whatever its reason, is hard on the child. Alexandrine looks like a white moth suspended in mid-flight. Is she praying? Or dwelling on the kisses, the soft caresses of her lover's hands? Or is she blaming herself again, the silly girl? Some imaginary transgression? Some trifling misdemeanor blown out of proportion?

I'll protect you, she thinks. *I'll make sure you won't be overlooked.*

A few minutes before nine, she motions to Queenie and orders her to check what is delaying the ceremony. Queenie rushes out of St. George's Hall as fast as her large bulky frame will let her. There is a murmur of excited speculation as the courtiers step aside to make way.

The mechanical music of the clock is still ringing in the air when Queenie comes back, looking flustered and uneasy.

"There is some slight disagreement, madame," she whispers, on tiptoe. "Platon Alexandrovich says it won't be long."

Paul leans forward to hear better. Maria Fyodorovna raises her hand as if she were about to cross herself. Alexander gives his grandmother a questioning look.

"I've heard some raised voices, madame," Queenie says with a gasp.

The child looks at them all, trying to comprehend what might be happening. But then the doors swing open and a sigh of relief escapes her. The courtiers resemble statues of themselves, all motionless, staring at the

538

door. The orchestra begins to play, but then it stops.

For only one person enters. It is Count Morkov. He approaches the throne, climbs the platform. There is a flicker of dark satisfaction about him. A warning, unheeded, has been proven right. A dire prediction vindicated.

It takes her a moment to understand the words Morkov is whispering in her ear: "The King protests. He says he is not trusted. He asks why he should sign the paragraph of intent at all."

For the next hour, messengers come and go, assertions bounce off one another, twisting, squirming, whirling with growing distrust.

The King says he has given his word already. Why is it suddenly not good enough?

Why does he have to sign a promise that he will keep his word? He is a man of honor. He will stand behind what he has promised.

It is not enough? He is not trusted, then?

Should he, perhaps, ask for the same from the Empress in return?

Alexandrine's eyes are growing bigger, flooded with silent questions. She will have to be taken care of, removed from this room. Crows will circle over carrion. The child needs to be away from prying eyes.

The Empress is sorry for her granddaughter, but in the end it is better to suffer a disappointment earlier than later, isn't it? Cut the ties when they are still weak. She will explain it to Alexandrine later. Right now she has to take care of the wreckage.

Her lips are parched. She is thirsty, but her thirst will have to wait.

By ten o'clock, when the peacock turns around, revealing his silvery tail, foreign Ambassadors sneak out of St. George's Hall to dispatch their coded news of Russia's humiliation into the night, hoping to come back for even more tantalizing tidbits. The Empress of All the Russias has been kept waiting for three hours by a stripling Swedish King forty-nine years her junior. What caricatures will turn up now: The Swedish King sticking his bare bottom at the old wrinkled hag? A David defeating a Goliath?

The wave of blinding anger hits her. That weakling, that puny full-lipped prig. That little King, that bastard.

There is silence in the Throne Room, heavy, black, suffocating silence. Alexander looks at her with concern, but he, too, implores her to right what has been wronged.

Zotov, good old Zotov, always ready with the remedies of a perfect valet, hands her a glass of water. She drinks from it, gulp after cool gulp, until the glass is empty.

There is terror in Alexandrine's eyes. In

540

them, Catherine sees the panicky fright of a child who finally learns that what has been smashed cannot ever be put right again.

This is not quite true, Alexandrine, she wants to say. *Defeat destroys you only if you allow it. There is a whole life ahead of you. Congratulate yourself on your narrow escape. You will still laugh. If a drop of my blood flows in your veins, you will.*

She manages to keep her face frozen, her eyes fixed on the chandelier, the glittering flames of candles reflected in the crystal. "Stop the negotiations," she tells Morkov. "Inform our Swedish guests that the Empress is indisposed."

It falls to Paul — who is still her official heir — to stand up and offer apologies to the Archbishop and the guests.

"Due to unforeseen difficulties . . . postponed . . ." she hears, though Paul's words seem to come from a distance, as if she were eavesdropping on them all. Prince Adam — she notes — is whispering something into Elizabeth's ear. Alexander's wife looks as if she is about to faint.

As soon as Paul stops speaking, she rises from the throne, feeling heavy and ancient, grown into the soil like a giant boulder, impossible to move. Alexander has offered her his arm, and she leans on her grandson with her full weight. Her breath is shallow.

With great effort she drags her swollen feet, one after another.

Behind her she hears a gasp, like the cry of a wounded bird, and a staccato rush of heeled shoes. The child has fainted and is carried away through the side door. Her father is carrying her; her mother follows like a hen, flapping her arms. "Watch out! Careful! Mind the doors!"

The crowd disperses to make room for the Imperial Family to pass. The faces of the courtiers flash grave, bewildered looks. Lost, searching for the implications this humiliation will have. Until she, their Empress, their *matushka,* can restore their pride.

Not now.

Later. In a few moments. Tomorrow.

This is what wounded animals do, withdraw into the thicket, lick the wounds to assess the damage.

A few more steps. Then she can lower herself into the rolling chair. For now, a few reassuring words to Alexander must suffice.

The flash of pain in her head is like a blow. Her jaw stiffens. Words she intended to say die in her throat. Bezborodko has pushed Morkov aside. He is saying something, but his words crumble into dust before they reach her ears. It is just as well. She doesn't care to discuss what has happened. Not yet. She has no need for consolations, either.

"Graman, are you feeling well?"

She can see terror in her grandson's eyes. She feels his hand clinging to hers. Something shifts in her, like a soft thump of soot falling down a chimney.

"Help me get out of here, Alexander," she says.

Leaning on Alexander, with Zotov propping her left side, she walks slowly out of the hall to where the rolling chair awaits.

If I cry, she thinks, *the others will sob; if I sob, the others will faint, and then everyone will lose both their heads and their bearings.*

What is dead is dead. I must think of what is still possible.

In her inner suite, as soon as the doors close behind her, she lets Alexander lift her from the rolling chair and motions to Zotov to take it outside.

The four wardrobe maids are waiting to release her from her clothes, wash away the makeup, unpin her hair. They, too, must have heard what has happened, for they stare at the carpet.

"Wait outside, until I call you," she orders, and they vanish.

"Go, get some rest," she tells Alexander, whose face is still changing color, from pink to white to red and then back to white. "There'll be enough to do tomorrow."

Her grandson hesitates, draws himself up.

His mind must be scurrying back to St. George's Hall and Alexandrine's sobs, for his fists clench.

"Go, dear," she repeats, knowing too well how bitter humiliation is, and watches him leave.

Still in her heavy robes, she shuffles into the Imperial Bedroom, leaning on the cane that Queenie — whom she hasn't noticed until now — has handed her. "Get Platon Alexandrovich here," she orders. "And leave me alone." Like ripples from stones thrown into the sea, her words make feet patter, doors open and close.

Platon Alexandrovich . . . Platon Alexandrovich . . .

A vain peacock of a man. Creamy, soft skin, and the sweetness of flattery.

Her folly, her weakness.

Keep him in your bedroom, matushka, *on his knees.* Grishenka's voice echoes off the tapestry that covers the gilded walls Empress Elizabeth liked so much. *Let him amuse you, bring you pleasure. Let him play the golden boy with his levees, his monkey. But never trust him with anything of importance.*

Why didn't she listen? Why did she let the passion long gone silence the voice of reason?

A soft tapping on the door. A whisper begging permission to enter. It's Vishka. "I've

544

been to Alexandrine's rooms, Your Majesty, but perhaps this is not a good time . . ."

"Speak," she snaps. Why is everybody suddenly so mindful of time being good or not? Has she ever shrunk from hearing the truth?

"The Grand Duchess won't stop sobbing." The creases on Vishka's face carry the stain of anger and pain.

"Is Alexander with her?"

"Yes, Your Majesty. And her maman."

"What do they tell her?"

"That there has been an unforeseen delay. A misunderstanding that needs to be corrected. But the Grand Duchess doesn't listen. This is the end, she sobs."

"Can they not give her something?"

"Rogerson bled her. Laudanum helped a bit, but not enough to stop her tears."

"Go to her," the Empress tells Vishka. "Tell the child to wipe her eyes with some ice and stop crying. Tell her I'm taking care of everything. Tell her I want to see her tomorrow. No more tears."

Vishka's heels make tapping noises on the wooden floor as she leaves. If Alexandrine has any wits left, she will listen to those who know better. Appear tomorrow in her pink dress, coiffed, as if nothing of any importance has happened. Manage a few casual conversations. Refuse to be drawn into conjectures. Dismiss what has happened as insignificant. Behave like a Queen and let the King see what he is in danger of losing.

The heavy doors open again. Le Noiraud saunters in, mumbling excuses. He has been a victim of a colossal perfidy. For the longest time, he was sure all would settle amiably. But the King has been utterly unreasonable.

Words flow, roll off his tongue, each an assault: *The King . . . the Regent . . . underhanded . . . stubborn. Presuming . . . daring . . . in spite of all I have done . . . in spite of all I was led to believe . . .*

Seated on her bed, propped by two fat pillows, Catherine listens and waits.

He is still trying to limit the damage. Admitting to failure is not part of Le Noiraud's strategy. Neither is admitting to negligence or pure asinine stupidity. His eyes are fastened on her, searching for signs of what she might want to hear.

It is useful to know how to make your face blank.

Finding no clues, Le Noiraud settles on derision. He calls Gustav Adolf a little weasel and a bastard. Awkwardly, he brings forth the sordid story of his conception. The gossip of a would-be mother sprawled on her marriage bed, entered by Baron Munck, who in turn is being entered by the King of Sweden. Why? Because the Great Gu couldn't bring himself to touch a woman.

"It's all true," Le Noiraud's voice scales up. "Even in Sweden they all know the little King is a bastard."

"Silence!"

Her scream makes him jump up. His face is white.

"You dare come here and tell me it is not your fault!"

Her voice, coming from her belly, is low and blunt, like a blow of a hammer that stuns the cattle before their throats are slashed.

"I've promoted you. I've raised you above your station. And you make me and Russia the laughingstock of all Europe!"

Le Noiraud shudders, still unable to believe that he has been rebuked. He is like a fish yanked out of water. Thrashing, hoping one of these jerky movements will save him. He sinks to the floor. His chin is trembling like that of a child about to cry. His eyes are blank with fear.

"What did they tell you about me?" he wails. "Was it Morkov? Or Bezborodko? They want me finished. They are jealous."

"Of *you*?"

"They criticize me because I dare to love you. They've always wanted to turn you against me. But I won't let them. You are all I have. You are all I care about."

Is he going to throw himself at your feet? Grishenka's voice mocks. *How much more does he think you will bear?*

"Correct me, Katinka," Platon pleads. "Teach me. You are the only one who wants me to be better. Without you, I'm dust."

A hound kills in the heat of pursuit. A hound does not bark, for it would hinder its own hearing of the furtive movements in the thicket. A hound pursues the rabbit in silence, anticipating its rapid turns. The reward is a crunch of tender bones, the taste of blood, still warm, the muscles, the fur. The dog devours it all.

"Your birthday is in two weeks. How old will you be?"

"Twenty-nine," Le Noiraud stammers.

"Suvorov tells me that in Italy, Bonaparte takes his army to the mountains. Spreads his forces out, so the Austrians spread their forces out. Then he concentrates his troops and strikes them at the weakest points. The man is unstoppable."

Le Noiraud is bewildered, but he doesn't dare ask what she means.

"Bonaparte," she tells him, her voice cold and cutting like the northern wind, "is only twenty-seven years old."

The wardrobe maids come back to undress her, take away the false hair, the jewels.

How could I not have seen it earlier? For the sequence of events that have just passed is as incomprehensible as its conclusion: The Empress of All the Russias has been snubbed

548

by a little Swedish King.

The maids are quick and silent. She has been pinned, locked in the armor of court dress, and it takes time to release the body from its crust. The string of black pearls is unclasped. The gown is removed. Jars and bottles open and close. The cold cream erases the pasted color that smooths her wrinkles. Her hair is released from pins and brushed with even strokes.

A few more minutes. A clenched fist stops the trembling fingers. One deeper breath slows the heartbeat a tiny bit.

Finally she smells of rose water and almond milk. A soft night bonnet covers her head; her body is wrapped in the white nightgown trimmed with lace. Her eyes skim over the painting of Sarah, hidden in the shadow while Hagar is lit by light. She should go to see the child, but she has no strength for it now. *Tomorrow,* she tells herself.

One by one the wardrobe maids disappear, having plumped the pillows and lifted the coverlet to remove the bed warmer. But now Queenie wobbles in with the evening glass of Malaga wine on a tray. "I've made arrangements to sleep in the antechamber tonight, should Your Majesty need me —"

"Leave me! *Now!*"

Alone, at last, she slumps to the floor. Her

thoughts are raw, bloodied. They tear her apart.

I trusted a fool. And now even my body has betrayed me.

Her tongue tastes of ash. She holds up her palms in supplication, but thoughts, these hovering vultures, swoop on her without mercy.

There is no Grishenka. There'll never be anyone like him. I've lost too much already. I've nothing else.

But even as she weeps, she remembers that vultures feed only on the carcasses of the dead.

. . . .

PART IV
NOVEMBER 6, 1796

. . . .

12:00 A.M.

Footsteps draw closer, heels turn, scrape the floor. A bony finger feels her throat, pulls the skin under her eyes. Candlelight blinds, the reflection of the flickering flame persists after the candle is gone.

The Scottish doctor clucks his tongue. To someone hidden in the darkness he mutters his bewilderment: "The human body is a mystery. Pools of hidden strength hide where nothing was expected but decay. The secretions of a woman's womb alter the flow of humors."

"How much longer, doctor?"

"No one can tell, Your Highness. The constitution is strong, and so is the pulse. The heart is still beating."

"In St. Petersburg," she hears Potemkin's throaty whisper, "you have to love the night or go mad."

Potemkin, her beloved Prince of Tauride.

Her lover. Her husband. Her best friend.

Am I dying, Grishenka?

Will I not see Alexander's children? Watch Alexandrine get married?

Smell another spring flower?

Is this how the end arrives?

12:05 A.M.

A thin man who sits beside the bed is no longer young. He has an upturned nose of a pug and an oblong face with snarling mouth revealing grayish, pointed teeth. A bubble of saliva has lodged itself in the corner of his mouth.

My son.

His name is Paul.

Her son, crippled by envy, a child of forced alliances and powerless times, mutters: "This is what I despise, Mother."

On his fingers he counts off: Courtiers and sycophants. Titles and honors. Mistresses and whores. The world of masked balls, of lechery and intrigues.

Furies. Harpies.

Women who refuse to see that they can never be equal to a man.

"The ancients have said it before, Mother. Listen to Plato and Aristotle.

It is only males who are created directly by

554

the gods and are given souls . . . the best a woman can hope for is to become a man.

A woman is an infertile male . . . The relationship between the male and the female is by nature such that the male is higher, the female lower, that the male rules and the female is ruled.

She shuts her ears to his venom, the miasma of frustrated dreams.

Her son has no power.

He cannot hurt her.

He doesn't know how.

Would Father have liked him? His grandson? This awkward man who flays his hands and breathes hard, snorting the air like a walrus.

A switched baby, Father.

A changeling.

Why didn't he die, instead of Anna? Perhaps I would've been luckier with a daughter? A child of love, not betrayal. Another Empress.

"You've always hated me, Mother. If I had a dog I loved, you would've tied a stone to its neck and drowned it."

There it is, unbidden, that same ancient pain that had seized her so many years ago, a harbinger of his birth. Does the body remember? The child's head splitting her open, tearing her flesh.

Someone's hands hold her shoulders; someone's lips mouth the prayers that bid her speed. Her child is slipping out of her. Ripping her open. The midwife kneels between her legs to receive that sticky little body still tied to her.

A moan. A flash of a knife's blade. A slap, followed by a tiny cry, a tinkering bell. Prayers cease.

Her son, his head smeared with her blood.

She is reaching her arms for him, desperate to see him through the sweat that stings her eyes. Her lips hunger to kiss his wet head. Her arms itch to hold him.

"Live," she urges him. "Live."

"My precious little Prince," Elizabeth croons. "My very own."

As if he had no mother. As if she, Catherine, were but a womb, a vessel to be filled and emptied at the will of the Empress.

And somewhere in all this there is another memory. Of warm fingers untangling her wet hair, of lips whispering consolations. "It's just for now. He is safe. He will live. I'll look out for him."

Varenka? Are you here, too? They told me you were dead!

12:30 A.M.

Don't think of Paul. He is no longer important.

In the corridors of the Winter Palace, young, strapping men trail her, trying to catch her eye. Spines straighten, chests thrust forward, sabres clink. Their love-smeared notes appear between pages of her books, under her pillow, or tied to her dog's collar.

Sometimes she toys with one of them, the boldest of the pack. Summons him into her innermost boudoir, inquires of his dreams. Pays attention to that first kiss of her hand. Is his touch firm or shaky? Does he linger, allowing the warmth of his lips to spread along her skin, or does he let haste win? Can he offer the pleasure of that first warm breath shared just before tongues intertwine and eyes close?

If a man wishes her to remember him, he has to find his own way.

But pleasure is not all. When passion is spent, will his next words surprise her? Will he spare her the trite confessions of love long concealed? Hints at immortal goddesses and the youths that worshipped them? Adonis, Endymion, Phaëthon?

Is he ready to love a woman?

The bedroom is sparsely lit, softened by shadows.

He is here, naked in her bed, lying on his

557

stomach, his head resting on his arms. He smells of *banya,* of birch leaves mashed into a pulp, of skin purified by steam. Catherine runs her finger along his spine, his shapely buttocks, then bends over and retraces that route with her tongue.

And then she waits.

This memory makes her chuckle: She is standing behind the thick marble column in the palace ballroom, her face covered by a black mask. A loosely draped domino reveals her disguise, the green tunic of the Preobrazhensky uniform faced with red, the long boots polished to an impeccable shine.

Her body cherishes its release from hooped dresses and tight stays. No panniers, no cumbersome folds of fabric, no whalebones digging into her stomach. It would've been so much better to be born a man. To always wear breeches and tight jackets. To walk in easy, confident strides.

The women in the ballroom flutter like giant butterflies, sweeping the floor with the hems of their rustling gowns. The foxy smell of sweat raises over the perfume and melting wax. It will linger in her hair and clothes for hours after the masquerade is over.

In the protective dimness of the room, the disguise has fooled her guests. A few of the women have already cast quick glances in her direction, their fans signaling their interest.

"Come closer," one has beckoned. "Do I know you?" signaled another.

To them she is just one of the dashing Guard officers on the prowl.

For a while, she watches the dancing women, their graceful movements, the bows and hops and quick half-turns. Heels click on the polished wooden floors as the dancers obey the music. Figures blending together, floating by, indistinguishable until one of them stops and leaves the circle, panting from exertion. A wreath in her raven-black hair is teeming with birds and fruit and peacock feathers. Her silver mask glitters with pearls. It is far too small to disguise the wild Tartar eyes of Princess D.

Desire comes unbidden.

Should I come up to you? Ask: Are you a shepherdess or a nymph?
I won't. You would only think it trite.
I'll watch you instead until you see me.

But D takes no notice of the masked officer's stare. Her eyes are drawn to a Turkish odalisque dancing alone. To a face hidden behind a veil, supple hips swaying to the clinking of tiny silver bells.

"Oh, how graceful she is," D says, and gasps.

"The one who praises is far better than the one praised."

D gives her a startled look. Her eyes quickly take in the Preobrazhensky greens showing under the domino. "You are pleased to joke, Mask. Who are you? How is it that you know me?"

"I'm speaking from my heart and influenced by its promptings."

"But who are you?"

"If you are kind to me, you will soon learn."

"Please say who you are."

"I shall, but first you must promise to be kind to a besotted soul."

These are bold words. Impertinent. Assuming far too much. The speaker of such words should be chastised.

D hesitates. Her fan flickers around her full lips.

Merely flattered? Or intrigued?

But at this moment, three shepherdesses approach. "There you are," they say to the Princess with the Tartar eyes, pulling her by the hand. "Come with us, quickly!"

A look of regret, a smile, a rustle of skirts, and D is gone.

A moment lost?

Making room for another?

But as she sits down on an empty chair by the wall, the Princess returns. She has abandoned her companions and has rejoined the circle surrounding the dancing odalisque. She has not forgotten the besotted "cavalier," either. It is not easy to let go of those who

560

profess admiration with such boldness.

When their eyes meet, there is a beckoning flicker of a fan. Not yet a sign, but enough of an encouragement to resume the game.

Now!

She stands up and approaches the dancers, making sure she is not too close to the Tartar eyes. When offered a questioning look, she pretends not to see it. But when D leaves the ballroom, she follows. Past the Guards standing at attention. Past the refreshment table, from which D picks up a pineapple slice and eats it greedily, letting juice drip down her chin.

Back to the ballroom.

You've stopped. You are waiting for me, but I won't come too close.

Now it is the Princess who cannot stay away. She maneuvers herself closer and closer, until they find themselves side by side, as if by accident.

She keeps her silence until, defeated, D turns to her, cheeks flushed, pupils wide. "Mask, can you dance?"

"Yes."

"Let's dance, then, shall we?"

The dance is a polonaise, slow and stately. Time lingers. The tips of gloved fingers can be gently pressed. An arm brushed in silence.

■ ■ ■ ■

Imagine what I'm thinking. Imagine what I'll tell you. Imagine what I'll do.

When the dance is over, D stops and hesitates. There is time to pull the top of her silk glove and kiss her white palm. There is time to mutter in a low, sultry voice: "What a happy man I am. You've granted me the honor of giving me your hand. Now I'm beside myself with joy."

A mistake.

The hand is withdrawn. The fan, swanskin with peacock feathers, drops to the floor.

"But you are too sure of yourself, Mask. Have you forgotten that I do not know you at all?"

There is not time to answer, for D is gone.

Is everything lost? But why leave with such haste, then? And why drop your fan? To test my resolve? Or to make sure I follow?

"One word, Princess, I beg you!" The palace corridor is empty but for the maids who wait for their mistresses, pelisses in hand. "Please. Have mercy on my heart."

"I still do not know who you are, Mask."

562

Still?

Have you been making inquiries, then?

"I'm your humble servant. Try me out, and you will see how well I'll serve you."

"You are gracious and your voice is pleasant, Mask."

"All this is a tribute to your beauty."

"Do you really think me beautiful?"

"Unequaled!"

"Please say who you are!"

"I'm yours."

"That is all very well, but what is your name?"

"I love and adore you. Show me that you care for me, and I'll tell you my name."

"Isn't that asking far too much?"

But desire, once stirred, is too hard to resist. There are too many empty rooms in the palace, too many passages leading to hidden alcoves. In the darkness of the night, caresses need no names, no pedigree.

There is pleasure in hearing gasps of surrender. There is pleasure in feeling the quiver of a woman's wet softness. There is pleasure in leaving her languid, spent, not knowing who has touched her.

Forever bewildered, forever puzzled.
Forever mine.

2:05 A.M.
A cool scented cloth touches her skin, mop-

563

ping up sweat. Queenie's hands tremble.

"A few more hours at the most, Your Imperial Highness," a man's cringing voice mutters. "Her Majesty is not suffering. We should be thankful for that."

"Leave," her son orders. "All of you."

Footsteps scurry, fade away.

Her son's eyes scrutinize her face, her bulging belly underneath the coverlet. His nose sniffs out her smell. Of urine and bile.

There is a pillow right beside her. Soft, pliant. It will take one push only. No one will see it. She cannot defend herself. Her body is useless. Her hands lie lifeless on the bed. Even if she managed to scream, it would be like screaming inside a vacuum tube.

Her son leans over her, and she can see his tobacco-blackened teeth.

Now?

Her heart beats wildly. Warm waves of urine sink into the mattress.

Now?

Her son licks his lips. He clears his throat.

"You've sinned, Mother," he says, then straightens up.

Relief washes over her. He will not kill her. He won't dare.

"God will punish you for what you have done . . . no woman will ever rule Russia again . . . I swear."

Her son is speaking fast. His voice is shaking. In phrases he must have rehearsed over and over again, he accuses her of "usurping the crown" that was rightfully his, of "defiling her august position," of "bringing shame on Russia" by her immoral conduct, of "pilfering the coffers of the state" to pay for her sinful pleasures. But his list of grievances is too long to be contained by the rehearsed words. The stiff phrases recede, give way to broken chunks of resentment. "You spied on my every move . . . You laughed at me behind my back . . . You let your lovers humiliate me . . . If I made a friend, you dismissed him . . . You didn't let me fight in the war . . . You took my sons away from me . . ."

Go back to Gatchina, Paul. Lord it over your troops. There is nothing for you here.

"Does the Empress of Russia have anything to say in her defense?" Paul asks in a loud voice he must consider solemn. His head jerks; his lips twitch.

You gave me my grandchildren. The only good that ever came from you. Alexander will rule Russia when I'm gone. You would've been a tyrant. Just like the man who called himself your father.

He turns to someone behind the screen, a seated shadow. "No answer," he says in that same affected tone.

565

Her eyes squeeze shut, blotting out her son's presence, but she cannot silence his voice. "Write that the Empress has nothing to say to her son's accusations."

Behind the screen, a quill scratches over paper.

3:10 A.M.

The light is dimming. Someone is taking the light away from her.

They are here in this room. They are gaping at her, peeping through the spying holes, two-way mirrors. Listening to the rhythm of her broken breaths. They want her alone. In the dark. At their mercy.

Her ill-wishers. Her defamers.

It is their hunger she fears.

They want to take all she has. They want the bed she lies on, the damask chairs, the gold cloth. They want her coffers, her paintings, her medals, her vases and urns, her dinnerware. They want her soft wool carpets, crystal chandeliers, bone-and-tortoiseshell-framed mirrors.

Her cameos.

Her china.

Her ostrich-feather fans, the rubies from her crown.

They want everything she has touched.

Greedy, sweaty hands. Grimy fingers. Grasping, clawing. Their eyes are as ravenous as their bellies. They wait for the moment when she is not looking.

They have sharpened their scythes and butcher knives on a whetstone. They imagine slashing her throat. Or plunging a knife inside her chest, right into her beating heart. Making her bleed like a slaughtered sow. Bayoneting the children, one after another.

Stop them, she hears Potemkin's voice warn from somewhere far away. *Now, Katinka. While there is still time.*

3:30 A.M.
What happened yesterday?
Before the pain. Before the fall.

Yesterday, the chill woke her up. It had settled in her bones, made them ache. The night must have been bitterly cold. Queenie, always weary of such wintry days, made her put on her thick quilted dressing gown trimmed with silver fox.

Someone came to see me.
Le Noiraud!
What did he want?

Her lover is propped on his elbow, smiling at her. His hand moves playfully over the sheet, fingers curling and uncurling like a cat's paw. When he dips his head, a raven-black lock tumbles over his brow. He always brushes it back with impatience.

His hair is soft and yet thick. Luscious.

He picks at something on the sheet, as if it were a scab over a closed wound. She takes his head in her hands and presses his face to her breast. He wriggles and then softens in her grip, kissing her exposed skin. He talks of battles and sieges, of fortresses yielding their treasures. "Why won't you let me fight?" he asks, his voice muffled against her breast. "You always let *him* do what he wants."

Him. Grishenka.
    Can't you see that?

When he leaves, she buries her face in the warm spot among the sheets, moist and musty, where he had lain. Empty now, cooling, stiffening from his absence.

3:32 A.M.

"Platon Alexandrovich is waiting outside. Shall I let him in?"

"Let him wait," Queenie mutters. "What good can he do now?"

Queenie's muttering is tinged with dark glee. The joy of seeing the once mighty fall.

Platon's face is gray. He sinks onto her bed, the very edge of it, on his knees. He must have had a nosebleed, for a red smudge of dry blood is still visible on his upper lip.

And yet even in his misery, his patrician elegance has not abandoned him. The Roman nose, the unblemished skin, as if chiseled out of the best Carrara marble.

Her smooth-faced Platon knows what is said of him.

Fear has settled in his black eyes, in his clasped hands. Fear and grief for what he has lost.

Catherine thinks of him cast out of the palace. Chased away into the empty streets, where rats on the prowl scurry. Running past houses shut for the night, their foundations crumbling.

Peter the Great's city has been built on shaky wooden poles, hammered into the marshes. If it is not constantly tended, it will collapse, slide back into the mud.

"Forgive me, Katinka," Platon sobs. "I've failed you, but please forgive me."

The candlelight shines on his beautiful face.

He casts a shadow; therefore, he is real.

8:15 A.M.

Borders shift, vanish, or arise where they have never existed before.

Her heart pounds like a giant bell.

Queenie only stares at her with terror. Vishka, always practical, hating to waste even a sliver of time, straightens the frills on her pillows.

Is she still in Tsarskoye Selo, on her green

ottoman? In the Gallery, overlooking the hanging gardens?

Someone is singing, in German.

Ach du lieber Augustine, Augustine . . .

She never could sing.

Notes make no sense to her ears. "It's like a screech of chalk on glass," Potemkin says, trying to describe to her what it means to hear a false note. "How can you not hear it?"

I don't know.

"So you, too, are not perfect after all," Peter sneers.

The singing fades and now her heels stomp the marble floors. Each step is easy, strong, clear from pain.

Floor-to-ceiling mirrors line the corridors of the Winter Palace, the profusion of reflected light shimmering like a glossy shield. This is how Empress Elizabeth once hoped to deter death. But in Russia, Death is a crafty old woman who cannot be frightened away.

"Don't be so haughty, Catherine," the old Empress warns her. "She'll find you, too."

Is life a gamble? Or a chess game in which movements can be foreseen, the opponent's hand forced? Answer me!

"You've chosen *her* over me, Sophie." Mother's voice is venomous with bitterness. "For that, I'll never forgive you."

There is no Sophie, Mother. Rest in peace.

Palace spies are everywhere. The stove stoker is lingering far too long with the kindling. The maid who takes away the chamber pot has fumbled with the escritoire drawer. Every book she reads has been leafed through. Mother trusts double-bottom trunks. "See, it's still there," she says triumphantly when the hair she has tied around her lock is untouched.

Spies linger in the service corridors, peek through cracks in the walls. Sometimes they fall asleep and she can hear them snore.

Russians do not like foreigners.

She has been warned before.

Life is a game.

In a gambling house, you keep your hands in your pockets.

If every player is cheating, how do you know whom to trust?

The woman who bends over her is wearing a blue waistcoat with a red collar. She looks feeble, and her puckered skin is ashen.

Varvara?

9:00 A.M.
"Hurry . . . Tell Bezborodko to wait . . . No

571

one can leave the palace without my permission."

Paul is issuing commands. His voice is sharp but not yet fully assured.

Is her son still terrified of her? Does he fear she can still recover? Or is it Alexander he is afraid of?

Through the slit in her half-shut eyes she sees her grandson's strapping figure. Standing at attention by her bed. Looking straight ahead. The eyes of a Palace Guard on duty, forbidden to stir.

Her true heir.

Light shines on Alexander, bounces off his polished buttons, the gold braid of epaulets. She remembers his child face, the dimples of baby fat, the jumps of impatience.

Now is the time to straighten what needs straightening.

The letter is folded, sealed, tied with a piece of black ribbon. She has written it herself, copied it in her own hand: *To be opened in case of my death, in the Council.*

Don't leave, Alexander. You have to be here when the letter is opened. Your father is a coward, but don't underestimate him.

9:20 A.M.
In the distant corner of the room, a child is

572

sobbing.

Alexandrine!

If this body still obeyed her, she would have called her granddaughter to her side. Ran her hand up her sweet face. Kissed the red, moist eyes.

Never cry.

Never show anyone where it hurts. Make them think you are strong. Walk away. Straight and proud. Like the Queen you should've been.

Learn from what happened. So little can undo the best laid plans. Push you onto a path you wouldn't have trodden. You cannot avoid all mistakes. Sometimes you have to lose. But you must always hide how much it hurts.

Pain is a ruler's secret.

"Do animals know they are alive?" Alexandrine asks someone in an urgent whisper. Her sister? Her brother? "Do they know that they are going to die? Can a dog love one person and then stop? Start loving another?"

Simple questions, and yet the answers are so hard.

11:20 A.M.

Grishenka, Prince Potemkin, her Prince of Tauride, towers over her, his face tanned

573

from the southern sun. He slides his arms under her armpits and pulls her up from the bed. Beside him she sees a shapeless bundle. "I'm taking you with me, Katinka," he says.

So you are not dead, Grishenka. They've lied to me.

He doesn't tell her where he is taking her, and she doesn't ask. She is broken: It is easier to obey.

"Your name is Apis," he says and opens her outer dress, helps her slide out of the heavy folds of fabric, the chains of gold and silver threads, the armor of embroidery. The bundle, opened, reveals a soft cambric shirt, a pair of breeches, a simple velvet jacket. The clothes smell of ashes.

"Put them on," he says, and she obeys.

When she is dressed, he hands her a yellow eye mask, with black stripes, a rim of brown felt along the edge.

Apis is Latin for *bee*.

The loose cloak he throws around her shoulders has a hood. It covers her head, shielding her from the afternoon light. When she stumbles, Grishenka stops and gives her his hand. "Hold on to me! I don't want to see Apis tumble down the stairs," he says.

11:25 A.M.

She must have slept, for the room she lies in has changed. Someone has opened the curtains, let in the pale autumn light.

574

"I've seen her, Graman," the child whispers.

You are trembling, Alexandrine. What has happened to you? Has anyone hurt you?

It is important that she listens to her granddaughter. It is important that she considers the child's every word.

"Xenia came to the palace gate, Graman. She looks just like they say. Her coat is all torn and tattered. It is too big for her, so she rolls up the sleeves.

" 'Pray for the Empress,' I asked her. 'Pray for her, so that she gets well again.'

"Blessed Xenia nodded, Graman. She didn't say anything but she nodded.

" 'Give me a sign,' I begged her. 'Let me know that all will be well.'

"And she gave me a sign, Graman!

"In the morning, I went to the garden and Bolik was there. By the gate. When he saw me, he ran toward me. 'Bolik,' I cried. 'Is that really you?' And he came up to me, trembling, wagging his tail. And I lifted him up, and he licked my face. He is so thin, Graman. I can feel his ribs. His fur is matted, caked with mud and blood. There is a gash on his head. Deep, crawling with maggots.

"But he is back.

"He survived.

"I wanted to bring him here. I wanted you to see him, Graman. But Maman didn't let me. She said it was not right, that you were

575

too ill. But I know you wanted him to come back."

The smells are of fried sausages, sauerkraut, and beer. The servants carry platters of food past her, casting quick glances in her direction. She can see them through half-closed eyes. Pinched, teary faces.

In the small room, her son is holding court.

"God works in inscrutable ways," Maria Fyodorovna announces with annoying solemnity to yet another visitor.

"You haven't eaten anything, Alexander? You'll need your strength, now!"

"We all do!"

"Sit down, Constantine. You make me nervous when you fidget like this."

They do not lower their voices. Don't they care that she can hear them? Perhaps — the thought is not implausible — her silent witnessing is a simmering pleasure. In lovemaking, the envy of the excluded heightens the sweetness of release.

Sometimes she hears Bezborodko's voice, explaining something, but she might be wrong.

Someone should watch them all.

12:00 P.M.
A clock chimes. Shutters rattle. November is a windy month.

576

Behind the screen, gray shapes move, edgy and tense, a puppet show of shadows. When she hears the shout "You have no business here!" the shapes gather speed. Something falls on the floor with a crash; glass shatters.

"Is no one minding the doors?"

"What are the guards doing?"

A coup?

The screen moves, threatens to fall, until someone's hands catch it. A graceful wiggling body lands on the bed with a whimper.

For Pani, faithful Pani, has fooled her minders, and she is here, licking her mistress's face with her warm, eager tongue. Cheeks, lips, eyelids. Dogs have no need for words of explanation. Pani knows, feels it through her skin. Her mistress is not where she should be. Her mistress is hurting. Licking a wound can heal it.

"Out! Get out of bed, Pani!"

Queenie is insistent, but Pani — pushed out of bed — returns on the other side and resumes her self-imposed duty.

"Out, you pest!"

Shooed again, the dog yelps and whines. Someone is ordered to hold Pani tight. To take the damned bitch away.

Why?

I must stop them from hurting Pani, she thinks, but the hand she tries to lift has disappeared. *Guillotined off,* she thinks, and the word looms cutting and vivid, flashing red.

12:13 P.M.

"Not a word so far. But Her Majesty can see us, I can tell."

"How long has it been now?"

"Quiet! You are making too much noise."

"The cook asks if he should send more smoked *balyk.*"

"The soup is too salty. Have they cried into it?"

"Her Majesty is still breathing."

"I wonder who will get the silver fox pelisse. It's so beautiful."

"Have you heard the bells? Russia is praying."

"His Highness has sent for the papers. It won't be long now."

This is your time, Alexander. Take the letter and go to the Council. Set it right. Don't waver. Don't be afraid.

I've never bet on the wrong horse before.

2:00 P.M.

"Where are you going, Alexander?" Paul asks.

Her son has come out of the side room, a chicken bone in his hands. His jaws move. He is still chewing his dinner.

"I'll be right back, Father."

"You didn't answer my question."

A servant rushes forward with a tray. The bone lands on it.

Paul snorts. He clears his throat, as if he were about to retch. How puny he looks beside Alexander. How insignificant. Harmless, if one is blind enough. If one forgets that there is no worse tyranny than the tyranny of the weak.

"At attention when I talk to you, Alexander. Do you wish to bring dishonor to our uniform?"

Heels click; the young, lithe body straightens.

"Do you wish to dishonor our Gatchina way, Alexander?"

"I do not wish it, Sire. I beg your pardon."

"At ease."

3:15 P.M.

"*Gospody pomyluy.* May God Almighty have mercy upon us," Vishka whispers. "Save us from all evil." Her eyes slide to the side room, where the Empire's fate is decided. In hissed conversations. In gasps of disbelief.

"Amen," Queenie echoes in a choked voice, clasping her hands.

They are wise. They speak in quiet whispers. In words that could still be turned around, denied if necessary.

"Her Majesty's private coffer . . ." she hears.

Her papers are being read. One by one, secrets are revealed.

You wanted to be Emperor, Paul? You wanted to destroy all I have built? Undo what I have

579

done? Where is your stomach for betrayals?

A fist slams on something hard. Glass cracks.

"How could you," Paul seethes. "My own wife!"

"I didn't sign it!" Maria Fyodorovna is wailing. "She wanted me to turn against you, but I didn't . . . See, it's not signed!"

Worthless words of no consequence. It's not Paul who matters now, but your son.

She braces herself for what must come next. An uproar. Alexander's voice ordering them all to stand still. Paul's scream as her will is taken to the Council, to be opened in front of witnesses. Her last words. Her legacy.

. . . upon my death . . . being of sound mind . . . I bequeath . . . to my grandson Alexander . . . Tsar Alexander I . . .

But there is no scream. Instead, what she hears is a stifled gasp followed by hushed voices. And then Alexander's plea: "I never wanted it, Papa. Graman forced me. You know the way she is. Please, let me burn it! Please!"

"No!"

She, their Empress still, has managed to conquer the limp muscles, to lift her head up.

Her scream pierces the air.

Queenie grips her hand in hers, covers it with kisses. Vishka is praising God for his infinite mercy.

The side room doors open. They all pour out.

"A miracle!"

Maria Fyodorovna is sobbing. Bezborodko is wiping his forehead, slick with sweat. Paul's cheek is beginning to quiver.

Alexander's eyes are wide with terror.

No!

But her scream has already turned into a choking gasp and what she wills to be words of command turn into a rattling noise. Heads shake and turn away.

Only Queenie is repeating the same words over and over again: "Her Majesty pressed my hand!"

3:50 P.M.

The memory surfaces from somewhere far away. Of the wet warmth of the maid's spit on her back and its lingering sour smell, like rotten cheese. Of roughness in the maid's cold hands, in the fingers that massage the spit into the skin.

The bed is soft. The feather mattress has been aired and smells of the wind, but the pleasure it could all bring doesn't last.

"Pull it tighter," Mother orders, deaf to pleas.

The leather corset has straps that bite deep into the flesh, chafing the skin. Pus is oozing from blisters; red welts on her shoulders have turned into open wounds.

"Lie still, Sophie." She hears her mother's impatient voice. "It'll only hurt more if you move."

"Why, Mother?"

"Because, Sophie, no one will marry a cripple."

Only she must be already married, for Peter, her husband, is standing over her. He is so young, a child almost, his face still free of pockmarks. He fingers the bed curtains, plays with the golden tassels. Braids them together and then lets them unwind. His fingers are long and shapely.

"I'm not a monster, Catherine," he says. "All I want is my flute, my Blackamoor, and my mistress. Is that too much to ask?"

Who has let you in, Peter?

Where are the guards? Have you bribed them?

"Are you ill, Sophie? Or could it be that you are again with child?" He shrugs and giggles as if his presence at her bedside was a practical joke. A cause of colossal merriment.

Peter's hands rise, protect his face. His lanky body folds. He is crouching on the floor. "I don't want to die!" he sobs. "Please, Sophie, let me live!"

Remember, Peter? Remember that crumbling house? Remember how fast you ran away? I could've died then.

"That's how you want to remember it."

That's the truth.

582

"The truth? The truth is that you've always wanted me dead, Catherine. And that you always got what you wanted."

They call her a wanton woman.

Insatiable in her greed.

Rumors hound her. Nasty, vicious rumors, meant to humiliate, put her in her place. The rumors of how she debases herself, seduces with power, for there is nothing in her aging body that can be freely desired. How she pays for the flattery that surrounds her, for the forced attention of her lovers.

How she robs the innocent to pay for her sins.

Emperor Peter III is dead. *Batushka*. The good Tsar. The father of his people. Cut down in his prime. Before he could bring happiness and justice to all his children.

This is Peter they speak about. Her foolish husband, who drank himself into a stupor night after night. Who executed rats when they chewed on his doll soldiers.

"You never forget your first kill," Father said once, after a hunt.

4:05 P.M.
Rogerson, a lock of his reddish hair falling over his forehead, lifts her hand and feels her pulse.

Here lies Duchess Anderson

Who bit Mister Rogerson.
I ought to tell him something.
I smell my own breath. It is fetid.
I see the canopy. Minerva is looking down at me.

How swiftly the rot sets in. Roses are covered in black spots. Peony blossoms turn into a shapeless mash. Flower beds are trampled with soldiers' boots. In the palace corridors, someone has gouged eyes from the portraits, slashed the painted faces. Children, lifeless, their bodies torn with bullets, pile up on the filthy floor. The girls' hair is speckled with blood.

Things are scattered everywhere: a chair with a broken leg, half-burnt candles, stained handkerchiefs. Silver hairbrushes with tangles of gray hair. Books with torn pages. Paper, sheets of paper, smeared with running ink.

"How can you live in such a mess, Sophie? Have you forgotten all I've taught you?"

You have to watch the servants. If they don't fold it carefully, taffeta will crease and split. All folds should be padded with muslin or buffered paper.

Silk doesn't like sunlight.

"Pick it all up!"
"Yes, Mother!"
But before she has time to begin, flames of fire lick the floor, consuming the carpets.

Bursting out of windows. The smell of gunpowder is everywhere. A man's voice begins a prayer; a woman joins in. Children scream. Rifles click, fire.

Run away, Catherine. Run before it is too late. Run before they steal your soul.

8:35 P.M.

Her lips are parched.

She longs for simple things. Wetting her fingers with spit to pinch out a candle. Watching the rays of light cavort in the mirrors of her Tsarskoye Selo study. The rich, mellow taste of dark porter, icy, fetched straight from the root cellar. Cucumbers smeared with honey.

A smell that reaches her nostrils is of an overripe apple. Bees circle it, tempted by the sweet drunken aroma of the darkened pulp.

Two bees, one beside the other. Closer and closer, until they seem one.

In the place of Thy rest, O Lord, where all Thy Saints repose, give rest also to the soul of Thy servant, for Thou lovest mankind.

Her heart still beats, her blood still flows through her body. She can see light and blurry faces. Some weeping, some smirking in triumph.

"We shall have a Tsar at last. Women have ruled Russia long enough."

585

"Our old *matushka* has amused herself sufficiently, I think."

"More than sufficiently."

I will pour out my prayer unto the Lord, and to Him will I proclaim my sorrows. For my soul is filled with afflictions, and my life has drawn near to Hades. And like Jonah I will pray: Raise me up from corruption, O God.

She is walking on a snow-covered field. She must find shelter soon. There are lights glittering in the distance. A village, maybe, or a few huts. There will be people there.

She takes a step, but her feet sink into the snow. There are things buried in it. Shoes. Bones. A steel helmet with ostrich feathers. A birch box with quills. A piece of amber with two bees inside, locked in an embrace.

Opening my lips, grant me a word to pray, O kindhearted Savior, for her that has now departed, that she find rest, O Master.

"A moon child," someone once called her.

Her skin was luminous then, no wrinkles marred her face, and yet unhappiness was crushing her heart. How clear they can be, the images that lay sunken somewhere in the depth of her mind. A drowned kingdom, distorted by watery films that reflect the light, blinding and teasing at the same time.

586

She grasps at the sheets, but they recede, leaving her sifting through sand on a beach somewhere by the cold Baltic Sea. The sand is hot on top, cooling as she dips her hand inside it.

The piece of amber she holds in her hand is of a rare beauty. Inside it, two bees lie together. Their bellies touch. Their legs are entangled. Locked in death. Welded. Inseparable.

She had a piece just like this once, she recalls. What happened to it?

Did she give it to someone?

To a friend?

A face that comes to her is fluid, taking on many features. Curly blond locks, a dimple in a plump cheek. A firm hand holding hers as she runs through long and winding corridors, into the street. She is not alone.

Varenka? Are you here?

It is winter. The horses are covered with blankets. Mist rises from their nostrils. The guards stomp their feet on the snowy ground, eye them both. Together they run into the street, past palaces lit with lanterns, past the frozen Neva, on which sentries burn fires for a bit of warmth.

"Come, Catherine," she hears. "I'll show you where I used to live."

Floating through time, over the rivers, the forests. The vast expanses of the steppes where the grass is fragrant and sweet.

587

They have drawn the curtains, and no light from outside penetrates the room. This is just as well. The sun moves relentlessly forward, and she does not want to think of such movements. She prefers to look at the painted ceiling of her room. The nymphs, the gods, the clouds that do not move or change or demand anything but admiration for their lightness and color and the passions that never fade.

I am of the night, she thinks.

Inside her, silence gathers. Sweet, warm, deceiving.

8:45 P.M.
Again we pray for the repose of the soul of the servant of God . . . that she may be pardoned of all her transgressions, both voluntary and involuntary.

There is death in her granddaughter's grieving eyes. Hesitation in Alexander's.

The world she leaves is so soft. It will be swallowed by the night. She imagines the rioting mob coming to get them all. Waving their torches. Light that does not illuminate but burns and destroys.

They do not care for her warnings.

For no matter how deep the loss, how startling the betrayal, doesn't life always turn away from the dead?

Here they are, ready to repeat the endless deeds of their everyday lives. Until their end.

Until emptiness and darkness claims them, too.

9:40 P.M.
Outside, the rain has turned to wet snow, dribbling down the glass like spit, spattering against the windowpanes.

She hears the shuffling of feet. Is it Queenie?

Queenie, who is in love with her. Her love is dark and sticky and suffocating. But it also brings what nothing else will: ultimate loyalty.

In her hands is a velvet cushion, green with a golden trim. Its corners are chewed to the gray stuffing. The dogs have been at it again.

In Paul's eyes she sees the madness that will bring about his death.

There will be other deaths. Multitudes of them. The walls of her palaces will be stripped of their finery, flames will lick the gold and silver, jewels will melt.

I've tried.
The light, too, can deceive.

Alexandrine, the sweet, beautiful child, is kneeling by the bed. Her golden hair is tied far too tight; her pearls look dull, as if someone tried to rub them too much. Her hands are clasped in prayer. Her face is white, just like little Olga's in her coffin.

The smell around her is not jasmine petals

but the sweet, heavy scent of *ladan.*

I've tried to turn you away from death, but I've failed.

The dog comes with her shoe, drops it at her feet, giving her a look of sad reproach. It is Pani? No, it is Duchess Anderson, her greyhound bitch. But how is this possible? Duchess Anderson is long dead and buried.

The bitch flops over on her side with a sigh and closes her eyes.

How is it possible, Queenie?

But the woman who stands beside her is not Queenie.

Look down on me from above, O Mother of God, and mercifully attend now unto the visitation that has come upon me, that, gazing on thee, I may depart from the body with rejoicing.

Without darkness, nothing comes to birth, and without light, nothing flowers. Jewels are important. Emeralds are fragile; they cannot be dropped. Gold has been melted down forever. That gold ring that is on your finger could have come from a pharaoh's golden necklace.

Hermes, the messenger of the gods, wrote on an emerald tablet. When Satan fell from heaven, an emerald dropped from his crown.

Nero watched the gladiator games through

an emerald lens.
Take my ring, Alexandrine.
Take it now.

"Come with me."
Grishenka's voice is soft, soothing.
She extends her hand to caress him. Stroke his back, slowly, his belly, his thighs. The creases of skin, the taut body, lying beside her. Her own body stretches in all directions, a sprawling fertile land with its rivers and mountains and valleys.

"I'm waiting for you, *matushka*. I've been waiting all these years."

The lengths of their bodies touch. He is moist and soft and yielding. His lips seek hers, like a suckling baby.
There are slices of red melon on a silver platter beside the bed. On chunks of ice, to keep them cold. He feeds her the sweet, cold, melting pieces. Smears the melon juice on her lips.

I've tried.
So hard.
To dispel the darkness.
To bring light.

Blood pulsates in her temples, drains into the sweet spot between her legs.

591

Nothing is alien. All is one. She is all.

"Don't speak, Grishenka."

His finger touches her lips. It is hard and cool from the melon ice.

It melts her.

She is one with the night.

The girl who runs through the snow-covered palace park is slim and agile. Fourteen years of age, not pretty, but graceful and bursting with energy. By the big pine tree, she jumps up to knock a thick cone off the lowest branch. The cone falls down and tumbles on the powdery snow.

The girl picks the cone up and raises it to her nostrils, for she has always liked the smell of resin. She doesn't care that it has stained her gloves and made them sticky. When her mother will chastise her for her "willfulness," as she is wont to do, she will keep her head down and think of something nice. Like the day the painter who had come to paint her portrait taught her how to mix colors on a palette, or when her governess took her for a walk into Zerbst to let her run along the old town walls and throw stones to the moat.

She should not be outside at all. She should be getting ready for the New Year's dinner. Her best dress has been hastily altered from her mother's old one, and it is not at all becoming, for purple makes her complexion look pasty. But how long does it take to slip on a dress and have her hair pinned up? The maids are grateful not to have to fuss for too long over her — as they have to with the Princess herself.

The palace entrance has been decorated with garlands of fir and pine. Two footmen in thick blue tailcoats and powdered wigs stand by the heavy carved doors. This is the first day of the New Year and dinner guests will begin arriving soon. Not quite as distinguished as the Princess of Anhalt-Zerbst would have wished, but life is a disappointment in so many ways. The baroque portal has just been fixed, the doors repaired, though beneath the Prince's study the masonry is crumbling, and some of the red roof tiles are missing above the garret.

The messenger rides through the wrought-iron palace gate. The maid who spots him through the kitchen window makes a grimace. "If it's bad news, mistress will be angry." The cook is thinking of the roast that —if dinner is delayed — will dry out; the Prince likes his meat juicy and slightly pink.

The messenger has been told to hurry.

The letter from Russia is addressed to Princess Johanna of Anhalt-Zerbst. *Awaiting the honor of Her Highness's immediate reply.*

AFTERWORD

Gentlemen, the Empress Catherine is dead
and His Majesty Paul Petrovich has
deigned to mount the throne of
All the Russias.

Catherine II of Russia died at 9:45 P.M. on
November 6, 1796, thirty-six hours after a
paralyzing stroke. It is impossible to deter-
mine now how much consciousness she
retained, although eyewitnesses reported an
attempt to speak and to squeeze one of her
attendants' hands.

On Catherine's death, her son Paul Petrovich
became Emperor Paul I, and for the next four
years tried to undo everything his mother
stood for. Catherine's funeral became the
first sign of this determination to erase his
mother's memory and legacy. At first, Paul
didn't want to give his mother a state funeral;
he relented after it was pointed out to him
that such a move would undermine the

monarchy. He exhumed the body of Peter III, crowned him in a posthumous coronation, and placed his coffin in the Winter Palace beside Catherine's. Later, the two coffins were on display in the Fortress of Peter and Paul before they were buried beside each other in the Cathedral of Saints Peter and Paul. The dates of their deaths were not inscribed on the tomb, giving the impression that the two reigned together.

In another manifestation of his hatred, Paul visited the imprisoned Polish general Tadeusz Kościuszko, apologized for his mother's actions toward Poland, and freed him and other Polish political prisoners. Paul also sent his messengers to Grodno and invited the Polish King Stanislav August Poniatowski to come and live in St. Petersburg as an imperial guest, offering him the Marble Palace as his official residence. The King, a broken man, died on February 12, 1798.

Alexander, who as Alexander I would vanquish Napoléon Bonaparte in 1812, paid dearly for his unwillingness or inability to honor his grandmother's wish to succeed her. Forced to watch the increasingly mad rule of his father, he agreed to a palace coup that ended with Paul's murder, an act for which he never forgave himself. In history's many twists, one of the plotters was Platon Zubov, Catherine's last Favorite.

■ ■ ■ ■

Adam Czartoryski, the friend to whom young Alexander confessed his sentiments on Russia's role in European politics, remained his friend. After becoming Tsar, Alexander made Czartoryski Russia's Minister of Foreign Affairs. With Alexander's knowledge and encouragement, Adam confessed his love for Alexander's wife, Elizabeth, a love they both shared and cherished all their lives. After Alexander's death in 1825, Prince Adam turned away from Russia and participated in the Polish uprising of 1831. By the time Prince Adam Czartoryski died in France, in 1861, an uncrowned King of Poland in exile, his Parisian residence, Hôtel Lambert, had become a center of political and artistic life. This is where Frédéric Chopin often gave his concerts and George Sand read from her novels.

Grand Duchess Alexandrine Pavlovna did not hear from Gustav Adolf again. Three years after her grandmother's death, she married an Austrian Archduke. She died in 1801, at the age of seventeen, giving birth to a stillborn daughter.

Gustav Adolf IV, King of Sweden since 1792, married Frederika of Baden and was forced to abdicate and flee Sweden in 1809 after what was considered an inept and erratic rule.

Constantine, who was once meant to rule Constantinople as the Emperor of the New Byzantium, continued to abuse his wife, Anna Fyodorovna, until, in 1799, she fled from him. In spite of many efforts to reconcile the two, Anna (who assumed her maiden name, Juliane Henriette Ulrike of Saxe-Coburg-Saalfeld) refused to return to Russia. She lived out her life in Germany as a divorced woman.

Constantine married again, a Polish commoner, Joanna Grudzińska. Alexander made him the Governor of Poland, and he lived in Warsaw, where Chopin was often brought to him at night to play the piano, and thus quiet his notorious rages. He died in 1831.

Queenie, or Anna Stepanovna Protasova, remained at court long after Catherine's death, a colorful and beloved presence. She became Maria Fyodorovna's confidante and offered her support in the difficult years after Paul's murder. Queenie died in 1826 at the age of eighty-one.

Vishka, or Maria Savishna Perekusikhina, Catherine's attendant and one of her many spies, died in 1826.

ACKNOWLEDGMENTS

Empress of the Night, even though it is a work of fiction, could not have been written without existing books on Catherine the Great, and I am much indebted to their authors, alive and dead.

Douglas Smith edited and translated *Love & Conquest: Personal Correspondence of Catherine the Great and Prince Grigory Potemkin* (Northern Illinois University Press, 2004), a fascinating account of the Empress's relationship with the man who had been the greatest love of her life. I have used numerous expressions and phrases from Catherine's letters to Potemkin and his responses to her throughout the novel. Equally compelling and rich in details is Sebag Montefiore's biography *Prince of Princes: The Life of Potemkin* (St. Martin's Press, 2000).

The report that the fictional Catherine reads on the relationship between Grand Duke Alexander and Prince Adam Czartoryski is based on Prince Adam's published memoirs: *Pamiętniki i memoriały polityczne 1776–1809 (Memoirs and political treatises 1776–1809)* (Warsaw, 1986).

Always in the background as I wrote this novel were many biographies of the last Russian Empress. The latest two, Virginia Rounding's *Catherine the Great: Love, Sex, and Power* (St. Martin's Press, 2006) and Robert Massie's *Catherine the Great: Portrait of a Woman* (Random House, 2011) were most influential, as well as Kazimierz Waliszewski's nineteenth-century accounts of Catherine and her son Paul.

My editors, Kate Miciak at Random House Publishing Group in the United States and Nita Pronovost at Doubleday Canada, have been invaluable in their help and guidance. I am indebted to their astute insights, guidance, and sharp eyes and immensely grateful for the time they have given me. I'd also like to acknowledge the tireless help and support of my agent, Helen Heller, and my husband, Zbigniew Stachniak.

Without their help, this book would not have come into being.

ABOUT THE AUTHOR

Eva Stachniak was born in Wrocław, Poland. She moved to Canada in 1981 and has worked for Radio Canada International and Sheridan College, where she taught English and humanities. Her first short story, "Marble Heroes," was published by *The Antigonish Review* in 1994, and her debut novel, *Necessary Lies,* won the Amazon.ca/Books in Canada First Novel Award in 2000. She is also the author of *Garden of Venus* and *The Winter Palace,* a novel of Catherine the Great, which has become an international bestseller. She lives in Toronto.

The employees of Thorndike Press hope you have enjoyed this Large Print book. All our Thorndike, Wheeler, and Kennebec Large Print titles are designed for easy reading, and all our books are made to last. Other Thorndike Press Large Print books are available at your library, through selected bookstores, or directly from us.

For information about titles, please call:
  (800) 223-1244

or visit our Web site at:
  http://gale.cengage.com/thorndike

To share your comments, please write:
  Publisher
  Thorndike Press
  10 Water St., Suite 310
  Waterville, ME 04901